ENVISIONING THE

Future

ENVISIONING THE

Future

SCIENCE FICTION AND THE

NEXT MILLENNIUM

edited by marleen s. barr

WESLEYAN UNIVERSITY PRESS   Middletown, Connecticut

Published by
Wesleyan University Press, Middletown, CT 06459
Copyright © 2003 by Wesleyan University Press.
All rights reserved.

Library of Congress Cataloging-in-Publication Data
will be found at the end of this book.

ISBN 0-8195-6651-9 cloth
ISBN 0-8195-6652-7 paper

Designed by Richard Hendel
Set in 10.3/13.5 Monotype Ehrhardt by
Julie Allred, B. Williams & Associates
Printed in the United States of America
5 4 3 2 1

FRONTISPIECE
Antony Gormley, *Quantum Cloud.* Photo by Stephen White,
courtesy Jay Jopling/White Cube (London)

For Nanette Schorr, woman of the future

CONTENTS

PART 4. Future Critical

American Science Fiction; or, "What Happened to the Flying Cars?"
Science Fiction/Millennia/Culture

marleen s. barr

To situate *Envisioning the Future: Science Fiction and the Next Millennium* in both personal and professional terms, I divide the preface into three sections. The first section links the new millennium to my own past history and potential future. In the second section, to illustrate my professional notion of how to link science fiction studies with cultural studies, I discuss George W. Bush's missile defense plan in terms of science fiction. Finally, in the third section, I offer my own science fiction vision to exemplify a juxtaposition between science fiction, culture, and the future. Antony Gormley's *Quantum Cloud,* which (as I will explain in the introduction) is emblematic of *Envisioning the Future,* also figures in the preface.

Millennia and Me

The human figure situated within *Quantum Cloud* represents the human condition positioned between open and shifting temporal and cultural currents. Since the figure is cast from Gormley's own body (Gormley seems to recast *écriture feminine* as *sculpture masculine*), it imbues the work with the personal. Gormley literally puts himself in his art; I discuss millenniums in terms of me.

As a baby boomer born three years after the midpoint of the twentieth century, the often repeated phrase "the year 2000" had special resonance. The phrase was a marker for a future that seemed too far away to ever arrive. At age ten, after doing the arithmetic, I thought, "Wow! In 2000, I will be forty-seven." Forty-seven was just too old to contemplate. Even during the 1990s, the coming of 2000 loomed large. Now the big date has come and gone. No one succumbed as a result of the hyped millennium apocalypse. All the supplies stockpiled in late 1999 are now as ridiculous as my childhood conviction that 47-year-olds are elderly. The new millennium arrived—and society survived. But we are not unscathed: the millennium positioned baby boomers face to face with their own mortality. No Peter Pans, baby boomers grew up and experienced firsthand that never-arriving never-never land called the year 2000. We cannot forget that for us the year 3000 (or even 2080) will never come. If, from the standpoint of 1963, the arrival of middle age and the millennium seemed almost unthinkable, the new postmillennium brings another unthinkable event to mind: we are going to die. No one imagined that 2001, not 2000, would bring catastrophe. September 11, 2001, caused Americans to fear apocalypse occurring —right here and right now.

The millennium as a signifier of mortality inspired me to embark upon this anthology. Science fiction provides my only inkling of what I will miss due to the fact that I will not witness 3000. As Jack Womack explains, "Although the genre isn't inherently predictive, I suspect science-fiction writers have a far better record than Futurists when it comes to having their general predictions come out right, or at least sort of right. I suspect, too, that this results from the fact that in the constant attempt to outdo reality, the unconscious mind cannot help but come into play—sometimes too often—and, by happenstance, the acorn appears on the surface even if the writer thought he or she was digging up something else. Look around: there are submarines, and footprints on the moon, and a tunnel that runs from London to Paris—all predicted by science-fiction writers" (Womack 2001, 38). Looking around inside science fiction provides the only means to see the far future.

I once approached Ad Reinhart's title "How to Look at Space" by looking at feminist outer-space fiction to find a means to survive in the patriarchal real world. Motivated by feminist science fiction texts, I navigated patriarchal riptides by swimming across prevailing currents—that is, I did not drown. I never (even in the recent past, shortly before my June 8, 2001, wedding date) imagined that, for me, *2001: A Space Odyssey* would allude to this question: How do I fit all of my possessions in my new and first husband's small Manhattan apartment? After September 11, 2001, this mundane query about domestic space became subject to revision: How do I cope with the empty space outside my living room window that the World Trade Center towers once filled? Now that middle age is here and my once breathtaking urban landscape view has turned into a graveyard, I turn my attention to the next new thing: mortality. Bringing cultural studies to bear upon science fiction provides the best means to interpret the far future I will not witness.

Back to 1964: When I looked out of my elementary school classroom window, I could almost see the 1964 New York World's Fair. Construction noise emanating from Flushing Meadow Park and the Grand Central Parkway often made it difficult to hear what my teacher said. I remember the futures the General Motors and Ford exhibits depicted. With these exhibits and *The Jetsons* in mind, I really expected an over-the-top science fiction scenario to characterize 2000. It was not to be. The New York State Pavilion—no *Men in Black* flying saucer—is currently a seedy edifice. I am disappointed that, in 2001, our space odyssey transpires in a space shuttle that orbits instead of venturing outward. I wish that the space shuttle more closely resembled the New York State Pavilion Hollywood recast as a flying saucer. In relation to outer-space exploration technology, the real 2001 falls far short of Arthur C. Clarke's *2001*. (More personally stated: Jane Jetson does not feel disappointed because space—the lack of closet space—just can't cut it in relation to space the final frontier.) The utopian phrase "space the final frontier" did not resonate with the reality of September 11, 2001, in which science fiction imagery became reality. Yet, even in the aftermath of the terrorist attacks—and in addition to emphasizing mortality—the new millennium reminds us of the mundane, non–science fictional nature of daily life.

Or, as Gail Collins explains, predictions about flying cars were inaccurate: "What I want to know is, what happened to the flying cars? We're about to become Americans of the 21st century. People have been predicting what we'd be like for more than 100 years, and our accouterments don't entirely live up to expectations. No airborne automobiles. No spaceliners to extraterrestrial vacation spots. . . . No housecleaning robots. . . . Our failure to produce flying cars seems like a particular betrayal, since it was so central to our image" (Collins 1999, A23). Our cars are more akin to the one Fred Flintstone, not George Jetson, drives. The predictors failed: "Hop into your personal helicopter every morning, fumble sleepily at the controls, and take off with millions of others into the same airspace. Just bide your time, said the prophets. Be patient. Bear up as well as you can for the time being. And just remember: by 1964, or 1980, or, at the latest, 2000, sing hallelujah! From the vantage point of (almost) 2001 A.D., these past predictions come across as not only delightfully foolish, but so ill–informed as to be troubling" (Womack 2001, 36). Predicting the future is not productive. This point is especially true because 3000, the next millennium, will not exist for us.

It is best to discuss the future in terms of the known—that is, the past and the present. The chronological given does, of course, have positive aspects. The

moon landing can assuage the disappointment the lack of flying cars evokes. To discuss the future, I will go back to the moon landing. More specifically, I will talk about Buzz Aldrin and me.

The photo of Aldrin and me I include here places us within demarcated space pertinent to the past, present, and future. The background-framed *Apollo* patches and picture of America's presence on the moon portray a bygone time. In contrast, a feminist science fiction critic pictured with the pilot of the first manned lunar lander addresses the present and, in turn, the future. Picturing together representatives of feminist science fiction criticism and masculine science fact strikes me as a new version of Grant Wood's *American Gothic* pertinent to the new millennium. Yes, Aldrin's star-and-moon tie is much spiffier than the overalls Wood's male figure wears. No, as you can see, I do not resemble Wood's female figure. (Even though I once wore my hair pulled back and parted in the middle, the resemblance between Wood's female figure and me is limited; she just does not look Jewish.) My *American Gothic* for the now focuses on what tool replaces the pitchfork the male figure holds in his thrust-forward hand: Aldrin holds a pen; I hold a model of the space shuttle, NASA technology of the moment. The astronaut and the feminist science fiction critic, then,

Buzz Aldrin and Marleen S. Barr

exchange the tools that play the biggest roles in our lives. Present and future reality in relation to this exchange of pen and NASA technology signals equality: we are both writers engaged with science fiction—not astronauts. (Aldrin, the author of *Encounter with Tiber* [1997] and *The Return* [2000], is a science fiction writer.) Our shared present engagement with writing and science fiction places moon explorer context and feminist text on common ground. In this new version of Wood's classic portrait, "gothic" is appropriately replaced by another genre: science fiction. My title for the picture, *American Science Fiction*, expresses how to look at space now.

When (at the time Aldrin traveled to the moon) I imagined the new millennium, I did not picture myself as a middle-aged astronaut. Women, of course, never had a chance to walk on the moon; I could not follow in a woman astronaut's footsteps. The new *American Gothic* I call *American Science Fiction* pictures sexism in retreat, a shifted patriarchal gaze. Wood's focused forward–looking male figure subordinates the female figure and her sideways vacuous glance. While Aldrin looks sideways with turned head, I—the woman—stare straight ahead with a dead-on look. In the manner of the pitchfork, I hold the tool of the moment firmly and upright. I look toward the future. I am not a woman men don't see.

This is the future in relation to the picture of Aldrin and me: immediately after the photo was taken, Aldrin excused himself to make a phone call. I heard him call frantically a computer technician to explain that his computer was malfunctioning. His conversation speaks to the new millennium that past pre-dictors of the future did not see: the hero astronaut par excellence becomes a mundane computer user. No one currently flies a rocket car to the Mars Hil-ton; most everyone, from time to time, says "AOL, I have a problem." The general public does not know the names of those who fly space shuttles; female and male astronauts are both equally anonymous. The outer-space hero is an anachronism. George W. Bush, in relation to his missile shield plan, emulates outer-space heroes.

Science Fiction Invades Bush's Missile Shield Plan

Quantum Cloud addresses the cultural connection to technological change and the future in terms of the "I.T. cloud." Thomas L. Friedman explains: "[C]orporate data, telephone calls and e-mail, which 10 years ago ran on sepa-rate networks, are now all running together on the same fiber-optic cables through the same routers. This is called the 'I.T. cloud'—a huge complex web of lines and routers, where, like a cloud, you see your voice, data or e-mail go-ing in one side and coming out the other, but never know how it works in be-tween" (Friedman 2001, A19). Communication networks used as recently as ten years ago are now obsolete. Ever changing communication networks—which Friedman describes as "like a cloud"—are, in the manner of the future, muta-ble and ungraspable. *Quantum Cloud* pictures "how it works in between": the human individual is in the center; Gormley portrays himself ensconced within the I.T. cloud of today (which will become tomorrow's changed entity). Bring-ing the I.T. cloud to bear upon *Quantum Cloud* addresses the present's relation-ship to the future; contemplating the future involves reading science fiction to discern how present culture impacts upon our ideas regarding what will ulti-mately surround our descendants situated within the "in between."

Friedman points to the I.T. cloud to explain why Bush's missile shield plan is ineffective. He argues that the I.T. cloud, not nuclear missiles, makes the United States more vulnerable: "The Bush missile defense plan is geared to de-fending the country from a rogue who might fire a missile over our walls. But the more likely threat is from a cyberterrorist who tries to sabotage our webs. The more tightly we are woven together, the more we become dependent on networks, the more a single act of terrorism can unleash serious chaos. . . . It will probably take a cyberattack that causes real chaos for us to see that our big threat is not a mushroom cloud but the I.T. cloud, and that threat will come up the web, not over a wall" (Friedman 2001, A19).

The tight technological weave Friedman describes—which I think the interweaved metal comprising *Quantum Cloud* represents—was nonexistent a decade ago. The I.T. cloud, then, exemplifies science fiction becoming real. This particular technology, newly made real science fiction, negates the effectiveness of Bush's plan; it shows that his plan touts an unsound basis for future policies regarding the military's presence in outer space. The newly made real science fiction imagery of September 11, 2001, shows that the missile shield plan is inappropriate; missile shields do not protect us from terrorists wielding box cutters and anthrax spores. Bringing science fiction to bear upon the missile shield plan provides an effective way to juxtapose science fiction and culture to understand how the present impacts the future. The missile shield's effectiveness is presently science fictional; the missile shield will provide the basis for America's future military presence in outer space. As Jack Hitt explains, "George Friedman, an intelligence consultant and the author of *The Future of War,* calls the national missile defense plan a 'Trojan horse' for the real issue: the coming weaponization of space" (Hitt 2001, 32).

Gail Collins, in her column "Beam Me Up, Rummy," humorously equates science fiction with reality to describe Bush's missile shield plan. She discusses the technologically implausible shield in terms of *Star Trek* technology: "I don't see why we're settling for a lousy missile shield. Why not decide to outfit our surveillance planes with Romulan cloaking devices, so that they could hover invisibly over the rogue nation's launch sites. If Saddam Hussein tried to pull a fast one, we could simply zap him with a photon torpedo" (Collins 2001, A27). Refiguring the missile shield plan in terms of *Star Trek* and science fiction provides a serious means to understand Bush's efforts to transform a technologically implausible undertaking into a viable governmental expenditure. Bush, after all, during his address to the nation about federal funding for embryonic stem cell research, framed his ideas in direct science fiction terms: "We have arrived at that brave new world that seemed so distant in 1932 when Aldous Huxley wrote about human beings created in test tubes in what he called a hatchery" (Bush 2001, A16).

The missile shield program, itself an example of technological mythology, is rooted in the American mythology characterizing science fiction. Bush's support for a missile shield falling outside the parameters of the technologically possible exemplifies the science fiction power fantasies that captivate male adolescents. Such immaturity is appropriate behavior for Bush. The president who is infantilized in relation to his father and his vice president, loves nicknames and baseball, routinely mutilates the English language, and brags about his low grades at Yale can be expected to succumb to power fantasies that attract immature males. It should come as no surprise that Bush seeks to pave the way for making photon torpedoes real. When he advocates constructing the shield, he authors a Walter Mitty–like science fiction scenario in which it really becomes plausible to deploy a Romulan cloaking device. Garden variety *Star Trek* accoutrements are just as impossible to build as an effective missile shield.

Star Trek is often described as *Wagon Train* situated in outer space. Bush and Dick Cheney—respective denizens of Texas's and Wyoming's western wide-open spaces—also combine science fiction with the genre of the western: they situate outer space as a new American West in which the rugged, individual United States controls rogue nations/Indians by calling in the technologically implausible missile shield/cavalry. Their militaristic western "fence in" and conquer manifest destiny approach to outer space greatly differs from John F. Kennedy's democratic eastern approach to managing terrestrial space. Kennedy established the Cape Cod National Seashore to provide real benefits for the general public; Bush wants to build a science fictional missile shield to provide monetary benefits for the military industrial complex. Kennedy inspired a technologically viable race to the moon that, rather like the Olympics, involved national pride. (*Apollo* astronauts left an American flag, not American military equipment, on the moon.) Further, during the Cuban missile crisis, Kennedy acted in the manner of an effective *Star Trek* starship captain: rather than initiating hostility, he threatened to use military force only after he had been provoked. (Although I am aware that some critics have argued that Kennedy acted with criminal recklessness and that the missiles located in Cuba were not provocative, I refer to the version of the crisis the Camelot myth promotes.) Bush (as opposed to Kennedy who—even though he manifested competitive masculine behavior regarding military involvement in Vietnam and the Cuba fiasco —did not initially provoke Khrushchev) ignores the fact that outer space is absolutely devoid of a contemporary Khrushchev. Bush, then, acts as a militaristic provocateur. Kennedy, via such initiatives as the innocuous *Echo* and *Telstar* satellites, situated outer space as an appropriate location for *Star Trek*'s vision of peaceful enterprise. Bush, in contrast, wishes to establish that outer space is an appropriate location for the *Star Wars* x-wing fighter—and Russian president Vladimir V. Putin supports his wish.[1] For Bush, "truly and finally mov-[ing] beyond the cold war" (Sanger 2001, A8) after the September 11th terrorist attacks means that Russia joins with the United States to fight terrorism —and that Russia allows Bush to proceed with the missile shield. Both Bush and Putin choose to ignore the fact that the terrorist attacks underscore the missile shield's ineffectiveness. Exactly how can a missile shield protect us from bioterrorism and random terrorist attacks that do not involve missiles? America's new war against terrorism has nothing to do with war waged in outer space.

Unlike Bush, Kennedy did not approach outer space in terms of unreal adolescent science fiction power fantasy. Kennedy, instead, actualized *Star Trek*'s beloved utopian and democratic ideals. His adherence to these ideals is a masculine enactment of Jacqueline Kennedy Onassis's sense of style, which is valorized to the extent that the New York Metropolitan Museum of Art's 2001 exhibition of her clothing is one of the most popular museum shows ever undertaken. The point is that *Star Trek* and the Kennedy family constitute the most enduring and admired myths of the second half of the twentieth century —and Bush's missile shield plan counters these myths. When Bush replaces the *Star Trek* version of high democratic ideals situated in outer space with the *Star Wars* version of American military aggression situated in outer space, he tries to actualize a science fiction scenario that opposes the most enduring late-twentieth-century American mythology. More simply stated: Americans do not like to have (as Bush advocates) arsenic placed in their water. Americans do not like to have America itself positioned as a rogue nation.

Bush's missile shield plan positions him as Darth Vader. Darth Vader is no John F. Kennedy. Bush/Vader opposes what multicultural studies scholar Ronald Takaki calls the "master narrative of American history," which involves "a democracy with lofty ideals" (quoted in Lee 2001, 57). In addition to Kennedy's handling of the Cuban missile crisis and *Star Trek*'s utopianism, the film *Pearl Harbor* (2001)—which emphasizes that America is not an initiatory military aggressor—also adheres to these ideals. Such factual and science fictional venerated master narratives of American history assert that positioning America as a military aggressor in an outer space that is devoid of a foreign military presence will certainly not enhance Bush's popularity. Bush is no Captain Kirk—terrorists are located inside caves in Afghanistan, not inside spaceships hovering above America.

Bush, however, acts in tandem with a branch of science fiction outside the *Star Trek* mode: the space soldier narratives involving high-tech future warfare that Robert Heinlein's *Starship Troopers* (1987) and the stories anthologized in *Isaac Asimov's War* (Dozois and Williams 1993) exemplify. In the introduction to their anthology *Space Soldiers*, "nine versions of the future of war" written by male authors, Jack Dann and Gardner Dozois state that "inevitably, one is led to conclude that the future will include war in space . . . and that therefore soldiers will be needed to fight those wars in space. Space soldiers. The poor bastards who will have to put their lives on the line to enforce policies made by politicians millions of miles . . . or perhaps even millions of light-years away" (Dann and Dozois 2001, 1). Bush's missile defense shield policy establishes him as the politician on the cusp of paving the way for a future in which the presently science fictional space soldier will become real.

Another type of science fiction portrays an alternative to this impending reality: the feminist science fiction that questions the need for space soldiers. Feminist science fiction asserts that outer space is a logical venue for feminist ideals and, hence, critiques the need for future war, forever war, and starship troopers. Instead of promoting the military pie-in-the-sky missile shield, Bush should read the feminist science fiction stories that are devoid of male presidents and male space soldiers. The notion that Bush would read feminist science fiction and initiate this genre's pacifist scenarios is, of course, a feminist Walter Mitty–like power fantasy—as unreal as zapping Osama bin Laden with a photon torpedo.

Reality, as we are aware, does emerge from science fiction. We have the submarines Jules Verne imagined. We have the communication satellites Arthur C. Clarke imagined. We are on the verge of having the human clones myriad science fiction writers imagined. We are on the verge of Bush initiating the need for the space soldiers he imagines. Presidents can institute adolescent male power fantasies.

In the face of this reality, feminists can turn to science fiction for inspiration and solace. I think of alternative Kennedy science fiction stories coupled with the pervasive science fiction cliché involving the spaceship landing on the White House lawn. (Since *Envisioning the Future* includes both essays and fiction, I interrupt this preface to offer a fictitious feminist future vision.) Hence: the spaceship gangplank descends and John F. Kennedy once again walks in front of the White House. When he is taken to America's current leader he says, "George, what you can do for your country is to initiate a policy analogous to establishing the Cape Cod National Seashore in outer space; set aside outer space as a wide-open space for everyone's enjoyment." Suddenly, in the manner of the science fiction film *Independence Day* (1996), spaceships commanded by women from technologically advanced feminist science fiction planets appear over Washington. In the best sense of science fiction combined with the western, extraterrestrial female spaceship commanders make Bush's day and force him to comply with Kennedy's vision. *Independence Day* features science fiction imagery. On September 11, 2001, terrorists made that fictitious imagery real.

Postscript: Talking Heads

Undaunted, I offer a science fiction scenario to explain how Gormley's body as it appears in *Quantum Cloud,* recast as a future female, would become a post-human female man. I turn to the science fictional disembodied head trope as it appears in a particular television situation comedy. No, I do not refer to the typical male head such as "The Big Giant Head" William Shatner plays in *Third Rock from the Sun.* To avoid this wrongheaded notion, I discuss a situation comedy that portrays feminist utopian community: *The Golden Girls,* the first successful situation comedy with an all-female cast.

In a two-part episode, "Home Again, Rose" (1992), the usual portrayal of feminist utopia in *The Golden Girls* becomes science fictional. During the first part of the episode, Rose suffers a heart attack and asks Dorothy and Blanche to make sure that her head is frozen after she dies. In order to be certain that all three women can be reunited in the far future, Rose makes Dorothy and Blanche promise that they will also have their heads frozen. The second part portrays the future meeting of the reactivated frozen heads belonging to Rose, Blanche, and Dorothy. According to Rose's future vision (which occurs when she is under anesthesia), the women's heads (sans their bodies) appear talking at their kitchen table—or, more accurately, on their kitchen table. The heads, mounted on silver trays, chatter away, explaining that they have not been given bodies. Where to find bodies for these future-projected female heads? The answer: off with his head. Or: attach the women's heads to the torso of the male figure *Quantum Cloud* depicts. Maybe in the future—circa 3000, for example—it will be possible to connect reactivated frozen human heads to inorganic bodies to construct immortal cyborgs. Think of the possibilities: male heads attached to female bodies and female heads attached to male bodies. The heads and the bodies could be different colors. And so ends sexism, racism, and ageism.

But: back to the future. Back from science fiction studies to cultural studies, back from feminist science fiction fantasy to female reality. Rue McClanahan, the actress who played Blanche, articulates a personal experience that forms a woman-centered alternative to Bush's missile defense and outer-space weapons plan. This is how McClanahan describes the visualization technique she used during her chemotherapy treatments for breast cancer: "I would draw my immune system fighting the cancer cells. Killing the cancer cells. And I would draw the chemo, the chemicals killing the cancer cells. So I made mine like little spaceships. Mine were little spaceships and they were zapping! Zap! Zap! Zap! These big, clumsy, dumb cancer cells. And these smart little immune system and chemotherapy things were just, you know, devastating these big, dumb cancer cells. You can picture it any way you want to. That worked for me" (Tuttle). Like Rose, McClanahan constructs a science fiction vision to help her cope with life-threatening illness. Like Bush, McClanahan imagines fighting an invading enemy in terms of science fiction. The differences in regard to how McClanahan and Bush imagine zapping spaceships are stunning, however. McClanahan zaps in outer space via a particularly personal and female cultural manner. Bush will not picture the idea that it is better to fund zapping real rogue cancer cells than it is to initiate a space war to zap rogue nations who have no presence in outer space. McClanahan and Rose articulate the respective women's real present and imagined futures patriarchal culture does not want to see. What to do? Or: how McClanahan and Bush look at space—differently. Look ahead. Look to a better future.

NOTE

1. David E. Sanger reports that "President Vladimir V. Putin of Russia emerged from more than an hour of talks with President Bush today saying they could reach agreements that would alter the 1972 Antiballistic Missile Treaty. If so, that would free the United States to test a proposed anti-missile system while meeting Moscow's demand not to abandon the treaty altogether" (Sanger 2001, A1).

WORKS CITED

Aldrin, Buzz, and John Barnes. 1997. *Encounter with Tiber.* New York: Warner.

———. 2000. *The Return.* New York: Forge.

Bush, George W. 2001. "Bush's Address on Federal Financing for Research with Embryonic Stem Cells." *New York Times* (10 August), A16.

Collins, Gail. 1999. "Grounded for 2000." *New York Times* (7 December), A23.

———. 2001. "Beam Me Up, Rummy." *New York Times* (8 May), A27.

Dann, Jack, and Gardner Dozois, eds. 2001. *Space Soldiers.* New York: Ace.

Dozois, Gardner, and Sheila Williams, eds. 1993. *Isaac Asimov's War.* New York: Ace.

Friedman, Thomas L. 2001. "Digital Defense." *New York Times* (27 July), A19.

The Golden Girls. 1992. "Home Again, Rose (1)." Written by Gail Parent. Directed by Peter D. Beyt (25 April).

———. 1992. "Home Again, Rose (2)." Written by Jim Vallely. Directed by Peter D. Beyt (2 May).

Gormley, Antony. 1999. "*Quantum Cloud* Sculpture Development: The Artist's Vision." Available from www.lusas.com

Heinlein, Robert A. 1987. *Starship Troopers.* New York: Berkley.

Hitt, Jack. 2001. "Battlefield: Space." *New York Times Magazine* (5 August), 30–35, 55–56, 62–63.

Independence Day. 1996. Twentieth Century Fox. Directed by Roland Emmerich. Written by Dean Devlin and Roland Emmerich. With Will Smith and Bill Pullman.

Lee, Chisun. 2001. "Romancing the Republic." *Village Voice* (12 June), 57.

Pearl Harbor. 2001. Touchstone Pictures. Produced and directed by Michael Bay. Written by Randall Wallace. With Ben Affleck and Kate Beckinsale.

Sanger, David E. 2001. "Putin Sees Pact with U.S. on Revising ABM Treaty." *New York Times* (22 October), A1, A8.

Tuttle, Gina. "Interview with Rue McClanahan." *Health Talk*. Available from www.healthtalk.com

Wolmack, Jack. 2001. "The Future Is History." *Artbyte* (February), 34–40.

ENVISIONING THE
Future

Now—and 3000
Science Fiction Studies/Cultural Studies

marleen s. barr

Envisioning the Future: Science Fiction and the Next Millennium presents fiction
and essays in a manner that combines the meaning of two titles—Ad Rine-
hardt's artwork *How to Look at Space* and J. L. Austin's *How to Do Things with
Words*—to juxtapose the words and space encompassing science fiction/cultural
studies. *Envisioning* focuses on how to do things with words to look at present
culture's relationship to the far future space fiction portrays. The contributors
—Rosi Braidotti, Harlan Ellison, James Gunn, Walter Mosley, Patrick Parrinder, Marge Piercy, Neil Postman, Eric S. Rabkin, Kim Stanley Robinson,
Pamela Sargent, Darko Suvin, George Zebrowski, and I—reveal how to look
at future cultural spaces.

Antony Gormley's sculpture *Quantum Cloud* is emblematic of their visions.
(See the frontispiece to this book.) As the LUSAS Engineering Software Products Web site explains, "*Quantum Cloud* is a 30 metre high × 16 metre wide ×
10 metre deep elliptical cloud sculpture which stands on four cast iron caissons
in the River Thames adjacent to the Millennium Dome in London. It is formed
from 1.5 metre long lengths of randomly oriented steel sections which diffuse
at the edges and condense into a 20 metre high human body form at the centre.
Modeled after Gormley's own body, *Quantum Cloud* is currently the tallest
sculpture in the UK" (LUSAS).

Gormley explains that the image of his body located in the center of *Quantum Cloud* "will be elusive, visible from some angles and not from others." He
continues:

> The finish will be galvanised, therefore reflective, the angled sides of the
> members will make it highly responsive to atmospheric conditions, both of

light and humidity. The outer antennae will vibrate and move in the wind. The work will rise out of an open-work grill supported by four 12 metre high cast iron columns that stand in the river adjacent to the Millennium Dome. It represents a shift in my work, from a preoccupation with mass, volume and skin to a concern with air, energy and light. Hovering above the cast-iron caissons that were bequeathed to us by the industrial revolution, the work alludes to the transformation of classical physics and its concern with the building blocks of matter to a new quantum reality: that everything is in flux and that solid objects are an illusion. *Quantum Cloud* is a project that can only be realised with digital design systems and I am very fortunate to be collaborating with energetic and ground-breaking engineers. The result, a combination of art and technology, will be a monument to the future, expressing the potential of the human being at the end of the twentieth century. (Gormley 1999)

The far future, too, is elusive; some of its aspects can be guessed at and others are unknowable. No stationary entities, *Quantum Cloud* and the future both shift according to random currents. The sculpture is grounded upon the cast-iron caissons inherited from the industrial revolution; the past is the future's bedrock. Our present is continually in flux and our future is an illusion. Gormley's monument to the future — which combines art and cutting-edge technology and addresses human potential as the new millennium begins — aptly represents this anthology's intention: to focus upon the present's relationship to the far future through a merged science fiction and cultural studies lens.

To exemplify this science fiction studies/cultural studies reading practice, *Envisioning the Future* presents four thematic sections: "Future Past," which investigates the relationship between past events and future scenarios; "Future Present," which addresses the reciprocity between the past and the future; "Future Perfect," which discusses women's futures; and "Future Critical," which investigates the future of future fiction. The authors who contribute to these sections are among the finest science fiction authors, scholars, and cultural critics writing today. My decision to place fiction and criticism in the same volume reflects the current cultural moment — the post–September 11, 2001, world — in which former assumptions about the fixed definitions demarcating the differences between fiction and reality no longer hold. The terrorist attacks exemplify science fiction imagery becoming real in a manner that we could not predict prior to their occurrence. Presently, then, an anthology about envisioning the future appropriately includes both imaginative literature and cultural criticism. This lack of adherence to usual generic classifications — a table of contents that exemplifies the term I call "genre fission"—reflects our new uncharted reality in which former rigid categorizations have become amorphous. If, for example, "war" no longer involves particular nation-states, then "anthology" need not be relegated to one particular textual genre. Further, since the far future is uncertain, fiction and nonfiction are equally useful tools with which to speculate about it.

"Truth," as postmodern theory reminds us, is subjective. The attacks of September 11th underscore this point: Osama bin Laden is at once a hero in the eyes of the terrorists and a villain in the eyes of the Americans. Stanley Fish, writing about the attacks, explains that there is no definitive standard for discerning which of several versions of an occurrence is true: "Postmodernism maintains only that there can be no independent standard for determining which of many rival interpretations of an event is the true one. The only thing postmodern thought argues against is the hope of justifying our response to the attacks in universal terms that would be persuasive to everyone, including our enemies. Invoking the abstract notions of justice and truth to support our cause wouldn't be effective anyway because our adversaries lay claim to the same language. (No one declares himself to be an apostle of injustice.) Instead, we can and should invoke the particular lived values that unite us and inform the institutions we cherish and wish to defend" (Fish 2001, A19). Fish's comments about envisioning the attacks are applicable to envisioning the future. There is no one way correctly to interpret the attacks; there is no one way correctly to speculate about the future. We can only approach the future by discussing the values and institutions we cherish and defend with the hope that these ideals will be operative in the future. *Envisioning* fosters this discussion. After all, with regard to the future, which (like definitive interpretation) must always be speculative, language and communication assume utmost importance. Language and communication are our only means to understand both the recent past's terrorist attacks and the far-future world—the next millennium—humanity might eventually inhabit. Talking about both subjects forces consideration of the newly past millennium and evokes such millennial issues as the end of the world, annihilation versus survival, and the place of technology and theology. Millennial issues are the focus of the media in the wake of the terrorist attacks; millennial issues are the focus of *Envisioning the Future: Science Fiction and the Next Millennium.*

Envisioning discusses the impossible: presently knowing the far future. Its contributors grapple with this question: How do we look at the presently potential space that will become the future?

Neil Postman, in "Building a Bridge to the Eighteenth Century," assumes an unusual position: understanding the future does not involve being forward looking. When he defines the eighteenth century as days of the far-future past, he suggests moving back to the future. He takes issue with those who look ahead to contemplate a forward temporal trajectory: "I am suspicious of people who want us to be forward looking. In fact, I literally do not know what people mean when they say 'we must look ahead' to see where we are going. What is it that they wish us to look at?" According to Postman, being forward looking involves looking backward, "turn[ing] our attention to the eighteenth century." Postman proclaims, for example, that the eighteenth century enables us to see that our current—and our future—devotion to information is not sensible. He believes that looking toward the far future involves understanding that eighteenth-century occurrences and worldviews will pertain to that far future.

James Gunn's story "The End-of-the-World Ball" investigates culture by having an end-of-the-world millennial ball's participants explore the relationship between future prediction and the fact of the known present. They question how paradigm shift occurs: "The questions remain: What changes the times? What brings about the sudden acceptance of this theory or that?" Answers to these questions involve blurring boundaries between fiction and reality. The catastrophe prediction experts gathered at the Millennium Celebration Ball act in the manner of literary critics. One of them contemplates the meaning of the president's decision to exit the premises where the ball is occurring: "What does that mean?" The answer: "Maybe nothing. . . . Maybe catastrophe." This answer, which encompasses two extremes, proclaims that there are no fixed definitions. Gunn's protagonist offers a suggestion that subscribes to poststructuralist theory which explains that reality is a constructed fiction: "[L]et's create a new world, for ourselves and whoever wants to join us." A glittering woman appears at the end of Gunn's story to address the heavens and portend the end of the world. She might be an angel—or one of the superior beings George Zebrowski imagines.

Darko Suvin's "Reflections on What Remains of Zamyatin's *We* after the Change of Leviathans: Must Collectivism Be against People?" discusses how appropriately to read Yevgeny Zamyatin's *We* during the new millennium, a time Suvin describes as a change of Leviathans. According to Suvin, *We* confronts a presently irrelevant Leviathan: "the opposition of positive individuality to negative collectivity of State centralization." The new millennium's appropriate Leviathan, in contrast, concerns being "ruled by the psychophysical alienation of corporate capitalist collectivism," which Suvin calls "the emptying terrorism." In other words, the Leviathan applicable to the new millennium emanates from McDonald's—not from a current Hitler. Or, in Suvin's words:

"The insipid food in *We*, made from petroleum and distributed by the State, does not collate to our problems with the overspiced and cancerogenously hormonized 'McDonald'sified' burgers pushed by brainwashing us in the 'free' market. Even less does it speak to the hungry and freezing unpaid millions of 'freed Russia.'" The specifically targeted groups who starved in concentration camps are superseded by everyone being "democratically free to be physically and psychically hungry while chewing abundant junk food." In our world dominated by twenty media monopolies rather than one dictator, the hamburger skillet, not the Nazi death camp oven, is the most potent insidious threat. The new Leviathan, then, is cultural and isolating rather than Fascist and brutal. Suvin, when he rereads *We* in terms of the new dominant global cultural homogenization, poses this question: "Who is in *We* the equivalent of the heretic Christ confronting the *apparatchik* Great Inquisitor?" Zebrowski, in his story "The Coming of Christ the Joker," depicts Christ appearing in the present and far future. Zebrowski answers Suvin's question.

His answer addresses another "we"—an alternative contemporary America, Zebrowski's fictitious reality, which is not a carbon copy of us. He imagines a heretic Christ—a Christ who, instead of being a deity, is a life form from a higher plane of existence—confronting the Great Inquisitor of our culturally homogenized time: the television talk show host. When Zebrowski's Christ, an entity whose technological abilities are vastly superior to our own, appears on television to speak with Larry King and Gore Vidal, he evokes the combination of capitalism and science Kim Stanley Robinson describes.

Like Robinson, Zebrowski emphasizes that combining science and capitalism does not usually yield universal human betterment. "Some of you know about vacuum energy and the impossibility of zero-fields. But you've always ignored your best minds, except when they make weapons for you. . . . I wish you people were as bright when it comes to your violent history and treatment of one another," says Zebrowski's heretic Christ. Both Zebrowski and Robinson emphasize that we combine capitalism with science to generate violence and mistreatment, not utopia.

Perhaps Zebrowski, the Austrian-born son of Polish parents who were kidnapped as slave labor for the German Reich (someone who experienced the culture that created the past's Nazi ovens and who lives in a present where the Golden Arches of McDonald's are pervasive), believes that humanity does not deserve an effective messiah. When Christ appears on *Larry King Live*, nothing of great pith and moment occurs; Christ offers banal jokes and performs slight-of-hand magic tricks. According to Christ, banality is an appropriate response to humans' trivial pursuits: "You're only a quantum fluctuation in a superspace vacuum, scarcely more than a greasy spot on the wall in one of our oldest cities. But we have let you be." Zebrowski's Christ (who, unlike Nazis, truly is a superior being) chooses not to eradicate humanity's future in a manner analogous to using Ajax to cleanse a greasy spot on a wall. Zebrowski's superior life forms are better than the biologically human Hitler who annihilated his fellow humans whom he defined as stains. Since Zebrowski's Christ believes that all humanity can be defined as a stain (perhaps a stain in the form of a grease spot dripping from Suvin's notion of the hamburger as new Leviathan), his benevolence may not be permanent. With a tone suitable to an annihilator more polite than Hitler, Christ suggests that the stain that constitutes humanity might indeed be wiped away: "'We might just have to let you go,' Jesus said, 'let you dissolve into nothing. . . . Have some faith in me when I tell you that you'll be much happier as nothing.'" Christ thinks that having no future is in humanity's best interest. Perhaps he correctly concludes that a species that conducted Nazi atrocities does not deserve to experience 3000, the next millennium.

In the manner of Zebrowski's "The Coming of Christ the Joker," Harlan Ellison's story "Goodbye to All That" echoes Arthur C. Clarke's *Childhood's End:* both stories depict humans entering the realm of a higher life form. Both Ellison and Zebrowski position a transcendent close encounter as a means to indict American culture: Zebrowski's Larry King and Gore Vidal chat with Christ on a television talk show (regarded by some viewers as what Ellison calls "The Intellectual Center of the Universe"); Ellison's Colman might meet God in McDonald's portrayed as "the Core, the Nexus, the Center." Both authors concur with Suvin's notion that homogenous corporate American culture is the new Leviathan. Colman's quest for Shangri-La includes a transcendent view of McDonald's Golden Arches, which unmistakably evoke Suvin's notion of the evil hamburger: he "saw above him . . . what appeared to be a golden structure rising from the summit, its shape a reassuring and infinitely calming sweep of dual archlike parabolas." Ellison's version of Zebrowski's "grease spots" are "excess drippings" emanating from a fast food restaurant's "deep fryer filled with sizzling vegetable oil."

The phrase "goodbye to all that" signals a farewell to all the local cultures corporate American engulfs. Even though Colman is situated in a real or fantastic exotic Asian wilderness, he knows that "the Baskin-Robbins 'flavor of the month' was tuna fish–chocolate" and that "Ben & Jerry had just introduced a new specialty flavor, Sea Monkey." Nothing—not even books—can abate the corporate presences that nullify local cultures; the death of Colman's yak—who dies despite the "lot of books" he consulted and the folk remedies he used "to resuscitate the imperial beast"—represents this situation. Goodbye to the yak and all that heterogeneous local cultural practice related to its use. Perhaps the yak literally dies from the burden of carrying material goods. Colman articulates his dependence upon all the things the yak had *schlepped*: *"I'll never make it with all this gear."* The yak's demise forces him to cope with all of his gear via a selection process: "He unshipped the dead noble beast and began, there on the slope, to separate the goods into two piles, seeing his chances of survival diminishing with every item added to the heap on his right." In the world of the hamburger as new Leviathan, selection and "survival"—deciding what will be relegated either to the right or to the left—involves a consumer categorizing "gear," not the Nazi concentration camp selection that categorizes Jews.

Jewishness is integral to "Goodbye to All That." Colman, while located within the fast food restaurant defined as the be all and end all of all things, decides that the following words are the most important ones to say to God: "Let me talk to the Head Jew." Many aspects of what was once particular to Jewish culture have become mainstream American culture. Bagels, for example, can be found in almost every American food store's frozen food section. *"Shrek,"* a Yiddish word, names a popular film released in the summer of 2001. *I Have No Mouth, and I Must Scream,* wrote Ellison. *Shrek* cannot scream either; the film cannot protest the fact that *"shrek,"* an ethnic cultural expression, has been subsumed within technocultural corporate globalization—that is, the new Leviathan.

Philip Roth's *Operation Shylock* is pertinent to the meaning of Colman's decision to equate talking to "the Head Jew" with talking to God. Roth writes, "God gave Moses the Ten Commandments and then He gave to Irving Berlin 'Easter Parade' and 'White Christmas.' The two holidays that celebrate the divinity of Christ . . . and what does Irving Berlin brilliantly do? He de-Christs them both! Easter he turns into a fashion show and Christmas into a holiday about snow . . . down with the crucifix and up with the bonnet! He turns *their religion into schlock.* . . . I . . . found more security in 'White Christmas' than in the Israeli nuclear reactor" (Roth 1994, 157–58). Hitler authors Operation Shylock (in which all Jews become villainous); Irving Berlin authors Operation Schlock (in which Christ—in the manner of Zebrowski placing Christ on a television talk show—becomes indistinguishable from popular American schlock culture). Irving Berlin, not Hitler, authors the texts most appropriate to contemporary American culture. Many American endeavors have been reduced to the inconsequential, turned into schlock. As Ellison so adroitly indicates, schlock is the black hole into which everything is now pulled. Even the word "schlock" has become schlockified. Where once the meaning of this word was clear only to, say, *shtetl* dwellers, educated *goyim* residing in, for example, North Dakota might be familiar with the word.

Colman's words "Head Jew" signal goodbye to all that Nazism—goodbye to all that World War II Hitlerian cultural stuff. Jewish culture is ensconced within American culture—and schlock pervades American culture. Or: frozen bagels found in North Dakota supermarket frozen food sections taste terrible in relation to those found in Manhattan's *Zabar's*. And: even good New York bagels have been culturally polluted in that they now come in such flavors as blueberry and "everything." (Thank God for the fact that an everything bagel still has nothing to do with "tuna fish–chocolate" flavor.) The new Leviathan is American cultural schlock (such as ever faster and larger fast food or Gary Coleman cast as the newly rich whitewashed black child in the situation comedy *Diff'rent Strokes*).

Schlock, not Hitler, now reigns supreme and has taken over the world. Hitler, as Mel Brooks's *The Producers* so creatively indicates, is now a laughing stock. As Brooks's Max Bialystock learns while trying to do everything he can to make *Springtime for Hitler* (the most schlock-sodden play he can produce) fail, schlock succeeds in America. *Springtime* succeeds because a schlockified Hitler is the most appropriate Hitler for our time. Ironically, Brooks is the "Head Jew" of Broadway because he "supersizes" the film version of *The Producers*— an idiosyncratic, nonhomogeneous, noncorporate work—to create the Broadway version. When Brooks inflates Max Bialystock, he inflates the value of his own individualistic entertainment value. The irreverent, individually authored *Producers* is no corporate Disney-sodden *The Lion King*—and Mel Brooks is no Michael Eisner. The uniquely individual artistic voice, then, is not a lost cause. Or: frozen bialys (a bialy is a less fattening, holeless version of a bagel) are not yet found in North Dakota supermarket frozen food sections.

"Let me talk to the Head Jew" reveals the meaning of the most potent scream emanating from and entering the American mouth, the locution that replaces *achtung* as the current most effective demand for attention: "May I super-size that for you?" These are the divine words Colman hears. "Super-size" indicates that fast food restaurants generate even more nutritional schlock; "super-size" is the new Leviathan that ultimately is as lethal as the Nazi oven. Everyone is vulnerable in relation to "super-size"—too much of the killing junk food that is taking over the world, the Golden Arches that appear everywhere. Look. Up in the sky. Is it a bird? Is it a plane? Yes. It's super-sized Americans crowded into an American Airlines flight, eating junk food.

Colman "spoke the only words that would provide entrance if one were confronting God." Because of the pervasive new Leviathan hamburger—an

Alice-in-Wonderland ingested item that only makes people larger—super-sized Americans may appear at the "entrance" to God's realm and find that they are too fat to enter.

I apply Ellison's title "Goodbye to All That" to George W. Bush's presidency. My story "Superfeminist; or, A Hanukah Carol" is a power fantasy in which it becomes possible to say goodbye to all that in regard to Bush's conservative agenda. I imagine that conservative aspects of the present are changed after Bush visits the future via a flight Superfeminist makes possible.

Pamela Sargent's story "Utmost Bones" presents a posthuman far future seen from the perspective of Kaeti, the last human connected to the Net who still retains her flesh and blood body. When Kaeti contemplates how humanity became so interconnected with machines, she is answered by Erlann, her ancestor who, in the manner of Neil Postman, advocates looking toward the past to understand the future. "How did we come to be as we are?" Kaeti asks. Erlann's answer: "When one looks back, it seems fairly obvious." The catastrophe experts who appear in James Gunn's "The End-of-the-World Ball" would feel at home in Kaeti's world. Like Kaeti, these experts ponder, in Gunn's words, "What changes the times? What brings about the sudden acceptance of this theory or that?" Gunn's experts provide an appropriate answer for Kaeti. Sargent writes: "The statistics were inexorable. If a certain finite number of people lived long enough, eventually some chance happening would kill them all." The version of "kill" operative in Kaeti's far-future world is alien to the experts.

Kaeti must discern whether or not human consciousness removed from bodies and juxtaposed with the Net is dead. From the perspective of this inhabitant of a world containing various new human species (such as posthuman bodies linked to the Net and animals who think and speak in the manner of humans), eradicating biological bodies is equivalent to death. Hence, Kaeti decides not to discard her body in order completely to merge with the Net. As the last existing compromise entity who possesses both a body and a Net link, she chooses to live as a Frankenstein monster trying to convince savage human survivors to connect to the Net. Her reason: she desires that someone who is like her will exist. She learns the complexity of the term "posthuman"—the fact that living as a Frankenstein monster is no fixed definition—as she discerns that her Net-connected body is as monstrous to the humans as the complete eradication of the body is to her. "How much of what I once was is left?" she wonders. When the human savages contemplate whether or not they should become linked to the Net, they might ask the same question. Kaeti decides that —because of the necessity of positioning disembodied human consciousness outside culture—"posthuman" is synonymous with subhuman: "She and those she had known had made no history of their own, nothing to match the accomplishments of their ancestors." Choosing to remain a human consciousness linked to a biological body, she equates losing the body with losing humanity: "if the brains in which their thoughts were first formed have been lost, then those people no longer truly exist. What the Net holds is no more than a host of simulacra. . . . [H]ow frightened she had been to know yet again that she was the last to inhabit the form of a human being—except of course for the unchanged and abandoned creatures who sat with her by the fire."

The "unchanged" mute primitives are in fact changed according to the reader's perceptions of them; they are closer to the definition of "creatures" than the talking animals Kaeti encounters. "Human" is a term open to interpretation. (Zebrowski's Christ would say that the bodiless Net-linked humans Kaeti encounters are more "human" then the people who perpetrated twentieth-century atrocities.) Sargent, when she recreates Olaf Stapledon's last man as the last woman, underscores that sexism is an atrocity. She concludes that genderless jettisoned biological bodies—not the female body Kaeti chooses to retain—are the alien Other. Kaeti's female bones, no Other in relation to contemporary patriarchy's assault on the female body, are the utmost bones.

When Marge Piercy grapples with what form love and sex will assume in the year 3000, she at first imagines that the future will involve a utopian cultural ideal for both women and men: "I like to imagine that in the future all people will have choices." Seeming to comment further on Joanna Russ's 1981 essay "Recent Feminist Utopias," Piercy's "Love and Sex in the Year 3000" includes this statement: "Utopia is work that issues from pain: it is what we do not have that we crave." Although we do not presently have equality in regard to love and sex, feminist utopias, of course, provide the best blueprints for achieving this desired feminist goal. Despite their value, some literary scholars still categorize feminist utopias as what Eric S. Rabkin's protagonist calls "crap." Like Rabkin, Piercy contests the idea that "[g]enre writing is generally looked down upon."

Written in a genre fission mode, "Love and Sex in the Year 3000" does not textually participate in the denigration of genre writing; Piercy's approach to science fiction studies and cultural studies involves the refusal to be confined by generic restrictions. Her piece at once presents her as a fantasist, essayist, literary critic, and autobiographer. Bringing the contemporary to bear upon Rabkin's notion that in the future science fiction and humanity will become one unified whole, she lauds speculative fiction novels by stating that they improve upon her essay's discussion of future love and sex: "I have played with some fantasies about sex in the year 3000, but finally, I believe that a good novel does it all better, which is one reason I read and write speculative fiction." Piercy, however, contradicts this assertion in that she provides powerful reality-steeped autobiographical detail: she explains that she shared her grandmother's bed and her mother was isolated to the extent that she argued with the televised images of evening newscasters. Piercy's genre fission approach involves interweaving women, culture, and the future by at once exalting speculative fiction and providing powerful glimpses of her own past female familial reality: her mother's and grandmother's stories now stand beside her novels' feminist utopian and dystopian visions.

Rosi Braidotti, in "Cyberteratologies: Female Monsters Negotiate the Other's Participation in Humanity's Far Future," argues that cyberteratology ("teratology" involves the scientific discourse about the origin and nature of monstrous bodies) provides a new way to understand the cultural penchant for juxtaposing the feminine and the monstrous. She asserts "that the female monster's presence marks the inception of a science fictional cultural trend that can impact upon the far future by reserving a place for female and minority subjectivities within that far future." Braidotti's theoretical approach to the female monster is quite congruent with Sargent's realization of the "monstrous" female protagonist Kaeti. Braidotti's ideas also coincide with the point that patriarchy would regard Piercy's notions of utopian feminist love and sex as being synonymous with "monstrous female." Kaeti, in Braidotti's words, elects not to become "a new 'posthuman' technoteratological phenomenon that privileges the deviant or the mutant over more conventional versions of the human."

In the manner of Piercy and Rabkin, Braidotti confronts some scholars' penchant for denigrating science fiction. She asserts that science fiction provides appropriate cultural illustrations of her insights regarding the relation between women and the monstrous. She also believes that science fiction addresses Giles Deleuze's theories of culture and Donna Haraway's "promises of monsters." Sargent, Piercy, and Braidotti all concern themselves with monsters' promises. They all—together with Robinson—agree that science fiction, as Braidotti states, "points to a posthumanist, biocentered egalitarianism." Braidotti's conclusion—"the presence of monsters can provide both solace and a model"—applies to discussing feminist science fiction in terms of cultural studies. My "monstrous" protagonist, Superfeminist, would concur too.

When discussing situating the temporal within science fiction texts, Patrick Parrinder, in "'You must have seen a lot of changes': Fiction beyond the Twenty-first Century," argues that a particular future date should be categorized as neither "near" nor "far": "a date such as the year 3000 is neither 'near' nor 'far' but typifies what I will call the intermediate future." He explains why Arthur C. Clarke and Robinson create intermediate-future fiction that employs precise dating and includes protagonists whose lives encompass much of the next millennium. Although Robinson's and Rabkin's contributions to this volume employ precise dating in the manner Parrinder describes, Sargent's "Utmost Bones" most aptly adheres to his new literary category. Sargent's protagonist Kaeti, who does not wish to jettison history and culture, behaves in a manner coinciding with Parrinder's point that "[h]istory and the cultural past are, by and large, superfluous baggage in an age of perfect reason. In anti-utopian fiction set in the intermediate future, historical memory has often been perverted and distorted beyond accurate recovery." Kaeti defines unrecoverable biological historical memory as a perversion and distortion of the definition of "human itself." Both Parrinder and Kaeti believe that the future should involve the cultural world we know: "What intermediate-future fiction perhaps now needs is a return to Earth, since paradoxically the future-realistic novel set in outer space has come to seem so mundane," explains Parrinder. His point is well taken in regard to American military culture, which desires to bring the *Star Wars* galaxy located far, far away home in the form of a missile shield and outer-space weapons positioned above our heads.

Adhering to Parrinder's notion that, in the manner of Clarke and Robinson, some science fiction writers present the far future in terms of specific dates, Rabkin imagines a far future that functions as a power fantasy for science fiction critics. His imaginative text, a next millennium review of two works about science fiction, argues that—even though "the very word 'crap' took on its modern meaning through science fiction"—science fiction is not crap. Hence, the future reviewer Rabkin creates asserts that contemporary science fiction culture is wrongfully denigrated. Science fiction itself makes it possible to read Rabkin's future of linked humans as a positive version of Sargent's bleak future vision of the Net. Rabkin's title "What Was Science Fiction?" is so much more benign than the question Sargent's Kaeti ponders: What was humanity?

Rabkin's version of Sargent's future Net, which he calls "the virtex," emanates from contemporary science fiction culture: "Even in the late twentieth century, so-called computer games, the vast majority of which adopted the subject matter and motifs of SF, involved networked humans, so that experiencing these hypernarratives was no longer a necessarily isolated experience." Late-twentieth-century science fiction culture, according to Rabkin's imagined scenario, leads to the twenty-third century's ubiquitous "biosm" (a means for people to interact with other natural and artificial intelligence). Science fiction, no crap, is "the main source of movement and sustenance for humanity in the twentieth century"—that is, science fiction is positioned at culture's apex. Rabkin predicts that science fiction will permeate future culture: "One recognizes it [science fiction] in every aspect of Solar Culture." He does not see fit to stop short at science fiction's domination of future culture: "SF is so much a part of us that it is no longer reasonable to speak of it as anything other than us." "What Was Science Fiction?" answers Kaeti's question: What will humanity become? According to Rabkin, humanity and science fiction will become a juxtaposed unit. Science fiction, an integral part of the cultural present, and the posthuman future will function as a positive and synonymous whole. Science fiction will metamorphose from toy (or, crap) to become SF "Я" us.

In the manner of Rabkin's text, Kim Stanley Robinson's imaginative text "Science in the Third Millennium" turns to a Borgesian fictitious book reviewer to describe a utopian future vision. Robinson's reviewer signals that the current definition of "human" is no longer applicable. The crux of Robinson's text, however, concerns considering the relationship between present cultural constructions and the word "humane." Robinson's protagonist explains that the combination of science and capitalism results in a new social system called permaculture. Permaculture comprises "[a]dequate food, water, shelter, clothing, health care, and education for all; increased longevity; the stabilization of Earth's ecologies; the inhabitation of the solar system: these and other major achievements of the millennium all followed from science's successful transformation of the social system of that time." The fact that so much of Robinson's future utopian scenario could presently be attainable American reality points to the dystopian aspects of our present. "[T]he great leaps in the biological sciences" now occurring *are* united with capitalism. The result, as Suvin and Zebrowski emphasize, is (in Robinson's words) "a dysfunctional social system."

Robinson's concludes his review by alluding to a fictional text positioned within his fictional text (called "History Judges You"). To provide an "exhibit A" vis-à-vis the guilt of the contemporary alliance between capitalism and science, I enable a nonfictional text to bear upon Robinson's fictional text: Michael Finkel's *New York Times Magazine* piece "Complications." Finkel's article, which juxtaposes science and capitalism, describes how the technology that makes kidney transplants increasingly successful creates a market in which the poor sell their kidneys to the rich. Finkel explains that a 44-year-old Turkish man, Mehmet Piskin, sold his kidney to raise money to save his young son Ahmet, who suffers from a degenerative bone disease. Piskin's effort certainly does not achieve the desired result. Four years later, Piskin cannot work because the operation caused him to lose his health. The Piskin family cannot afford electricity. Ahmet Piskin's illness prevents him from attending school. Mehmet's wife, Sebnem, describes the impact the merger of science and capitalism has had on her family: "Everything is worse now than before. . . . Mehmet was a healthy person, and now he is like this. . . . Ahmet is crippled. We've basically been reduced to begging" (Finkel 2001, 40, 52). The contemporary coupling of science and capitalism creates real posthumans: impoverished people reduced to a subhuman existence who inhabit the now. Robinson's nonhuman protagonist is more privileged—treated in a manner more human and humane—than the Piskin family.

Envisioning the Future ends as it began—with an unexpected temporal stance. Like Postman, Walter Mosley looks toward the future through the lens of the past; "Black to the Future" indeed moves back to the future. Black people have been excluded from empowerment during the historical past; science fiction enables them to imagine—and actualize—the future: "Black people have been cut off from their African ancestry by the scythe of slavery and from an American heritage by being excluded from history. For us science fiction offers an alternative where that which deviates from the norm is the norm." Science fiction enables black people to emerge from a past historical void to create the future as a black norm. Mosley, who as the child of black and Jewish parents himself experiences a background that deviates from the norm, extends the spectrum of literary color scheme: due to his efforts, recognition for the mainstream "color purple" now also includes recognition for the science fictional *Blue Light* (2000). Ellison seems to describe an expanded color scheme in relation to science fiction: Colman sees "the Singular Scheme of Cosmic Clarity" located "[h]igh above him, blazing gloriously in the last pools of sunlight whose opposite incarnations were fields of blue shadow." When more black writers create science fiction, the dark "fields of blue shadow" (or, the paucity of black science fiction that Sheree R. Thomas [2000] refers to as "dark matter") will become gloriously blazing blue light (black authors' contribution to science fiction that Mosley's *Blue Light* exemplifies).

It is, of course, not possible accurately to predict what will occur in the year 3000. Mosley, however, offers a future vision involving a more manageable time frame: "Within the next five years I predict there will be an explosion of science fiction from the black community." Conforming to the power of genre fission, the science fiction black people create has the power to blast racism to smithereens—in the present and for the far future. Black science fiction writers (with the noted exceptions of Octavia Butler and Samuel Delany) are just starting to imagine brave, new, better egalitarian worlds that can become the future world.

Black science fiction visions are joining feminist science fiction visions in articulating that a future dominated by white men is a wrongheaded idea. I would like to situate *Quantum Cloud* within a more egalitarian (that is, more devoid of sexism and racism) future. Perhaps, unlike the meaning of "quantum," the particular white male figure situated in the center of *Quantum Cloud* is not a fixed, elemental unit. The present has been a time for changing previously fixed definitions of proper social roles and rules. Perhaps, in the future, we will ensconce someone other than a white man at the center of cultural momentum. Perhaps, in the future, science fiction and cultural studies will merge in a manner that makes it possible for the center of *Quantum Cloud* to be, instead of a present man, a future female.

WORKS CITED

Clarke, Arthur C. 1953. *Childhood's End*. New York: Ballantine.

Diff'rent Strokes. 1978–1986. Directed by Gerren Keith and Herbert Kenwith. Written by Bernie Kukoff. With Gary Coleman and Conrad Bain.

Ellison, Harlan. 1967. *I Have No Mouth and I Must Scream*. New York: Pyramid.

Finkel, Michael. 2001. "Complications." *New York Times Magazine* (27 May), sect. 6:26–33, 40, 52, 59.

Fish, Stanley. 2001. "Condemnation without Absolutes." *New York Times* (15 October), A19.

Gormley, Antony. 1999. "*Quantum Cloud* Sculpture Development: The Artist's Vision." Available from www.lusas.com

LUSAS Engineering Software Products. "The Design and Analysis of *Quantum Cloud: A Sculpture by Antony Gormley*." Available from www.lusas.com

Mosley, Walter. 2000. *Blue Light*. New York: Warner.

The Producers. 2000–. Directed and choreographed by Susan Stroman. Written by Mel Brooks and Thomas Meehan. Music and lyrics by Mel Brooks. With Nathan Lane and Matthew Broderick.

Roth, Philip. 1994. *Operation Shylock: A Confession*. New York: Vintage.

Russ, Joanna. 1981. "Recent Feminist Utopias." Pp. 71–85 in *Future Females: A Critical Anthology*, ed. Marleen S. Barr. Bowling Green, Ohio: Bowling Green State University Popular Press.

Thomas, Sheree R. 2000. *Dark Matter: A Century of Speculative Fiction from the African Diaspora*. New York: Warner.

one

FUTURE PAST

Building a Bridge to the Eighteenth Century

neil postman

I start from the assumption that, like so many others, readers are concerned about what will happen to us in the new millennium and beyond. There certainly is a great deal of frantic talk about the twenty-first century and how it will pose for us unique problems of which we know very little but for which, nonetheless, we are supposed to carefully prepare. Everyone seems to worry about this topic—businesspeople, politicians, theologians, and especially educators. So if you will not think me patronizing, I should like to begin by putting your minds at ease: I doubt that the twenty-first century will pose problems for us that are more disorienting or complex than those we faced in the twentieth century or, for that matter, in many of the centuries before that. But if anyone is excessively nervous about the new millennium, I can give you, right at the start, some good advice about how to confront it. The advice comes from people whom we can trust, and whose thoughtfulness, it is safe to say, exceeds that of Ted Turner or even Bill Gates. Here is what Henry David Thoreau told us: "All our inventions are but improved means to an unimproved end." Here is what Goethe told us: "One should, each day, try to hear a little song, read a good poem, see a fine picture, and if possible, speak a few reasonable words." Socrates told us: "The unexamined life is not worth living." Rabbi Hillel said: "What is hateful to thee, do not do to another." And here is the prophet Micah: "What does the Lord require of thee but to do justly, to love mercy and to walk humbly with thy God." And I could tell you—if we had the time (although you know it well enough)—what Confucius, Isaiah, Jesus, Mohammed, the Buddha, Spinoza, and Shakespeare told us. It is all the same: there is no escaping from ourselves. The human dilemma is as it has always been, and it is a delusion to believe that the technological changes of our era have rendered irrelevant the wisdom of the ages and the sages.

Nonetheless, having said this, I know perfectly well that because we do live in a technological age, we have some special problems that Jesus, Hillel, Socrates, and Micah did not and could not speak of. For example, all of us are aware that scientists in Scotland successfully cloned a sheep. Another group of scientists in America has cloned a monkey. And apparently, a high school student, in order to gain some extra credit, claims to have cloned a frog. We can expect, if not this year or the next, that the cloning of human beings will be a reality, especially now that the genome project has advanced so far. Now, I think we can say that we have here a genuine twenty-first-century problem. It would be interesting—wouldn't it?—to speculate on what Jesus or the Buddha would say about this development in human reproduction. Well, we will have to address this matter without them. How will we do that? Where will we go for guidance? What use shall we make of this technology? Here is an idea I imagine most of you will find unacceptable, if not contemptible: cloning humans, a science fiction scenario that is about to become reality, opens up a whole new field of "human spare parts." The way it would work is that every time someone is born, a clone of this person would be made. The clone would be kept in a special, confined, and well-guarded place so that it could provide spare parts for the original person as needed throughout life. If the original person loses a kidney or lung, we would simply take it from the clone. Now, I know you will protest that the clone is, after all, a real human being. But that would only be the case if we *define* the clone as a human being. There is nothing new in human beings' defining other human beings as nonhuman things. In all cases of genocide, that is exactly the procedure. Aldous Huxley wrote about how to do such things, although he did so ironically and bitterly. In our own time, Marvin Minsky and others working in the field of artificial intelligence have prophesied quite enthusiastically that humans will become merely pets of their computers, so that the definition of the worth and capacity of humans will change.

I hope you are thinking that my proposal is simply a bad joke and that any such proposal, seriously made, is a product of a depraved mind. Of course, I agree with you. But here is a question: Where did you get the idea that this proposal would be the product of a depraved mind? I imagine most of you believe that infanticide is also a depraved idea, in spite of the fact that it has been practiced for many more years in human history than it has been forbidden. Where did you get the idea that infanticide is horrible? Or that slavery is a bad idea? Or that the divine right of kings is a bad idea?

What I am driving at is that in order to have an agreeable encounter with the twenty-first century, we will have to take into it some good ideas. And in order to do that, we need to look back, to take stock of the good ideas available to us. I am suspicious of people who want us to be forward looking. In fact, I literally do not know what people mean when they say "we must look ahead" to see where we are going. What is it that they wish us to look at? There is nothing yet to see in the future. If looking ahead means anything, it must mean finding in our past useful and humane ideas with which to fill the future.

I remind you here of Bill Clinton's metaphor—building a bridge to the twenty-first century. Let us take his metaphor more seriously than he does. If we build a bridge to the twenty-first century and beyond, what will we carry across the bridge? Surely he cannot mean that the bridge will be used merely to take into the twenty-first century virtual reality, cellular phones, high-definition television, and all the rest. He must have had in mind that our technology will be accompanied by some ideas with which to make the journey. But he didn't mention them. Perhaps he meant some of the ideas developed or promoted in the twentieth century—like the principle of indeterminacy or Nietzsche's assertion that God is dead or Freud's insistence that reason is merely a servant of our genitalia or the idea that language is utterly incapable of providing accurate maps of reality. Perhaps not. In any case, I do not think the ideas of the twentieth century will take us very far. After all, the twentieth century was a horror. Who would have thought, in 1900—the year, by the way, of Nietzsche's death and the publication of Freud's *Interpretation of Dreams*—that the twentieth century would feature continuous mass murder, far exceeding anything humanity had witnessed in the previous two millennia? Who would have thought that the three great transcendent narratives of the twentieth century would be Fascism, Nazism, and Communism? Who would have thought that the theme of the twentieth century would be "Technology über Alles"? No, I do not think we will get much help from the last century. I speak as an enemy of that century, but even if you are not, you must admit that it is hard to be its friend. (I do, however, recognize that the twentieth century's feminist innovations motivate many women to feel well disposed to the time period.)

Where, then, shall we look? Well, of course, there is the advice of the sages I referred to earlier. But they are too far apart from each other and from us in time, space, and culture to offer coherent and relevant instruction. Their words can comfort and calm, which is why I mentioned them, but I doubt that we can be energized by them.

There is, of course, the fifth century B.C.—the time of the great Athenians. I know that they are the classic example of Dead White Males, but we probably should pay them some attention anyway. These are the people who invented the idea of political democracy. They invented what we call Western philosophy, and what we call logic and rhetoric. They came very close to inventing what we call science. They wrote and performed plays that, almost three millennia later, still have the power to make audiences laugh and weep. They even invented what, today, we call the Olympics, and among their values none stood higher than that in all things one should strive for excellence.

But for all of this, their most luminous intellect, Plato, was the world's first systematic fascist. They saw nothing wrong in having slaves, or in killing infants. Their conception of democracy relegated women to silence and anonymity. And they despised foreigners. Their word for those who could not speak Greek was "barbarian." They were also technological innocents. The Athenians produced no important technical inventions (excluding the use of "technical" to mean such inventions as sculpting tools and pottery dyes), and they could not even devise ways of using horse power efficiently.

Still and all, there is much to be said for our using the Greek Way, as Edith Hamilton called it, as a guide to the future. And certainly, to ignore the contribution Athens made to our journey toward humanity would be a catastrophe. But the Athenians are also too far from us and too strange and too insular to use their ideas as a social or intellectual paradigm. The same may be said for the Middle Ages—in my opinion a much maligned era (the Crusades and the burning of heretics notwithstanding). I would remind you that John Maynard Hutchins used the medieval period and its ideas as a guide for education when he reformed the University of Chicago in the 1930s and 1940s. He did so because he found in the Middle Ages a very high degree of integration in its worldview. Medieval theologians developed an elaborate and systematic description of our relationship to God, to nature, to each other, and to our tools. Their theology took as a first and last principle that all knowledge and goodness come from God and that, therefore, all human enterprise must be directed toward the service of God. Theology, not technology, provided people with authorization for what to do or think. That is why Leonardo kept his design of a submarine secret, believing, as he did, that it would not gain favor in God's eyes. It is why Pope Innocent II prohibited the use of the crossbow, claiming it was "hateful to God" and could not be used against Christians. Of course, he saw no problem in using it against infidels. But the point is that in a theocratic worldview, technology was not autonomous, but was subject to the jurisdiction of a binding religious system. Can you imagine anyone saying today that cloning humans should be prohibited because it would not find favor in God's eyes? Well, of course, some people do say that, but we are inclined to discredit them as naive fundamentalists or fanatics. Which is why I think the medieval way cannot offer us much guidance. In a theocratic world, everyone is a fundamentalist. In a technological world, and in a multicultural world, fundamentalism is a side issue, confined to those places that are still theocratic and are therefore regarded as a danger to world harmony.

Where shall we look for guidance about what to do and think in the twenty-first century, especially guidance about our relationship to technology? This question is as significant as it is daunting—and it is especially difficult for those who are strangers to history. "Every culture," Lewis Mumford wrote, "lives within its dream." But we often lose our dream, as I believe happened to us in the twentieth century. And we are in danger if we cannot reclaim one that will help us go forward. What else is history for if not to remind us of our better dreams?

With this in mind, I humbly suggest that we turn our attention to the eighteenth century. With this suggestion, some of you will think me hopelessly regressive. But it is *there,* I think, that we may find ideas that offer a humane direction for the future, ideas that we can carry with confidence and dignity across the bridge to future centuries. They are not strange ideas. They are still close to us. They are not all that difficult to remember. What we need to bring them to life is a refresher course, which I will attempt, although what I will say is more in the nature of a syllabus than a course.

The eighteenth century is the century of Goethe, Voltaire, Rousseau, Diderot, Kant, Hume, Gibbon, Pestalozzi, and Adam Smith. It is the century of Thomas Paine, Jefferson, Adams, and Franklin. In the eighteenth century we developed our ideas about inductive science, about religious and political freedom, about popular education, about rational commerce, and about the nation-state. In the eighteenth century we also invented the idea of progress and, you may be surprised to know, our modern idea of happiness. It was in the eighteenth century that reason began its triumph over superstition. And, inspired by Newton—who was elected president of the Royal Society at the beginning of the century—writers, musicians, and artists conceived of the universe as orderly, rational, and comprehensible. Beethoven composed his First Symphony in the eighteenth century, and Bach, Handel, Mozart, and Hayden composed their music in the eighteenth century. Schiller, Stendhal, Swift, Defoe, Fielding, Samuel Johnson, Voltaire, and William Blake were among its major writers. Gainsborough, Hogarth, David, and Reynolds were its most well-known painters, and Christopher Wren, its most eminent architect.

We are talking about the time referred to as our period of Enlightenment. In truth, it may be said to begin toward the end of the seventeenth century with the ideas of John Locke and Newton and extend into the nineteenth if we wish to include—as I think we ought to—the ideas of John Stuart Mill and Alexis de Tocqueville. And so the eighteenth century is a kind of metaphor referring to the time, as Kant put it, when we achieved our release from our self-imposed tutelage. It is the time of which historians have said that the battle for free thought was begun and won. By the end of that time, the modern world had been created. This is the century that Isaiah Berlin summed up in these words: "The intellectual power, honesty, lucidity, courage and disinterested love of the truth of the most gifted thinkers of the eighteenth century remain to this day without parallel. Their age is one of the best and most hopeful episodes in the life of mankind."

If this is so, we can hardly afford to neglect it, which is why this is the century I recommend to your notice, your study, and your advocacy. It is the century educated people ought to know about. I will try to show how two or three of its ideas may be useful to us. But I must say, first, especially because the thought has probably occurred to you, that I am well aware that inhumane beliefs and institutions existed in the eighteenth century. The burning of witches was still happening in the eighteenth century. France burned its last witch in 1746, Germany in 1775, and Poland in 1793. In Italy, the tortures of the Inquisition continued until the end of the eighteenth century. Slavery still existed, at least in America. The oppression of women was standard practice, as was child labor. And, of course, most nations were still ruled by despots. But it was in the eighteenth century that the arguments were generated that made these inhumanities both visible and, in the end, insupportable. Yes, Jefferson had slaves. But he knew that he *should not* have slaves. He tried to include a denunciation of the African slave trade in the Declaration of Independence, urged that slavery in Virginia be prohibited, and was well aware that one of his predecessors as president had freed his slaves and that his other predecessor would find it unthinkable to have slaves. Yes, Frederick the Great ruled over Prussia with an iron hand. But he employed the greatest enemy of despotism, Voltaire, as his court philosopher. If you can imagine it, this would be analogous to Lenin relying upon John D. Rockefeller to teach him economic theory. Yes, children as young as seven or eight worked from sunup to sundown in factories and mines. But the idea that child labor is inhumane came from the eighteenth century, in particular from Rousseau, who gave us the idea that children must have a childhood. And yes, Thomas Paine's *The Age of Reason,* which was an uncompromising attack on the Bible and churches of all kinds, led to his being vilified and dismissed as one of America's founding fathers. But the First Amendment to the American Constitution forbids any interference with one's religious beliefs. You can take any century you please and make a list of its inhumanities. The eighteenth is no exception. But it is *there,* and in no other, that we have the beginnings of much that is worthwhile about the modern world.

If we remember that, how, then, can it help us? I should like to offer a few possibilities. Perhaps the most useful contribution the eighteenth century can make to our future is in the confidence it placed in the powers of language. I do not think I need to tell you that in our own time, language is under deep suspicion, and even thought to be delusional. Jean Baudrillard, who seems to be required reading in our universities, tells us that not only does language falsely represent reality but also that there is no reality to represent. In the eighteenth century this idea would have been considered nonsense, if not a form of mental illness. While prose was not an invention of the eighteenth century, it was there that it was brought to its finest expression. And in their development of prose, philosophers, scientists, and even theologians placed the greatest possible emphasis on clarity. They did not take language for granted. They knew as well as any French postmodernist that language has the capacity to create both illusions of truth and distortions of reality. But they did not, at any point, believe that language was nothing but a snare and a delusion. They believed that, through the disciplined use of language, humanity could gain insight into how the world works, including the human heart. And, indeed, the spectacular advances made in science and technology in the eighteenth century show us that they knew what they were doing. In the eighteenth century, Fahrenheit invented the mercury thermometer, inoculations against smallpox began, Stephen Hales figured out how to measure blood pressure, Lavoisier discovered that air consists mostly of oxygen and nitrogen, Linneaus created his great scientific taxonomies. And, of course, as we all used to learn in school, James Watt perfected the steam engine. The birth of the modern world has its origin in faith in language, and the successes that such faith produced led to an unprecedented sense of hope—indeed, to the idea of human progress. But the eighteenth century philosophers did *not* believe as so many do today, that technological innovation is the same thing as human progress. Technological change —its pace and consequences—was not taken for granted, was considered an issue, was thought to be a matter to be seriously discussed. In fact, many of the inheritors of the Enlightenment became severe critics of technological growth. William Blake wrote of the "dark, satanic mills" that stripped men of their souls. Matthew Arnold warned that "faith in machinery" was humankind's greatest menace. Ruskin, William Morris, and Carlyle railed against the spiritual degradation brought by industrial progress. Balzac, Flaubert, and Zola documented in their novels the spiritual emptiness that a technological culture produces.

You can, perhaps, get the clearest idea of the seriousness and skepticism with which intellectuals regarded technology by reading Lord Byron's speech to the House of Lords early in the nineteenth century. He spoke against a proposed law that would apply the death penalty to anyone deliberately breaking a machine such as those people called "Luddites" were in the habit of doing. Byron tried to show how the rise of factories made workers useless and desperate, and how their way of life was being destroyed. Byron was not a Luddite himself and, in fact, understood the advantages of machinery. But he saw in technology a Faustian bargain — economic growth on one hand; the loss of self-respect and community vitality on the other.

I recommend the speech to you, and suggest further that you compare it to the way in which Al Gore speaks of the future of computer technology. Or Alvin Toffler. Or George Gilder. Or Nicholas Negroponte. Or, for that matter, the average school superintendent who believes that computers will, at long last, solve the problem of how to educate children. Rousseau would have laughed at that, as would have Pestalozzi, the greatest educator of the century. Jefferson and Voltaire would have thought the idea insane. It is unfair, of course, to compare almost anyone today to these men, but if you do, you cannot fail to get the impression that our conception of progress is unidimensional. We seem to have concluded that everything must make way for technological growth, including the human spirit.

This difference in outlook can be seen not only by contrasting ideas about progress but also by contrasting ideas about information and democracy. The period known as the Communications Revolution did not arrive until the end of the Enlightenment, beginning, as it did, in the middle of the nineteenth century with the invention of telegraphy and photography. Nonetheless, the philosophers of the Enlightenment were not aware that they lived in what *we* would call an age of information scarcity. If they did, they did not see it as a problem. The magazine was invented in the eighteenth century. Books were abundantly available, and most believed that all of this was sufficient. Literacy, of course, was understood to be the key to citizenship in a democratic society. I have always found it astounding that the *Federalist Papers,* eighty-five essays written by Alexander Hamilton, James Madison, and John Jay, *originally* appeared in a daily New York newspaper in 1787 and 1788. Can you imagine such essays being printed in any newspaper today? The point I am making is that in the eighteenth century, information was not always thought of as a commodity to be bought and sold. It was not thought to be useful unless it was imbedded in a context, unless it gave shape or texture or authority to a political or social idea, which itself was required to fit into some worldview. No one was ridiculed more, especially by Jonathan Swift, than the pedant, the person who collected information without purpose, without connection to social life. The idea of a contextless information society would have struck Swift and Voltaire as ludicrous. Information for what? for whom? to advance what idea? I feel sure they would think of us as garbage collectors, information junkies—a nation endlessly talking about nothing worth talking about. I remind you here of Thoreau's famous remark when he was told about telegraphy. He said, "We are in great haste to construct a magnetic telegraph from Maine to Texas; but Maine and Texas, it may be, have nothing important to communicate. . . . We are eager to channel under the Atlantic and bring the old world some weeks nearer to the new; but perchance the first news that will leak through into the broad flapping American ear will be that Princess Adelaide has the whooping cough." I shudder to think of what he would say if he knew about our information society.

And I should add here that, by itself, information was certainly not thought of as an asset to the democratic process; that is to say, it was not confused with useful knowledge and wisdom, nor with argument. If Hamilton, Madison, and Jay could know of the Internet, I do believe they would be intrigued. But I do not think they would easily see how the network advances the cause of a democratic polity. Not long ago, Lawrence Grossman published *The Electronic Republic* in which he enthusiastically argued that computer technology will bring an end to representative democracy and restore the Athenian ideal of participatory democracy. Computers, he prophesied, will allow us to have instant and continuous plebiscites on every issue, so that we will have no need for Congress. Voters will decide if we should join NAFTA or send troops to Bosnia or impeach the president. If Jefferson and Hamilton could read Grossman's book, they would at long last find something to agree upon: that the computerization of citizenship will restore nothing worth the name democracy.

There prevails among us what Langdon Winner calls "mythinformation" —no lisp intended. It is an almost religious conviction that at the root of our difficulties—political and otherwise—is the fact that we do not have enough information. This, in spite of everyone's having access to books, newspapers, magazines, radios, television, movies, photographs, videos, billboards, junk mail, and all the rest. If we do not know it ourselves, the eighteenth century can make it clear: this devotion to information is utter nonsense. If people are starving, it is not caused by insufficient information. If crime is rampant in the streets, it is not caused by insufficient information. If children are abused and wives are battered, it has nothing to do with insufficient information. And if our schools are not working and democratic principles are losing their force, that, too, has nothing to do with insufficient information. If we are plagued by such problems, as indeed we are, it is because something else is missing. And we might be able to find it in the eighteenth century.

Now it was the custom in the eighteenth century for people to give very long speeches—even much longer than this essay—but I have no intention of inflicting this tradition on you. So I will wind down by making two final points: the first is that I do not believe, of course, that the eighteenth century can give us all the answers we will need. I am not saying we should *become* the eighteenth century. Only that we should use it for what it is worth; and for all it is worth.

Second, I do not know if anything I have said will have any practical value for you. But I do wish to sum up the four ideas we can get from the eighteenth century that have relevance for us. The first is the importance of language, and I mean by that a focus on reading and writing, which are the keys to intelligent growth. The second is the idea that we need to cultivate a certain distance from technology, which can be gained by knowing something of its history. We do not need a nation of technological cheerleaders. We need people who can use technology without being abused by it. The third is the development of people who know the differences among information, knowledge, and wisdom. To say that we live in an information age is meaningless, if not dangerous, unless one has a sense of what information is for. And the fourth is the idea that as technology changes the meaning of democracy, we require people who are aware of what we may gain and what we may lose from such changes. We require people who have the knowledge and courage to know what changes to support and what changes to resist.

It goes without saying that each of these ideas would be amplified and assisted if we all knew something about the eighteenth century. After all, that is where these ideas come from. I am quite sure we will need them in the years ahead as well as in the very far future.

The End-of-the-World Ball

james gunn

December 31, 2000

9 P.M. William Landis stepped out of the express elevator that had transported him, like a redeemed sinner, from the lobby of the World Trade Center to the bar and restaurant at the peak of this man-made mountain, this towering skyscraper, this 110-story monument to international networking and the power of commerce. As the year 1000 had reached its end, believers had gathered on mountaintops to await the Second Coming; one thousand years later, skeptics had built their own mountain and assembled at its summit to celebrate a moment consecrated in their forgotten faith.

For this occasion the entire top floor of the World Trade Center had been taken over by the Twenty-First Corporation for its end-of-the-millennium celebration. The tables had been removed to form a ballroom and the main bar was supplemented with smaller tables around the periphery. Between the bars were buffet tables laden with food that featured a wide variety of cuisines prepared by Manhattan's most famous chefs. On the periphery of the room wide windows during the day had offered views of a winter storm over New Jersey, clouds over Coney Island, smog over midtown, ships in the harbor, and helicopters flying below. Tonight the sky was clear, and the stars shone down in all their awesome splendor.

This evening everything was free. The occasion must be costing the Twenty-First Corporation a fortune, Landis thought, not only for the food and drink but for the rent of this prime location on the restaurant's most profitable evening of the year. The public relations benefits could not possibly be worth the costs. Landis made a mental note to add to his final chapter, when he got back to his hotel room and his portable computer, a paragraph or two about potlatch and the earning of status by ostentatious gifts and entertainment. Or maybe the richest corporation in the world knew something he didn't know and was spending its resources in a final "you can't take it with you" gesture.

Just outside the elevator doors stood a Gothic arch carved from ice. It dripped, but the drips were caught by clear plastic and led to reservoirs at either side. On the arch had been engraved, as if in marble, and the letters out-lined in black to make them readable, "*Lasciate ogni speranza, voi ch'intrate.*"

Landis looked at the inscription, and wondered how many other guests would read, and recognize, Dante's Italian. On the other side of the arch, a naked young woman wearing a black mask ran squealing from a fat and sweaty satyr. Landis felt a brief chill as he stepped through the archway. Hell had frozen over.

On the other side of the arch a young man in the quietly elegant blue-and-white corporation uniform accepted the engraved invitation Landis extended to him. A woman who was passing the entry stopped and stared at Landis. She was in her early forties, perhaps, and behind her gauzy mask and pale make-up, and a simple crimson, calf-length cocktail gown, was a face and figure that promised remarkable beauty.

"You're William Landis," she said. "The writer. I heard your talk this af-ternoon."

He was of medium height and slender, with blue eyes and brown hair, and he was dressed in formal black. "Guilty," he said.

"I'm Elois Hays," she said.

"The actress? I saw your play night before last."

"Guilty," she said. "You're not in costume."

"This was a costume ball?"

"You know it was. The end-of-the-world ball." She put a hand on his black-silk sleeve.

"Then I am," he said. He looked down at her hand and covered it with his.

"You were supposed to dress up as your favorite catastrophe," she said ac-cusingly. "What catastrophe do you represent?"

"Ladies first," he said.

"I'm radiation sickness," she said.

"No sores?" he asked. "Leave it to the good-looking women to choose a ca-tastrophe that does not diminish their beauty."

"Leave it to the men to be grotesque," she replied. "Or refuse to participate."

"Well, as for that," he said, "I am in costume. I decided to come as Satan."

"Where are your horns," she said, "and forked tail?"

"I'm a modern Satan. No external stigmata."

"No mask either."

"The devil doesn't need a mask. But then, I'm more of a devil's advocate."

"For what?"

"For hope. I'm not sure this is the end of the world."

"What makes you think that's hopeful?"

A masked and costumed couple brushed past them, entering the ballroom. The man was dressed like a Visigoth, the woman like a captive Roman, her robes artfully ripped to display tempting expanses of rosy flesh.

"Is the thought of the world's survival that wearisome?" Landis asked.

"Not to me," she said. Her pale hands were an art form. "Though I wouldn't care very much, I think. But what better time to end the world than the conclusion of the second millennium?"

"Is there a good time for catastrophe?"

"If you've spent as many years as I have on the stage, you would know that timing is everything. No one should linger after her exit line."

The naked young woman raced past them again. She was giggling. The satyr was farther behind and panting heavily.

"They're at it already," Hays said.

Landis looked at his watch. "If the world is going to end in three hours, even the minutes are precious."

She tucked her hand under his arm. "Is that your philosophy? Eat, drink, and be merry?"

"It's one of them," he said. "I think we all have a bit of that feeling. Particularly on an evening like this. Besides, who are we to criticize these others? I don't know about you, but I'm not without sin—or at least a hope for sin."

She made a ruefully attractive face. "For one thing, that fat satyr is my former husband. For another—well, I've always been fascinated by intellectual men."

He patted her hand. "And I by actresses. But you're a real actress, and I'm only a popularizer of other people's ideas."

"Perhaps we should both have faith," she said.

"In this place where Dante said we should abandon all hope? But if you will be my companion for the rest of the evening, perhaps we will find faith or hope before it is over."

9:15 P.M. Persistent reports of Russian troops assembling on the border of Georgia have just been confirmed by United Nations surveillance satellites. Earlier announcements by the United States met with skepticism by a number of nations and denials by the new Russian right-wing leaders. An emergency meeting of the Security Council has been called, although any action voted by the Council is certain to be vetoed by the Russians. This comes at a time of continuing revolution or guerrilla warfare in half a dozen Latin American nations, the never-ending religious wars of the Middle

East, undeclared wars in Southeast Asia, and the reports of Chinese Army maneuvers near the Russian border. Out of any one of these could come a provocation that might lead to an exchange of nuclear missiles.

9:30 P.M. The open floor was almost as big as a football field. It might have dwarfed some groups, but there were many dancers, most in costume. Strangely, no orchestra played, and each couple was doing a different step to a different rhythm. It was like a medieval drawing of the dance of St. Vitus.

Paul Gentry studied them from his position with his back to one of the broad windows framing the night. He was a tall, dark-complexioned man with gloomy features and eyebrows like black caterpillars. He wore a dark business suit and a rope shaped into a noose dangling like a tie from his neck. "I beg your pardon," he said to a slender, blonde woman standing nearby, "but could you tell me why those people are behaving like idiots?"

She turned and held out a small, sealed, plastic bag. Gentry took the bag and looked at it. Inside were a pair of earplugs with dials. His eyebrows moved up.

"You put in the earplugs and dial whatever channel you want," the woman said. "There are fifty channels, half for music, half for voice. You can listen to your favorite music or news or discussion, or the commentary to what you see on the screens."

She waved a hand at the glowing theater-sized screens spaced around the room above the temporary bars and in the spaces between windows. One showed places and streets that seemed Parisian; they were filled with people and revelry. A second presented motionless groups gathered on high places; many of the people were staring at the sky. A third displayed throngs in Oriental apparel and appearance, while others framed mob violence or church services or quick cuts of missiles and tanks and people dying in battle. One seemed to be portraying various kinds of threats to the continuation of human existence, from the icy majesty of advancing glaciers to the waterless sands of deserts, from the abandoned children of crowded slums to the slime of polluted rivers and seas. Here and there, scattered among the others, lines of letters scrolled up screens with news about impending catastrophes like the words written on the wall at Belshazzar's feast.

It must have seemed to the dancers on the ballroom floor as if they were located at the center of the world, as if from the top of this artificial mountain they could see around the entire globe. But none of them seemed to be paying any attention.

"Of course," the woman said, "the views from other parts of the world are tapes sent back earlier. What with the record number of sunspots and solar flares, electronic communication with the rest of the world has been cut off."

Gentry handed the unopened bag back to the young woman. "No, thanks," he said. "I'll spend my last hours in this millennium doing my own talking and seeing." He looked back toward the dancers. "But isn't it typical of our times that they are all individuals, together but separate, each dancing to his or her own music?"

"You're Paul Gentry, aren't you?" the young woman asked. "The—"

He shrugged his heavy shoulders. "Ecologist. Environmentalist. Give me whatever name you think fits."

She smiled. It was an expression that transformed an otherwise businesslike face. "How about propheteer? That's what *Time* called you."

"If you like," he said. "And what is your name and occupation?"

"I'm Sally Krebs, and I'm in charge of a camera crew for CNN." She was wearing a yellow jumpsuit that could have been either evening wear or a uniform.

"Where's your crew?" he asked in his sardonic baritone.

"They're around. You just don't see them. What's wrong with individualism? Aren't people better off?"

"Materially, perhaps, but actually not in any meaningful sense. In most periods of the past, people have had enough to eat, and they have enjoyed a much greater sense of security."

"We can destroy ourselves," Krebs said, "but we can choose not to do so. Surely our ancestors faced perils like flood, plague, and barbarians over which they had no control at all. That must have given them the terrible fear that they existed at the whim of supernatural forces."

"They accepted these calamities as part of the natural order," Gentry said. "The security I am talking about is being part of a sturdy social matrix that is capable of surviving the blows of nature or of fate."

"But not," Krebs added, with a sly smile, "of technology."

"True. Science and technology could be created only by individuals, and once created could not be stopped until they brought us to this point. To this." He waved a hand at the ballroom. "The idle rich consuming their idle riches. Is this the finest accomplishment of Western civilization?"

"Maybe it isn't very serious," Krebs said. "But it's not contemptible, either. Today people have what no one ever had before: choice."

"When people can do anything, they find that nothing is worth doing. People are social animals. Like wolves and monkeys, we belong in groups, and when the groups are gone, and the reason for the groups is gone, we find that the reason for humanity is gone."

"What you see here is just a small part of life," Krebs said. "The ceremonial part."

"Ceremony is a group function we have lost. We get together as individuals making gestures at group feeling but discover that we cannot really surrender our individualism."

"The group should determine what we think and feel?"

"The group thinks. The group feels. The group survives."

"Why exalt the group above the individual?"

"What leads to the destruction of the species—indeed, if our best scientists are right, to the destruction of all life on Earth—is automatically wrong and evil."

"So that is your favorite catastrophe!"

"Self-destruction every time," Gentry said. "That's why I wear this noose." He fingered the rope around his neck.

"I thought that was to make it handy for the lynching party."

"Me?" he said in mock surprise.

"No one is going to be happy when your jeremiads come true."

"We stand on different sides of most fences, my dear," Gentry said, "but on this one we stand together. You know what they do to bearers of ill tidings."

"That's my profession."

"And pointing out the consequences of human folly is mine."

"You've done very well out of preaching catastrophe."

"And you've clearly done well out of reporting it."

She laughed. "It's no wonder people find you fascinating. Your ideas are so unrelievedly pessimistic that anything that happens comes as a relief."

A slow smile broke the dour lines of his face. "My dear, I'm glad you find me fascinating, but why are we standing here talking when we could be making love?"

Krebs laughed. "I said 'people,' not me. Besides, I'm working."

"You won't always be working."

"We've been filming and recording this conversation," Krebs said. "May we have your authorization to telecast it?"

Gentry smiled. "Everything I say is on the record. Including my final suggestion."

"End of interview," she said into the air.

"But not, I hope, the end of our relationship."

She offered him the possibilities of an enigmatic smile.

"The only time we have a certain grasp on reality," Gentry said, "is when we hold each other, pressed together flesh to naked flesh."

9:45 P.M. The reputation of environmentalists is not what it used to be. Like the boy who cried "wolf," they have shouted "catastrophe" once too often. From *Silent Spring* to *The Population Bomb* and *The Poverty of Power,* their texts have raised specters that, though frightening, turned out to be only skeletons in the closet. Undeterred, Paul Gentry, the most prominent of the breed today, recently called attention to a substantial die-off of plankton in the Gulf of Mexico, a sharp decline in krill production off Antarctica, an increase in radiation to which the average citizen is exposed in his lifetime, and an increase in acid rain after the small reduction that followed governmental restrictions on coal-fired generating plants in the early years of this decade. He has lots of other data, but it all adds up, he says, to death by pollution in the next century. In the next decade, he says, we should expect such problems as decreasing agricultural yields in a period when water has become scarce and fertilizer has become almost prohibitively expensive, a decrease in an already limited harvest of seafood, and an increase in the wholesale destruction of wildlife. That is, he says, if we don't destroy ourselves first.

10 P.M. Murray Smith-Ng stood at the seafood buffet loading his plate with shrimp and salmon. He was short and round, and his gray eyes glittered. He was dressed in the dark cloak and conical hat of a medieval astronomer, but his face had been darkened as if by a severe burn. Nearby but at a respectful distance, like a well-trained dog awaiting his master's signal to be fed, was a young man dressed in the scorched rags of a nuclear survivor. They displayed to good advantage his slender legs and muscular chest. His name was Lyle, and he had been a student in Smith-Ng's seminar on catastrophism.

"Dr. Smith-Ng, may I help you to some of this lobster?" Lyle asked.

Another young man, dressed in imitation furs to look like an ice-age savage, paused in the process of picking up a plate. "The Dr. Smith-Ng?" he asked.

"I'm sure there aren't any others," Smith-Ng said.

"The catastrophist?"

"The only one of those, too."

"Maybe you could answer a question that's always bothered me," the young man said.

"If I can," Smith-Ng said.

"I thought catastrophe theory was a mathematical discipline."

"Oh, it is," Smith-Ng said, setting down his plate to wipe mayonnaise from his chin. He picked up the plate again. "At least, that's how it started. Gradually people began to see practical applications for the mathematics, and that's where I did my work."

"What kind of applications?" the young man asked.

Smith-Ng popped a shrimp into his mouth. "Read my book, young man."

"Like volcanoes and meteor strikes," Lyle said impatiently. "Plagues and wars. Tornadoes and earthquakes."

"Some processes are continuous," Smith-Ng said around a mouthful of poached salmon. "They can be charted as familiar curves: straight lines, sines, hyperbolas. . . . Some are discontinuous. They start suddenly and break off just as abruptly."

"Like chain reactions and critical mass," Lyle said. "And the dinosaurs."

Smith-Ng gave Lyle the look of respect reserved for the good student. "And other life forms," he said. "The dinosaurs are simply the most dramatic. For a century after Darwin published his theory of evolution, scientists believed that evolution proceeded at the same even pace: as conditions changed, certain secondary genetic characteristics were selected to cope with them. Scientists of that kind were called 'uniformitarians' or 'gradualists.' Then, with the discovery that certain species, and at some periods most species, disappeared simultaneously and, in evolutionary terms, almost overnight, evolutionists all became catastrophists."

"If you had read *Catastrophe: Theory and Practice*, you'd know that," Lyle said.

"The discontinuous process is more prevalent than we ever suspected," Smith-Ng said, "although there was evidence enough around. Learning, for instance. Everyone had noticed that no matter how much you learned, you were still in a state of ignorance until something magical happened and all you had learned suddenly fell into place. Everyone had observed the plateau theory of learning but pretended that learning proceeded smoothly."

"It was the same way with catastrophe theory," Lyle said. "Suddenly everybody was a catastrophist."

"Some earlier than others," Smith-Ng said.

"But don't the times have something to do with it?" the other young man said.

Smith-Ng lifted his face from his plate.

"I think I read that somewhere," the young man said.

"Some ideas seem to have a better chance in certain periods than in others," Smith-Ng admitted cautiously.

"Now I remember," the second young man said. "In a series of articles William S. Landis has been writing about catastrophe, he quotes a theory about 'steam-engine time' that he attributes to a fellow named Charles Fort."

"'In steam-engine time people invent steam engines,'" Smith-Ng said. "And he applies that to catastrophism. 'In catastrophic times, people invent theories to explain catastrophes.' But what you've got to understand is that Landis's book is catastrophism masquerading as uniformitarianism. It merely pushes the origin of the catastrophe back to the mystical. The questions remain: What changes the times? What brings about the sudden acceptance of this theory or that? I prefer to put my faith in something I can measure."

Landis and Hays had stopped nearby, unnoticed, to listen to the conversation when they heard his name. "The question is, Smith-Ng," he asked now, "what catastrophes do your theories predict for the end of this evening?"

"You must be William Landis. I recognize you from your photographs," Smith-Ng said genially. "Of course you would be here. This will make a great concluding chapter for your book."

"If it all doesn't conclude here," Landis said. "But what's your prediction? Surely you have run everything through your equations."

"As for catastrophes," Smith-Ng said, "I predict all of them. But not for quotation."

"You certainly won't be quoted if you are no more precise than that," Landis said and smiled.

"You heard my talk this morning," Smith-Ng said. "I saw you in the audience. And that was for the record."

"You were talking in terms of centuries," Landis said. "Can't your theory do better than that?"

"And you want to pin me down to hours? Ah, Landis!" He waggled a pudgy finger at him. "But if you insist, I would hazard a guess that the world will end promptly at midnight."

Lyle chuckled appreciatively.

"But how?" Landis persisted. "That's too quick for a new ice age or the hothouse effect. Meteor? Nova? Nuclear war? Can't you pinpoint it a little better than that?"

"By the Second Coming, of course," Smith-Ng said and laughed. But he sounded as if he would be pleased if his theories were proved correct, no matter what happened to him or the rest of the world.

Lyle eyed him as if he were the end of Lyle's world.

10:15 P.M. The mathematician who titles himself a "catastrophist," in a speech today to the fancifully named "Twenty-First Century Conference" at the World Trade Center in New York City, called attention to what he termed "a sharp rise" of one-half degree in the world's average temperature over the past decade. The speaker, Dr. Murray Smith-Ng, noted that the rise in temperature is paralleled by a similar rise in the amount of carbon dioxide in the atmosphere over the same period. He called these increases "catastrophic changes" and an indication of what he called the beginning of the "greenhouse effect" that will turn Earth into an embalmed twin of Venus. Disagreement was registered from the floor, however, in particular from one expert in atmospheric phenomena who said that his measurements and calculations indicated the beginning of a new ice age instead.

10:30 P.M. Barbara Shepherd presided over a gathering of true believers on the rooftop of the skyscraper. The weather was comparatively warm for December, but the stars, slightly distorted by the air currents rising past the sides of the building, glittered coldly overhead.

The terrace was protected from the gulfs of space by a waist-high wall. Tracks for the tower's movable window-washing machine ran along the edge of the wall. A turntable occupied each corner. Steam issued from chimney pots scattered here and there about the roof, as if there were a direct connection with the nether regions. In the middle of the roof was a turnip-shaped metal tower and a sixty-foot metal pole for microwave transmissions. The metal pole was studded with ten red beacons.

Shepherd stood on a platform draped in white linen facing the forty-odd chairs almost filled by her audience. She wore a flowing white gown with wide and diaphanous sleeves. When she raised her arms, they looked like gauzy wings. The platform had been placed close to the south wall of the terrace. Sometimes she looked as if she were about to soar above the audience like Gabriel.

Landis and Hays stood in the distant doorway by which they had reached the tower's top. "Has she really lost touch with reality?" Landis asked softly.

"She says that she's finally found it," Hays replied.

"This is the time foretold," Shepherd said, needing no amplification, her voice ringing as if it were the instrument of Gabriel itself. "This is the day of judgment. Scarcely more than an hour remains for the people of this world to repent their sinful ways and accept salvation. Ninety minutes from now the world will end, and everybody will be sent to their eternal homes. To heaven, to hell. It is our choice, each one of us."

She paused, as if gathering her thoughts, and then continued more quietly. "When I was a girl," she said, "I thought that the purpose of life was to shape my body into a perfect instrument, so that it would do whatever I told it to do. And I worked hard, and I came as close as anyone."

"You can't get much closer than Olympic gymnastics," Landis whispered to Hays.

"And then I thought that the purpose of life was to understand the way the universe had been created and the laws by which it worked, and I went to school and learned everything I could."

"Can you imagine going from the Olympics to a Ph.D. in philosophy from Berkeley?"

"And then I thought that the purpose of life was to express my creativity, and I became an actress and lived other people's lives for the sake of audiences."

"She was a pretty good actress, too," Hays said, "but she ran out of parts and maybe out of her range."

"Each of those things in turn proved to be folly, and I decided that the only purpose of life was to seek pleasure, and I lost myself in that."

"That was what she was really good at," Hays murmured.

"And I nearly lost myself for all eternity," Shepherd said, "but now I know that the only purpose of existence is to prepare us for the life to come." Her voice lifted a fraction. "And that time is almost at hand. All we need is belief and faith."

"Where do you think all this is leading?" Hays asked.

"I don't know," Landis said, looking at his watch, "but it's getting on toward eleven. Do you want to go join the revels—or perhaps find a quiet spot for some conversation?"

Hays shivered and he put his arm around her shoulders. "It's like a good play," she said. "I've got to see the curtain go down. Anyway, what better place to greet the new millennium than the top of this mountain?"

10:45 P.M. The approaching end to the second millennium of the Christian era has produced a resurgence of religion, including increased attendance in formal church services and unscheduled outbreaks of what has been compared to the mania of the Middle Ages, such as speaking in tongues, fits, snake handling, and preaching on street corners. A kind of public resignation to the end of the world, however visualized, has been accompanied by an outbreak of militant fundamentalism in some Christian countries as well as in Islamic nations in the Middle East, involving an increase in terrorism, a quest for martyrdom, and the threat (or promise, as some see it) of Armageddon. One of the most unusual public conversions has been that of Olympic athlete, actress, and playgirl Barbara Shepherd, who plans a prayer meeting for the top of the World Trade Center during an exclusive, invitation-only End-of-the-World Ball.

II P.M. The pace of the evening accelerated as the hands of the invisible clock passed eleven in their inexorable progression toward midnight. Food and drink of all kinds was constantly replenished in all the bars and buffets. Drugs were almost as openly available as alcohol, and only slightly less in evidence than the food and drink; in some of the bars, they were laid out to be smoked, inhaled, or ingested or, even, with the aid of neatly clad nurses and sterile syringes, injected.

But this was not a junkie's paradise. These were the world's leading citizens, and the drugs were available, like the food, only to enhance their enjoyment of this moment that would not come around again for another thousand years. To be sure, a few, out of boredom or terror, or loss of self-control, overindulged themselves in drugs as some did in food or drink, and rendered themselves insensible to the approach of the millennium's end, collapsed in a corner or nodding in a chair or over a table like any common drunk. One died of an overdose, and another of a cocaine seizure. If the world survived this millennium, the Twenty-First Corporation would be tied up in courts throughout the century from which it took its name.

Some sought their surcease in other ways. Sexual couplings that earlier in the evening had been consummated discreetly in staircases and rooms made available in the floors immediately below, began to overflow into more public areas and to be joined by third and fourth participants as the evening proceeded. In some places the floor became a sea of writhing bodies, as if the protoplasm that had evolved into the shape of humanity was returning, in the space of a few hours, to the amoeba-like stuff from which it had come.

"There is more to this of panic than of passion," Gentry said, looking on from the periphery.

Krebs took a deep breath. "I'm beginning to feel a bit of that myself."

Gentry smiled, lifting his eyebrows at the same time. "The panic or the passion? Are you ready to take me up on my offer?"

"And join the anonymous heaps of flesh?"

"I was thinking of something a little more private."

"I thought you were in favor of groups," she said.

"Even primitive societies approved the privacy of some functions."

Suddenly she pointed to the ballroom. "Isn't that—?"

"I believe it is," Gentry said, tracing her finger to the shape of a tall, lean person in the sepulchral costume of Death itself. "It's the president, all right. It would be difficult to hide that figure and that way of moving."

"But why is he here?" Krebs asked.

"Isn't everybody?" Gentry responded.

"Even you and me, yes," she said distractedly. She spoke into the microphone pinned inconspicuously to her lapel. "Bob," she said, "get a camera on that figure of Death dancing with the willowy lady in green. That's got to be the president, and that's not the first lady. Lloyd can do what he wants with it, but we're going to feed it to him."

11:10 P.M. The New Genes Laboratory in California has announced the development of a hybrid wheat that resists drought, heat, and most, if not all, diseases, including mosaic, but most important fixes its own nitrogen fertilizer with the aid of symbiotic bacteria. The National Disease Control Center in Atlanta has issued a general warning to physicians about a new viral infection, popularly called the Moscow flu, that is affecting large centers of population and particularly schoolchildren. Its victims display many of the symptoms of influenza, but the disease has produced early mortality rates higher than pneumonia, AIDS, and what was once called Legionnaires' disease. A consumer watchdog group blames the new disease on genetic experimentation, and a spokesman for the Preservation of Democracy, on Soviet bacteriological warfare.

11:20 P.M. Smith-Ng had progressed to the meat buffet and loaded his plate with rare roast beef. He still was followed by the two young men. "Isn't that the president?" Lyle asked suddenly.

"Of course," Smith-Ng said, swallowing. "You can tell by the men in dark suits around the edges of the crowds."

"What do you make of that?" the other young man asked.

"Either he thinks he won't be recognized, or he doesn't care," Smith-Ng said.

"Why wouldn't he care?" the other asked. "When the activities at this place get reported, nobody present will be able to get elected garbage collector."

"Maybe the news that he wasn't here would be worse politically," Lyle said. "As if he wasn't invited."

"Now you're beginning to think like a catastrophist," Smith-Ng said. "But not enough like one."

"What do you mean?" Lyle asked.

"What if a catastrophe occurs?" the other young man said. "Then it wouldn't matter, and he might as well enjoy himself." He gestured at the displays of flesh and folly. "Like everybody else."

"And?" Smith-Ng prompted in his best Socratic manner.

"And what, sir?" Lyle asked.

"And what if he knows it?" Smith-Ng concluded with gluttonous satisfaction.

Lyle looked at the figures on the ballroom floor as if he had just begun to consider the possibility that catastrophe theory might turn into reality.

11:30 P.M. The Orbital Observatory adds some new concerns as the Western world approaches the end of the second millennium of the so-called Christian era: sunspot activity has picked up after the relative quiet of the past decade, an indication, say some authorities, of possible solar instability that might result in a solar flare or even an explosion that could wipe out all life on Earth. Nonsense, say other experts; that hot ball of gases in the sky is good for another eight billion years yet. An increase or decrease in its output of a few percent could be fatal to life on Earth, however. The Observatory also is watching a possible explosion at the heart of our Milky Way galaxy that might reach us any day now; or a massive black hole ejected from galactic center could be upon us before we know it. Meanwhile, work is pressing toward completion of the world's pioneer space habitat, which some proponents say is the first step toward ensuring humanity's survival, perhaps even its immortality. The good news, at least for some, is that the Observatory now has discovered a second star, other than Earth, with planets, and confidence is growing among some cosmologists that the formation of planets, around some kinds of suns, at least, is a normal process.

11:35 P.M. On the highest terrace, Barbara Shepherd's voice had grown more intense as midnight grew closer, as if, indeed, some truth was struggling for expression, some message was demanding to be heard. Members of the informal congregation had shifted uneasily from smiles to frowns, from chuckles and comments to uncomfortable glances at their neighbors, and some had left for more enjoyable pastimes. Others, as if hearing about what was occurring on the terrace, had arrived to take the empty places, and almost every chair was filled.

"This is the millennium described in Revelations. For a thousand years Satan has been bound and cast in the bottomless pit. Now that millennium has expired and Satan has been loosed to deceive the nations of the Earth and to gather them together to battle. Is this not the world we see about us? Deceived by Satan? Gathered to do battle?"

Hays studied the people seated in the chairs. "Are all these people believers, do you suppose?"

"I think they're here for the same reason we are," Landis said.

"And why is that?" Hays asked.

"To see how far she's going to go."

Shepherd raised her wings. "Can we doubt the predictions in Revelations? That fire will come down from God out of heaven and devour us all? Some of you think that when the fire comes down from the sky it will be missiles and hydrogen bombs raining down upon us, that we will be destroying ourselves, but it will be God's fire and His triumph—and our triumph, too. Because the devil who deceived us will be cast into the lake of fire and brimstone, and we will all be judged.

"If you think that I am afraid to be judged, you are right. I have sinned."

"That's certainly true," Landis whispered.

"I have fornicated, and I have committed adultery," Shepherd said. "I have profaned the temple of my body with drugs. I have borne false witness and denied my God. I have broken all of the commandments and discovered others to break that would have been commandments if the ancient Hebrews had known about them. But fearful or not, I welcome judgment as the beginning of the eternal glory to come."

She had been a beautiful woman and she was beautiful now, filled with a passion as real as any she had experienced in the arms of a man. It shook her body as she spoke and made her voice tremble. "In that day of all days, we will stand before the throne of God, we the dead, small and great, and we will be judged by the works written in the book of life.

"The sea will give up its dead, and death and hell will deliver up their dead, and every person will be judged according to their works. And whosoever is not found written in the book of life will be cast into the lake of fire. And so it is up to you. Will you repent before it is too late? Will you write your name in the book of life? Will you join me in life everlasting? Or spend eternity with Satan in the fires of hell?

"Because if you do not believe me, if you do not believe that Satan walks the Earth, if you do not believe that the fire of God will rain down on the Earth this very night, if you do not believe that this is the day of judgment and that this begins our eternal lives in heaven or in hell, look yonder!" She stretched out one gauzy arm toward the space near the door.

"There stands Satan with his paramour!"

In spite of themselves, the audience turned to look at the figures of Landis and Hays watching the scene with detached fascination. "She recognized you," Hays muttered.

"And you," Landis said.

11:40 P.M. The World Energy Council announced today that the price of oil, which began its present climb in 1997, has reached $150 a barrel. For all except special or emergency needs, oil no longer is classified as a fuel. After the panicky hiatus of the 1980s and 1990s, the United States has resumed building nuclear-generating plants. The rest of the world, which now boasts 90 percent of nuclear-generating capacity, never stopped. Generating plants that once burned oil have been abandoned or converted to coal, sometimes in a liquefied form, in spite of the cost in human life and acid rain. Synthetic fuels once more are being pursued. Meanwhile research presses forward into the elusive thermonuclear process for fusing hydrogen. Laboratory operations have demonstrated that the theory works by getting back more energy than is consumed, but so far efforts to scale up the methods to commercial size have proven too expensive. The search goes on, however, since success would solve the energy problems, now pressing hard on the arteries of the world, for the next thousand years.

11:43 P.M. The ballroom floor was crowded now that the magic hour had almost arrived, as if the assembled guests were seeking the protection of numbers or the sacrament of ceremony. The filmed scenes flickered from screen to screen around the walls in dizzying procession until they blurred into a continuous panorama of motion uniting all the places of the world into one frantic montage of anticipation.

Here and there fights broke out between men and between women, and even between men and women, over drunken insults or sexual privileges. Women were raped, sometimes by groups of men, and occasionally a man was attacked by a group of women. Weapons carried for show were put to ancient uses; men and women, injured, staggered away for aid, or, dead, lay where they had fallen. Blood seeped into sticky puddles, and vomit and excretions dried upon the floors. Uniformed attendants who had worked diligently at keeping the tables filled and the complex clear of refuse had stripped away their emblems and joined the melee struggling desperately to forget the desperate hour. Here two thousand years of civilization disintegrated into barbarism.

And others went on with their own lives, pursuing their own visions of catastrophe.

11:45 P.M. Vulcanologists have had a great deal to watch recently. Old volcanoes in Hawaii, Mexico, Italy, Iceland, Indonesia, Nicaragua, Costa Rica, Chile, and Japan have erupted or shown signs of imminent activity, and new volcanoes have opened smoking fissures. So far none has demonstrated the destructiveness of Mount St. Helens and El Chichon in 1983, but vulcanologists do not rule out that possibility. One or more eruptions the equal of Krakatau in 1883 or Tambora in 1815 might inject enough ash and smoke into the atmosphere to rival the nuclear winter predicted by many scientists in the 1980s to follow a nuclear war.

11:47 P.M. On the balcony Krebs listened to her earphone and then looked quickly at the ballroom floor. "He's leaving," she said.

"Who's leaving?" Gentry asked.

"The president. As if he's in a hurry. One of the Secret Service men ran over to him and spoke a word or two—nobody could pick up what was said—and he's almost running out of here."

Gentry shrugged. "It probably doesn't mean anything. Maybe he doesn't want to get caught in the midnight crush."

She made a face at him. "You're supposed to be the realist."

"Are you ready then for my realism?"

She looked at him for a moment without speaking, and then she said, "If you were anybody else, I might say 'Yes,' and to hell with the job. But if the world survives I'm going to go back to the Midwest and find a more meaningful way of life, and you, for all your above-it-all earnest cynicism, you use people—you use life itself—for your own selfish satisfactions."

He seemed speechless for the first time that night, and then he said, without his customary condescension, "Do you think I don't know that? My cynicism doesn't come out of superiority, but out of fear. I'm afraid. I've always been afraid."

"Maybe so," she said, "but you'll have to live with it like everybody else. I've got to go. I've been told there's something happening on the rooftop."

11:50 P.M. Astronomers today announced the discovery of a new comet that promises to be larger and brighter than Halley's comet. The comet, as yet unnamed, may be making its first pass through the solar system, possibly disturbed in its billions of years' orbit in what is known as the Oorts Cloud by a distant companion sun to Sol called by some scientists "Nemesis." Preliminary calculations indicate that the new comet may pass close to

Earth, but alarmist reports of a possible collision have been dismissed by scientists as "next to impossible."

11:52 P.M. Smith-Ng looked up from the dessert table in the restaurant on the second balcony. "What did you say?" he asked Lyle, who still tagged along behind him.

"The president. He's gone. What does that mean?"

"Maybe nothing," Smith-Ng said, wiping a glob of whipped cream from his upper lip. "Maybe catastrophe."

"Shouldn't we—couldn't we—find some place quieter? More alone?" Lyle's teeth made an uncontrollable chattering sound, and he put his hand on Smith-Ng's shoulder as if he were steadying himself.

Smith-Ng looked at Lyle and then toward the ceiling as if seeking guidance. He placed his hand tentatively over Lyle's. His face approached the young man's as if moved by some external power, and he kissed him with the curiosity and then the intensity of an unsuspected passion he had just discovered. He drew back as if he could feel his world shattering in pieces around him and shook himself. "I understand that something interesting is happening on the roof," he said shakily. "Perhaps we should go find out what it is."

11:54 P.M. On the eve of the twenty-first century the United Nations Office of Population announced that the world's population has passed six billion. Of these six billion, it said, more than half were undernourished and one billion were actually starving. These figures, a spokesman said, raise serious questions for world peace as well as for the number of deaths by starvation and disease if world population doubles again, as predicted, in the next thirty-five years.

11:56 P.M. By the time the cameras arrived, the audience had swollen to fill all the chairs and the standing room that surrounded them. Krebs with Gentry behind her had reached the terrace just a few moments earlier, and Smith-Ng and his disciple were only a few steps behind.

The terrace had rippled minutes ago with the news of the president's hurried departure, but now it was quiet with the hushed expectancy of something momentous about to happen, as if by listening hard one could hear the last grains of sand trickling through the hourglass of the universe.

In the ballroom two floors below, the crowd was frantic in its effort to greet the new millennium with life and laughter, like savages at the dawn of civilization trying to frighten away disaster with noise or appease it with celebration.

Below Saturnalia was in progress. Here on the rooftop a congregation as solemn as that of any true believers awaiting the day of judgment on mountaintop was contemplating the eternal.

People were here because of who they were, choosing this kind of celebration rather than other kinds below, because of the occasion and its star-reaching site, and because of Barbara Shepherd. She stood now like a sacrificial virgin, her hymen restored with her faith, her arms outstretched, her hands clenched into fists, her voice lifted in exultation.

"Now has the moment come," she said, "the time arrived, the stroke of the clock about to sound as we listen. Now we must demonstrate our faith or lose all faith forever and be forever damned. Faith can save us yet. Faith will save us. Have faith! Have faith!"

"I'm frightened!" Hays said to Landis.

"What are you frightened of?" he asked gently, tightening his arm around her as if to create a fortress for two.

"Everything," she said. "The world ending. The night exploding. Bombs. Change. Everything."

"Don't be afraid," he said. "Maybe we found each other too late, your sense of the drama of life and my search for its purpose. But if we make it through this night, I have a suggestion: let's create a new world, for ourselves and whoever wants to join us."

"I'd like that," she said. "If we make it through."

"I'm frightened, too," he said. "But it's not catastrophe I'm afraid of. What I fear is our love of catastrophe."

Barbara Shepherd turned and ran toward the back of the platform like the acrobat she once had been. As she reached the middle, she did a flip backward, landed on her feet, and flipped again. The second took her off the end of the platform. For an instant she seemed to disappear from view. Then her figure reappeared, propelled upward with surprising speed, head high and facing the audience with the composed features and confidence of a saint, rising, rising, clearing the railing that surrounded the rooftop and floating free in the air beyond it. Her gown fluttered; her arms reached out and, like wings, seemed to support her body in the crystalline air, even to lift it toward the heaven she addressed.

The audience waited, shocked into immobility, shocked out of skepticism, expecting miracles and fearing them, fearing catastrophes and expecting them.

But as the stroke of midnight sounded and maddened noise broke out in the city below and in the ballroom behind like celebration or like explosions and machine guns and the screams and dying cries of victims, and the spinning world seemed to hesitate in anticipation of catastrophe, the figure of Barbara Shepherd faltered in the air before it fell, with growing velocity, glittering, through the night.

THE END

Afterword

The terrible events of September 11, 2001, seem to have been foreshadowed by the end of "The End-of-the-World Ball," which itself is the final chapter of *The Millennium Blues*. The novelette and the novel are the products of some thirty years of meditation on our terror of and fascination with catastrophe, and its association with millenniums. But science fiction writers are not prophets. They are in the business of contemplating the human condition confronted by change. In the application of their art, they construct scenarios to dramatize the ways in which the human species will be tested and shaped by forces currently at work within our world or by those yet to be encountered. "The End-of-the-World Ball" was one of those scenarios, and if its final scene seems to resonate today, that is partly because of the novel's meditation about catastrophes of every sort and partly because of the accident of choice over time. In my early version of the chapter, written in the 1970s, I placed the scene in a new, towering building to be constructed by the Twenty-First Corporation on a renovated Times Square. But as my novel emerged, chapter by reluctant chapter, and the world and I entered the 1990s, I realized that such a structure not only would not be built but that it was not plausible that it might be built in the time remaining before the end of the millennium. By then, however, the World Trade Center towers had been added to the New York City skyline, and I even had an editorial dinner at Windows on the World. I considered moving the scene to the Great Pyramid of Egypt (where some actual millennial tours planned to end) or the Sears Tower in Chicago, or the Petronas Tower in Kuala Lumpur, but in the end I could not abandon New York. The World Trade Center was the natural choice. A chapter in the novel is devoted to a woman (Dame Nostra) who claims to foresee catastrophe. I reject any such claims for myself and am a skeptic about the claims of others: it may be instructive that of such coincidences—like the stopped clock that is right twice a day—are reputations made.

James Gunn

two

FUTURE PRESENT

Reflections on What Remains of Zamyatin's *We* after the Change of Leviathans
Must Collectivism Be against People?

darko suvin

The Revolution—that is: I—not alone, but we.
—*A. A. Blok, diary note, 1918*

I see in the near future a crisis approaching that unnerves me and makes me tremble for my country. . . . Corporations have been enthroned and an era of high corruption will follow. . . .
—*A. Lincoln, letter to Colonel W. F. Elkins, 1864*

The case against saying we *seems overwhelming. . . . The epistemological and political need to say* we *remains, however. Neither a theory nor a politics of irreducible singularity seems very promising.*
—*N. Scheman, "The Body Politic," 1988*

First premise (epistemological): The rereading of a text that, within radically altered circumstances of a reader, suddenly begins to look significantly different —prompting perhaps a reconsideration of the ethical, political, or other values earlier allotted to it by the same reader—poses a puzzle about the nature of textual meaning. It foregrounds an axiom of semiotics that seems counterintuitive only because our "intuition" has been shaped by positivistic prejudice: there is no object-"text" out there, independent of the collective or allegorical subject-eyes beholding it. (This does *not* mean there's nothing out there!) I'll be speaking here of a novel, but text may be taken in the semiotic sense of any articulated signic entity able to stand still for the purpose of analysis. No fixed and unmoving central text, analogous to Ptolemy's Earth or to an unsplittable atom or personality, can be opposed to an environing "context" (or even the more recent and modish "intertext"), unless one is to say that the context permeates the text by existing beneath and between each sign–unit and determining their shapes and meanings. Such is the case of the context of any specific sociolect of some natural language: Russian or English or indeed the Spanish of Pierre Ménard's word-by-word reconstruction of Cervantes's *Don Quijote*, which nonetheless gives the nineteenth-century reader, as Borges rightly argues, a quite different novel from the reader of Cervantes's age. A text, in brief, exists in the interaction of signifiers visible on its surface with the individual or collective beholder, who allots signification and meaning to the ensemble and articulation of the signifiers. All text studies—and thus also, perhaps more clearly than other genres, SF studies—are historico-semiotic studies or, if you wish, cultural studies.

Second premise (political): We have gone through—the globe is still going through—a change of Leviathans that rule and subsume us, which might be dated with 1991 in Russia as the final stage of a world-historical change datable (maybe) with 1973. I extrapolate "Leviathan" from Hobbes's meaning to that of any collective, politico-economic as well as ideological, hegemony, the World Whale inside which all of us are condemned to live. The transfer into the entrails of a new, but just as pernicious and probably more micidial, whale is surely of the utmost significance for understanding the position of all of us under the missing stars.[1] To the contrary, this orientation can be of use as a defense against being totally digested by the devouring global whale, the capitalist socioeconomic formation in its new Post-Fordist shape, and indeed as modestly emboldening us to work toward preparing its downfall, from an assumed point of view based upon lineaments of some different, better, today necessarily utopian collective. This would be in line with Wallerstein's argument that the prevailing "antistatism" (the loss of ideological ascendancy and even legitimacy by the State) is necessarily a prelude to the downfall of the capitalist world-system, since the latter has never been able to exist only through the Invisible Hand of the Market without crucial State support to weaken the claims of the workers, transfer citizens' taxes to the capitalists, and defend them against stronger "foreign" competitors (Wallerstein 1998, 32, 46–47, and passim). Whether this view may be too optimistic or not, it is at any rate what I am attempting to contribute to by clearing up some premises.

It follows that our very ambiguously new Post-Fordist age—a return of the stalest meat spiced with the sharpest sauces—unambiguously forces an alert critic into new ways of envisaging and talking about text/context. The new ways have unfortunately not been fully worked out by anybody that I can see. The best I can do is to adopt a "braided" structure, which should not be too surprising for readers of Le Guin's *The Dispossessed*, Piercy's *He, She and It*, the Strugatskys' *Snail on the Slope*, or the even more complex shuttling in Russ's

Female Man (as well as for readers of verse, say with the *abab* rhyme). Indeed perhaps the compositional principle of all fictional utopias (including anti-utopias) is necessarily the braiding of showing and telling, lecture and action. And if you believe, as I have often argued, that all SF is not only historically a niece of utopia but is also ineluctably written between the poles of utopia and anti-utopia, then to the degree this is correct, it further follows that such braiding or more generally patching is also the compositional principle of SF.

All of this finally means that the pretense at a "final" explanation of anything has been well lost. But my project is even more modest: I think it may be too early to achieve a full new overview of *We* (for one thing, most regrettably, many writings by Zamyatin still remain inaccessible or indeed unpublished),[2] and I wish this contribution to be simply a first shot across the bows by a devil's advocate—whom my subject himself would salute as necessary. For Zamyatin himself was and constantly remained both a convinced heretic and a convinced utopian socialist.[3]

So then: just how different is today, after the sea-change of whales inside which we Lucians, Sindbads, Pantagruels, or Nemos live, the text of Yevgeny Zamyatin's novel *We*? For one question, which is a technical way of putting it within the debates of Utopian Studies: is it still a living anti-utopian novel when nobody can even pretend that the utopia it was anti to is still a major, observable actuality?

1

It is well known (and rehearsed from Gregg to Beauchamp) that *We* takes its central agential constellation as well as some of the most important value horizons from a heretical reworking of the orthodox Christian myth of Eden, which echoes powerfully in Milton and Dostoevsky.[4] In mildly semiotic or narratological terms, one could characterize it as a conflict between a Protagonist (God)—who is both the supreme power and the supreme value—and an Antagonist (Satan as the Serpent tempter) over the Pentateuch's and the Bible's overriding Value—the obedience of Man (Adam) to God. I find it useful for further discussion to present this as a little graph (see table 1).

Already in *Paradise Lost*, as is well known, Satan had ambiguously acquired some traits of a political heretic not too dissimilar from examples in the English Revolution of Milton's age; focusing on those traits, Blake could then read Milton as being of the Devil's party without knowing it, and Mary Shelley could rework the Miltonic template into Dr. Frankenstein as a bungling and culpable Creator and his Creature as a righteous antagonist more sinned against than sinning. This may suffice here as a shorthand to indicate how, be-

TABLE 1: Agential Constellation behind *We*

Scheme of Conflict

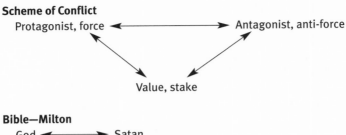

Protagonist, force ⟷ Antagonist, anti-force

Value, stake

Bible—Milton

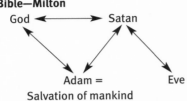

God ⟷ Satan

Adam =   Eve
Salvation of mankind

tween Milton and Zamyatin, the huge earthquakes of the second, overtly polit-ical series of revolutions, centered on 1789 and its results, had changed the landscape. The great lesson from the failure of the radical *citoyen* project, from the bourgeois compromise with the old rulers, was for the Romantics that the heaven's god(s) turned tyrants. Some of the best Blake or Percy Shelley be-longs here, while Byron's and then Baudelaire's pseudo-Satanism, echoing throughout all European culture, is the strategic hinge to all later *poètes mau-dits*. Russian poetry (from Pushkin and Lermontov to Zamyatin's elder con-temporaries) and the equally great prose of "Romantic realism" after Gogol (cf. Fanger 1965) were both exasperated, in a country that hadn't managed even an initial bourgeois revolution, and powerfully swimming in the same current. Theirs was a bitter protest, sometimes revolutionary but in the fin-de-siècle Symbolists more and more just privately (for example, erotically) blasphemous —even though its principal names, Bryusov and Blok, came to sympathize more or less actively with the October Revolution. As a rule, the world "out there" was felt as offensive and the real values as residing in the poetic persona's "inner" creativity—Shelley's ambivalent "caverns of the mind" (in Frye 1970, 211), or in the Symbolist poet as hypnotic visionary.

Zamyatin became—as did his colleagues Belyi and Bulgakov—a "terminal point" (to adapt Frye's argument for *1984* [1970, 204]) of this Romantic subver-sion. Substituting life in the Unique State, a futuristic glass city walled-in against the outside "Green World" (supposedly because of devastation in century-long wars), to life in the Garden of Eden, he followed the Romantics by resolutely disjoining power and goodness in the new agent that took the place of God as both ruler and addressee of people's absolute worship—the totally planned State, and its head and symbol, the dictator Benefactor, "the new Jehovah, coming down to us from heaven" (Zamyatin 1983, 140).

Even further, if we take the proper narratological approach that the Protagonist is that agential force which initiates most of the narrated action, the new Protagonist is laicized from God to Man: as in *Frankenstein*, he is a male scientist-creator, the mathematician D-503, chief constructor of the first spacecraft whose possession is supposed (rather vaguely) to ensure victory to the possessing side. As in Blake, Percy Shelley, or Byron, he is faced with tyrannical paternal authority; but he will also, as in the more conservative Mary Shelley, get faced with his own inadequacies. The Powers-That-Be still rule, but their basis in Man's obedience is in the story both shown as increasingly shaken and shown up as simply repressive: their dogmatic pretense to divine infallibility, transferred from Christianity to science, has turned them into the negative Antagonist, taking the place of Satan from the Judeo-Christian myth. The new Adam is not only an exemplary (that is, primarily allegorical) Protagonist but also his own supreme Value. This constellation, prefigured in Frankenstein's Creature, is here derived from the Man-God Jesus opposed to the Church in power in Dostoevsky's Grand Inquisitor legend (see Gregg 1988, 66–67), but Zamyatin's atheist individualism reduces salvation to what narratology calls narcissism. It is articulated as obedience to the protagonist D-503's own (that is, humanity's) sensual or "shaggy" nature, which is therefore easily swayed by the supposedly satanic but in Zamyatin liberatory figures from the Miltonic model. The ideal goal or *salus,* the Grail of this quest, is not sinless life in a renewed Paradise but the dismantling of the fake paradise of all-pervasive, Leviathanic politics in favor of either passionate life and/or a freer or more "natural" political life. The salvation of the allegorical Protagonist lies no longer in listening to a collective, institutionally codified and enforced story but in fashioning a new story for himself through sexual passion, which is magically analogous to ideological heresy and political subversion; erotics takes the place of theology and largely of politics also (see table 2).

TABLE 2: Agential Constellation in *We*

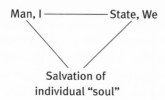

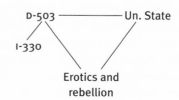

This is not only a most ingenious refashioning of the best-known narrative constellation or "master narrative" of European culture from Palestine to the industrial and bourgeois revolutions. It is also articulated in a masterly, almost Cubist texture of splinters (cf. Parrinder 1977, 137, and the brief discussion in Suvin 1979), which has aged as well as the best wine. Further, it also reuses, through the sole narrator's (tardy) education by events, possibly the second most powerful European narrative, which spelled the religious one in bourgeois individualism from Bunyan and Fielding on, was best codified probably in Goethe's *Wilhelm Meister*, and meandered through innumerable variants down to Heinlein and today: the voyage of the hero to a true understanding of himself, the "educational novel" (Bildungsroman) of what might be called individualistic religion. The hero is simultaneously—and not wholly convincingly —"humanly" representative and yet atomically individual, an investment of the authors' core personal values and yet an example for all the readers insofar as they are all supposed to be individuals, only individuals, and nothing but individuals. In the best Modernist and dystopian fashion, the educational voyage is at the unhappy end aborted, but its values should have inoculated the reader. We approach here possibly the central contradiction or *aporia* of individualism, clearly shared by Zamyatin: in the end, we are all unsplittable atoms (say of hydrogen), but every atom is possessed of a different, unique, and most precious soul. And yet the soul needs exterior validation—God, or more prosaically, social life (cf. Marx's *Holy Family* in Marx 1978, 148 and passim).

Finally, Zamyatin throws into this rich mix the pairing of the Protagonist with an erotic seductress. I shall return to this in section 5.

2

However, if my argument that the "contextual" side shapes all parts and aspects of the text has any merit, the long duration model of the preceding section is always renewed by major synchronic constraints produced in a new historical period. In order to attend to this overriding determination, I propose to you my (not at all original, I'm happy to say) first sketch of the change of Leviathans. It won't have the elegance of Zamyatin's construction, but it may have the persuasiveness of recognizability. I'll begin the closest I can to the new dispensation of global Post-Fordist rule, and my initial argument is taken from an Internet article by Michel Chossudovsky. He is not alone in convincingly arguing that we are in the midst of a possible worldwide crisis whose scale already makes it "more devastating than the Great Depression of the 1930s. It has far-reaching geopolitical implications; economic dislocation has been accompanied by the outbreak of regional conflicts, . . . and in some cases the destruction of entire countries. This is by far the most serious economic crisis in modern history."[5] It is not simply that, in what I see as an omen, 2,300 billion dollars of "paper profits" could in a few weeks after mid-July 1998 evaporate from the U.S. stock market: a plague on its house (except that we all live in this house).

More to the point right here, since we're speaking about Russia, from 1992 to 1998 "some 500 billion dollars worth of Russian assets—including plants of the military-industrial complex, infrastructure and natural resources—have been confiscated (through the privatization programs and forced bankruptcies)" (Chossudovsky 1998, 2). They were plundered by new domestic as well as the Western speculative capitalists, not interested in long-term investment and production but only in immediate profit: the percentage of investments into durable production is half of that of the United States, so that productive fixed capital is being reduced by 5 to 10 percent of Russian gross domestic product (GDP) per year. The industrial production, GDP, and real wages have since the collapse of the Soviet Union plummeted by at least half and continue to fall. The 2000 Russian median income is about $50 (U.S.) per month and also falling: incomplete estimates put the *majority* of population in present-day Russia, more than 80 million people, under the poverty threshold, and probably 30 percent more at a very bare subsistence level; "50–80 percent of school-age children are classified as having a physical or mental defect" (Cohen 2000, 23). The life expectancy for males has fallen to 55 years, the level of the famine countries of mid-Africa, compared to the life expectancy of 74 years in Cuba. The World Health Organization reported in 1997 an unmonitored rise in diseases for 75 percent of Russians who in the new "free" Leviathan live in poverty without social services, including a 3,000 percent rise in cases of syphilis (Redford, 1997; cf. McMurtry 1999, 270), while Holmstrom and Smith (1999, 6) report a doubling of suicides and tripling of deaths from alcohol abuse: the population in Russia is falling by about one million people per year (but no humanitarian outcries have been heard from the NATO governments and media)! Obversely, 2 percent of the Russian population has possessed themselves of 57 percent of the total national economic wealth. This super-rich gangster-capitalist oligarchy in banking and export-import has, in collusion with the global corporate raiders dealing almost exclusively in asset-stripping and speculation, illegally transferred out of its country at least 250 billion dollars, and possibly double that amount (Clairmont 1999, 18; cf. Flaherty 2000, Holmstrom and Smith 1999, Menshikov 1999, and Skuratov 2000). Russia is a country in moral and material ruins.

In cases of refractory States that refuse embedding into world capitalist finances, mercenary armies may still be used, as in Nicaragua, Iraq, or Serbia. But Russia is the prime object-lesson that, as a rule, the takeovers by our new Leviathan of private corporate capital substitute for invading armies' complex speculative instruments for "control over productive assets, labor, natural resources and institutions" (Chossudovsky 1998, 2). Its new paradigm is "concentration of control combined with decentralization of production" (Kagarlitsky 2000, 4). The often obnoxious State-centralized planning by bureaucracy has been replaced by the no less huge and more powerful global planning by hundreds of millions of "globalization" bureaucrats, from corporations and stock markets to international bodies, whose cost is by now 20 percent of the commodities produced (McMurtry 1999, 287). Banks, not tanks; computer terminals or cell phones instead of artillery or bombers: the devastation for the lives of millions of powerless people outside the relatively very small ruling class is identical. After Mexico and Eastern Europe, this "financial warfare" has in a few months of 1997 "transferred over 100 billion dollars of East Asian hard currency reserves into private financial hands. At the same time, real earnings and employment plummeted virtually overnight, leading to mass poverty in countries which had in the postwar period registered significant economic and social progress" (Chossudovsky 1998, 3).

The crises of the 1990s mark "the demise of central [national] banking, meaning national economic sovereignty," that controlled money creation on behalf of what was at least susceptible of being an overt will of that society. The demise is by no means confined to the "inferior races" of Africans, Asians, or Slavs. It is by now threatening both the Nazis' and the World Bank's favorite "honorary Whites," Japan, as "a handful of Western investment banks . . . are buying up Japan's bad bank loans at less than one tenth of their face value." It is also hitting countries such as Canada, "where the monetary authorities have been incapable of stemming the slide of their national currencies. In Canada, billions of dollars were borrowed from private financiers to prop up central bank reserves in the wake of speculative assaults" (Chossudovsky 1998, 3–4).

Who funds the IMF bailouts, asks Chossudovsky? Where did the money come from to finance these multibillion-dollar operations from Mexico to Indonesia or Japan? Overwhelmingly from the public treasuries of the G7 countries, constituted by working citizens' taxes (businesses as a rule pay no taxes), and leading to significant hikes in the levels of public debt. Yet in the United States, say, "the issuing of U.S. public debt to finance the bail-outs is underwritten and guaranteed by the same group of Wall Street merchant banks involved in the speculative assaults." These same banks will "ultimately appropriate the loot (e.g., as creditors of Korea or Thailand)—i.e., they are the ultimate recipients of the bailout money (which essentially constitutes a 'safety net' for the institutional speculator). . . . [As a result], a handful of commercial banks and brokerage houses have enriched themselves beyond bounds; they have also increased their stranglehold over governments and politicians around the world" (Chossudovsky 1998, 5). The new Leviathan is at least as powerful as the old one and even less accountable to democratic control from below. It ruthlessly subordinates the whole of civil society and democratic self-determination to the objectives of financial capital (cf. Clarke 1989, 356 and passim; Kagarlitsky 2000, 29–31; McMurtry 1999). It needs and uses States for public brainwashing and coercion to destroy the Keynesian and ensure the globalized Leviathan (cf. Kagarlitsky 2000, 14–19): internally as back-up apparatuses for plundering the taxpayers and keeping them quiet by electoral charades and police, and externally as pressure and finally war machines against recalcitrants.

3

If my preceding section seems a detour, this is due to the rigid, strongly ideologized boundaries of our disciplinary division of labor, which fortunately doesn't prevail in Utopian Studies. For, the change of Leviathans—of the hegemonic collectives or "We"s inside which we all live—is at the root of my revisiting *We*, and revisioning it with this new insight. From the 1950s on, many of us defended Zamyatin against those who didn't recognize his pregnancy— not only against Stalin but against all religious and cryptoreligious dogmatisms. If we ever get nearer to a *Handmaid's Tale*–type society, no doubt we'll have to return to some form of such defense. But today, we have to delimit within Zamyatin not only by holding fast to what is still relevant in his vision but also by recognizing that there are at least relevant limits to it. His novel's title is an ellipse, unfolded in the text as a sarcastic unveiling into which he positions the reader: it should fully be "the false We vs. the True or Inner I" (cf. Parrinder 1977, 135). My thesis is that the central emotional and notional axis indicated by this device, the opposition of positive individuality to negative collectivity of State centralization, doesn't seem relevant anymore: both of its poles are by now untenable. One small set of examples, composed of a number of significant, more or less overt uses of this opposition in the novel follows.

It begins in Entry 1:[6]

I, D-503, Builder of the Integral, . . . shall merely attempt to record what I see and think, or, to be more exact, what we think (precisely so—we, and let this We be the title of my record).

—and continues in a number of places where D-503 is still or again a loyal "number"-cog in the mechanism of the State, for example in Entry 20 when he compares "I" to a gram and "We" to a ton:

> ... on one side "I," on the other "We," the [Unique] State. ... And the natural path from nonentity to greatness is to forget that you are a gram and feel yourself instead a millionth of a ton.

While there is a lot of semi-overt reference to collectivism in the presentations of Taylorism (the Table of Hours, the machine-like work rhythms on the construction site—Entries 7 and 15), a clear indication of D-'s disarray comes about in Entry 18, a Gogolian grotesque of dismemberment:

> ... imagine a human finger cut off from the whole, from the hand—a separate human finger, running, stooped and bobbing, up and down, along the glass pavement. I was that finger. And the strangest, the most unnatural thing of all was that the finger had no desire whatever to be on the hand, to be with others.

This opposition is conceived exclusively in terms of a power struggle and irreconcilable conflict: either "We" will eat up (dominate, enslave) "I," or "I" will eat up (subvert, destroy) "We." Either "'We' is from God, and 'I' from the devil" (Entry 22), or the obverse: no dialectics may obtain. The former case prevails at the beginning of the novel, as indicated by the first two quotes. The latter case develops slowly and bursts into the open before the middle of the novel (Entry 16) when D-503 develops the malady of "soulfulness" and an increasing anxiety that can only be allayed—and his isolation rendered tolerable and indeed emotionally validated—by what one might call the privatized mini-collective of the erotic couple: D-503's desire for I-330. A further "We" is less than clearly and somewhat inconsistently sketched out when D- and Zamyatin proceed to interpret the opposed, "natural" and "shaggy," Mephi in terms of a unanimous collective where "everybody breathes together" (Entry 27), so that D- "cease[s] to understand who 'They' are, who are 'We'" (Entry 28).[7]

This absolutistically individualist horizon was indeed Zamyatin's enthusiastic creed, identified as the supreme value of the Russian intelligentsia. In an essay that echoes the language of *We*, he spelled it out both in national terms—"the stormy, reckless Russian soul" (no less)—and in class terms: "This love, which demands all or nothing, this absurd, incurable, beautiful sickness is ... our Russian sickness, *morbus rossica*. It is the sickness that afflicts the better part of our intelligentsia—and, happily, will always afflict it" (1970, 223). In a number of other pronouncements, he speaks of such an idealist "romanticism" as the true artistic attitude toward the world (see, for example, Shane 1968, 52 and 53).

On the contrary, the combinatorics of what I shall simply call Value versus Social Horizons is much richer than the Manichean opposition between "We" and "I" (and other ideological binaries such as public versus private, reason versus emotion, *et j'en passe*—so that a strong suspicion arises that all such binaries are finally untenable). I cannot imagine any self-aware collective movement (political, religious, and even professional) without a communitarian "We" epistemology that it necessarily implies and invokes. This doesn't mean that some such "Us" orientations cannot be pernicious—examples abound throughout history down to today, the latest being the super-corporate collectivity of the international financial market to which I shall return. However, the "Me" epistemologies and orientations may not only be as pernicious, they are also self-contradictory in a way that the "We" ones are not: for, as Aristotle observed, people who can live outside of community are either beasts or gods. This does not mean that any easy black-and-white way out obtains; indeed, I believe that both the strictly collectivist and the strictly individualist ideologies situate themselves in the same double bind, from which we must step out.

In other words, even if we agree to the dubious dichotomy of "We" and "I," the combinatorics allows for at least four cases of pairing the collective and the individual. In table 3A, the Upper Left + Upper Right case or (++), a good collective interacting with good individuals, is the best imaginable one, Paradise or Utopia. The Lower L + Lower R or (–) one, the corrupt collective interacting with corrupt individuals, is the worst case, Hell or total dystopia. I would argue that the World Bank/IMF/WTO system is today fast approaching this condition, while hypocritically pretending that it is if not the best imaginable at least the best of all realistically possible worlds (we are in Candide country here). Zamyatin, however, considers only the diagonal cases, LL+UR (–\+, bad collectivism stifling good individualism) that masquerades to boot as UL+LR (+/–, a good collectivism voiding bad individualism). This is what his strong but

TABLE 3A: Combinatorics of Social Life (overview)

Social Horizons

Collective	Individual	
+	+	Good
		Value
–	–	Bad

TABLE 3B: Combinatorics of Social Life (listing)

Possible pairings:
(++) Upper ⟷ = Earthly Paradise
(– –) Lower ⟷ = Earthly Hell
(+/–) Diagonal U.L. to L.R. = pretense of Unique State
(–\+) Diagonal L.L. to U.R. = reality of Unique State

reluctantly admiring critic Voronsky, in certainly the best Soviet response *We* received, called the usual bourgeois equation of Communism with a super-barracks (1972, 171 and ff.). For, Zamyatin is here dealing with a nightmarishly distorted version of Leninist War Communism equated with medieval Catholicism (a type of configuration that Stalin did his best to bring about ten years later). However, this assiduous reader of Dostoevsky ought to have taken into account that Christianity moved between the poles of the Grand Inquisitor, from whom his Benefactor is derived by way of metallurgic metamorphosis, and Jesus, whose method has been fairly called a "Communism of Love" (Bloch)—much different from the privatized frenzy of the D-I couple (see table 3B).

4

For, what is the Leviathan—briefly glimpsed in section 2 above—that we are facing today? No doubt, it is again a negative collectivism, but in a different form from the still existing one of the brute militarized State gang that returned from colonial ventures to rule Europe in the industrialized and Taylorized World War I, which echoes strongly in this novel by a naval engineer: "The soldiers on the front lines recognized that the [First World W]ar was like work in an abominable factory" (Gray 1997, 121). The high cost of Nazism and high-tech destruction has taught our ruling classes that the empowerment by direct physical violence, including mass torture and murder, is to be used only when some of the forcibly impoverished countries, regions, and cities today threaten to revolt. While when necessary we in the richer North can remain in comfortable cahoots with the Francos, Pinochets, and Suhartos of the world, we are today overwhelmingly ruled by the psychophysical alienation of corporate capitalist collectivism. It is, politically speaking, a variant disguising the leaden weight of gang power—but morally indistinguishable from it—by a "velvet glove" in the archipelago of upper-class and (shrinking) middle-class enclaves, while retaining open militarized suppression outside those enclaves. Directly relevant to our immediate concerns here is that this hegemony also functions by fostering the ideological illusions of "individual expression" in the middle classes, while re-

other-steered at least to the same degree as in the Catholic Mid-
ler Stalinism.

ordist collectivism means unemployment, totalizing alienation
spossession in the working place — including bit by bit but quite
ing places of intellectuals such as universities or research groups.
ising political impotence of not only the working classes proper
rofessional-managerial" classes (with the exception of some im-
of mercenaries among the CEOs or the media, sports, and sci-
uivalent to the military generals). Its insidious alienation con-
'd tentatively call *emptying* negative collectivism as opposed to
tive collectivism of mass paleotechnic uniformity dreaded and
t in *We*. While the ruled are encouraged to indulge in faddish
n also uniform) surface garishnesses of dress or music consump-
are a faceless, diffuse congerie of interlocking directorates: one
Mr. Greenspan (of the U.S. Federal Reserve) or M. Camdes-
) as the Benefactor — the capitalists have learned that Hitler was
a tool. To what Çapek in his *War with the Newts* called the "male
horde or a t brutal collectivism, there gets substituted in the North a genderless rule by gray suits and attaché cases, which can co-opt women like Mrs.
Thatcher or Ms. MacKinnon. It's "the impersonal Nothing represented by
the manager" (Kracauer 1977, 160), and articulated for us in Kafka and Beck-
ett or the best cyberpunk and Piercy. As opposed to the despotic configuration
Dostoevsky and Zamyatin attributed to medieval Catholicism, exasperated in
overt Fascism and Stalinism, it suppresses individuality by brainwashing the
disoriented majority into Disneyfied consumer contentment or at least stupe-
faction, and driving a minority of us into unhappy isolation.

Instead of Medieval choral music or Zamyatin's State odes and music-
making machines instilling the sense of the rulers, the emptying terrorism uses
senseless muzak. Instead of universal ideologies hiding race, nation, and gender
by rejecting it Outside, as in the city-State of *We*, racism, sexism, and ethnic
exclusivism get now foregrounded in the rule over the motley crowds of our
megalopolises and their identity politics. Instead of the Sexual Hours we have
commodified pornography and S/M (cf. Kern 1988, 20). Instead of the Unique
State's Institute of State Poets and Writers, today in the United States — and
thus almost in the world — twenty interlocking media monopolies (in television,
movies, publishing) and their bankers "constitute a new Private Ministry of
Information and Culture" (Bagdikian 1992, xxviii). Everybody is democratically free to be physically and psychically hungry while chewing abundant junk

food. The Catholic God acquires in this perspective a certain grim nobility, not to mention the truly noble Nirvâna of Gautama the Enlightened (Buddha).

Nonetheless, to the old plus new Leviathans of negative collectivism we ought in reason and with passion to oppose the possibility of (++), the utopia of a radically better communal arrangement, "an association in which the free development of each is the condition for the free development of all" (Marx, *The Manifesto of the Communist Party*, in Marx 1978, 238). Or, as Aleksandr Blok noted while writing his great poem "The Twelve," testifying to the ubiquity of Zamyatin's theme in that historical moment but also to the availability of a diametrically opposed poetic vision on it, "The Revolution—that is: I—not alone, but we" (quoted in Dement'ev 1967, 420).[8] Today, it has become clear that collectivism is in our overcrowded—massified and urbanized, electric and electronic—mode of life absolutely unavoidable. The only choice we have is between the bad collectivities, suppressing freedom from as well as freedom for, and the good collectivities that, whatever form they may take, would be in feedback and mutual induction with non-narcissistic personalities: it is either "We" against "I" or "We" in feedback with "I"; either Zamyatin or Blok. In such a feedback, as Le Guin put it, "to be whole is to be part." On top of classical heresies and liberal revolutions, from Gautama and Spartacus to J. S. Mill, we have in this century a number of quite good, if alas too brief, examples of "temporary liberated zones" (the Temporary Autonomous Zones of Hakim Bey) from which to draw lineaments of such a positive collectivism. Eschewing written blueprint sketches, such as Lenin's *State and Revolution,* and even the best imaginative articulations, which are to be found in the SF of Mayakovsky, Platonov, Russ, Le Guin, Charnas, or Piercy, let me foreground here only the experiences of actual liberation movements. These comprise all noncorrupted unions, cooperatives, or similar people-power struggles and culminate in the popular revolutions whose promising beginnings and sad suffocations from without and within mark the twentieth century, from the Russian and Mexican series to Yugoslavia, China, Cuba, and Vietnam. One could also argue in favor of a positive collectivism in religious terms, where all believers are members of a higher unity: "Members of a Church congregation enter upon a 'We' which signifies the commonality of creatures that both sublates and founds all the distinctions and unifications which cleave to the proper name" (Kracauer 1977, 167). This old and powerful tradition, of which Zamyatin was certainly cognizant and against a decayed, unbearably autocratic form of which he was reacting, is—for example—recalled in 1837 by Emerson in a protest against a state of society "in which the members have suffered amputation from the trunk, and strut about so many walking monsters" that directly recalls the *We* entry on a finger sundered from the body. Finally, this "good We" is also a commonplace of most socialist movements. In "warm Marxist" terms, Brecht's poem "Ballad of the Waterwheel" articulates a utopian plebeian "We" of suffering and rebellious solidarity:

> Ach wir hatten viele Herren
> Hatten Tiger und Hyänen
> Hatten Adler, hatten Schweine
> Doch wir nährten den und jenen . . . (Brecht 14:207)

> (O we had so many bosses / They were tigers or hyenas / They were eagles, also swine, / But we fed this one and that one . . .)

Many other works of his, such as the radio-play *Ocean Flight* or other poems, delve at greater length into the "We" versus "I," indeed "We" versus "It" syndrome. As Jakobson commented about another Brecht poem, "'we' is here an unalienable part of 'I' as well as of 'thou.' But . . . [this is] the inclusive 'we,' which includes the addressee . . ." (1981, 668–69). Zamyatin's Unique State is what Sartre would call a serial collectivity, one in which each member is alien to others and himself, as opposed to the very unclear possibility of Sartre's "fused group" among the Mephis (1960, 306–19, 384–96).

Of the "fused" or inclusive traditions I will choose here only the nearest to us in space-time, the quarter-revolution of Western feminism, and use for that purpose the representative texts by Mary Mellor, Adrienne Rich, and Sally Miller Gearhart.

I shall begin with Mellor's book for "a Feminist Green Socialism," which contrasts, in the wake of Carol Gilligan, a "male-experience . . . ME-world" to "[a decentralized and safe] WE-world." The "We"-world was prefigured by Fourier and Marx, "but subsequently sidelined by later Marxists and socialists" and reactualized in "the interests and experience of women" (1992, 250). I would object to the traces I find here of an undialectical tendency to lump all women together as positive—though I imagine feminists might want to except Thatcher, Schlafly, and I much hope also the Fortune 50 female CEOs or the corporate astronauts (certainly Rich does so; 1985, 15–16)—and, more cutting, to lump all men as more or less lost causes. Still, I'd accept Gilligan's opposition of personality-types whose relationships are centered on responsibility and care versus those who are centered on "integrity" as separation, self-actualization, and (in my terms) conflict, and who ultimately depend on "direct exploitation of [not only, D. Suvin] women's time and labor" (Mellor 1992, 270–71).

My critique is much advanced by Rich's dialectical keynote speech at the Utrecht 1984 conference. Her engagement with the pronouns "I" and "We" begins with a twin axiom: "there is no liberation that only knows how to say 'I,'" and "[t]here is no collective movement that speaks for each of us all the way through"; and issues in the conclusion: "We—who are not the same. We who are many and do not want to be the same" (1985, 16–17). One can find in Rich also a wonderful meditation, based on her visit to the Sandinista Nicaragua, on what she identifies as "the deepfreeze of history." Her description exemplarily encompasses both the bad approach to collectivism and a new "We" resisting it and is thus most cognate to my discussion of *We:*

> Any U.S. citizen alive today has been saturated with Cold War rhetoric, the horrors of communism, the betrayals of socialism, the warning that any collective restructuring of society spells the end of personal freedom. And yes, there have been horrors and betrayals, deserving open discussion. But we are not invited to consider the butcheries of Stalinism alongside the butcheries of [W]hite supremacism and Manifest Destiny. . . . Discourse itself is frozen at this level. . . . Words which should possess a depth and breadth of allusions, words like socialism, communism, democracy, collectivism—are stripped of their historical roots. . . . Living in the climate of an *enormous either/or* [italics mine], we absorb some of it, unless we actively take heed. (1985, 14)

In a more restricted, genre discussion, Gearhart points out that the practice of most feminist utopian fiction is characterized by a tendency both toward "collective values as opposed to the individual values [of] male writers," and toward a group protagonist, somewhere between participatory democracy and "out-and-out anarchism" (for example in Charnas, Gearhart, Russ, Wittig). She recognizes there are also different methods, as in Le Guin, but argues that even there (in my words) a full focus on the empathetic, "I am Madame Bovary" protagonist never obtains (1981, 42–43). Gearhart reconducts all such changes in figuration to a "we feeling" that identifies women as vehicles of humanity for collective cooperation "with the earth, with animals, and with each other" (1981, 41). I won't go into ways by which her little essay could be supplemented and even respectfully criticized (beyond the remnants of a "We-I" dichotomy, I think it's by now fatally self-defeating to confine our hopes to women only and in particular to posit lesbian feminists as the vanguard of this struggle) but only note that I'd accept the points cited as a part of any good collectivism.

5

In this light, and facing the Leviathans of today and not yesterday, it seems to me decisive that Zamyatin lived at a historical moment when nonindividualist utopianism, in a wide spread from theocracy to warm Marxism (from Solovyov through Lenin to Bogdanov), had been debated and when its possibility, however precarious, was on the agenda of the post-1917 revolutionary openings. In numerous articles, he situated himself within this debate and pleaded for a radical utopia, one of tomorrow and not—as the Bolshevik one—of today; and I don't wish to retract my argument from *Metamorphoses* that *We* judges its nightmare from the vantage of such a utopian-socialist tomorrow. Yet he was unable to imagine a workable utopian variant (the "soft primitivism" of the country Mephi is obviously not such, which is acknowledged in the novel by the attempt to take over the city). This is both the strength and the weakness of *We*. The strength resides in his fierce concentration on the creator-diarist D-503, the weakness in the consubstantial absence of views and norms alternative to the Romantic individualism Zamyatin and this creature of his come to share. The hiatus or indeed contradiction between his overt doctrine of permanent heresy or revolution and his covert untranscendable doctrine of individualism grows into what Marx called "the Robinson Crusoe fiction," not only born of alienated relationships typical of capitalism but also acquiescing in the dichotomies that constitute the alienation. E. J. Brown may be one-sided when he focuses on the "belated Rousseauism" of the fact that "[t]here is no adequate attempt in [Zamyatin, Orwell, or Huxley] to examine the concrete social or economic factors that would lead to the debasement of human values: they offer only an abstract argument in favor of the simple and primitive as against the complex and cultivated" (1988, 222); but he's also right.

I argued in section 1 that Zamyatin is a terminal point of such Romantic individualism. My examples were drawn mainly from English Romanticism, but except for Byron, Zamyatin was more familiar with the German tradition, in Goethe's *Faust* (from whose denying figure his Mephi took their name) and in the late Nietzsche's distinction of elite versus herd, which exactly matches the relationship both of D-503 to the gray masses of the Unique State and of I-330 to the colorful subversives she leads (though D- oscillates guiltily while I- is sardonically uninhibited). The novel's Romanticism has been rightly found in the contrast between innocence and experience, in the pathetic fallacy equating nature with D-'s moods, in the "noble savage" notion present both in the Mephi primitivism and in D-'s shagginess (Edwards 1982, 44 and 62; cf. Hoyles 1991, 108), and in the lineage of Zamyatin's heroes, which comes from the solitary and brooding, rebellious or even salvational, Byronic types in Russian culture, such as the male outcast—often the sensitive artist—right down to Gorky (cf. Barratt 1984, 355; Scheffler 1984, 91). This was blended with Zamyatin's overwhelming inspiration from Dostoevsky.

Paradoxically, however, in comparison to that theocratic populism Zamyatin's atheist stance is both less clear and more elitist. Who is in *We* the equivalent of the heretic Christ confronting the *apparatchik* Great Inquisitor? D- is too weak for this role, and the true heretic I- and her Mephi Green World are not only finally defeated but also to my mind an ambiguous brew of incommensurable, if potent, erotic and political traits. In this section I shall focus on I-, an object of much libidinal investment inside and outside the text, who has disturbed a number of critics as functionally a self-interested political Snake yet axiologically part of the book's core values, sex (and brains) as heretic rebellion: the point is that she is, richly but confusingly, both.[9]

Zamyatin spoke of pathos and irony as the cathode and anode between which the literary current is created (1970, 130); but if the irony suddenly loses relevance, pathos is the only (inert) pole that remains. As some of his novel's other central devices, the femme fatale I-330 (cf. Praz 1970, ch. 4) is taken from the overheated, reach-me-down quasi Romanticism of the European fin-de-siècle, and in particular from the Russian Symbolists' mysterious and supremely alluring Beautiful Lady (prekrasnaia dama—cf. Zamyatin 1970, 32), also descended from the Byronic semidemonic female (Lamia), and characterized by stock Decadent props such as the sharp liqueur (probably out of Huysmans's *A rebours* [1884]; English as *Against Nature*). This figure-type is, of course, a figment of the (male) imagination reacting after the mid-nineteenth century against the threat of transgressive female independence. However, I- is overdetermined in complex ways, so that it is imperative to distinguish, in the tradition begun by Propp, her narratological plot position and her characterological role.

I-330 is narratologically placed in the position of Eve from the biblical-Miltonic model. In his essay "On Synthetism," Zamyatin claimed this literary movement of his was sublating in a Hegelian fashion—assuming and transcending—the tragically unattainable "Eve as Death" from Vrubel and Blok; so that instead of Schopenhauer they were following the ecstatic Nietzsche. But whatever the theory,[10] the transcendence is not noticeable in *We*. Rather, it hesitates between Symbolism (mystery) and Cubism (new understanding). Furthermore, the plot of *We* is quite consciously taken (see Entry 18) and re-functioned from popular penny-dreadfuls: it is a political spy-thriller with a vamp who comes to a bad end, as popularized at the time by the sensational Mata Hari case. (By the way, this became, mainly through Orwell, the template of much subsequent SF in the "new maps of hell," most often losing the redeeming qualities of *We* and just keeping the stereotype of individual—anguished protagonist—plus female sidekick versus State machine.) The seductive satanic force from Genesis, Milton, and the Romantics has been fully laicized and displaced from the position of antagonist (now reserved for the rulers), though echoes of its former status richly if somewhat confusingly persist. In *We* the most alluring sexual and political seductress I-, aided by the eponymous S-for-Satan-4711, turns out to be politically and ideologically positive. Thus I- oscillates between two narratological positions. Traditionally, she would have been an aide or satellite to D-: Juliet to his Romeo, or better Eve to his Adam. But in *We*, consonant with her characterological upgrading as pillar of heretic strength, she is Snake rather than Eve (besides its role in Eden, the Snake was also a nineteenth-century theater role of faithless femme fatale); that is, I- becomes an *al pari* co-protagonist, who in fact initiates all the political and most of the erotical actions in the plot—though not a co-narrator.

Characterologically, I-330 is much stronger than the sensitive and indecisive D- who is, in a subversion of the usual gender roles, "feminized" by her beesting of pollination, her vampirical pointed teeth, her sexual initiative fulfilling him, and her politico-ideological leadership and guru or commissar status (cf. Hoisington 1995, 83). Yet she is also, against the grimly Puritanical Unique State, the emancipated flapper in a world of Symbolist decadence, materialized in the Ancient House (a commonplace of the SF-cum-utopian tradition from William Morris through Wells's *Time Machine*), and whose forbidden and intoxicating qualities are emblematized by the sharp green liqueur (absinthe?). A further way of characterizing her is to oppose her, in a series of very effective love-and-jealousy triangles—taken from the theatrical conventions of vaudeville, melodrama, and boulevard comedy near and dear to Zamyatin the playwright—to O-90 (and subsidiarily to U-). This also employs Dostoevsky's usual contrast between two strong female types: the gentle, mild, and humble woman versus the predatory woman with demonic traits, corresponding to epileptic hypersensitivity of her male prey. It is O- who is the Eve to D-'s Adam (Entry 19) where I- is Lilith. O- is round and rosy where I- is straight line and associated with extreme colors, O-'s love and sex are comfortable where I-'s are "bitterly demonic and untamed" (Edwards 1982, 65, from Billington 1970, 502), O- is transparent where I- is opaque, O- is maternal where I- is nonprocreative though intellectually and erotically "pollinating" D- (cf. Hoyles 1991,

104–5). In Entry 19, however, O- begins to take on some traits of I-: she is energized and subverted simply through her love for D- and the child she bears, the maternal becoming the political (somewhat like Gorky's *Mother*). Finally (Entries 29 and 34), I- saves O- and her child among the Mephi.

The unresolved ambiguities about I-330 may be understood as the confusion of two forms of Zamyatin's overriding positive principle of energy: political subversion and erotic passion. In Zamyatin's novel, these two forms and goals, copresent only in the pivotal I-, are equated. But they can coincide only if, as Orwell realized, a love affair is also a political subversion of the State. Empirically, this is nonsense in any mass State; in this respect, Huxley's *Brave New World*, where sex is a drug in the hands of rulers, has proven much nearer to our unromantic concerns today than Zamyatin or his imitation in Orwell. The novel can only work if D-503 is taken as the axiologically representative subject of the Unique State, that is, not a "realistic" character but an allegorical protagonist. As constructor of the politically crucial spaceship, he is much too important to be simply Everyman: rather, he is the allegorical Intellectual, without whose support no revolution can win. Both as creator of spaceship and as creator of the diary entries, D- is the archetypal creative individual, enthusiastic scientist, and reluctant artist. Written around the same time as Joyce's *Portrait of the Artist as a Young Man*, Zamyatin's novel might be called, among other things, a "portrait of the artist as (sexually) awakening dystopian." After seducing D- sexually, I- therefore sets about persuading or educating him politically — with mixed success. But the sexual carnality remains entirely non-allegorical; it is a (no doubt very appealing and brilliantly executed) carryover of Dostoevskian possession, a matter of depth psychology and possibly theology but not of politics. Within the political strand of the plot, the carnal affair with D- must necessarily be backgrounded, so that his function becomes that of a patsy, used for the advantages he can bring the Revolution by delivering the spaceship to its side. The Benefactor tells him so, though D- doesn't really want to hear it.

However, Zamyatin uses the political strand of the plot much as I- uses D-: as means to a higher end — the sexual growth into a "soul." His aim is to show a sincere believer turned inside out by what is missing in the Unique State: the pleasure of the senses, a feedback loop between the brain and sexual *jouissance*, the colors, tastes, smells, and hormonal delights experienced by his body, an eversion that would translate as a subversion. Very realistically, D- really wants only such "soulful" erotics, and he is dragged into politics reluctantly and with relapses. That he would be dragged into subversion at all belongs to the penny-dreadful, melodramatic hinge between politics and example. But sexuality in

We is not heretical in the utopian "constructivist" or "synthetist" sense announced by Zamyatin's essays. Rather, it is strung between proclamations of freedom and experiences of death: D- associates it with caveman violence, fever, and death (not only the "little death" of epileptic and orgasmic fits).[11] At the end, the exemplary sexual pair D-I is sorted out into death as liquidation (I-) versus indifferent looking-on (D-). Erotics and individualism seem defeated, while the political struggle remains undecided.

Besides the emblematic I-330, the Mephi outside the Wall are supposed to be another incarnation of the union between great sex and liberatory politics. But apart from her preaching, in a philosophically to my mind unimpeachable but politically rather vague way, the necessity of permanent revolution, what alternative program are we given in the Mephi world, even in glimpses? Back to the land? For a mass industrialized society? Even to pose such questions shows that *We* is concerned with politics only in the sense of individual protest against its course, but not really in the high philosophical or cognitive sense claimed by Zamyatin. A critic in the mid-1990s could therefore rightly observe that Zamyatin and similar dystopians had "lost almost [all] of their interest and relevance" shortly after their publication in the Russia of the late 1980s: "[I]t is as if 'we' had won the battle against the 'One State,' but what we find beyond the Green Wall is increasingly not what we expected. . . ." (Lahusen 1994, 678; ellipsis in the original). This is what I attempted to discuss earlier by way of the "We" versus "I" dichotomy.

6

Zamyatin commented in 1932 that *We* "is a warning against the twofold danger which threatens humanity: the hypertrophic power of the machines and the hypertrophic power of the State" (Lefèvre 1932, 1). The comment may say more about how the author's stresses had shifted in the intervening dozen years—and pursuing his ideological shifts after the mid-1920s, apparently to the Left, might prove very revealing—than about the much more ambiguous treatment of technoscience in the novel.[12] This fascination with and yet mistrust of technoscience can be taken beyond State sponsorship of massive drives such as the Soviet Five-Year Plans and the U.S. Manhattan Project or Marshall Plan, so that it remains applicable to our concerns today: the Post-Fordist capitalist corporations' full symbiosis with computers, automation, and gene manipulation; and of course to the ever more horrifying ways of mass military murders in "small" (but tomorrow perhaps again global) wars.[13] Yet shouldn't we focus on who (what social group) deals with the machines of technoscience, how, what for, in whose interest, and to whose detriment? Finally, amid all the mathematics, architecture, and construction technology, it may be still cognitively useful, and thus acceptable, that *We* is inhabited by faceless crowds marching four abreast. Perhaps one can even accept as realistic for 1920 that these crowds then resolve into women in various variants of sexual desire — named stereotypically by "soft" I, O, and U vowels — or of janitoring, and into men as doctors, poets, or secret-service "Guardians" — named by "hard" consonants D, R, and S. After all, *We* is a unique, grotesque, Cubist kind of allegory (though again, Zamyatin had some doubts about Picasso and especially abhorred Le Corbusier's architecture of cubes [1970, 134–35]). But it is built around a central absence: except for some brief and not very enlightening scenes in the shipyard, there are within the horizons of Zamyatin's novel no economics, nor productive labor, nor working people — no accounting for the distribution and maintenance of the food, housing, "aeros," telephones, electric whips, walls for fencing in, and streets for marching. The anonymous (unnumbered?) masses are there only as a backdrop for D- and I-. The "I versus We" translates as private versus public. Most perniciously perhaps, reason is insistently identified with "We," and emotion (or imagination) with "I." This aspect in Zamyatin is late, impoverished, ideological individualism.

However, I wouldn't like to end merely on a negative note about a dialectically contradictory masterpiece I still in many ways admire. If the humanization of the overwhelmingly center-stage protagonist has been defeated and the temptress firing his imagination and organizing rebellion has been cruelly suppressed in the best Jehovaite tradition, at least two important aspects remain relevant and fertile today. The most important may be signaled by the inferences hidden in its technology of writing: for all meaning resides in the form, and form cannot be disjoined from meaning. As Voronsky was one of the first to have pointed out, Zamyatin was a master of the word, the sharp observer of incisive details. His Cubist texture and some other aspects (for example, the astounding believability of the rather improbable D-503 and I-330; or the two-edged use of mathematics, see Suvin 1979) have only rarely been matched since in any SF — utopian or dystopian or anti-utopian. A postrealistic or properly Modernistic texture, say, can be found in a very few items after the 1960s: much William Burroughs, one text by Golding (see Parrinder 1977, 139), some Bester or Le Guin (for example, "New Atlantis"), Harlan Ellison, and Kathy Acker. Thus, like his revered Wells, Zamyatin has rightly entered world literature. In fairness, I should also note that while the story of D- and I- ends in total defeat, the novel's ending remains ambiguous, not quite closed: the battle rages on, and 0–90 has left the State to bear D–'s child. Most important: as I also argued in *Metamorphoses,* the defeat *in* the novel isn't the defeat *of* the novel—that is, of its potentially liberatory effect on the reader. The warnings against capitalist industrialization, with its military drill incorporated in the machines, and of the Soviet enthusiasm for it, clash strangely and richly with the precision of the thematic development, the economic clarity incorporating even the "irrational number" into a system of lucidly functional oppositions, and many other matters of "style" (cf. Heller 1983, 235–37) that evince a Cubist or Constructivist confidence that is not only utopian but also deeply complicitous with, indeed unthinkable without, the very urbanization and industrialization whose one, malevolent variant they so doggedly stigmatize. They bear the imprint of Zamyatin the mathematical engineer and shipbuilder, the extoller of the persecuted theoretician of science Robert Mayer, and constitute the hidden positive, utopian socialist, values in the name of which the repressive aberrations are envisaged and judged. I doubt this would provide any comfort to the present-day savage corporate capitalism subjugating national states, the new Leviathan.

And second, more restrictedly but perhaps more acutely, the old State apparatus is neither fully nor definitely off the agenda of present history. The Global Corporate versus State Leviathans don't spell each other as participants in a relay race or train connections. Rather, they relate at least as intimately as do geological strata, where a new formation can for long stretches be interrupted by remains or even re-emergences of the old formation upheaving and sticking up as whole mountain ranges.[14] Though the "translational" corporations are still mainly "national companies with a transnational reach" (Meiksins Wood 1998, 7, and see Krätke 1997), the partnership and collusion between the capitalist global corporations and the nation-States seems to me finally dominated by the former. Yet, as we have seen in the mendacious and cruel war against Serbia, the old State Leviathan can be summoned into operation at the touch of a cellular phone call or of a computer button whenever the new Leviathan needs it: they are, after all, still instruments of class rule, brothers under the skin. State apparatuses have largely become local enforcing committees of the big oligopolies conveniently designated as the IMF/WTO/World Bank group; it may in fact turn out that the new Leviathan is a true dialectical sublation of the old one, both denying and preserving it in selected aspects. Dialectically, the old Leviathan is also, at given propitious places and times, available for useful work, bundling and accelerating a large national consensus in order to improve life, for example, to institute Medicare or social insurance. That is especially the case in some approximations to popular sovereignty in poorer states brutally attacked by the subversive forces of international capital. This was prefigured by the Mexican and Kemalite revolutions, this is what Lenin's State decayed into at its best moments of defense of the Soviet Union, and this is what continued into the postwar experiences of the "non-aligned" peoples from Tito through Nkrumah and Nehru to Castro. But where are the snows of yesteryear?

Yet Zamyatin's generous indictment of life in a "super-barracks" society is of a much diminished importance for getting our bearings in a super-Disneyland society. *We*'s bad collectivism recycles what are by now "paleotechnic" (Mumford 1963) or Fordist elements and attitudes predating speculative finance capitalism. The insipid food in *We*, made from petroleum and distributed by the State, does not collate to our problems with the overspiced and canceroge-nously hormonized "McDonald'sified" burgers pushed by brainwashing us in the "free" market. Even less does it speak to the hungry and freezing unpaid millions of "freed" Russia.

NOTES

My thanks go to colleagues connected with the Society for Utopian Studies November 1998 meeting where this article was first presented in a briefer version: Naomi Jacobs; Carol Franko, whose writing led me to Adrienne Rich's article, which she kindly sent me; and Savas Barkçin, my copanelist, whose paper on Kemalism reminded me of what became my next-to-last paragraph. Thanks also go to Patrick Flaherty for sending me some unpublished papers of his on Russia today, from which I learned much. I am responsible for nonattributed translations. Except for direct quotes and the book title, arguments about the philosophical "We" and "I" in and out of Zamyatin are always put in quotes with initial caps. The characters D-503 and I-330 are named (or "numbered") in full the first time they occur in any paragraph, and after that written only as D- and I-.

1. After completing the first draft of this article I read Krätke's excellent analysis of the limits of globalization (1997, esp. 40–55), which proves that the multinational corporations have fully globalized only the currency and capital markets. The circa six hundred big corporations and "institutional investors" are owned and managed, and further they produce, research, and invest overwhelmingly in one zone of the "triad" (North America, Europe, Japan and East Asia), indeed eighty out of the one hundred biggest mainly in one country; exceptions can be found in the food and drink, computer, and some other consumer goods' firms (McDonald's!). Based on such data, the splendid book by Kagarlitsky rightly argues that the "argument about 'the impotence of the state'" both hides its abuse by financial capital and hobbles struggles for a countervailing, democratic nation-state (2000, vi and passim; cf. also Went 2000, 48–50). I dissent only from his analysis of the Bosnian civil war and a few other minor matters.

Amongst them is his term of "New Big Brother" rather than New Leviathan: true, it is more immediately comprehensible but also, as I argue in section 4, much too personalized for the capillary politics of globalization.

2. A smattering of letters to and about Zamyatin was published in Russia and abroad beginning with the *glasnost* years. Yet there is still a great deal of unpublished writings by Zamyatin in the archives at Columbia University, in Paris—including a ten-page film synopsis of *We* called *D-503* from 1932—and in Russia.

   It might also be useful to immerse Zamyatin more decisively into his precise locus. First of all, *We* and some of his most significant essays were written in and as a response to the period of War Communism circa 1917–1921, the time of fierce military struggle, direct State dictatorship, and the crudest collectivist hyperboles (for example by the "proletarian" poets and the enthusiasts for Taylorism). Stalin's post-1928 or post-1934 reign of terror is a rather different period—for one thing, open opposition à la Zamyatin wasn't tolerated anymore. There are indications that a number of Zamyatin's later and not yet fully accessible works (such as the unfinished novel about Attila) again turned to a critique of the West. Second, he would profit from much more comparison to his contemporary Futurist poets or Constructivist painters (cf. Heller 1983); and within SF and utopia/anti-utopia, only some first parallels have been drawn to two other major Russian SF works of the 1920s with world-historical horizons that were deeply preoccupied with, respectful of, yet not necessarily starry-eyed about the price of revolutionary politics—Alexey Tolstoy's *Aelita* and Ilya Ehrenburg's *Trust D. E.* (cf. Striedter 1983). All three were written by intellectuals who had been living not only in Russia but also in western Europe, of which they were rather critical. All three oscillated in their attitude toward the Bolshevik authorities, Zamyatin being the most resolutely and stridently critical of them.

3. A remarkable unpublished article draft from 1921 propounds: "Only those who do not believe or insufficiently believe in socialism want an orthodox socialist literature and fear unorthodox literature. I believe. I know: socialism is inevitable. It has already ceased to be a utopia, and precisely because of this it is the business of true literature to build new utopias. . . . [T]he future has become the present, it has acquired flesh, earth, steel, it has become heavy, current—and that is why it no longer . . . carries the pathos of utopia and imagination—so that it is necessary to build for man a new utopia of tomorrow and the day after tomorrow" (Russian original in Malm'stad and Fleishman 1987, 107–8).

4. So far as I'm aware, having followed criticism on Zamyatin in the main European languages, most critics—including the meritorious Slavists, most of whom are listed in the bibliography of *Metamorphoses*—who speak about his relation to Dostoevsky mention only aspects from *The Brothers Karamazov, The Possessed,* and *Notes from the Underground* (but see the pioneering Shane 1968). Yet Zamyatin knew his Dostoevsky very

well indeed, and I think a thorough confrontation of *We* with Dostoevsky's whole opus is a desideratum that one hopes the Slavists could put high up on their agenda, just after the publication of Zamyatin's collected works, even though grants might have dried up with the Cold War. It would be a shame if we had to find out that most Slavists had in reality been more interested in Kremlinology than in literary cognition when they extolled Zamyatin.

5. Chossudovsky (1998, 1); cited hereafter by the number of "virtual page." Chossudovsky is professor of economics in Ottawa; see also for Russia his *Globalisation of Poverty* (1997, ch. 11). My thanks to him for generously permitting extensive quotation.

6. Given the several translations in print and used pell-mell in criticism so far, I shall be citing by "Entry" (as the chapters in *We* are called) and not by page of the Ginsburg translation I used. I've checked them all against the original Russian (Zamyatin 1967).

7. Huntington's subtle analysis notes a number of such positive "We's" in the novel, issuing in the Entry 37 query "Who are we? Who am I?" This jibes with his argument that the confusion in the novel is a deliberate strategy but seems too strong a reading to me. It is tempting to posit an "unconscious" Zamyatin-the-artist working against the ideologist, but it may be too easy. Nonetheless, as Huntington's analyses of "thou" also suggest (1982, all 132–34), we have only scratched the surface of this rich artifact: it may surprise us yet.

8. Many similar statements, not all by second-rate poets, could be found at the time; full titular coincidences are, for example, the great movie director Dziga Vertov's *We: A Variant of the Manifesto* of 1922, and Mayakovsky's poem "We" already appeared in 1914.

   It must be acknowledged that all bad variants of collectivism, prominently including Stalinism, stress the individual's subsumption under a Leviathan: the tell-tale semantic sign here is the insipid and covertly religious hypostasis of the collective into a singular unit, either named Leader or allegorical Party, as, for example, in Becher's *Kantate 1950:* "Du grosses Wir, Du unser aller Willen: / . . . / Dir alle Macht, der Sieg ist Dein, Partei!" ("Thou great We, Thou will of all of us: / . . . / All power to Thee, victory is Thine, O Party!").

9. Critics' opinions about the role of Zamyatin's splendid I-330 have been diametrically opposed. A brief sample of a few more recent ones yield some extreme pro and con opinions. *Pro:* in Ulph, one of the most stimulating critics, I find references to "dialectic duality—siren & revolutionary . . . Superwoman . . . Belle Dame Sans Merci . . . one of the most sadistic, frenetic & comical seductions of the faltering male by the determined vamp in Western [?!] literature" (1988, 82–85 passim). In Hoisington, whose entire article is praise of I-330 as real heroine of novel "both in the sense of the mover and the character who best exemplifies the novel's governing values," I- "is the stimulating, fertilizing force"; "a rebel . . . who chooses to remain true to her beliefs, to

suffer and to die rather than recant" (1995, 82–85 passim). *Con:* For Mikesell and Suggs I- is failed trickster, "the love she demands [of D- has] destructive effects," "the world desired by I-330 and her Mephi . . . harbors . . . violence & deceit," and "finally she is not a facilitator but, like the Benefactor himself, a tyrant" (1982, 94 and 98). For Barratt, I- is "a Mata Hari figure, who has been using her sexual attractiveness as a means"; her ultimate aim is freedom but paradoxically "her initial act . . . was to *enslave* [D-] by luring him against his will into compromising his allegiance to the One State" (1984, 346 and 355). For Petrochenkov "I-330's most ominous feature [is] . . . the vaginal teeth that castrate. . . . Her mouth is associated with a knife and dripping blood . . ." (1998, 246–47).

It should be noted, first, that the critics' opinions don't follow their gender; and second, that most pro critics note I-'s ambiguous (both-and) characteristics, while the con critics concentrate on the negative ones. The problem seems to me to be which of the undoubtedly present two aspects of I- predominates within the plot and the ethicopolitical concerns of Zamyatin—and then, our concerns today.

10. See Zamyatin (1970, 82); cf. also Scheffler (1984, 29, 92, and passim) and Rooney (1986). To my mind, Zamyatin's handling of Hegelian historiosophy as well as of Nietzsche's Superman versus herd is rather simplified. He was a *bricoleur* in the philosophy of history and of politics. While this may be quite enough for writing one novel, it will not do to extrapolate his pronouncements as indubitable cognitions about the State Leviathan in general and the Soviet State in particular; as a theorist he catches fire only when he can integrate his overriding Modernist avant-garde allegory of entropy versus energy with other symbolism.

11. It would be interesting to compare this with Walter Benjamin's views on the woman's body in Baudelaire's civilization as "death-body, fragmented-body, petrified body" and "a metaphor for extremes," issuing in the Baudelairean abyss (or, I would add, Zamyatin's vertigo); the quotes are from the approach to this aspect of Benjamin in Buci-Glucksmann (1986, 226 and 228). A crucial question for *We,* so far as I remember not yet posed, would here be: "Who is D-'s diary really addressed to?"

12. As a number of critics from Lewis and Weber (1988) on have remarked, insofar as the ideology of "mechanized collectivism" is the target, *We* is a polemic with the school of Proletkult poets propagating the extension of Taylorism (cf. for those themes also Scheffler 1984, 186–91)—the pet focus of Zamyatin's sarcasm from his English 1916 stories on—into all areas of life. *We* is not a polemic with supertechnological ways of life in Russia, quite nonexistent there until recently, but was in fact meant by Zamyatin equally, if not more, for the capitalist "West" (cf. Myers 1993, 75–77).

13. As in all nations that had quickly to recapitulate "Western" modernization, and thus serve to show its underlying structure, modern science was in Russia too first introduced for military purposes as part of a centralized State; the first use of the term

nauka (science) was in a 1647 military manual in the sense of "military skill" (Billington 1970, 113). It is most eye-opening that the one thing the two Leviathans, Zamyatin's Fordist one and our Post-Fordist one, have obviously in common (remember the imperialist interplanetary rocket D- is building!) is the massive war technology and nationalist propaganda playing it up, both of which they're not only engaged in but in fact deeply dependent on; this is the visible tip of the iceberg of continuing murderous class-rule.

14. Perhaps the succession of not only modes of production but also of their main stages might best be understood as imbricated articulation rather than simple abolition (cf. Jameson 1999, 67). My little geological metaphor is worth whatever it's cognitively worth: any metaphor or model has limits of applicability. But if we were to proceed to a metalevel of theorizing, it should be noted that Marx's key notion of "social formation" refunctions the geological "formation" of his admired Lyell, which wittily fuses a historically specific process and its result. In geology, terms like primary and secondary formation suggest simultaneously the nature/structure and the evolutionary collocation of rock strata (cf. Godelier 1979, 343); if not metaphors they're at least puns. In that sense the historical figures of the two capitalist Leviathans of centralized Fordist State and globalized Post-Fordist speculative finances are both distinct ideal types and inextricably commingled within the latter's contradictory domination over the former.

WORKS CITED

Bagdikian, Ben. 1992. *The Media Monopoly*. 4th ed. Boston: Beacon Press.

Barratt, Andrew. 1984. "Revolution as Collusion: The Heretic and the Slave in Zamyatin's *My*." *Slavonic and East European Review* 62, no. 3:344–61.

Beauchamp, Gorman. 1973. "Of Man's Last Disobedience." *Comparative Literature Studies* 10:285–301.

Becher, Johannes R. 1950. "Kantate 1950." *Neues Deutschland* (27 May).

Billington, James H. 1970. *The Icon and the Axe*. New York: Vintage.

Brecht, Bertolt. 1989–1998. *Werke*. Grosse kommentierte Berliner und Frankfurter Ausgabe. Berlin: Aufbau V, and Frankfurt/M: Suhrkamp V.

Brown, E. J. 1988. "*Brave New World, 1984* & *We*." Pp. 209–27 in *Zamyatin's "We,"* ed. Gary Kern. Ann Arbor, Mich.: Ardis. [Article originally published 1976.]

Buci-Glucksmann, Christine. 1986. "Catastrophic Utopia: The Feminine as Allegory of the Modern." *Representations*, no. 14:222–29.

Chossudovsky, Michel. 1997. *The Globalisation of Poverty*. London: Zed.

———. 1998. "Financial Warfare." (E-mail posting from 22 September.) Available from http://www.southside.org.sg/souths/twn/title/trig-cn.htm or chossudovsky@videotron.ca.

Clairmont, Frédéric F. 1999. "La Russie au bord de l'abîme." *Le Monde diplomatique* (18 March), 18–19.

Clarke, Simon. 1989. *Keynesianism, Monetarism and the Crisis of the State.* Aldershot, U.K.: Elgar.

Cohen, Stephen F. 2000. "American Journalism and Russia's Tragedy." *The Nation* (2 October), 23–30.

Dement'ev, A. G., et al. 1967. *Istoriia russkoi sovetskoi literatury.* Vol. 1. Moskva: Nauka.

Edwards, T. R. N. 1982. *Three Russian Writers and the Irrational.* Cambridge: Cambridge University Press.

Fanger, Donald. 1965. *Dostoevsky and Romantic Realism.* Cambridge, Mass.: Harvard University Press.

Flaherty, Patrick. 2000. "Putin, Praetorianism and Revolution" (September). Unpublished.

Frye, Northrop. 1970. "The Drunken Boat." Pp. 200–217 in Frye, *The Stubborn Structure.* Ithaca, N.Y.: Cornell University Press.

Gearhart, Sally. 1981. "Female Futures in Science Fiction." Pp. 41–45 in *Proceedings of the Conference Future, Technology and Women.* San Diego: Women's Studies Department, San Diego State University.

Godelier, Maurice. 1979. "Formazione economico-sociale." Pp. 342–73 in *Enciclopedia Einaudi.* Vol. 6. Torino, Italy: Einaudi.

Gray, Chris Hables. 1997. *Postmodern War.* New York: Guilford.

Gregg, Richard A. 1988. "Two Adams and Eve in the Crystal Palace: Dostoevsky, the Bible, and *We.*" Pp. 209–27 in *Zamyatin's We,* ed. Gary Kern. Ann Arbor, Mich.: Ardis. [Article originally published 1965.]

Heller, Leonid. 1983. "La prose de E. Zamjatin et l'avantgarde russe." *Cahiers du monde russe et soviétique* 24, no. 3:217–39.

Hoisington, Sona Stephan. 1995. "The Mismeasure of I-330." Pp. 81–88 in *A Plot of Her Own: The Female Protagonist in Russian Literature,* ed. Hoisington. Evanston, Ill.: Northwestern University Press.

Holmstrom, Nancy, and Richard Smith. 1999. "The Necessity of Gangster Capitalism: Primitive Accumulation in Russia and China." *Monthly Review,* no. 9:1–15.

Hoyles, John. 1991. *The Literary Underground.* New York: St. Martin's.

Huntington, John. 1982. "Utopian and Anti-Utopian Logic: H. G. Wells and His Successors." *Science-Fiction Studies* 9, no. 2:122–46.

Jakobson, Roman. 1981. "Der grammatische Bau des Gedichts von B. Brecht 'Wir sind sie.'" Pp. 660–71 in Jakobson, *Selected Writings.* Vol. 3, ed. S. Rudy. The Hague: Mouton.

Jameson, Fredric. 1999. *The Cultural Turn.* London: Verso.

Kagarlitsky, Boris. 2000. *The Twilight of Globalization.* London: Pluto.

Kern, Gary. 1988. "Introduction." Pp. 9–21 in *Zamyatin's "We,"* ed. Kern. Ann Arbor, Mich.: Ardis.

Kracauer, Siegfried. 1977. *Das Ornament der Masse.* Frankfurt: Suhrkamp.

Krätke, Michael R. 1997. "Kapital global?" Pp. 18–59 in E. Altvater et al., *Turbo-Kapitalismus.* Hamburg: VSA.

Lahusen, Thomas. 1994. "Russian Literary Resistance Reconsidered." *Slavic and East European Journal* 38, no. 4: 677–82.

Lefèvre, Frédéric. 1932. "Une heure avec Zamiatine." *Les nouvelles littéraires,* no. 497 (23 April):1, 8.

Lewis, Kathleen, and Harry Weber. 1988. "Zamyatin's *We,* the Proletarian Poets, and Bogdanov's *Red Star.*" Pp. 186–208 in *Zamyatin's "We,"* ed. Gary Kern. Ann Arbor, Mich.: Ardis. [Article originally published 1975.]

Malm'stad, Dzhon, and Lazar' Fleishman. 1987. "Iz biografii Zamiatina." Pp. 103–51 in *Stanford Slavic Studies.* Vol. 1. Stanford, Calif.: Stanford University Press.

Marx, Karl. 1978. *Selected Writings,* ed. D. McLellan. Oxford: Oxford University Press.

McMurtry, John. 1999. *The Cancer Stage of Capitalism.* London: Pluto.

Meiksins Wood, Ellen. 1998. "Labor, Class, and State in Global Capitalism." Pp. 3–16 in *Labor in the Age of "Global" Capitalism,* ed. Meiksins Wood et al. New York: Monthly Review.

Mellor, Mary. 1992. *Breaking the Boundaries.* London: Virago.

Menshikov, Stanislav. 1999. "Russian Capitalism Today." *Monthly Review,* no. 3:81–99.

Mikesell, Margaret Lael, and Jon Christian Suggs. 1982. "Zamyatin's *We* and the Idea of the Dystopic." *Studies in Twentieth Century Literature* 7, no. 1:89–102.

Mumford, Lewis. 1963. *Technics and Civilization.* New York: Harcourt.

Myers, Alan. 1993. "Zamyatin in Newcastle." *Foundation,* no. 59:70–78.

Parrinder, Patrick. 1977. "Imagining the Future: Wells and Zamyatin." Pp. 126–43 in *H. G. Wells and Modern Science Fiction,* ed. Darko Suvin. Lewisburg, Pa.: Bucknell University Press.

Petrochenkov, Margaret Wise. 1998. "Castration Anxiety and the Other in Zamyatin's *We.*" Pp. 243–55 in *Critical Studies: The Fantastic Other,* ed. B. Cooke et al. Amsterdam: Rodopi.

Praz, Mario. 1970. *The Romantic Agony.* New York: Oxford University Press.

Redford, Tim. 1997. "Europe Faces Disease Invasion from East." *Guardian Weekly* (17 April), 7.

Rich, Adrienne. 1985. "Notes toward a Politics of Location." Pp. 7–22 in *Women, Feminist Identity and Society in the 1980's,* ed. M. Díaz-Diocaretz and I. Zavala. Amsterdam: Benjamins.

Rooney, Victoria. 1986. "Nietzschean Elements in Zamyatin's Ideology." *Modern Language Review* 81, no. 3:675–86.

Sartre, Jean-Paul. 1960. *Critique de la raison dialectique*. Paris: Gallimard.

Scheffler, Leonore. 1984. *Evgenij Zamjatin: Sein Weltbild und seine literarische Thematik.* Bausteine zur Geschichte der Literatur bei den Slaven 20. Tübingen: Böhlau V.

Shane, Alex M. 1968. *The Life and Works of Evgenij Zamjatin*. Berkeley: University of California Press.

Skuratov, Iurii. 2000. *Variant drakona*. Moskva: DP.

Striedter, Jurij. 1983. "Three Postrevolutionary Russian Utopian Novels." Pp. 177–201 in *The Russian Novel from Pushkin to Pasternak*, ed. John Garrard. New Haven: Yale University Press.

Suvin, Darko. 1979. *Metamorphoses of Science Fiction*. New Haven: Yale University Press.

Ulph, Owen. 1988. "I-330: Reconsiderations on the Sex of Satan." Pp. 80–91 in *Zamyatin's "We,"* ed. Gary Kern. Ann Arbor, Mich.: Ardis.

Voronsky, A[leksandr] K. 1972. "Evgeny Zamyatin," trans. P. Mitchell. *Russian Literature Triquarterly*, no. 3:157–75.

Wallerstein, Immanuel. 1998. *Utopistics*. New York: New Press.

Went, Robert. 2000. *Globalization*, trans. T. Smith. London: Pluto & IIRE.

Zamyatin, Yevgeny. 1967. *My*. New York: Inter-Language Literary Associates.

———. 1970. *A Soviet Heretic: Essays by Yevgeny Zamyatin*, ed. and trans. M. Ginsburg. Chicago: University of Chicago Press.

———. 1983. *We*, trans. M. Ginsburg. New York: Avon.

The Coming of Christ the Joker

george zebrowski

By 2001 A.D. some 44 percent of Americans believed that I
would be coming back in the new millennium. That's better
than the ten just men my Father tried to find.
—*Jesus Christ*

"Well, you know, God is at best an exaggeration," said Gore Vidal to his talk show host.

"What do you mean?" Larry King asked.

"You know—omnipotent, omniscient, biggest, best—all extremes. Imaginative exaggerations each." He crossed his legs and sat back with a sigh.

"Don't you believe in God, Mr. Vidal?" Larry King asked in a hushed voice.

"Believe? Oh, come now, Mr. King, I shan't be dragged into that can of worms."

"It's certainly more than that," King said.

Gore Vidal smiled his distant, deep smile. "Now look, Larry. You know what the wars between religions were about, don't you? About which side had the better imaginary friend."

King laughed uncomfortably as he got the point. "I've heard that joke."

Vidal grimaced with mock mercy. "Okay, let's be fair. It was about which side had the one true imaginary friend."

King shrugged. "Same difference. So you think faith is a sham?"

Gore Vidal said, "I'm sure that I could make a better defense of faith than mere insistence."

As Larry King hesitated before the poised intellect of his guest, someone who might have been taken for Jesus in a lineup appeared slowly in the chair next to Gore Vidal.

The audience gasped. Larry King stared. Gore Vidal looked over and said wearily, "Magic tricks? I'm going to be part of a magic show? Good God, give me a break."

Larry King reached over and grabbed Vidal's wrist. "But you . . . didn't you see him just fade in? That's what he did, that's what he did! Faded right in next to you!"

Vidal sighed and pulled his wrist free. "Fade in? I had to type that in my scripts for ten years so I could make enough money to live as I please." Then he glanced over at the smiling man sitting next to him and said, "Good evening, Sir. I don't know why you're here, but I hope they're paying you enough. My name is Gore Vidal."

"Yes, I know," the bearded, smiling man said through yellowing teeth.

Just as Larry King began to say, "Look here, buddy, I don't know how you got in here, but the soup kitchen's down the street," the visitor disappeared.

In the twinkling of an eye, before Gore Vidal had a chance to look at him again.

"Faded right out!" King exclaimed. "Right on out there . . . "

"There's no soup kitchen down the street," Gore Vidal said as Christ the Joker came to all parts of the world.

He came to ridicule, not to teach or save, following the principle that a good horselaugh is the best weapon against stupidity.

Heads of state found themselves floating naked above their capital cities, screaming as pigeons alighted on these human dirigibles.

At Grant's Tomb in New York City, Jesus walked up to a cop on the beat while eating a hot dog and wiped his mustard-covered hand on the back of the policeman's blue uniform. The Irish cop turned around, and Jesus finished the job on the front of the uniform.

"Now look here, friend," the cop said. "I'll be runnin' you in for that!"

"Oh, come now. If you've heard my parable about the mustard seed, you'll know why I did it."

"Is that a fact?" the cop said as he reached out to arrest the empty air.

On Wall Street, Jesus appeared on the main floor of the stock exchange and scrambled the big board. Amidst the shouts and moans that followed, he unscrambled the board, then with a hand motion sent it into chaos again, just so there would be no mistaking that he had done the deed.

"Terrorist!" cried the money mob, clearing a circle around the Nazarene.

"Put it back!" a lone voice pleaded from some private hell.

As all eyes looked to the salvation of the big board, the chaos continued.

Simultaneously at the Vatican, Jesus appeared in the Pontiff's earthly garden.

"Who are you?" the Pope demanded, putting away his Palm Pilot.

"Who do I look like?" Jesus asked.

"I think you had better leave," said the Pontiff, looking around for his guards.

"Very well," Jesus said, and dissolved.

When the guards arrived, they found the Pope buck naked, attempting to cover himself with a few fern branches.

At Donald Trump's third wedding reception, Jesus appeared at the champagne fountain and turned all the waiting bottles into boxed wines.

At the annual conference of American governors, combined in this year with a convention of prison wardens, Jesus replaced the keynote speaker, William Bennett, and said, "The measure of a criminal justice system is whether it commits new crimes against the convicted. Fresh crimes harm those who commit them as much as they harm the punished. Surely you can understand that much?"

Then he did a magic trick—the destruction of all documents, physical and electronic, by which 60 percent of all people incarcerated were imprisoned. "Thus I free the undeserving," he said to the delegates, "and there will be nothing you can do about it. The lawyers will do their work with a good conscience."

"Who do you think you are!" Mayor Rudolph Giuliani cried from the middle row.

Jesus raised his right hand and said, "I am who *will* be."

"What's that?" Rudy asked.

"As my father *was* when the Burning Bush spoke," Jesus continued. "He was who *is*, and I am who *will* be."

"Ah, shut up, Giuliani!" a voice cried out. "You'd arrest Jesus, Mary, and Joseph if they came to New York."

Rudy said, "The homeless are not, I repeat, not those holy figures."

The audience booed.

Jesus raised a hand. "The mayor of New York forgets that what he does to the least of mine he does to me."

Suddenly silent, the audience shrank back from the intruder. Giuliani rolled his eyes, insisting to himself that no one powerful would show solidarity with the weak and worthless without a political motive. Only legends and myths did that. Tricksters he did not have to worry about.

Silently, Jesus looked at the audience—as he did on Wall Street, and in the Papal Garden of the Vatican where the Pontiff prayed on all fours, and in a thousand other places throughout the world. At Grant's Tomb he leaped into the cop's arms and kissed him on the lips. The policeman let him go. Jesus did not fall.

"Lord have mercy!" cried the wardens and governors, still shrinking from the hand that seemed raised to strike.

Jesus popped back in on *Larry King Live*.

Gore Vidal crossed his legs and said, "You know, you're quite good. You remind me of a novel I once wrote called *Messiah*. But there's one fatal flaw in your act."

Jesus lowered his hand and turned to the famous author. "Flaw?" Jesus asked. "Act? There can be no flaw."

Gore Vidal sat back and smiled.

"Well, aren't you going to tell me?" Jesus asked.

"Don't you know everything?"

"I don't pry," Jesus said.

Vidal leaned forward. "Exactly what I mean. You cannot be Jesus Christ, despite your tricks. But you do have his persona right. At least I've always liked to believe that Jesus was an annoying character, even to his friends."

Jesus sat back and gazed with interest at the man of wit. "So why am I not he?"

"As you said," Vidal explained, "you don't pry. Now if theism were true, and God—your Dad, I suppose—made us all, then the first thing he would do is to convince us of his nonexistence. At the very least he would make of his being a thing of doubt. This would then leave room for moral freedom and faith. After all, everyone bets on a certainty, and you wouldn't like to be worshiped as a sure thing. There's no test in that."

"Go on," Jesus said.

"Therefore, God's absence is the best proof we have of his existence." Vidal yawned. "That is, if you wish to play theological games."

"So what does all this have to do with me not being myself?" Jesus asked.

Gore Vidal grinned, and there was a twinkle in his eye as he asked, "Now, you're sure you don't want to pry into my mind and find out—and prove something to me?"

"No," Jesus said.

"Well, there you have it. Since you've interfered with human affairs, you cannot be God or his Son. An interfering God is inconceivable, so you can't be Jesus."

"I interfered once before," Jesus said.

"So people say. For my part a God of second thoughts cannot be God. Therefore you're a very clever impostor. For all I know you're David Coppersteel . . . or some such magician."

"Don't get him angry!" a woman cried from the audience.

Elsewhere throughout the world, Jesus continued his guerrilla raids, playing pranks upon humanity in place of exhortations, teachings, or plagues. These last had always been later explained as natural events anyway, so they had never done any good. Even great theologians had marked them as "physical evils" having nothing to do with God, whose evils would surely have been "intentional."

This time Jesus had begun with slapstick. But he quickly began to see that perhaps something stronger was needed—irony, even bitter black comedy.

Maybe.

He thought about this as he sat next to Gore Vidal, and in a thousand other locations. Humor, it had been said by these very same creatures who had been set in motion by his father (creation was hardly the word for what he had done), was the highest form of reason. It provoked sudden, unexpected exposures of stupidity. Unfortunately, these insights lasted only long enough to produce very slow net progress in human affairs. These creatures might very well destroy themselves before self-improvement kicked in decisively.

"Mercy!" cried the peoples of the world, as ironic bitterness pierced their lives in a million ways. "Why teach us in this way? Why did you not make us right to begin with, oh Lord?"

Jesus answered that to do so would have simply created the so-called angels all over again. Then, as with the angels, it would have been necessary to give them free will, so that they would escape the triviality of guaranteed goodness. And look what happened when the angels had been set free. One faction stayed loyal. The other set up shop elsewhere. Both continued to meddle. No, he was not yet ready to give up on goading humanity to see the right—which was per-mitted—and have them choose it for themselves. It was risky, but maybe it would come out right this time; after all, not all the angels had chosen wrongly.

Jesus adjusted the time, enabling him to sit next to Gore Vidal even as his plan of provocation played throughout the world.

After a few unmeasured moments that might have been years, or miniature infinities, Gore Vidal said, "Okay, I do sense that you're doing something to the world, to my mind, and perhaps to time itself. I would consider it good manners if you would at least be up front about it. Of course, I can't think of you as the traditional Christ. That would be beneath whomever or whatever you are."

The man was brilliant, Jesus thought. For a man, that is. That was the trou-ble with these experiments. It was impossible to know where they might lead; yet they had to be left to run their course to have any value.

"I've always suspected," the brilliant and intuitive man continued, "that humankind was some kind of put-up job. Will you confirm this?"

"Mercy!" the unprotectedly satirized cried in Christ's mind.

"Watch it," the Father said within him. "I wouldn't want to have to try to drown them a second time."

What the brilliant and remarkably intuitive man had said made Jesus think that it would be better to tell these creatures the complete truth about who they were and where they came from. That way they would at last be disabused of their misguided ideas about the powers of the Trinity. The brilliant and witty man sitting next to him was right. Show these creatures any great unexplained power and they tended to exaggerate.

"We have hundreds of callers," Larry King said.

The speakerphone crackled. "How do we know you're God, or Christ, or whatever?" asked a male voice, and a bald-headed little man in pajamas was suddenly sitting in Larry King's lap.

The man got up and dropped to his knees with conviction.

"See that?" Jesus said to Gore Vidal. "It would have been better for him to doubt and find his faith, but you people always need a convincer."

The man vanished.

"But very shortly many will doubt I did that," Jesus said, "even if they replay the scene."

"Well," Gore Vidal said, "you do admit that it's a shabby miracle, since there are countless ways to explain it. A miracle must be made of sterner stuff. It must be inexplicable."

Larry King pulled himself together and said, "Is this why you've come, to nudge us into goodness . . . again?"

Jesus sighed. "I'm of three minds about it, and maybe I should lose all patience. We've tried to help you by visiting your scale of life, but it did no good then and might do no good this time either. Laughter doesn't seem to open your eyes, except fleetingly, and then you forget to live the lesson. So I will let you all know how things are, just who and what you are."

"Really?" Gore Vidal asked, eyes wide as his skepticism warred with his growing wonder.

Jesus said, "Starting over at the manger wouldn't work today. You're not children anymore."

"I quite agree," Gore Vidal said. "The lessons of that Bronze Age document, the Bible, have rarely instructed us to do more than kill each other."

Disturbed by Gore Vidal's critical attitude (he couldn't tell which side the writer was on), King shifted in his chair and gazed at Jesus, determined to humor his mad guest. "So what did you . . . you or your Father, and that third thing, think you were doing when . . . you created the universe?"

"The universe?" Jesus said. "Hardly that. A world."

"All right, a world," King said.

"Being creative," Jesus said. "You can understand that, I suppose," he added, glancing at the brilliant and intuitive man next to him. "I've now reentered your scale of existence from what you would call a much larger one. You are an escaped creation, but we've left you to yourselves because we consider it wrong to destroy anything self-sustaining, however humble. It's a matter of before and after. After is very different. It's later."

King's jaw dropped. "You've got to be kidding, buddy."

"Not at all," Jesus said. "You're only a quantum fluctuation in a superspace vacuum, scarcely more than a greasy spot on the wall in one of our oldest cities. But we have let you be. Our mistake was to make you free too early in the game. And of course you don't like freedom. You want to be told what to do all the time, as if your own decisions, especially those about how you should treat each other, don't count unless they have some kind of divine pedigree. And you yearn for enforcers."

"But you say you're Christ," King said. "So you know what's right and wrong."

"See what I mean?" Jesus said to Gore Vidal. "Yes and so what?"

"And you punish us when we die, right?" King asked.

"Of course not," Jesus said. "Most of you just dissipate into nothing."

King stared at him.

"What?" Jesus asked. "Isn't that bad enough? To go and not to know, I mean."

Gore Vidal had a sick look on his face and held his stomach, as if he was about to hurl.

"Are you all right?" Jesus asked.

"No," Gore Vidal grunted and bent forward.

Jesus touched his forehead. "There, is that better?"

The brilliant and intuitive man sat back. "Yes, thank you."

"How did you do that!" King asked.

"No more difficult than putting a Band-Aid on a cut," Jesus said. "You'd call it a kind of channeling."

Shaken, Gore Vidal asked, "How . . . do you power all these miracles?" and rubbed his chin.

Jesus said, "We lay off the energy expenditure to another scale."

"Oh, I see," Gore Vidal said. "So it's paid for."

"Yes. Supernatural in your eyes, but quite something for something rather than something for nothing. It's pay as you go, even if you do rob Peter to pay Paul." Jesus smiled.

"Can anyone learn?" Gore Vidal asked.

"In principle, yes."

"This scale . . . of things," King said, "does it go on forever?"

"Yes, it does. How else could we lay off the energy we need to do things? It's a standing infinity."

King looked confused, so Jesus said, "Things get bigger forever, and they get smaller forever. Got it?"

"And you made us, and kept this from us?" King asked.

"You'd only have destroyed yourselves sooner," Jesus said. "You have to grow into that level of power usage. Some of you know about vacuum energy and the impossibility of zero–fields. But you've always ignored your best minds, except when they make weapons for you."

Larry King took a deep breath.

Gore Vidal fidgeted. "I was not a good science student," he confessed.

"Another caller!" King cried. "Go ahead, you're on!"

"Do animals have souls?" a woman asked, then burst into tears.

"What is it, dear?" Jesus asked.

"My cat Dino died a few days ago, and my minister . . . well, I asked him where my cat was now, and my minister said *nowhere*! Because animals don't have souls. He said that about Dino, for Christ's sake!"

Jesus said, "Animals have as much soul as all living things, because they're part of the same evolutionary programs we made. It doesn't matter whether it's pigeons or people. They achieve their share of soul, however small."

Gore Vidal looked at him as if to say that this wasn't much of an answer, because it still left the soul undefined, but it seemed to console the woman, who heard what she wanted to hear and cried out, "I knew it! Thank you so much," and hung up. Jesus looked at Gore Vidal, as if he knew what the man of wit was thinking, and said, "You do have to earn a soul, my dear man. It must be built up in the complexities of learning and response to life, along with a good memory. A soul must be deserved."

"Are you now prying?" Vidal asked.

"No, your objection was plain on your face."

"Let me ask you something," King said. "From what you've said about these levels, or scales—then there may be someone . . . above you?"

"Of course," Jesus said. "But they haven't visited us."

"No, no," King said, "that's not what I meant. I mean is there someone above it all? I mean a God, a real one above all the levels of infinity?"

"You've got to be kidding," Jesus said. "That's not even a question."

"It certainly is," Larry King insisted, smoothing back his hair.

Gore Vidal leaned forward and said, "Larry, keep in mind that by the meaning of the word *infinity* it goes on forever, up and down from us. There can't be an overall God, just the infinity. An overall God would limit it, and then would himself have to be an additional infinity."

"Oh," King said, then sat back looking confused. "No," he said after a moment, "there can't be an infinity. And how could you know if there was one?" He laughed. "Count it? Measure it?"

"That's a puzzle," Jesus said. "If we could travel indefinitely in scale, up and down through the multiverses, we might still never know whether they went on forever, since we might reach the last one in the next jump. After an eternity of travel, we would still not be certain."

"There," Larry King said to Gore Vidal, "I knew it!"

"However," Jesus said, "the principle that you call induction would suggest, after a while, that one is facing an infinity. Besides, an infinite superspace is necessary to explain universes, to avoid the problem of origin, which then becomes inexplicable in finite systems. Local origins are acceptable, but there must be an inconceivable infinite vastness to support local origins. All reality is local."

Gore Vidal smiled. "Either God always existed and is the ground of being, or the universe always existed and needs no explanation, in the same way that we would not ask where God came from. Choose one. Or are they both one and the same?"

Jesus looked at him. "I wish you people were as bright when it comes to your violent history and treatment of one another."

"So is there life after death?" Larry King asked.

"Mostly no," Jesus said. "You'll have to gain the glory of greater life spans on your own."

"Will you help us?" Gore Vidal asked, looking at Jesus with eyes that knew their mortality.

"I tried to give you life once," Jesus said, "but you misunderstood and turned it into all kinds of mystical jargon."

"Jargon?" Larry King asked.

"Words like divine love, grace, providence became meaningless as they were enlisted to serve your thieving power politics."

King sat back, looking appalled.

Jesus continued, "According to your Bible, my Dad supposedly said to me, in so many words if not exactly, 'I'll forgive them their sins, now and forever, if you're willing to die for this humanity on the cross. Just speaking up for them won't be enough. I'll know you mean it when you actually suffer and die for them. Of course, later on we'll get you up again, but you will have experienced the human pain.' And so on, as if my coming was a mission of some kind." Jesus paused, then said, "But of course he said no such thing to me. I was not a sacrifice for your salvation, which still seems a long ways off to me. You got this Lamb of God sacrifice idea from your agricultural festivals, or some such."

"If Christ has not been raised," Gore Vidal intoned, "then our preaching is in vain and your faith is in vain. Corinthians 15:14, I believe."

"But you did rise?" King asked, ignoring him.

"Yes, yes," Jesus said. "But what happened to me back then was a complete accident, later embellished."

"But you did get up from the dead," King insisted.

"What else could I do?" Christ said. "Later it seemed that maybe it would set a good example, encourage you to thinking about the shortness of your lives and spur you to getting yourselves a decent life span, for a start, and more later."

"Huh?" King asked.

"I wanted to set a good example," Christ said.

"Let me get this straight," King said, sounding dazed. "The way you talk suggests that you . . . made us somewhere, like on a table somewhere, in some large corner beyond our stars."

Jesus nodded. "We made a program, with every initial condition specified, then let it run. It wasn't the most impressive phenomenal realization of the noumena that I've seen. We might have started with a better Word. Still, you did get away from us, and there is much to be said for independence of action. While some of you do think, you're mostly hopeless."

"Oh, come now," Gore Vidal said. "Here I must side with Larry and say that you don't expect us to believe that our whole universe of stars and galaxies is some greasy spot on a wall?"

"One of you actually guessed something like the truth," Jesus said, "a mystic named . . . "

But even as Gore Vidal named the noumenously inclined scribbler, Jesus was also at a nearby hospital-hospice telling jokes to the sick and dying. At first a few of the patients laughed, but as the jokes found their mark one man cried out:

"I'm pissed off! They say you're Jesus Christ and you've been appearing all over the world. So you should be performing miracles instead of crackin' funnies." He looked around at the suddenly silent ward. "We're dyin' here! You should help us!"

Jesus raised a hand and said, "A laugh is nothing to sneeze at, my friends. Laughter has curative powers."

Slowly, the chain reaction started, and the sick ward chuckled, laughed, then roared explosively.

Gore Vidal sat back smugly and said, "So you've come to pillory us for our sins?"

Jesus said, "I've come to make you laugh, to wake you up."

"What's pillory?" Larry King asked.

"You're doing it to yourself," said Gore Vidal.

Jesus shouted, "Laughter is divine, a kind of grace born of the unexpected, invasive understanding that steals into us and cannot be denied. A revelation, no matter how trivial the joke."

"What does he mean?" King demanded.

"I tried other ways of helping you think for yourselves," Jesus continued. "I revealed myself in various ways, to different people. But it did no good. They made the same thing of my good advice."

"And what was that?" Larry asked him.

"Religion," Jesus said. "The bureaucratization of ethics."

"What's wrong with religion?" King demanded. "You, of all people . . . "

"It's only a wish-fulfillment way out of your difficulties, death among them. You'll have to work harder than just imagining a better place to go to. You'll have to learn enough to make one for yourselves."

"Tell me," Gore Vidal began, "how is it that you do miracles, given that you're not what we really mean by God?"

"I say again, they're not miracles," Jesus insisted. "Not in the sense that natural laws are inexplicably suspended. When you visit another scale, you can go around, behind, below, lower scales . . . and well, open doors in the physical laws."

Gore Vidal looked skeptical, as if he had just awakened. "All this you've made us think you've done, it's some kind of hypnosis, isn't it? And it's not really happening."

He waited, as if expecting the illusion to dissolve.

"It's the best I can do to explain it to your level of understanding," Jesus said.

Larry King guffawed. "Well, he certainly put you in your place!" He was still trying to do a tube show, even though human reality itself was in the balance and about to be found wanting.

"So what will come of your visit, this time?" Gore Vidal asked.

"We might just have to let you go," Jesus said, "let you dissolve into nothing."

"What!" King cried.

"So you've come to threaten us," Gore Vidal asked, "rather than make us laugh? We're supposed to die laughing, I suppose."

"Don't underrate nothingness," Jesus said. "It's a great peace. There are vast stretches of it in the up-and-down scales. Still, it's hard to achieve. Something always persists, some suffering echo of a bad job, impossible to erase, since one would have to achieve what some of your finest today would call a zero-point field."

"A what?" King asked.

"A hard wipe," Jesus said, clicking his tongue.

"Erase us?" Larry King cried. "How cruel! Who do you think you are?"

"Might we not appeal our case to your father?" Gore Vidal asked, "or to some being above your . . . scale, who might be more . . . of a God than you are? Maybe there's a God above all the scales, or outside them?"

Jesus sighed, then said, "I don't think so. Why do you say it's cruel? Your misery will be at an end. I will prevent a future of suffering damnation for humanity, going on as it has in pain."

"But you can't see all futures," Gore Vidal said, "so maybe in some we'll succeed."

"You're right about that," Jesus said. "There is an infinity of possible futures. To see or try to change them, or prevent them, would put me in search mode forever. You're quite a bright fellow, but no, I mean this world right here."

"And by damnation you mean nothing more than our continued, fragile existence?"

"Of course," Jesus said. "As one of your great ones said, 'First you dream, then you die.'"

"Did it ever occur to you," King began, "that we might wish to continue as we are?"

"Everything occurs to me," Jesus said. "Evil always wishes to perpetuate itself. Have some faith in me when I tell you that you'll be much happier as nothing."

"That's sheer sophistry," Gore Vidal said. "We won't be around to appreciate a state of nothing."

"Trust *me*," Jesus said. "I'll know you're better off. Appreciate the thought now, while you can. You won't be able to later. You know, bright as you are, for a man, you really should listen more closely. Worlds teeter on a Word."

King took a deep breath. "Are you flesh and blood, now?"

"If you doubt it," Jesus said as he took a Smith & Wesson revolver from under his armpit and slid it across the table to Larry King, "you can shoot me through the head." King caught the weapon before it landed in his lap. "Feel free," Jesus said. "That's what you're supposed to do, act freely, even if it looks to me like repetitive motion."

King put the black gun gently on the table. "Let me ask you if there's any point to the universe, I mean from your perspective . . . uh, in the scale . . . of things." He stared at the gun.

"Oh, I don't think there are *things* really. It's all nearly nothing to begin with, with no beginning or end, needing no explanation of anything except local origins. The only thing that really seems to matter is being the right size."

"Right size?" King asked, his eyes still worrying the gun before him.

"Morally and physically, we're bigger than you, since we know how things have gone in the scale below us, at least down to several trillion levels."

"And above?" asked Gore Vidal.

"We do not inquire upward," Jesus said impatiently.

"Ah—so you fear something after all, or someone?"

"No, we just don't care to know more of what's there. What good would it do us?"

"But you do know?" Gore Vidal said.

"Hierarchies," Jesus answered, "—endless, petrified hierarchies from endless duration. I prefer the humilities of below."

"And you ignore the true God who rules above it all!" Larry King added belligerently.

"No," Jesus said. "An eternal being would be an absurd mystery to itself. I am that I am. An all-powerful, eternal, and even all-knowing being would still be unable to answer the question, why am I like this? Such a being would be an enigma to itself."

"But that doesn't rule it out, does it?" King asked, delighted by his own cleverness.

Gore Vidal smiled and said, "Well, I suppose that would all depend on what the meaning of the word *is* . . . is, wouldn't it?"

"We already have eternal existence," Jesus said. "It's the unique, infinite superspace—the *mysterium tremendum*. You've heard the story—the roof of the world . . . is supported by seven pillars, and the seven pillars are set on the shoulders of a genie whose strength is beyond thought. And the genie stands on an eagle, and the eagle on a bull, and the bull on a fish, and the fish swims in the sea of eternity!"

"Mysterium tremendum!" King exclaimed ecstatically.

"Latin," Vidal added, "for a right smart piece of time, as Lionel Barrymore once said about eternity."

Jesus said, "The most important part of that story is the infinite sea, in which the fish swims. Without that infinity, nothing would be possible."

"I see," Gore Vidal said. "The buck stops there, since the infinity simply is, and needs no further explanation. It always was."

Jesus said, "That is what the word *is* truly means."

"I think I see what you mean," Larry King added.

"Wait a minute," Gore Vidal said. "I know that story. It's from *The Thief of Bagdad*, a 1940 movie!"

"Yes," Jesus replied. "I've seen quite a few. They're so much better than the shapeless dramas that are your lives. I've even seen some of the movies you wrote."

Gore Vidal waited to hear what Jesus might say about his movies, but after a few moments of silence asked, "And my novels? Read any?"

"No," Jesus said, "no novels. I do envy the best moviemakers their god-like eye."

Gore Vidal grimaced. "Who do you fear?" he asked, pressing the question as if he had discovered something.

"Unpleasant, unkind people, if you must know," Christ said. "One of us got like that and fled upward into the scales a long time ago. We don't know what he's doing there, and we don't care as long as he stays away."

"One of you?" King asked. "Could that by any chance be Satan?"

"We don't know his name anymore," Jesus said with a wave of his hand.

"I don't quite understand this fleeing upward," Gore Vidal said, "despite your pilfered fish story. Who inhabits the upward?"

"It's all pretty mysterious," Jesus said. "The same infinity, the infinity! It's a kind of endless horror of unknowing for us who know so much, a cloud without edges. It's the one thing all our knowledge can't encompass. Not even our deep travelers will ever dive to the top or bottom of physical infinity."

"Deep travelers?" asked Gore Vidal.

Jesus smiled and pointed to himself.

"Then why do any of you bother . . . to travel?" King asked.

"It might still not be an infinity," Jesus said. "The idea haunts many of us, that infinity might only seem to be one, and that at any moment the end may not be far off."

"And if you came to the end of it," King asked, "what would you learn? That there's more beyond?" He laughed, proud of himself for getting it.

"Alas, yes. No matter how far we travel, the end may be an infinite way off. And if we found it suddenly nearby, there would likely be more beyond it."

"You've said *we* rather often," Gore Vidal said. "Who is this *we*?"

"The Trinity," Jesus said. "And each of us is also made up of quite a few lessers. We've been massing for a long time now."

"Massing?" Gore Vidal asked.

"We share each other," Jesus said. "You've had some imitative experience of that in your worship of cultural idols."

"Another caller!" King cried. "Go ahead, you're on."

A deep voice said over the loud crackle. "Hi, I'm from North Carolina . . . "

"Let me fix that for you," Jesus said, and the interference died.

"Thanks! Lookee here, I've been dead for donkey's years now, and suddenly here I am in my fallin' down old house with my dead girlfriend, who just said to me, 'Jesse Helms, how did we get back here?'"

"How do you think?" Jesus asked.

"My question is this. How can you be Jesus Christ? From what I've experienced firsthand you're just some kind of powerful alien . . . or some hogwash like that."

"So what's your question?" King asked.

"Who does he think he is, coming here and doing all these crazy things? Shoot him through the head and see what he does!"

"Go right ahead," Jesus said, pointing at the gun on the table.

"Don't get him mad, Jesse!" a woman's voice cried out. "He'll send us to hell!"

There was a long silence.

"Call his bluff, King!" Helms cried. "Do it and settle this crap once and for all."

"Lordy, lordy," chuckled Gore Vidal.

"Jesus! Jesus!" cried the crowd in Central Park. "What can we do?"

"First," Jesus said, "you get a big needle. As big as you can find, so you'll have a chance, at least. Then you get a very small camel—I'm trying to be helpful —then pass the beast through the eye of the needle—and you're home free."

Gore Vidal said, "Jesus, that's a really bad one."

"But Lord, Lord!" cried the mob, "We can't do that. No one can."

"It's a parable," Jesus said.

"Easy for you to say, Lord!" the mob cried.

"But remember," Jesus said, "I am who will be. And you can do the same."

"Mercy, Lord!" cried the crowd. "Save us!"

Larry King asked, "What about eternal life?"

"Aren't you going to shoot me?" Christ asked.

"Read his mind," Gore Vidal said.

"Can't tell which possible world this might be," Jesus countered in what seemed a moment of confusion. "But to answer your question. Eternal life? A nice ambition—a prerequisite to any kind of civilized life—but no one will give it to you. Certainly I won't. You'll have to accomplish all that on your own— or you won't know what to do with it."

"Providing you let us live," Gore Vidal said, using the word that might or might not be related to providence.

"Shoot him!" cried Jesse Helms over the crackle-free phone line.

"How can we achieve eternal life on our own?" King asked.

"You'll have to learn how."

"You've done it, then?" King asked.

"A long time now. It's a basic of truly intelligent life. But don't rush things. There are virtues to having a beginning and an end—certain qualities of dynamism. True, they must be paid for by being brief. Short lives in intelligent species are a way of shuffling the genes until something worth permanence emerges."

"Hmmm," said Gore Vidal wonderingly. "But not always . . . "

"And you can raise the dead?" King asked.

"That's part of it," Jesus said.

"No use in shooting you, is there?"

"Shoot him!" Helms cried. "So we'll know he's a goddamn liar!"

"It's worse if he's telling the truth," said Gore Vidal.

"You're forgetting the Trinity," Jesus said, shaking his finger at the camera.

"He's got backup," Gore Vidal said with a smile.

"Eternal life is a matter of bending time," Jesus said.

"Please demonstrate?" King asked, picking up the gun and pointing it at him. "Correct me if I'm wrong, but I get the feeling you want me to use this. You will get up from the dead, won't you?"

"I'll show you once more before I leave. Try not to get it all wrong." He stood up and faced the host's desk.

King hesitated, and his hand trembled.

"Here, give me that," Jesus said, grabbing the gun by the barrel and pulling it up to his chest.

"Wait a minute!" King cried as he let go and crashed back into his chair.

The gun fired, opening up Jesus' chest. The bullet came out through his back, whizzed over Gore Vidal's head, and shattered a studio light. A sudden shadow covered the scene. Jesus fell forward across the veneer wood desk and lay there for a moment.

Then he stood up and smiled.

And in the next twinkling of an eye, Jesus Christ rose into the air and vanished with a whoosh, abandoning Jesse Helms to the prison of this life and leaving Larry King with an open and locked jaw.

Trembling uncontrollably, Gore Vidal leaped up from his chair and shouted, "My Lord! My Lord! Take me with you!"

After three days of solemnity, during which the world sought to explain away the Millennial Coming of Christ the Joker, the man buried in Grant's Tomb arose, walked marveling to the public library on Fifth Avenue, and asked a pedestrian, "What happened?"

No one had noticed his blue Union general's attire.

Jesus appeared at his side, presented Ulysses S. Grant with his favorite cigar, and lit it for him with a flutter of flame from nowhere.

"Thank you," Grant said, taking a puff. "How do you do that? Who are you?" There was another man beside Jesus, heavyset, gray-haired, and pale, looking a bit shaken but relieved.

"Deep travelers, like yourself now," Jesus said. "You'd better come with us."

Grant looked at him inquiringly, and then at his companion. "You think that would be best?" he asked as he flicked the ash from his cigar.

Jesus nodded. "You and Mr. Vidal are about the best to be had from . . . here."

The two men looked at each other, and the shadows fled from their faces.

Then Jesus took them by the hand and together the threesome slipped downward through worlds-within-worlds, searching the lower infinities, where swimmers from above would always be gods.

Goodbye to All That

harlan ellison

"Like a Prime Number, the Ultimate Punchline stands alone."
Daniel Manus Pinkwater

He knew he was approaching The Core of Unquenchable Perfection, because the Baskin-Robbins "flavor of the month" was tunafish-chocolate. If memory served (served, *indeed!* if only! but, no, it did nothing of the sort . . . it just lay about, eating chocolate truffles, whimpering to be waited on, hand and foot) he was now in Nepal. Or Bhutan. Possibly Tannu Touva.

He had spent the previous night at a less-than-opulent b&b in the tiny, forlorn village of Moth's Breath — which had turned out to be, in fact, not a hostelry, but the local abattoir — and he was as yet, even this late in the next day, unable to rid his nostrils of the stultifying memory of formaldehyde. His yak had collapsed on the infinitely upwardly spiraling canyon path leading to the foothills that nuzzled themselves against the flanks of the lower mountains timorously raising their sophomore bulks toward the towering ancient massif of the thousand-peaked Mother of the Earth, *Chomolungma*, the pillar of the sky upon which rested the mantle of the frozen heavens. Snow lay treacherously thick and deep and placid on that celestial vastness; snow blew in ragged curtains as dense as swag draperies across the summits and chasms and falls and curved scimitar-blade sweeps of icefields; snow held imperial sway up here, high so high up here on this sacred monolith of the Himalayas that the natives called the Mother-Goddess of the Earth, *Chomolungma*.

Colman suffered from poriomania. Dromomania was his curse. From agromania, from parateresiomania, from ecdemonomania, from each and all of these he suffered. But mostly dromomania.

Compulsive traveling. Wanderlust.

Fifty United States before the age of twenty-one. All of South America before twenty-seven. Europe and most of Africa by his thirtieth birthday. Australia, New Zealand, the Antarctic, much of the subcontinent by thirty-three. And all of Asia but this frozen nowhere as his thirty-ninth birthday loomed large but a week hence. Colman, helpless planomaniac, now climbed toward The Nidus of Ineluctable Reality (which he knew he was nearing, for his wafer-thin, solar-powered, internet-linked laptop advised him that Ben & Jerry had just introduced a new specialty flavor, Sea Monkey—which was actually only brine shrimp-flavored sorbet) bearing with him the certain knowledge that if the arcane tomes he had perused were to be believed, then somewhere above him, somewhere above the frozen blood of the Himalayan ice-falls, he would reach The Corpus of Nocturnal Perception. Or The Abyss of Oracular Aurochs. Possibly The Core of Absolute Discretion.

There had been a lot of books, just a *lot* of books. And no two agreed. Each had a different appellation for the Ultimate. One referred to it as The Core of Absolute Discretion, another The Intellectual Center of the Universe, yet a third fell to the impenetrable logodædalia of : The Foci of Conjunctive Simultaneity. Perhaps there had been too *many* books. But shining clearly through the thicket of rodomontade there was always the ineluctable, the inescapable truth: there *was* a place at the center of it all. Whether Shangri-la or Utopia, paradisaical Eden or the Elysian Fields, whether The Redpath of Nominative Hyperbole or The Last and Most Porous Membrane of Cathexian Belief, there was a valley, a greensward, a hill or summit, a body of water or a field of grain whence it all came.

A place where Colman could travel to, a place that was the confluence of the winds of Earth, where the sound of the swaying universe in its cradle of antiquity melded with the promise of destiny.

But where it might be, was the puzzle.

Nepal, Katmandu, Bhutan, Mongolia, Tibet, The Tuva Republic, Khembulung . . . it *had* to be up here, somewhere. He'd tried everywhere else. He'd narrowed the scope of the search to a fine channel, five by five, and at the end he would penetrate that light and reach, at last, The Corpus of Nocturnal Perception, or *whatever;* and then, perhaps only then, would his mad unending need to wander the Earth reach satiation.

Then, so prayed Colman deep in the cathedral of his loneliness, then he might begin to lead a life. Home, family, friends, purpose beyond *this* purpose . . . and perhaps no purpose at all, save to exist as an untormented traveler.

His yak had died, there on the trail; he presumed from sheer fright at the prospect of having to schlep him up that great divide, into the killing snow-fields. The yak was widely known to be a beast of really terrific insight and excellent, well at least pretty good, instincts.

Death before dishonor was not an unknown concept to the noble yak.

Colman had tried several simple, specific, and sovereign remedies to resuscitate the imperial beast: liquor from toads boiled in oil to help reduce the fever; leaves of holly mixed with honey, burned to ash in oast ovens and rendered into syrup; the force-feeding of a live lizard tongue, swallowed whole in one gulp (very difficult, as the yak was thoroughly dead); tea made from tansy; tea made from vervain.

Absolutely no help. The yak was dead. Colman was afoot in the killing ice-fields. On his way to Utopia, to Shangri-la or, at least, The Infinitely Replenishing Fountain of Mythic Supposition. There had been just a *lot* of books.

He reconciled the thought: *I'll never make it with all this gear.* Then, the inevitable follow-up: *I'll never make it* without *all this gear.* He unshipped the dead noble beast and began, there on the slope, to separate the goods into two piles, seeing his chances of survival diminishing with every item added to the heap on his right. He lifted his tinted goggles onto his forehead and stared with naked eye at the massif looming above him. There were more than a few hysterical flurries of snow. Naturally: there was a storm coming.

He knew he was nearing The Heart of Irredeemable Authenticity because the happily-buzzing laptop informed him that not only had geomancy been declared the official state religion of Austria, but that Montevideo had been re-named Happy Acres. An investment banker in Montreal had been found dis-membered, parts of his body deposited in a variety of public trash bins and dumpsters, but Colman didn't think that had anything of the significant omen about it.

The storm had broken over him, sweeping down from the pinnacles less than two hours after he had crossed the great divide, broached the slope, and begun his ascent toward the summit now hidden by thunderheads. Abrading ground-glass flurries erupted out of crevasses; and the swirling lacelike curtains of ice and snow were cruelly driven by a demented wind. He thought he had never known cold before, no matter how cold he had ever been, never anything like this. His body moaned.

And he kept climbing. There was no alternative. He would either reach The Corporeality of the Impossible Metaphor, or he would be discovered eons hence, when this would all be swampy lowland, by whatever species had inherited the planet after the poles shifted.

Hours were spent by Colman coldly contemplating the possible positions his centuries-frozen (but perfectly flash-frozen) corpse might assume. He recalled a Rodin sculpture in a small park in Paris, he thought it was an *hommage* to Maupassant or Balzac, one or the other, and remembered the right hand, the way it curled, and the position of the fingers. He envisioned himself entombed in just that way, sculptural hand with spread fingers protruding from the ages of ice. And so, hours were spent trudging with ice-axe in hand, up the killing icefields, dreaming in white of death tableaux.

Until he fell forward and lay still, as the storm raged over him. There was silence only in that unfrozen inner place beyond the residence of the soul.

When he awoke, *not* having frozen to death at all, which eventually struck him as fairly miraculous (but, in fact, easily explained by the storm having blown itself out quickly, and the escarpment just above him providing just enough shelter), he got to his feet, pulled the staff loose from the snow pack, and looked toward the summit.

High above him, blazing gloriously in the last pools of sunlight whose opposite incarnations were fields of blue shadow, he beheld the goal toward which he had climbed, that ultimate utopian goal he had sought across entire continents, through years of wandering. There it was, as the books had promised: The Singular Scheme of Cosmic Clarity. The center, the core, the hub, the place where all answers reside. He had found lost Shangri-la, whatever its real name might be. He saw above him, in the clearness of the storm-scoured waning day, what appeared to be a golden structure rising from the summit, its shape a reassuring and infinitely calming sweep of dual archlike parabolas. He thought that was what the shapes were called: parabolas.

Now there was no exhaustion. No world-weariness. He was not even aware that inside his three pairs of thermal socks, inside his crampon'd boots, all the toes of his left foot and three of his right had gone black from frostbite.

Mad with joy, he climbed toward those shining golden shapes, joyfully mad to enter into, at last, The Sepulchre of Revealed Truths. There may have been a great many books but, oh frabjous day, they were all, every last one of them, absolutely dead on the money. The Node of Limitless Revealment. Whatever.

It was very clean inside. Sparkling, in fact. The tiles underfoot were spotless, reflective, and calming. The walls were pristine, in hues of pastel solicitude that soothed and beckoned. There were tables and chairs throughout, and at one end a counter of some magnificent gleaming metal that showed Colman his ravaged reflection, silvered and extruded, but clearly wan and near total exhaustion. Patches of snowburned flesh had peeled away on both cheeks, chin, nose. The eyes somewhat unfocused as if coated with albumin. The Sanctum of Coalesced Revelations was brightly lit, scintillant surfaces leading the eye toward the shining bar of the magic metal counter. Colman shambled forward, dropping his ice staff; he was a thing drawn off the mountain barely alive, into this oasis of repose and cleanliness, light and succor.

There was a man in his late thirties standing behind the gleaming metal counter. He smiled brightly at Colman. He had a nice face. "Hi! Welcome to The Fountainhead of Necessary Perplexity. May I take your order, please?"

Colman stood rooted and wordless. He knew precisely what was required of him—each and every one of the arcane tomes had made it clear there was a verbal sigil, a password, a phrase that need be spoken to gain access to the holiest of holies—but he had no idea what that *open sesame* might be. The Gardyloo of Ecstatic Entrance. Wordless, Colman looked beseechingly at the counterman.

He may have said, "Uh . . ."

"Please make your selection from the menu," said the man behind the counter, who wore a classic saffron robe and a small squared-off cardboard hat. Colman remembered a film clip of The Andrews Sisters singing "Boogie Woogie Bugle Boy," wearing just such "garrison caps." The counterman pointed to the black-on-yellow signage suspended above the gleaming deck. Colman pondered the choices:

THE OXEN ARE SLOW, BUT THE EARTH IS PATIENT

CHANCE FAVORS THE PREPARED MIND

IT TAKES A HEAP O' LIVIN' TO MAKE A HOUSE A HOME

DEATH COMES WITHOUT THE THUMPING OF DRUMS

I LIKE YOUR ENERGY

THE AVALANCHE HAS ALREADY STARTED; IT'S TOO
LATE FOR THE PEBBLES TO VOTE

EVERY CLOUD HAS A SILVER LINING

DON'T LOOK BACK. SOMETHING MAY BE GAINING ON YOU.

YES, LIFE IS HARD; BUT IF IT WERE EASY, EVERYBODY
WOULD BE DOING IT

LIFE IS A FOUNTAIN

TRUST IN ALLAH, BUT TIE YOUR CAMEL

THE BARKING DOG DOES NO HARM TO THE MOON

THE MAN WHO BURNS HIS MOUTH ON HOT MILK BLOWS ON
HIS ICE CREAM

NO ONE GETS OUT OF CHILDHOOD ALIVE

SO NEAR, AND YET SO FAR

MAN IS COAGULATED SMOKE FORMED BY HUMAN
PREDESTINATION . . . DUE TO RETURN TO THAT STATE
FROM WHICH IT ORIGINATED

French Fries are à la carte.

Colman drew a deep, painful breath. To get to this point, and to blow it because of a few words . . . unthinkable. His mind raced. There were deep thoughts he could call up from a philosophy base on the laptop, the aphorisms and rubrics of six thousand years of human existence, but it was only one of them, only one—like a prime number—that would stand alone and open to him the portals of wisdom; only one that would be accepted by this gatekeeper of *Universal* Oneness; only one unknown core jot of heartmeat that would serve at this moment.

He tried to buy himself a caesura: he said to the saffron-robed counterman, "Uh . . . one of those . . . 'Life is a Fountain'? I know that one; you've got to be kidding, right? 'Life is a fountain . . . '? "

The counterman looked at him with shock.

"Life *isn't* a fountain?"

Colman stared at him. He wasn't amused.

"Just fooling," the counterman said, with a huge smile. "We always toss in an old gag, just to mix it up with the Eternal Verities. Life should be a bit of a giggle, a little vaudeville, whaddaya think?"

Colman was nonplussed. He was devoid of plus. He tried to buy another moment: "So, uh, what's your name?"

"I'll be serving you. My name's Lou."

"Lou. What are you, a holy man, a monk from some nearby lamasery? You look a little familiar to me."

Lou chuckled softly again, as if he were long used to the notoriety and had come to grips with it. "Oh, heck no, I'm not a holy man; you probably recognize me from my bubble gum card. I used to play a little ball. Last name's Boudreau." Colman asked him how to spell that, and he did, and Colman went to his rucksack, dropped on one of the tables, and he pulled out the laptop and did a Google search for the name *Lou Boudreau.*

He read what came up on the screen.

He looked at what he had read on the screen for a long time. Then he went back to the counter.

"You were the player-manager of the World Champion 1948 Cleveland Indians. Shortstop. 152 games, 560 at bats, 199 hits, 116 runs. You were the all-time franchise leader with a .355 batting average, slugging and on-base percentages and a .987 OPS! What are you doing here, for gawdsakes?!"

Boudreau removed the little paper hat, scratched at his hair for a moment, sighed, and said, "Rhadamanthus carries a grudge."

Colman stared dumbly. Zeus had three sons. One of them was Rhadamanthus, originally a judge in the afterlife, assigned the venue of the Elysian Plain, which was considered a very nice neighborhood. But sometime between Homer and Virgil, flame-haired Rhadamanthus got reassigned to Tartarus, listed in all the auto club triptychs as Hell. Strict judge of the dead. No sin goes unpunished. From which the word "rhadamanthine" bespeaks inflexibility.

"What did you do to honk him off?"

"I went with Bearden instead of Bob Lemon in the first game of the series against the Boston Braves. We lost one to nothing. Apparently he had a wad down on the game."

A slim black man, quite young, wearing a saffron robe and a cardboard garrison cap, came out of the back. Lou aimed a thumb at him. "Larry Doby, center fielder. First Negro to play in the American League." Doby smiled, gave a little salute, and said to Colman, "Figure it out yet?"

Colman shook his head.

"Well, good luck." Then, in Latin, he added, "*Difficilia quae pulchra.*" Colman had no idea what that meant, but Doby seemed to wish him well with the words. He said thank you.

Lou pointed toward the rear. "That's our drive-thru attendant, Joe Gordon, great second baseman. Third baseman Ken Keltner on the grill with our catcher, Jim Hegan; Bob Feller's working maintenance just till his arm gets right again, but Lemon and Steve Gromek'll be handling the night shift. And our fry guy is none other than the legendary Leroy 'Satchel' Paige . . . hey, Satch, say hello to the new kid!"

Lifting the metal lattice basket out of the deep fryer filled with sizzling vegetable oil, Satchel Paige knocked the basket half-full of potatoes against the edge of the tub to shake away excess drippings, and grinned hugely at Colman. "You see mine up there?" he said, cocking his head toward the signage of wise sayings. Colman nodded and smiled back.

"Well," said Lou Boudreau, saffron-robed counterman shortstop manager of the 1948 World Series champion Cleveland Indians, who had apparently really pissed off Rhadamanthus, "are you ready to order?"

Time had run out. Colman knew this was it. Whatever he said next would be either the gate pass or the bum's rush. He considered the choices on the menu, trying to pick one that spoke to his gut. It had to be *one* of them.

His mind raced. It *had* to be one of them.

He paused. It was the moment of the cortical-thalamic pause. *Why* did it have to be one of them?

Life *wasn't* a fountain.

There was only one thing to say to God, if one were at the Gate. At the Core, the Nexus, the Center, the Eternal Portal. Only one thing that made sense, whether this was God or just a minimum-wage, part-time employee. Colman straightened, unfurrowed his brow, and spoke the only words that would provide entrance if one were confronting God. He said to Lou Boudreau:

"Let me talk to the Head Jew."

The peppy little shortstop grinned and nodded and said, "May I super-size that for you?"

three

FUTURE PERFECT

Superfeminist; or, A Hanukah Carol

marleen s. barr

To the *New York Times* editor:
Re "Bush, in Reversal, Won't Seek Cut in Emissions of Carbon Dioxide"
(front page, March 14, 2001): This decision suggests that, while President Bush
insists that he will "leave no child behind," he evidently has no qualms about
leaving them a ruined Earth.
Stephen C. Wilson
New York, March 15, 2001

Professor Sondra Lear, a feminist science fiction authority, was exceedingly
depressed. Denying that George W. Bush had been appointed president, she
could not fathom how to cope with the situation's reality. Luck was with Sondra, though. Something seemingly unreal was about to ensue.

Ensconced within her office at SUNY Manhattan's midtown campus, Sondra heard a knock on her door and voiced permission to enter. A gray-haired,
heavyset woman who spoke with a discernible New York accent greeted her.
Sondra, of course, immediately recognized that she was face to face with none
other than Betty Friedan.

"Hello, Ms. Friedan. What can I do for you? Do you need information about
feminist science fiction?"

"I am not Betty Friedan," said the woman.

"Friedan is an exceedingly recognizable person. You can't be her clone. They
have so far cloned only sheep, not famous feminists. Please do not insult my
intelligence by denying your obvious identity."

"I am not human. I am not Betty Friedan."

Sondra decided to humor her guest. "Okay. Then who—and what—are
you?"

"I am Lara. I come from the planet Krypton. Because you are a feminist
science fiction expert, I sought you out to be my first human contact. I have arrived on Earth to help feminists survive George W. Bush's presidency. Since
I decided to appear in the guise of a celebrity feminist, I entered a phone booth

and changed into Betty Friedan. Phone booths, as the *Superman* movie emphasizes, are now hard to find. Luckily, I located one in the New York Public Library."

"I would not be worth my salt as a science fiction critic if I were unaware that you have powers and abilities far beyond those of ordinary feminists. Can you bend steel in your bare hands? Can you leap over tall buildings in a single bound?"

"Yes."

"Lara, I want to believe you. X-ray vision is the customary accoutrement for someone from Krypton. The office located on the other side of this wall belongs to my nemesis, conservative critic Hutcheson River Parkway III. Can you see through the wall and tell me what is in Hutcheson's office?"

Long red beams emanated from Lara's eyes.

"There is an appointment calendar on Hutcheson's desk open to today's date. He has written the following: 'To do list: (1) 10 A.M. department meeting. Vote against Sondra's pet issue. (2) Write a negative letter to be placed in the tenure file of the department's feminist assistant professor. (3) Snub Sondra in the hall. (4) Design a syllabus devoid of women authors. (5) Attend Ku Klux Klan meeting.'"

"You *are* Superfeminist! I'm so glad Hutcheson thinks that science fiction is garbage and never reads it. That man doesn't know from Superman and Kryptonite. He can't use Kryptonite to rob you of your superpowers," said Sondra.

"One must be grateful for small things. Excuse me. I'm going to the New York Public Library on Forty-second Street to use the phone booth," responded Lara.

Lara returned dressed in a red cape and a blue lycra bodysuit emblazoned with the letters "SF."

"I just wanted feminist SF to be regarded as a kosher discipline. I never imagined that SF would stand for a real Superfeminist. With Bush in the White House, Superfeminist has arrived just in time to fight for truth, justice, and the American way," said Sondra.

"Absolutely. Helping that assistant professor is a job for Superfeminist. I'm flying to the administration building to use my heat vision to burn the negative letters Hutcheson's cronies have already placed in her file."

Lara flew out of Sondra's window before returning almost instantaneously.

"Time to save America. I'm still a little unfamiliar with the eastern seaboard. Which way do I fly to get from Manhattan to Washington?"

"Even though you are not a bird and you do not need a plane, please know that it is necessary for you to fly south."

"Washington or bust. Nice to meet you, Sondra."

After again leaping out of Sondra's window in a single bound — and flying south — Lara landed on the White House lawn and entered the Oval Office. Secret Service agents, who are not trained to be on the lookout for a superhero (no less a feminist one who can fly over the White House fence), never noticed her.

"Hello W," Lara said.

W was surprised to see a gray-haired woman inappropriately dressed in a too tight pantsuit — and the cape appalled him. He reacted rather calmly, though. "I can tell from your attire and accent that you are a New Yorker. I guess that I'm not in Texas anymore. Is there some newfangled politically correct anti-ageism requirement for White House interns? Are *you* an intern? Do you expect that I have some sort of mother complex and your gray hair will turn me on? Do you expect that your too tight and too blue suit will have the impact of Monica's thong? The answer is no. No means no — I think."

"I am not an intern. I am not here to seduce you. Frankly, my dear, Al Gore is more my type. I like his hunkish Superman look."

W, crestfallen after being reminded that with Gore as his competition he could not win a Superman look-alike contest, asked, "What does SF stand for?"

"Superfeminist."

"Superfeminist? I have enough trouble with Hillary. And now I am confronted by a non-intern of my mother's generation who calls herself Superfeminist. What's your name?"

"Lara. But you can call me Betty Friedan."

"Friedan. Friedan. I might have heard that name before. And you look vaguely familiar. Have we met? What do you do?"

"I am a superhero. You might recognize me in that I look exactly like a famous feminist."

"Nope. Can't be. I've never seen a feminist — with the exception of Hillary, that is."

"There is a first time for everything. Even though you have traveled abroad infrequently, can't you tell that I am an alien?"

"You don't look like an alien to me. And, as governor of Texas, I've encountered some Mexican Americans. I get along with aliens. I'm a compassionate conservative. I suppose that if I have to talk to Democrats, I can talk to you. But remember that I'm the president and what I say goes."

"Not so. I am stronger than you. Anything you can do as president, I can do better. I can do anything better than you."

"Fly on Air Force One?"

"No contest."

"Drop a bomb?"

"Easy as pie."

"I have to phone Dick Cheney and ask him what to do."

"There is no time. You don't even have time to go to a phone booth to call your father. We are going on a trip immediately."

"I drank. I never inhaled. Still, I can see that you are a real trip. Clinton had to contend with Linda. I have to deal with you."

"Linda is the past. We are going on trips to the years 2060 and 3000 to see your future."

"Like in *A Christmas Carol*? That's one of the books Laura told me about."

"Our dealings have nothing to do with Christmas. In my Betty Friedan form, I am a *Jewish* liberal feminist alien superhero. You will be experiencing a Hanukah carol."

Lara picked up W and flew out of the Oval Office window. The Air Force categorized a flying feminist holding a president as a UFO. Upon landing, Lara told W that he had arrived in Washington in the year 2060.

"Who are those two female twin eighty year olds? Why are they crying?" W asked.

"The elderly twins are your daughters, Barbara and Jenna. They are crying because Jenna's granddaughter, Laura, just died from an illegal abortion. John Ashcroft overturned *Roe v. Wade*. This future exists because of you. And things do not get better. It is time for us to see Washington in the year 3000."

Lara and W touched down after their second flight. They saw nothing but crumbling white stones embedded in sand.

"Where are all the people? Where are all the trees? Where is everyone and everything?" W inquired to respond to the void he viewed.

"Your disrespect for environmental issues set the stage for the death of every living thing in America."

"I get the point. I want a different future. Tell me that this future can be altered and I will do anything."

"Anything?"

"Yes."

"Become a feminist and a Democrat."

"I agree. I surrender."

Lara and W embarked upon their return flight. After landing in the Oval Office, W phoned Dick Cheney.

"I'm the president. Not you. You're fired. Gloria Steinem is taking your place." W hung up and turned to Lara. "Okay, Superfeminist, are you satisfied? What do I do now? I'm not used to making my own decisions."

"Appoint feminists to all Cabinet and Supreme Court positions. Sondra Lear, for example, would make an excellent secretary of education."

Sondra accepted W's offer. Faster than a speeding bullet, she solved America's education crisis. Her solution: "pay teachers more." Sondra—and all American feminists—lived happily ever after, secure in the knowledge that Superfeminist was flying overhead. Hutcheson River Parkway III and his cronies were sent to the Phantom Zone. Lois Lane won the Pulitzer Prize for reporting how Superfeminist was infinitely more effective than a *Star Wars* national missile defense system. All American future females lived good lives.

Utmost Bones

pamela sargent

At first, Kaeti did not know where she was, although her surroundings looked familiar. She lay on a soft mossy surface that seemed to be a bed of some kind; as she sat up, she glimpsed green hills through an opening in a pale wall. A tent, she thought as she glanced up at the opaque white expanse overhead. Then she lowered her eyes to gaze at the landscape outside the open tent flaps.

Kaeti had been in a place like this before, perhaps many times. Just as she was about to call out to the Net, she restrained herself. She had come here to explore, to see if she could find some of what she had lost without the Net's assistance. Again she had the odd and irrational sensation that her Link was concealing important data from her, perhaps in an attempt to protect her, but from what?

Kaeti had shed much of her past, and would soon have to dispose of her more recent memories to make room for new experiences. She had performed this task intermittently for so long that she could no longer recall exactly how many times she had shed parts of herself, although it would be simple enough to find out. Lately, she had been feeling as though she might have given up too much, that certain details that she had retained were now fragments unconnected to anything else.

There was, for example, the persistent image of someone called Erlann. Whenever she thought of his grayish-blue eyes and gentle smile, a poignant warmth rose up inside her, making her think that she had once had a strong attachment to Erlann. But she could not remember exactly what kind of emotional bond theirs had been, how long ago she had known him, when she had last seen him, or where he might be now.

She could open herself to her Link and find out everything about Erlann, yet resisted. More was coming into her awareness as she realized how often she had been calling on her Link lately to restore what she had forgotten, to fill in what she had chosen to forget. She had come here, she realized then, to find out whatever she could by herself, to rely on her own efforts instead of depending on the Net.

I want to know, she thought with a fierceness that surprised her, but still could not say exactly what it was that she so desperately wanted to discover.

She had been in this place, or one much like it, with Erlann long ago. "Erlann," she whispered, and then realized that she had opened a channel to her Link.

Erlann appeared before her, smiling, and was walking toward her before she closed the channel once more. As he vanished, Kaeti felt a strand of the Net tugging gently at her through the Link inside her. She opened a channel again, willing to listen—she had not yet summoned up enough courage to close herself off from her Link completely—but still held most of herself back.

Her Link whispered, "We can give you Erlann."

"But that's not what I want," Kaeti said. "Tell me who he is."

"Erlann was one of those who shared your genes. Long ago, you referred to him as a great-grandson, and later, your term for him was—"

"Was," Kaeti interrupted. "Every time I ask you to inform me about someone I know, you use the past tense." So it had been for a while now, ever since she had begun to close the channels to her Link more often. She had made other inquiries about others who had been of some importance to her, to whom she had once been tied by strong emotional bonds. How odd it was that so many of those people had apparently been lost; even more striking was the fact that every single one of her queries had yielded an answer in the past tense. He was your great-grandson. She was your dear friend who once collaborated with you on designing mind-tours and various sensory experiences. He was your bondmate; she was your sister. He was. She was.

Kaeti knew that she could have asked for all of them, and they would have appeared to her just as the simulacrum of Erlann had a few moments ago. She could be with anyone she wished at any time, but it seemed to her that others came to her only when she summoned them through her Link. Once, that had been enough for her, calling on the Net's memories to present the people she had known. Once, she had been able to imagine that, wherever they actually were, some of them might be calling up a simulacrum of her through their own Links in order to reacquaint themselves with the Kaeti they remembered.

Now she wanted more than that.

She had come here to look for others like herself, and suddenly felt fear. The people whom she had known might have left this world altogether. The friends and lovers, the children and their descendants, the ancestors, mentors, and admirers—might no longer exist. There would always be echoes of them, for the Net of Minds preserved all that was known and had been known; the Net could not erase them altogether. But perhaps the echoes were all that remained.

"Are there any of my kind left?" she shouted, opening a channel.

"Yes," her Link replied, "of course."

She closed herself off again, got up, and went to the tent's opening to peer outside, feeling as though she was just waking from a long sleep filled with vivid dreams. The scenarios provided by her Link never seemed like dreams when she was experiencing them; only later, when she closed her channels and was left with only her own senses, did she feel them to be subtly and almost undetectably false. And yet there were also those times when she could not tell the difference between her memories of actual events and the experiences the Net had provided. Maybe that difference was unimportant, but she had found herself disturbed by the notion that many of her memories were only the products of the Net interacting with her own imagination, rather than being traces of actual events.

Kaeti crept outside the tent and gazed out at a grassy green plain. The tent, made of a silken white cloth, had been pitched near several tall trees; a gently sloping hill led from the tent down to a brook. Even with her channels closed, she seemed to sense her Link inside her, a tiny gemlike node glowing near her cortex, her bond with the Net. What must it have been like for her distant ancestors to be without Links, completely imprisoned in the shells of their own bodies, with only their senses and the intermittent and imperfect fancies of their imaginations to guide and divert them? Even in the scenarios through which she had experienced simulations of past lives, she had always been dimly aware of her Link, and it had seemed to her afterward that this might be a slight flaw in those simulations, that her awareness of her Link should have been temporarily excised from those experiences for the sake of more verisimilitude.

How reckless of me, she thought. Even to pretend that she was cut off from the Net completely might be too frightening an experience to endure. She shivered reflexively, and noticed then for the first time that her body was entirely encased in the silvery skin of a protective suit, and her feet covered by thick-soled boots.

"You're certainly not taking any chances," a soft voice murmured.

Kaeti started, knowing that the voice had not come from her Link. She turned and saw a small gray-furred animal with green eyes. The animal's tail flicked back and forth as the creature slowly padded toward her. A cat, she thought, and felt pleased that she could identify the animal by herself without automatically retrieving the information through her Link.

"Was that you who spoke to me?" Kaeti asked.

"You don't see anyone else around here, do you?" The cat sat down and began to lick one of its paws. "What I meant was that even though you must have a Link, you're wearing a protective garment as well, which seems an excess of caution. The Link would summon—"

"I've closed all my channels," she said. "I am not communing with the Net at the moment."

The cat tilted its head and stared at her with its yellowish-green eyes. "Even so—"

"Have you seen any people near here?" Kaeti asked.

"People?"

"Beings that resemble me."

The cat's whiskers twitched. "No, I haven't seen any people who resemble you." The answer was ambiguous, but before Kaeti could say anything else, the cat bounded away and disappeared among the trees.

The cat could not be a wild creature, or it would not have been able to talk to her. She wondered who had asked for the cat, for whom the Net had made the creature, whether the animal had been abandoned or had simply run away to live on its own.

Kaeti wandered down to the brook and dipped a cupped hand into the water, then drank. Nothing in the water could harm her; parts of her body had been repaired and replaced so often that she would have been nearly invulnerable to physical damage even without the microscopic organisms inside her that maintained and rejuvenated her.

How much of what I once was is left? she wondered, and that thought seemed a repetition of a question that had come to her many times before. Perhaps there was more of her in the Net than remained inside herself; the Net was the repository for all of the fears, hopes, loves, and accomplishments she had forgotten.

A fragment of a conversation from long ago came to her then, spoken in a low voice that seemed familiar, although she could not recollect whom the speaker had been. "Believing in some sort of reincarnation never made any sense to me," the voice was saying. "If you have to forget everything from your previous life in your next incarnation, then in effect you're dead anyway."

How many of her past selves were dead? How many others whom she still thought of as alive had died? Human beings had abolished physical death caused by disease and aging long ago, and the Net of Minds continued to maintain and develop the biological implants and nanotechnology responsible for indefinitely expanded lives. But death was still present in her world. If one lived long enough, sooner or later an accident would happen, or a system on which one's existence depended would temporarily fail. The statistics were inexorable. If a certain finite number of people lived long enough, eventually some chance happening would kill them all.

She sat down by the brook. For a while, she was unable to move. There was a difference between considering statistics on mortality with her channels open while resting in a secure environment that responded to her every mood, and in sitting out here, in an open space with the channels to her Link closed. She shivered again as feelings of fear and despair flowed into her. The temptation to open a channel so that her Link could banish such disturbing emotions was strong.

Yet Kaeti resisted those impulses. She had come here to discover what she had lost, what the Minds might be keeping from her. She had come here to look for others like herself; that was part of her purpose. If she reached out to her Link, she would lose that desire again, would give it up easily, would eventually allow the Net to envelop her in its comforting cocoon of experiences and diversions. She had the sensation that this had happened before, that she had gone on this same sort of search earlier only to give it up in the end.

She glanced to her side and saw that the cat was sitting near her on the grassy bank. "Why are you out here?" she asked.

The cat replied, "I could ask you the same thing."

"I'm asking you."

"I don't remember," the cat said, "but I do have a picture of another in my mind, another two-legged one like you. I think that I had such a companion once."

"Do you have a Link?" Kaeti asked, suddenly wary. Her Link would not violate the blocks she had put on her mental channels, but there was nothing to prevent the Net from observing her through another Linked being.

"Of course I don't have a Link. I'm a cat."

"I knew a terrier with a Link long ago." That fragment had floated up from the pool of her memories unattached to anything else. "So it's possible—"

"That wouldn't make much sense, would it?" the cat interrupted. "The whole point of asking for a creature like me or like that terrier is to have a companion to pet and nurture and train and play with and enjoy that isn't wild and feral, a creature with whom one can communicate through speech, but that also isn't at all like oneself. Give me a Link, and you've basically admitted that I'm not that different from you, whatever I may look like, in which case you might as well have asked the Net for a lover, a friend, or a child instead of a cat. My guess is that the relationship of that Linked terrier and its person didn't end happily."

"No, it didn't," Kaeti admitted. "The person wanted a particular kind of comrade, one that offered a kind of unconditional love and devotion, and the dog couldn't be like that once she was Linked. She fell under the influence of the Net, she learned that she could ask her own questions of her Link directly instead of having to depend on her human being for answers. And when she realized that she had been deliberately created with certain limitations, that she would never be able to become entirely . . . "

Kaeti fell silent for a moment before continuing. "After that, the terrier resented what had been done to her, and then she didn't want to have anything to do with her person any more." Kaeti felt a sudden conviction that she had been the one who had asked for the terrier, that she was the person who had been abandoned by that dog in the end.

The cat stared coldly at her, as if growing bored. "I don't at all mind being alone," the cat murmured, "but people do seem to get awfully lonely when they're by themselves," and then the creature left her, scurrying up the bank and into the tall grass until lost from view.

"That's what it is," Kaeti whispered. "I've grown lonely." More was coming to her now, more of what she might have forgotten. She had felt in need of more solitude, had wanted to withdraw from others for a time, but could not recall exactly why. There had been no discordant elements in her sanctuary, nothing to disturb or upset her, nothing recalcitrant that she was unable to control. When communing with the Net had not been enough company for her, she had summoned the images of those whom she had known and loved. But she had tired of that congenial environment, had soon been longing for the company of other people in the flesh, and then —

What had happened after that? Why did she still feel impelled to close the channels to her Link instead of accessing those memories? Why was she out here relying on little more than her own senses and recollections, instead of using the Net to help her find those she sought?

The answer came to her, but she was ready for the recollection this time, prepared to withstand the shock of remembering again. The Net had searched and had been unable to find other people for her; she might be the last of her kind. She had closed herself off after hearing that, before she could verify the truth of that revelation.

But now, remembering what she had been told, Kaeti had the feeling that her Link had been trying to tell her more, and that she might have closed her channels before hearing the rest. But what more could her Link say to her? The Net could not give her others like herself, people who were still alive, and if that were true, then there were no other people.

Unless, impossible as it seemed, there were people without Links, people who lived as that gray cat did, with no Net to teach and to guide them.

Somehow, she managed to steady herself and, as she grew calmer, even felt pride in being able to bring herself back into balance without the aid of her Link. How many times had the Net told her that she was alone, the last of her kind? How many times had she chosen to forget that, and then to search for others?

"Kaeti," a remembered voice said inside her, "you are being obstinate." Another person had said that to her long ago, but she could not recall who had spoken the words.

The air was growing colder. A cool breeze brushed her face; her protective skin would maintain her body temperature, but there might be other dangers out here, ones for which she was not prepared. Severe storms, earthquakes, cataclysms of all kinds—even with the Net's protection, such disasters came often enough to take the lives of some. The numbers of human beings had been diminishing for a while; that much she still retained in her memory. The experiences of parenthood, of both having genetic offspring of her own and serving as a mentor and nurturer to the young, lay far in her past; life had too many other pleasures and challenges to offer. So perhaps with fewer and fewer young ones to replace them, people had finally died out.

No, Kaeti thought; she would not have come out here, would not have begun her search, without some assurance from her Link that the effort would not be futile.

The sky was darkening. She did not want to be out in the open when night came. As she was about to retreat to the tent, something glinted in the distance on the horizon.

She narrowed her eyes slightly. There it was again, a flash of light; she wondered if someone was signaling to her. There might be others out searching, also thinking they were alone and hoping to find companions.

She turned and hurried toward her tent. As she approached, the tent's flaps opened to admit her. As she went inside, the flaps closed against the night. If others were out there, she preferred to seek them out during the daytime. Maybe they would come here; she tensed for a moment, afraid again. But the tent would warn her if anyone approached, and would throw up a protective shield.

How helpless I am, Kaeti thought. She lay down on her bed of moss, brooding about her uselessness. She and those she had known had made no history of their own, nothing to match the accomplishments of their ancestors; history had long been a mere entertainment, only a source of details for their diversions.

She drifted, not fully conscious and yet not asleep. With her channels closed, silence enveloped her, a silence so complete that the only sounds she heard were her own breathing and her heartbeat and a soft but oddly soothing throbbing inside her ears.

"How did we come to be as we are?" A voice was coming to her from memory, and she realized that it belonged to the person she had known as Erlann. "When one looks back, it seems fairly obvious," he continued. "First our ancestors created diversions that distracted them from reality, which then led to developing even more sophisticated diversions that became far more pleasant than reality, once the technology was available to do so. By then, the actual world had become decidedly more unpleasant for many people, which of course tempted those who were able to do so to retreat from the world outside themselves even more."

"I have always thought of the past as a more heroic age." That was her own voice, objecting. "Humankind was embarking on great deeds and accomplishments. There was all of our solar system to explore, and after that—"

"That time was a heroic age only for the few," Erlann said, "for those who were willing to take the risks of leaving Earth, even if it meant risking their own lives and safety. It was a time of accomplishment for those who created and wove the earliest strands of what would become our Net of Minds, and for those who uncovered the secrets of life extension. But even they, in the end, surrendered to the experiences the Net offered to them. Even they turned inward at last."

"All of them?" Kaeti asked.

"I asked the Net that very question. Is there anyone who resisted the experiences the Net offered in order to contend with reality? Were there human beings who chose not to live that vicarious existence? And my Link informed me that the Net could not recall any such people."

"That's an ambiguous answer," Kaeti said. "They are not remembered. That doesn't mean that they didn't or do not exist."

"But consider this," Erlann continued. "Contemplate your own life, Kaeti. How often have you retreated? How often have you chosen to face what lay outside?"

How often have I? Kaeti asked herself as she rested inside her tent. She had left safety before, she had gone on other searches, but she had always retreated again, shedding her memories.

More was coming to her; that was the trouble with trying to rid herself of certain recollections. Echoes were left behind, troublesome fragments that drifted inside her and could not be connected to anything coherent. She had searched for other people, and somehow she sensed that at least one such search had been successful. But she had lost whomever she had found afterward, and become a solitary again. She lived with the constant feeling of having misplaced familiar things.

A howl cut through the night. Kaeti sat up. She would be safe inside the tent, but her heart beat faster for a few moments before slowing again. She heard another howl, lower and softer this time, the sound of an animal.

She got to her feet and crept toward the front of the tent; the flaps lifted as she stepped outside. The Moon was up, fat and yellow in the sky, and another memory came to her of the people who had gone there long ago and tunneled out dwelling places under the lunar surface and observed the heavens with the great dishes of their telescopes. Where were those people now? Had they left to embark on a great voyage across space? Or had they retreated into the world that the Net could create for them? Perhaps they had done both, closed themselves off in an interstellar vessel and then turned inward even as their ship carried them out into the universe. Whatever had happened, no people remained on the Moon now; of that she was certain. She had known it as soon as she caught sight of Earth's dead satellite.

The gray cat was outside, prowling, visible in the moonlight. The animal howled again, then turned to the south. "Look over there," the cat whispered.

She looked south and saw a patch of flickering light. A fire, she thought, and hurried away from the tent, picking up her pace until she was running. A thought came to her of another fire, of people huddled around the flames, seeking warmth and safety as their earliest ancestors had done. There might be people out here; she would no longer be alone.

When Kaeti was still far from the fire and had slowed to a walk, she saw a dark two-legged shape moving toward her across the plain. She had not even considered any possible danger to herself, but suddenly sensed that she had nothing to fear from this apparition. She stopped and waited until the creature was only a few paces away from her, and knew that she was looking at another like herself.

"You are a person," she said, "a man," for she saw now that the other wore a beard on his face.

He made a sound that might have been a greeting, or only a sigh.

"What are you doing out here?" she asked.

The man was clothed in a garment that resembled her own protective skin, but his seemed looser, as though the garment did not quite fit him. He waved one arm in an arc, and then turned away; she saw that he wanted her to follow him.

She kept behind him as he led her toward the fire. A patch of land around the fire had been cleared of growth, and a hollow dug in the ground to hold the fire. Others sat around the fire, a person with long pale hair and another smaller one with hands stretched toward the flames; both of them wore the same kind of ill-fitting coverall as the man did. Kaeti kept her Link closed, knowing already that she would not be able to speak to them through it, that these people had no Links. How long had they been out here? How had they survived without being able to call on the Net for food and shelter?

The bearded man went to the other two people, then squatted near them. Kaeti hesitated, then knelt on the other side of the fire. Objects were scattered over the ground, shiny pieces of metal, shards of what might have been pottery or plates, torn rags. Apparently they had sustained themselves by taking whatever they could find in abandoned sites, in the cities and parks and isolated refuges where people had once lived. The three stared at the fire, keeping their heads bowed, refusing to look at her.

Kaeti said, "I thought that I might be all alone, that there was no one left, but my Link—"

The man thrust out an arm, as if warding her off.

"I came out here to find others like myself," she said in a gentler voice. But she could do nothing for them without opening a channel and calling out to her Link. Steadying herself, Kaeti reached out through her Link to the Net of Minds—

—and remembered.

The three humanlike creatures and their fire vanished. Kaeti stood on a rocky ledge, holding out a hand to a shadowy form hiding in a cave. "Come with me," Kaeti called out, even knowing that the woman could not understand her, that she would have to summon a vehicle to carry them both to safety.

The ledge disappeared—

—and she was standing in a windswept desert as dunes shifted before her like waves. The funnel of a dust storm was sweeping toward her and the five frightened people huddled near her. Kaeti waved at them with her arms, trying to tell them with her gestures to come to her, so that she could protect them from the storm with the force field that her vehicle could put up around them. The wind rose, blinding her for a moment with a veil of sand—

—and she was sitting with Erlann at the edge of a forest, watching as two men ran from them across a plain of tall grass. Occasionally the men turned, shook their spears in Kaeti's direction, then hurried on their way.

Erlann said, "They'll die if they stay out there."

"I know," Kaeti murmured.

"I think that this is the last time I'll come looking for unchanged people with you."

Unchanged people, she thought. The term was not entirely accurate. Some of the people she had discovered in the course of her earliest searches were unchanged, the last survivors of those who had never been Linked to the Net, but she had found no such people for a long while. The human beings she hunted for now were creatures who had been made as they were, playthings for those who had grown bored with simulated experiences, human beings who meant about as much to the people who had asked for them as did their talking dogs and cats and other pets. Their creators always tired of such pets in the end; unlike the people in simulated experiences, such beings usually became recalcitrant, their earlier placidity overwritten by sullen resentment or even outright hostility. When they were abandoned, some of them would ask for Links, and become a full part of the human community sustained by the Net of Minds, but others fled to untamed regions, bewildered and lost. Those who ran away were usually those who had been so dominated by their creators that they had no sense of what they might become, no knowledge of the Net of Minds, no realization that they were anything other than beings entirely dependent on the Linked people around them for their very existence. By the time Kaeti had found such people, their lives were controlled by fear and despair.

"What have I done?" asked those who could grasp some of Kaeti's words. "What is wrong? Why was I loved and then cast out?"

"Unchanged people," she said aloud to Erlann. "Call them what they really are, people who were thrown away. It makes me disgusted with my own kind."

"I pity them, too," Erlann murmured, "but I won't come looking for them anymore."

"Why not?" she asked, hearing a harder and flatter tone in his voice that she had not noticed before. "Don't you still care about them?"

"Of course I care," he replied. "It's only that there probably aren't that many of them left. Any whom we find now are going to be the most fearful, the most recalcitrant creatures, who perhaps can't adapt to what we want to give them."

"You're so certain of that," Kaeti said. "Surely anything we can do to help them is better than what they have."

"Are you so sure?"

"Look at them," she said, "living as they do, suffering, facing death after too short a time—"

"—living as most people once did," Erlann finished. "Eventually, any who are left will either die out, or they'll have to learn how to survive on their own, when there's nothing left to scavenge from or steal. And maybe their descendants will make another history for themselves."

"You don't believe that. You're just finding excuses for giving up our search."

"Farewell, Kaeti." He turned away from her and moved toward the forest. There was a finality in his voice that told her that she would not see him again.

The memory vanished. She was once again sitting by the fire with the three creatures she had found. The man's narrowed eyes watched her warily, but he was showing no fear of her. A memory came into her then, overlaying this scene with a vision of two people walking away from her across a flatland of high grass. She had followed those two people, calling out to them, wishing that Erlann had been with her to advise her on what to do.

"I followed them," Kaeti said aloud, "and when I realized that they wouldn't willingly come with me, I called on the Net for help, and then I stunned them until a craft was sent to carry them to a secure environment. I stayed with them, but I wasn't of much use. The woman kept screaming and the man withdrew into himself, refusing to move or do anything to sustain himself. Finally I had to let them go."

The three strangers were silent. The man seemed to understand her, but she might only be imagining that.

"You see," Kaeti continued, "forcing you to come with me wouldn't do any good. You have to decide that for yourselves."

She stood up, noticing that the sky was growing lighter. Perhaps the lost people would follow her to the tent. "Please come with me," she said, feeling that the soft tone of her voice might draw them. "You may feel frightened at first, but when you've eaten, when you've had some rest, you'll see that there's nothing to be afraid of."

"When they've eaten," another voice said, "when they've had some rest, when they realize what they are, they'll leave you."

"Erlann," Kaeti whispered, knowing his voice, and then she opened a channel and braced herself, waiting for the dammed up memories to flood into her.

At first, she heard only a sigh, and then sensed a tendril of the Net through her Link. "Forcing you would not do any good," her Link murmured. "You must decide what to do by yourself." Already she could feel her emotions being dampened; the fear that had started to rise inside her was fading.

No memories rushed into her; instead, she found herself sitting in a room, alone, thinking of Erlann and all of the others who had left her, whom she would never see again.

The Link said, "We can give you Erlann, and anyone else you remember."

"No, you can't," Kaeti replied. "They're gone now. They might as well be dead."

"But they are not dead. They are a part of the Net, a part of us."

"No," she insisted. "You have only fragments, memories, bits and pieces of what they were. They're no longer alive."

"But they are alive, woven into the strands of the Net. They chose to join us. You could do the same."

"They didn't choose to join you," Kaeti said. "They chose to die. Maybe some of them didn't realize that that was what they were deciding to do, or maybe they knew and didn't care, but they're dead all the same. Their memories, their experiences, their innermost feelings, everything they'd ever known or ever done—you preserved all of that, but that doesn't mean that they themselves are part of you."

"They are alive," the Link said.

"They may seem alive to you, but they're not. Whatever is there, whatever you may call it—an essence, a soul, or whatever obsolete and inaccurate term you prefer—what is left in you is not what was. Those constructs inside you, those bits you've preserved—those aren't the people I remember. Their bodies, their brains—they aren't a part of the Net. I'm a materialist in these matters —if the bodies are dust, if the brains in which their thoughts were first formed have been lost, then those people no longer truly exist. What the Net holds is no more than a host of simulacra."

"Or ghosts," the Link said.

"I don't believe in ghosts."

"Every one of them chose to join the Net completely. All of them chose to give up the rejuvenated and rebuilt carbon-based shells that were their bodies. Much of what they were was already woven into the Net. They were simply shedding the vestiges of bodies that were no longer necessary."

"I don't accept that," Kaeti said. "Maybe some of them had lived so long that they mistook indefinitely extended life for immortality, but I suspect that many of them, maybe even most of them, were well aware that they were choosing to die."

"They are with us, part of the Net."

"Those are only echoes, copies of what they were," Kaeti said. "I asked you if there are any of us left, and you told me that there were. I probably asked that question many times, and every time you assured me that there were others of my kind. I knew that you wouldn't lie, that you would not deceive me, but I didn't consider that you might have been misled, or drawn the wrong conclusions, or simply chose to think what you wanted to believe."

"We were not thinking of the human memories woven into the Net," her Link murmured, "when we told you that your kind still lives on."

Kaeti sighed. "Then you must have meant people like this, the strays." She glimpsed the shadowy forms of the three lost people squatting near the fire, all of them watching her now.

"We were not thinking of those creatures, either."

"Am I alone?"

"No, you are not alone. We are with you. Now ask yourself this—how much of what you once were long ago is left?"

"I don't understand," Kaeti said.

"But you do understand, you have asked this question of yourself many times before. How much of your former physical self remains? The answer, as you have said many times, is almost nothing. Every cell in your body has been recreated, all of your physical capacities are aided and amplified by microscopic machines. More of your memories live in the Net than inside your own brain. If you are the strict materialist that you claim to be, you might claim that the entity known as Kaeti died long ago, since so little of what was her remains in you."

"No," she whispered, "I am still myself." She remained connected with her past self, still the same conscious being, persisting through all of her body's changes. But perhaps the continuity she felt was an illusion imparted to her by the Net; a restored Kaeti might have no memory of her earlier self's death.

But she had not died; she was certain of that. She knew now that she had gone through all of this with the Net before, and come to that same conclusion.

"Your kind still lives on," the Net sang through her Link, "in you, in all of those whose memories are part of the Net, in all that we hold."

Kaeti said, "I am seeking other people."

"But we are here. We are your children. The Minds of the Net, the Links that connect us, all of that is the progeny of humankind. That is what is left of your kind. You have come to this knowledge many times before, and then you choose to forget again."

"Not this time," Kaeti said, growing dimly aware of all the past times she had come to this realization, of how frightened she had been to know yet again that she was the last to inhabit the form of a human being—except of course for the unchanged and abandoned creatures who sat with her by the fire. "I won't forget this time." She was no longer afraid to remember what she had been told so many times before, but felt a twinge of despair.

The man made a noise in his throat; one of his companions held up a hand. Kaeti forced herself to look at them as revulsion rose inside her. "I keep looking for people like you," she said, "because I can't bear the thought that I'm all alone. Then I find you, and take you to safety, and watch over you as you acquire Links of your own, and sooner or later, all of you decide to weave yourselves completely into the Net, and I am left alone again." For a moment, she seemed to be viewing her three companions through a veil, and had the sensation that she was coming to the end of another simulation, and then the sense of a reality outside herself returned.

"Are there any other unchanged people left?" she whispered to her Link, but the Net could not answer her question. The compulsion to remain as she was, to continue her searches, was strong, and she wondered if she was doing a penance for earlier misdeeds of her own, or atoning for the mistakes of all humankind. She would have to keep on searching until she was certain there was no one left for her to rescue, and that time might never come.

The sky was growing gray in the east. She beckoned to the three people. "Come with me," she said, and was relieved to see them all get to their feet, ready to follow her. She would have human companions for a while, to guide and nurture, and perhaps these people would not choose to leave her, to vanish into the Net. She could hope for that, and if that hope ended in disappointment, she could begin a new search for other survivors.

"There is no one else," and the voice saying those words surrounded her, but she would not believe that, not now, not yet. She waited as the man covered the embers of his fire with handfuls of dirt, then began to lead the three toward her tent.

When she awoke again, she knew once again what had happened.

"Show me what is," she said, hoping that this time she would not retreat into yet another search.

Earth was a great physical desert, part of a rejected reality. All oases were within, secret meeting places bright and green, where beings without bones swam in lakes of glass, surrounded by the night of faint hurrying galaxies.

Love and Sex in the Year 3000

marge piercy

Trying to figure out what things will be like in a thousand years is a silly and futile endeavor, but it is also absorbing. If people did not enjoy imagining the future, there would be no science fiction and no speculative writing. We almost always guess wrong. In my favorite short story of William Gibson, "The Gernsbach Continuum," a man finds himself in the future projected by 1930s designers, what he calls "raygun Gothic," a future that never happened instead of our own: the world projected by the World's Fair as World War II was just beginning in Europe.

Imagine a monk in an abbey in England in 1000 trying to decide what the world would be like in the year 2000. Yes, there are still people, dogs, cats, horses, and cows and that's about it. The forests that covered much of England have vanished. Sherwood Forest has a few trees more than Manhattan—if you leave out Central Park. His world was governed by the natural cycle of light and seasons and the cycle of the Catholic Church. What was important to him about his life and his ideas is largely irrelevant to us, and he would not understand a single commercial or a book he would pick up—except perhaps some poetry. Poetry changes every generation, but it does not improve or progress. It just changes its styles, trappings, and some of its obsessions, but we can still enjoy Sappho and Homer—they are today's news as much as when they were written—or recited.

Nonetheless, some of our concerns are constant from the days of Og the Gatherer with her rudimentary carry bag. Am I loved? Are my children safe? Will I have enough to eat? Am I in danger? What will happen to me when I die? Indeed, we share many of our concerns with other mammals such as dogs and cats: Am I loved? Will I have enough to eat? Am I in danger? How do you smell? What does this taste like? Am I going to get laid? Can I get back home? Who is coming onto my territory?

I think we can readily assume that many of these concerns are likely to be with us as long as we have bodies, but how we attempt to satisfy ourselves and each other changes sometimes slowly, sometimes in epicycles, sometimes with great rapidity. We can play with a lot of variables, but none of them is truly any likelier than any other. The reason for speculation is more to consider options in the present than it really is to predict the future with reliability. People have enough trouble predicting the stock market for the next six months or six weeks, or the likelihood of a marriage combination working out in two years. But that doesn't stop anyone from taking a flier in the market or getting married. From the moment we pick up the phone to talk to someone or walk out the door in the morning, we are taking chances—some with the odds in our favor and some really long shots. We attempt to predict the near future constantly and our future next year, next decade, twenty years hence in order to make plans involving work, houses, finances, retirement, but we know such planning is more hope than accuracy. To project ourselves forward a thousand years is fantasy.

Notions of what women are and what men are and what both should be have varied wildly, as have ideas about what constitutes satisfactory sex and worthwhile attachments. Men have married women as baby machines, usually for producing a male or males; as the title holders of land; or as someone capable of bestowing money or a title on their mate. Men have married women because the women were famous, notorious, viewed as prizes. Men have married a set of tits or long blond ringlets or slender ankles or a face they thought perfect. The rest of the person tagged along like a string of cars behind the engine of specific fetishistic desire. Men have married women seeking a victim, a receptacle of their rage. Men have married women to own, to conquer, to symbolically and in the flesh possess something they wanted but could not otherwise have, from their mothers to their oppressors or the forbidden strange. The more distant we are from each other, the greater the gap of experience and perceptions between the sexes, the more bizarre the reasons for wanting.

Women have mostly married men because they had to, mates chosen by their family, their dynasty, their clan; or because they were pregnant or because they were given as a bond between groups. Women have mostly married because they had to economically. My own mother had been sent to work at fifteen as a chambermaid, but there was no way she could ever have supported herself, because she had not even a high school degree and no skills that would be recognized or rewarded in the marketplace. She married three times, and each time she was disappointed. But she was, after age forty-five, a woman without choices.

I like to imagine that in the future all people will have choices. I like to imagine that people will be bound to each other in sexual and familial relationships by affection and not by economic necessity. We all know women and sometimes men impoverished by divorce. We all know couples who stay together in spite of the fact that they cannot stand each other and have not enjoyed each other's company or body or mind in years, because of the children, because they don't want to sell a trophy house, because they have such a super apartment or loft in New York, because scandal would tarnish one of the other's chance at something external to the marriage—or because they simply judge they cannot afford to split their assets in half and live in a style they are used to and do not want to give up. I like to imagine that whatever bonds are formed between people in the distant or even the near future, society will permit people who detest each other to part without one or the other being forced into penury. Far from viewing the divorce rate as a sign of moral decay, I find people living together who detest each other far more deplorable—and just as hard on the children.

If we are to live longer and longer, and a 200-year or more life span becomes normal, certainly overpopulation will have to be dealt with finally, or we will all smother under the weight of each other's bodies. Similarly, it was one thing to swear to be faithful forever when the life span was thirty-five to forty years; quite another now that it is seventy-five; and quite, quite different if the life span is doubled or tripled. Certainly our notions of marriage and family will have to change into something perhaps unrecognizable to us today. What someone may want at twenty-five might be immensely different from what they want in a mate at one hundred and twenty-five.

I'd like to imagine that we will be less stupid in many different ways. I like to imagine that we will accept varieties of people without condescension or terror or hatred or contempt. Now, although we live on a planet where paramecia have seven sexes and amoebae only one, we tend to project a dichotomy of two discrete sexes into the future, onto other planets and galaxies, into the infinite. Most people seem unable to worship a deity without ascribing sexual characteristics, usually, in our time, male. God has a beard and presumably a penis. This is such a weird concept to me I cannot begin to understand it emotionally or intellectually. For me any notion of the eternal has to contain all sexes or none.

We can easily locate each of us along a continuum where nobody is entirely masculine or male and no one is entirely feminine or female. I imagine the holy as containing all of that continuum. I imagine a future in which people are not defined primarily by who or what they go to bed with or what they do there. I imagine we may finally grow up into a warm and kindly tolerance for other people's sexual behaviors. As a British actress (I believe it was Mrs. Patrick Campbell) said, I don't care what people do, as long as they don't do it in the street and frighten the horses. To me, as long as somebody doesn't do something to somebody else that they don't want done, it's none of my business. I yearn for a tolerant and friendly society, but I see little sign that we are headed in that direction.

I must imagine that we will grow up and stop trying to make other people behave as we want to behave—or as we think we ought to want to behave. I fantasize that we will stop policing each other for what we consider aberrant behavior—and I never forget that the psychologists, doctors, and sex experts (including good old Dr. Freud) defined as abnormal the sexual responses of 75 percent of the female population, because they did not fit what the "experts" wanted to find, the ability to have a vaginal orgasm upon penetration. I hope that in the unimaginable future, we will not judge each other as controlled by our particular set of genitals. Perhaps we shall change them with the fashions.

People have always adorned and fixed up their faces, their bodies. What pleases in one culture is deemed a deformity in another—large buttocks, large hips, large bellies, large breasts; or small asses, flat tummies, hipless boyish stick figures have all been admired as have small lips, big lips, hairiness and hair-lessness, short and tall stature. I want a woman's fate to lie in her brain and her character, rather than in her genes and her ability to starve her body into sub-mission. I would rather see a nation of female bodybuilders than a nation of anorexics—not because muscles turn me on, but because in one case some-thing positive results and in the other, virtue consists of absenting oneself, and the less there is of you, the weaker and tinier you are, the better.

I assume that we will go on fiddling with ourselves to an unprecedented de-gree. We will remove and add hair wildly, change its color, its length, its texture; we will change our bodies the way we change our clothes. Perhaps our descen-dants will alter their sex not once like Virginia Woolf's Orlando but several times—in order to conceive, in order to experience the other side, out of con-cupiscence or boredom, to please another or oneself. If we all can look just about any way we please, perhaps the standards of beauty and acceptability will mu-tate and open up. Perhaps we will tolerate wild exceptions to the norm and even cherish them as creative. We will assume that every person looks the way they do because they choose to look that particular way at that particular time, so we will consider ourselves less superior to those we judge less attractive than ourselves and feel less envy toward those we think more nearly perfect.

Will we conceive? Will we grow babies within us and give birth? Maybe there will be, as I imagined in *Woman on the Edge of Time*, baby machines, brooders. Maybe some will use them and some won't. If we are all living for a couple of hundred years, we are going to have to regulate reproduction. Many more people will wish to reproduce late in life rather than early, for convenience in their work lives.

It's obvious we're going to play with our genes. I can't imagine any woman who wouldn't prefer a safe contraceptive with no side effects to cloning, but no doubt we will get cloning long before we get the safe and 100 percent sure birth control. I suspect cloning appeals to men, who therefore can have offspring alone, offspring they imagine loving as they love themselves.

I am assuming that not terribly far into the future, women will control their fertility, finally, and be able to turn it on and off like a faucet, probably from some mental choice operating embedded technology. All the present torture mechanisms used by fertility doctors will look like the iron maiden to future generations. If they had to go through all that, our descendants will ask, why did they bother? They will not understand the anguish of the infertile, because they will breed when they want. I don't think it will take that long to conquer the mechanisms of fertility. It is going to be increasingly important as populations continue to overwhelm the available space and as individuals live longer and longer.

Women's fertile years have lengthened, and one can assume they will continue to push further into the fifties, sixties, and eventually seventies. My grandmother was fifty-three when she had her last child, the only one she had the time to spoil. I find the idea of childbearing at fifty-three appalling just because I don't think I could cope with a baby at that age, but she did cope, and many women will. Some women obviously will put off childbearing for a long time; some will want the current male option of starting a second family with a second spouse after the children of the first marriage have grown. Whatever I may want or not want personally, I want more choice for all of us and respect for different choices. The hostility expressed by some to the idea of older women giving birth sounds to me just like the general hostility toward older women in our society, who are considered ugly and useless.

I don't think the nuclear family works very well. It hasn't existed for long, and it breaks up all the time, leaving women poor and their children poorer. We will have to invent new types of family groupings that provide more stability to our young in their long helplessness. We are not about to go backward and drop the possibility of divorce. We will not, I believe, imprison people as they once were, caught in the grip of religious belief that two people once bound shall stay yoked no matter what their opinion of each other and no matter what grief that may cause to each other and those trapped with them. I don't know what kind of grouping we will invent. Perhaps group marriages. Perhaps a rebirth of some kind of extended family providing contact with children to those who do not choose to have children or are urged not to, because of overpopulation or diminishing resources. Perhaps something entirely different. Whatever it may be, I feel sure that the common forms will permit more inclusion of people of different ages than tends to be the case now.

Ageism partly comes from failing to know any old people well or intimately. I had a close relationship with my mother's mother, who shared my room and my bed for part of every year. I have never had that fear of the old, that contempt verging on hatred that is so common in our culture. My grandmother was more loving than anyone else in my life, but she was also a stubborn, eccentric, and willful being, a storyteller, a gossip, a woman with history and politics and a strong attachment to Orthodox Judaism. She was not a grandma dolly or a creature of sentimentality to me. She would be talking to you and deep in conversation, when a radio soap opera, *Helen Trent,* would come on, and she would run to listen to it. She was also, as her sight diminished, a terrible cook. My mother was always asking her to sew things, but she vastly preferred to sew clothes for my dolls than make curtains or other useful things.

I have always had friends much younger and much older than I am, but I often notice that people I know of the generations after mine are most comfortable with those of a narrow age range. Whatever we develop to replace the nuclear family of current sacred name, it has to work in the long run and include more people. Certainly it will not be the present situation in which a woman may find herself caring for her children, often alone, and then when they leave the nest, if she is lucky, or before that, if she is unlucky, having an aged and perhaps ill parent for whom, once again, she is solely responsible.

What do I think the world will be like in a thousand years? Truthfully, the most fruitful ways to approach the future for me are speculative fiction or utopian fiction. Isaac Asimov once said that all science fiction falls into the categories "what if," "if only," and "if this continues." I have written in all three categories. *Dance the Eagle to Sleep* is a kind of "what if." *Woman on the Edge of Time* is mostly "if only," with the brief venture into dystopia being "if this continues." *He, She and It* is "if this continues." To me, fiction is my only legitimate access to future possibilities, because it admits it is "made up" and is the fruit of imagination.

In the nineteenth and early twentieth centuries and again in the 1970s, a number of feminist utopias were created. I notice that in recent years fewer of them are appearing. I believe that the urge to create them, while coming from a sense of what we do not have in our lives, depends on a certain ambient optimism or sense of movement and hope. When women are politically active in a way that seems to bring forward motion, then we have more energy and more desire to speculate about the kind of society we might particularly like to live in. When most of our political energy goes into defending gains we have made that are under attack, whether we are defending the existence of women's studies, access to safe medical abortions, or affirmative action, there seems to exist among us less creative energy for imagining a fully realized alternative to what surrounds us.

The utopias that men have created over the centuries tend to be tremendously organized down to the street plans, tend to be hierarchical: cities of god where everything is minutely planned and perfectly utilized. The utopias women imagine tend to be looser, more fluid groupings where women can do things forbidden us, anarchical places of hard work and new means of giving birth, socializing children, finding companionship, love, and sex, with different attitudes toward aging.

All feminist utopias spend a great deal of time worrying about child care—as women do in real life. I cannot think of a utopia created by a woman where a woman is solely responsible for her offspring. None of them contains that awful isolation many women report as occurring after giving birth when they find themselves left alone with a stranger, a new live baby who demands everything at the top of his or her lungs. In fact, one characteristic of societies imagined by feminists is how little isolated women are from each other. Instead of the suburban dream turned nightmare in which each house contained a woman alone and climbing the walls, or the yuppie apartment house where no one speaks but each has perfect privacy in her little electronic box, the societies women dream up tend to be long coffee klatches or permanent casual meetings. Everybody is in everybody else's hair.

Another characteristic of feminist utopias: freedom from fear of rape and domestic violence. All of them seek to eliminate domination of one person over another. People live in small groups, larger than nuclear families and less closed in but small enough for everyone to know everyone else, as in extended families. Society is decentralized. Order is kept far more by persuasion than by force. Nurturing is a strong value. Communal responsibility for a child begins at birth.

These feminist visions tend to be ecologically conscious, assuming a partnership between nature and the social world—excluding, of course, the older ones such as Charlotte Perkins Gilman's *Herland*. Often the societies women have imagined are quite pastoral. This is no accident, since what I view as one of the many functions of feminist art is to create that experience of the underlying ground of unity, among women, among all living creatures, among all of us who with our planet make up one being, Earth as she rolls along.

The societies portrayed in feminist visionary novels are usually communal, even quasi tribal. Often a strong emotional connection to the natural world is stressed. In James Tiptree's short story (James Tiptree was Alice Sheldon) "Houston, Houston Do You Read?" the spaceship of a feminist society contains not only chickens but also an enormous kudzu vine, and the women who run the ship are excited about getting a goat soon.

One concern of *He, She and It* is what we are doing to the world we inherit and pass on, and what that will really mean to the daily lives of ordinary people. One of the strongest messages that we all receive through our pores as well as through our ears and eyes from the media is that ordinary necessary work is demeaning and those who do that work are fools and that ordinary people are made of inferior stuff and only the extraordinary, the celebrities, are made of different stuff. Fame is an attribute of the body and soul that ennobles through and through.

The only work that ennobles is unnecessary work, for instance, media work or financial manipulation. One of the most lucrative activities in our culture is taking over functioning companies that actually make something, playing with the stock, and then moving them off to Guam or dismantling them altogether. This destruction is highly rewarded by our society. Feminist utopias are almost all concerned with the dignity of necessary work, as they tend to be concerned with integrating the aging into society and with socializing children as a mutual and glad responsibility.

Similarly, classlessness is pervasive in feminist visionary fiction, especially that written in this century. Many of the utopian novels women have written are deeply concerned with sharing the prestigious, the interesting, the rewarding opportunities, but also sharing the maintenance, the housework, the daily invisible labor that underlies society.

Another characteristic of contemporary utopias is sexual permissiveness. The point of that permissiveness is not to break taboos but to separate sexuality from questions of ownership, reproduction, and social structure. The feminist utopias that are not entirely lesbian often assume, as in Ursula Le Guin's *The Dispossessed*, some mix of monogamy and what practitioners these days call polyamy, homosexuality and heterosexuality and bisexuality. Many feminist utopias portray lesbian relationships matter of factly and without apology. For a number, the societies described contain only women, such as Sally Miller Gearhart's *Wanderground*. *Herland* was probably the last asexual utopia created by a woman.

Some of these imagined societies emphasize sex as connection. These tend to be the ones that have an essentialist view of women as inherent nurturers. Others emphasize pleasure. They envision women's sexual energy loosed and free to redefine sexuality individually and collectively.

Obviously, some feminist utopias contain men and some do not. None of them contains men as we commonly think of men today, as the dominant, normative head of society. In none of them will you find the power structure that in any way resembles the congressional committees that have lately been debating a woman's right to terminate a pregnancy when the fetus is not viable or when her life or health is threatened. As Joanna Russ suggests in her title, *The Female Man*, women are the norm.

In general, all utopian fiction seeks either to create a society with an entirely different class structure (such as Plato's Republic) usually with the writer's social class having more power than is the case in the contemporary setup—in Plato's instance, in his Athens. But most feminist utopias seek to destroy class roles in the interest of equality.

Who wants equality? Those who do not have it.

Joanna Russ has written in "Recent Feminist Utopias": "I believe that utopias are not embodiments of universal human values, but are reactive; that is, they supply in fiction what their authors believe society lacks in the here and now. The positive values stressed in the stories can reveal to us what, in the authors' eyes, is wrong with our society. Thus if the stories are familial, communal in feelings, we may safely guess that the authors see our society as isolating people from each other, especially (to judge from the number of all-female utopias in the group) women from women. If the utopias stress a feeling of harmony and connection with the natural world, the authors may be telling us that in reality they feel a lack of such connection."[1]

In a similar vein, we might say that the classlessness of feminist utopias issues from the insecurities, competitiveness, and poverty women experience. In the society we all know, our own, women congregate on the bottom. We hold the lowest-paying jobs. We huddle with our children in shelters for the homeless and for battered women. We constitute the bulk of the elderly poor. We speak of the feminization of poverty, but behind that Latinate word are millions of households of women struggling to get through another week, choosing between paying for heat and buying food, neglecting their own teeth and chewing aspirin, if they can buy aspirin, so that their children may have cereal, if not milk to put on it. Then there are growing numbers of women not held by any house but out there without shelter or safety of any sort.

The utopias' sexual permissiveness and joyfulness are poignant comments on the conditions of sexuality for women: unfriendly, coercive, simply absent, reactive rather than initiating, and I might add regarded as a function of young women but not of older women and never of old women. A valued place and continuing integration for the aging is another common concern in feminist utopias.

The women who write them know they likely will live long enough to grow first middle aged and then old, and that this society scorns and demeans older women. The more you know and the wiser you grow, the less valuable you are considered to be.

In a society in which women commonly experience streets as potential mine-fields of violence about to explode; in which a city apartment has to be fortified like Fort Knox to protect not wealth but just one's own body and life; in which the first sexual experience for many children is the abuse by someone in their own home from whom they could reasonably expect protection and secure af-fection; in which any date can turn into an attack, no wonder women dream of a society in which sex is a chosen pleasure — chosen by a woman.

In our society, aging by women is seen as shameful. We are enjoined not to develop, not to mature, not to spread out, not to age. The images we buy un-reflectively kill some of us and cripple many more. We are now in a time when people spend hours a day pursuing a perfect body, which is defined as some-one who photographs well, since the camera adds fifteen pounds. We are as puritanical about food and weight as previous generations were about sex. Fat is supposed to be a sign of weakness, indulgence, sin. It takes an enormous amount of time to try always to look younger than you are and to try to carry less weight than your body comfortably wants to carry. It is supposed to be healthy. It is certainly a replacement for educating your mind, developing your interests, becoming closer to other people. If you spent the amount of time a week you may spend on the pursuit of a prepubescent body on learning a for-eign language, in writing something meaningful to yourself and to others, prac-ticing piano, changing society, this country would be a far different place. I wonder why the media pushes thinness, called fitness. Of course it is partly a class issue: any affluent woman can buy a trainer, time in a gym, fitness equip-ment at home, someone to fill in for her while she exercises; the ordinary working-class woman may have two jobs, kids to care for on her own, and no money to spend on a health club or a NordicTrack.

Being thin is not cumulative and you can never rest. The French you learned at twenty returns easily if you go to France. Retired athletes go as rapidly to flab as anyone else. So it is a permanent occupation; and truthfully, the em-ployee at McDonald's who has what is judged by this year's standards as a per-fect body is still an employee at McDonald's and likely to remain so. The myth is that the young and pretty and thin inherit the earth; but it ain't necessarily so. More likely it is the kid who sits at the computer instead of running around the block. Fat and pimples never kept anyone from writing a superb novel or mapping a chromosome or making a million.

We judge women who have, we say, let themselves go. Go where? I cannot remember a recent utopia that accepted the common idea in our culture that a woman's value is primarily as a decorative object, perfectly preserved. Most such novels are concerned with reintegrating the age segregation so typical of our recent society, with finding value in experience that our society finds only in the unused body.

Utopia is work that issues from pain: it is what we do not have that we crave. It is the labor of hunger, as images of feasts, roast legs of lamb, mountains of pies are. A book came out a couple of years ago consisting of recipes that women remembered in concentration camps, while they were being systematically starved to death. Utopia is where we are not that we long to go.

It is by imagining what we truly desire that we begin to go there. That is the kind of thinking about the future that seems to me most fruitful, most rewarding. I want a future long before the year 3000 in which women are not punished for having women's bodies, are not punished for desire or the lack of it, are viewed as independent protagonists in their own spiritual, intellectual, romantic, sexual, and creative adventures.

Why do I think speculative and utopian fiction important? In the standard hierarchy of literature as rated by its critics, neither has a lofty position. Genre writing is generally looked down upon. Utopian fiction tends to lay its assumptions right on the table. Some utopian works are closer to speculation and others to vision. Contemporary critics often assume that there is something wrong with fiction that has an ideological content, as if all fiction does not. All fictions embody assumptions about what is right and what is wrong, who are the good guys and who are the baddies, who deserves to win and to lose and what do winning and losing consist of, what are the prizes and what are the punishments, what is masculine and what is feminine, what's okay to do in bed with whom, who's smart and who's stupid, and who's okay to make fun of.

Since we cannot know the future and any guess we make beyond our lifetime is likely to be no more than a joke, the purpose of making a concrete future, whether in an essay, in fiction, in film, or on television, is to create images of what we might want or what we might intensely dislike, so that we may decide how to get where we discover we might want to go and how we might avoid the place we see as hell on earth. If we have no idea what there might be other than what we see and hear everyday, then we will only be able to demand more of the same: more and bigger McDonald's and Wal-Marts, bigger trophy houses and skinnier trophy wives, bigger SUVs and thicker pollution, louder, more invasive ads on everything that can be so labeled, ads in every media and on every surface of our clothing, our bodies, and our minds.

As a working-class Jewish girl from Detroit without money, without position, without any nets under me in society, a woman who wanted to write and wanted to survive, what I desperately needed when I was twenty-one and could not find was a sense of possibilities, of alternate universes of social discourse, of other assumptions about what was good or primary, of other viable ways of making a living, making love, having and raising children, being together, eating, cleaning up, relating to a landscape, dying, burying and mourning my dead, remembering, forgetting, and imagining.

I still need this today. What we think we are determines what we see as making us, what in the past has led to us. What we think we can be comes from what we think we are. What we think we want to be and what we don't want to be makes us choose among available pasts and futures. What we see as possible puts blinkers on us. The invention of possibilities is often liberating in itself. One of the most striking differences between living in the 1950s and living in the 1960s was in the range of options ordinary people thought were open to them. The closing down of options was an important loss in the 1980s. I hope that the new century will open up possibilities again in what we can imagine, what we can wish for and then work toward. All we think we can want now is newer, more plastic-looking sex partners and many, many more objects. Yet many of us are unsatisfied and many of us are deeply, angrily dissatisfied.

Still, the larger intention of creating a utopia is not that different from the underlying desire of much of my other fiction and my poetry, a desire to take control of the stuff of our dreaming mind, the stuff of our fantasies, the stuff of the stories we tell ourselves about our lives, the myths that shape what we expect to experience and to remake those myths, those stories, those dreams and fantasies from my own perspective. To re-imagine, to subvert, to make over the myths of our culture is one of my ongoing passions, whether I am working with Eve or Ruth, with Jacob wrestling the angel or the princess and the frog, with Golem/Frankenstein/Robocop or with the French Revolution or with World War II, with the symbols of the Tarot or the myth of scientific objectivity. The media constantly feeds us stories and myths that shape what we think we are and what we imagine we can be. It is a matter of opening the box or at least demonstrating where the sides are.

When we talk about the future, when we project a set of expectations onto 1984 or 2001 or 2476 or 3000, we are really discussing what values we think underlie society and our own actions. One of the most useful ways we can approach such a task is to ask ourselves what are the underlying myths we are working inside. Do we believe in progress? As a woman, that is a little hard for me, believing in progress, because women have had periods of much greater freedom in the past followed by periods of intense repression. As a woman, it is also hard for me not to believe in progress, because when I consider the options, the choices that were open to my grandmother in the *shtetl* in Lithuania where she was born, the choices available to my mother in a tenement in Philadelphia, and the choices that were open to me, born in the inner city of Detroit—all of us in poverty but what a difference in what we might aspire to and what we might experience.

I do recognize that progress is a myth. There is no inevitable evolution of society toward more freedom, more choice. Even twenty years ago everyone thought we would soon have a shorter workweek and more leisure. What we have instead is corporations that have cut back their workforce for more profit and more and more people forced to work longer hours and to rush to get more done in the same amount of time. We don't work less hard; like Alice, we run twice as fast to stay in the same place. But at the same time, I see that if many people strive together toward something useful to them, whether it is a higher minimum wage or more coverage of needed health care, it is likely to happen.

To what myths do you subscribe and how do you experience them? Is sexual desire good or bad? When you make love, are you knowing or having or investing or colonizing? Are your real allies in this world the people who do exactly what you do in bed with the same kind of partner? When you love, when you give affection and attention, are you spending, using up something that is fixed capital, or are you exercising muscles that will grow stronger with use or are you planting a seed that will grow? Often the myths we live by are concealed in the metaphors we use to describe daily behavior. These underlying assumptions determine the future we can imagine as well as the future we are likely to get.

Of course, it may be that the obsession with media will simply continue to grow, and we will want and need less and less to do with each other. It is highly probable that a programmed cyborg or android could perform sexually much better than any person, if pleasure is the only goal. This is of course not an original idea. Although we don't yet have fully functional life-sized sex toys, I am sure we will have them halfway through this coming century, if not sooner. To perform well sexually does not require a great deal in the way of artificial intelligence. The male praying mantis goes at it vigorously long after his head has been consumed by his mate. Some men prefer inflatable dolls right now. It is a question of how much intimacy, how much conversation and communication we require to satisfy us.

After all, we live in a society in which many people report their closest relationships are with their pets or with personages or characters they see on television. I understand the person/animal bond. My cats are friends. If I can't share my poems or my worries with them as I do with human friends, or argue politics or speculate—as I am doing in this essay—neither are they too busy to give me their time and affection. But I can't imagine feeling intimacy with someone encountered on television. I write that, and a moment later I remember my mother's later years isolated in Florida where she knew no one, with a husband contemptuous of her. She was starved for conversation and interaction, so she would sit there watching the evening news and arguing with the anchors and the reporters. Sometimes any simulacrum of communication and exchange has to satisfy us, because we can't get anything better.

Certainly many of my intimate friends I communicate with not in person but via e-mail. It is fast, easy, and time-independent. It may be 6 A.M. and I'm up, but my friend Karen doesn't get up until three or four hours later and does her e-mail at midnight or 2 A.M. Our different schedules used to preclude us talking in a trivial, daily way; now it does not. I do not join with those who decry e-mail and long for more "personal" forms of communication. Why is e-mail more technologically dependent than the telephone? Or the letter that depends on the postal service to deliver it on paper manufactured in a paper mill and now probably composed and printed on a computer? We do not seem to feel the need to carve our communications in stone or bake them in cuneiform tablets or send them via smoke signals. But communication is the same in its essence whether we are dealing with the written or spoken word or with telepathy. It is an exchange of words by which we give and get feedback.

While we need this exchange, we will find ways to do it. While we fall in love, we will desire this exchange. As I said when I began this essay, what people think is satisfactory sex is determined partly by their own biology and reaction time and early experiences and partly by the culture. In cultures that regularly perform clitoridectomy, pleasure for a woman must indeed reside only in the mind or in fulfilling the roles expected of her. Whether a woman expects an orgasm or doesn't will have a major influence on how she views having sex, whether she shuts her eyes and thinks of England or the Super Bowl, or whether she seeks sex actively—the terror of many a man over the centuries—and views her own pleasure as an integral part of any physical relationship.

How much we value romantic love is partly personal and partly culturally fed. I have had otherwise sane friends tell me that they needed chemistry, and some otherwise nice, friendly, intelligent guy would not do without that chemistry. By that one of them meant love at first sight, which means your programming kicking in and overriding any common sense you may possess. The other meant instant satisfaction the first time. I think a couple can negotiate sex as well as who does the dishes and whether the toilet seat is up or down. Your partner doesn't have to guess you prefer oral sex or that you like your contact very gentle or silent or with dirty talk or a bit rough. That's the advantage of having language. Since I believe much romantic love is adolescent and counterproductive, I would be happy to jettison it culturally. Someone who needs it to feel valued would imagine a future rife with valentines and soft music or aroma calliopes and simulated "romantic" environments to order, romance on the holodeck. "Dinner in the castle tonight, my pet?"

We all make up the future, and sometimes it is a delicious dream and sometimes it is a nightmare. In every case, it is our own hopes and fears we are casting as a long shadow down the road. I have played with some fantasies about sex in the year 3000, but finally, I believe that a good novel does it all better, which is one reason I read and write speculative fiction.

NOTE

1. Joanna Russ, "Recent Feminist Utopias," pp. 71–85 in *Future Females: A Critical Anthology,* ed. Marleen S. Barr (Bowling Green, Ohio: Bowling Green State University Popular Press, 1981).

Cyberteratologies

Female Monsters Negotiate the Other's Participation in Humanity's Far Future

rosi braidotti

A teratological imaginary grips urbanized Western postmodernity. (I use "teratology" to mean the scientific discourse about the origin and nature of monstrous bodies.[1]) The monstrous, grotesque, mutant, and downright freakish (also known as the postmodern Gothic) have gained widespread currency in urban postindustrial cultures. Leslie Fiedler (1979) points out that since the 1960s a youth culture has evolved that entertains a strong—albeit ironic and parodic—relationship to freaks. Feminist culture offers no exception. Susan Sontag (1976) notes that the revival of cultural interest in freaks in literature and cinema of the 1960s coincides with the outlawing of the famous Coney Island freak show. The physical suppression of the freaky beings facilitated their metaphoric consumption. Just like other endangered species, the eviction of freaks from their highly policed territories functions as a license for their commodification as the subject matter of popular art and culture.

One of the sources of the great popularity of the postmodern Gothic is that its structural ambiguity lends itself to multimedia applications: to visualization, dramatization, serialization, transformation into musicals (Andrew Lloyd Webber's *Cats* and *Phantom of the Opera* come to mind) as well as into various video games. Early cinema (like *Nosferatu* and *The Golem*) swarms with all kinds of monstrosities. The shift from marginality to the mainstream occurs in the 1970s with W. P. Blatty's *The Exorcist* (1971) and Ira Levin's *Rosemary's Baby* (1967) and *The Stepford Wives* (1972). A new generation of accomplished film directors was ready to take up the challenge: Steven Spielberg, David Cronenberg, Brian De Palma, James Cameron, David Lynch, Ridley Scott, Tony Scott, Kathryn Bigalow, and others. The audience was primarily the baby boomers, that is to say the first postwar generation that grew up with television and its endless reruns of grade-B films. As Noel Carroll points out (1990), this gene-

146

ration engaged with feminism, civil rights, and other momentous social and political changes.

Freaks, geeks, androgynes, and hermaphrodites crowd the space of multiple Rocky Horror Shows. Drugs, mysticism, Satanism, and various brands of insanity are also included. Murder and cannibalism, made visible during the 1960s by Romero in *Night of the Living Dead*, became eroticized by Greenway in the 1980s and became mainstream by the 1990s (with *Silence of the Lambs*). An analysis of the current fascination with the freakish half human/half animal or beast figure alone would be quite lengthy. We may think, for example, of comic strips (the Ninja Turtles); classic television series like *Star Trek;* covers of records, CDs, and LPs; video games and CD-ROMs; video clips and computer-generated images of Internet and virtual reality as further evidence of the same trend. They are connected to the drug culture, as much as to its spin-offs in music, video, and computer cultures. A great deal of this culture flirts with sexual indeterminacy, which has been prevalent since David Bowie's path-breaking Ziggy Stardust.

Contemporary culture shifts the issue of genetic mutations from high-tech laboratories to popular culture. Hence, the relevance of new science fiction and cyberpunk monsters who raise metamorphosis to the status of a cultural icon. Altered states are trendsetters; video drugs now compete with pharmaceuticals. This cyberteratology imparts a new twist to the century-old connection between the feminine and the monstrous. There is indeed a distinct teratological flair in contemporary cyberspace (a proliferation of new monsters) that often merely transposes into outer space very classical iconographic representations of monstrous Others. Whether utopian (*Close Encounters*) or dystopian (*Independence Day*), messianic (*E.T.*) or diabolical (*Alien*), the intergalactic monstrous Other is firmly established within the imaginary of today's media and the electronic frontier. Lara Croft of the CD-ROM *Tomb Raiders* inaugurates the digital heroine character, post-Barbarella but also post-Ripley and, I will argue, thoroughly Gothic. In this essay, I assert that the female monster's presence marks the inception of a science fictional cultural trend that can impact upon the far future by reserving a place for female and minority subjectivities within that far future.

The contemporary trend for borderline or liminal figures of sexuality is also quite significant. I am especially interested in the replicants, zombies, and vampires (including lesbian vampires and other Queer mutants) who seem to enjoy special favor in these post-AIDS days. This is not only the case as far as "low" popular culture genres are concerned; it is equally true of relatively "high" literary genres, in such authors as Angela Carter, Kathy Acker, Martin Amis, Bret Easton Ellis, and Fay Weldon. The established success of genres such as horror, crime stories, science fiction, and cyberpunk also points to a new "post-human" technoteratological phenomenon that privileges the deviant or the mutant over more conventional versions of the human. Susanne Becker argues that these forms of neo-Gothicism also express some of the libratory potential of the postmodern condition in that they return to the social agenda issues of emotion and excess. She also argues that "one of the secrets of the Gothic's persistent success is gender-related: it is so powerful because it is so feminine" (Becker 1999, 2). Part of this feminine power consists, according to Becker, in excess that exceeds the boundaries not only of the classic Gothic genre but also of pulp, porn, parody, and other postmodern subgenres. Such blurring constitutes a serious gender-related challenge for cultural criticism.

On this score, feminism is very much a part of this culture. Contemporary feminist culture is just as passionately, parodically, and paradoxically involved with the cybermonstrous universe as any other social movement or cultural and political practice in postindustrial societies. Feminism shares fully in and actively contributes to the teratological technoimaginary of our culture in that it emphasizes hybrid and mutant identities and transgendered bodies. Witness Linda Dement's fabulous computer art: in *Cyberflesh Girl-monster* Dement plays with body boundaries and the contours of the corporeal, presenting graphical surfaces where erudite theoretical quotations mingle with organs that are re-assembled, grafted, and montaged to constitute monstrously unfamiliar forms. This is a relevant expression of the confected location of femininity in postmodernity.

Gender trouble, a sort of transsexual imaginary (rather than 1970s-style lesbianism), has entered feminist culture. "Queer" is no longer the noun that marks an identity they taught us to despise; it has become a verb that destabilizes any claim to identity—even and especially to a sex-specific identity. The alliance between Queer sexuality, drugs, and cybertechnology was announced in the psychedelic, narcotic film *Liquid Sky* (Slava Tsukerman 1993), where lethal alien biomachines spread like a virus through the postindustrial urban landscape. These machines seduce and induce cosmic orgasms and then kill the humans at orgasm point, making them disappear. The aliens feed upon the euphoria-producing chemicals secreted during orgasm.

The contemporary version of "no more nice girls" provides a colder, more ironic sensibility with a flair for sadomasochism. Mae West has replaced Rebecca West as feminist mother. As Madonna claims in her *Sex* album (1993), cyber-feminism in all its multiple rhizomatic variables promotes a monstrous or hy-

brid imaginary. Bad girls are in, and bad girls carry/are carried by a teratological imaginary. As Marina Warner explains: "In rock music, in films, in fiction,
even in pornography, women are grasping the she-beast of demonology for
themselves. The bad girl is the heroine of our times, and transgression a staple
entertainment" (Warner 1994, 11). The iron-pumping giant Ninja mutant Bar-
bies are upon us!

The monstrous or teratological imaginary expresses the social, cultural, and
symbolic mutation ensuing around the phenomenon of technoculture (Penley
and Ross 1991). Visual regimes of representation are at the heart of this mutation. From the Panoptical eye Foucault explores in his theory of "bio-power,"
to the ubiquitous presence of television, surveillance video, and computer
screens, it is the visual dimension of contemporary technology that defines its
pervasive power. With the continuing electronic revolution reaching a peak, it
is quite clear that this disembodied gaze constitutes a collision of the virtual
spaces with which we coexist in increasing degrees of intimacy. In this context,
feminist analysis describes both the pleasures and the dangers of "visual politics" (Vance 1990) and the politics of visualization—especially in biotechnology
(Franklin, Lury, and Stacey 1991). Whereas the emphasis on the powers of visualization encourages some of the theoretical masters of nihilistic postmodern
aesthetics—such as Kroker and Kroker (1987) and Baudrillard (1995)—to reduce the bodily self to a mere surface of representation and to launch a sort of
euphoric celebration of virtual embodiments, the feminist response has been
more cautious and ambivalent. It consists of stressing both the liberating and
potentially one-sided application of the new technologies (Haraway 1992; Zoe
1992). Feminists promote the need to develop figurations of contemporary female subjectivities that can do justice to the complexities and contradictions of
our technological universe.

Contemporary Science Fiction

La science fiction a toute une évolution, qui la fait passer des devenirs animaux,
végétaux ou minéraux, à des devenirs de bactéries, de virus, de molécules et
d'imperceptibles.
—*Deleuze and Guattari (1980, 304).*

One needs to turn to "minor" (not to say marginal and hybrid) genres—
such as science fiction, science fiction horror, and cyberpunk—to find fitting
cultural illustrations of the changes and transformations presently taking place.
I also think these genres provide an excellent field in which to test and apply
Deleuze's work on culture, embodiment, and becoming. Deleuze himself ac-

knowledges the importance of science fiction when he praises these texts for their nomadic force; science fiction is indeed all about displacements, ruptures, and discontinuities. As a "low culture" genre, moreover, it is also mercifully free of grandiose pretensions—of the aesthetic or cognitive kind—and thus ends up providing a more accurate and honest depiction of contemporary culture than other, more self-consciously "representational" genres (such as the documentary).

Furthermore—for the purpose of my argument about the quest for positive social and cultural representations of hybrid, monstrous, abject, and alien Others in such a way as to subvert the construction and consumption of pejorative differences—I think science fiction offers an ideal breeding ground to explore what Haraway describes affectionately as "the promises of monsters." I will argue forcefully for the relevance of Deleuze's theory of becoming to science fiction texts and films.[2] I will also argue with Deleuze about the issue of the sexually differentiated nature of these processes. I will, finally, challenge Deleuze's idea of sexually undifferentiated "becomings" by pointing to significant evidence of gender-specific patterns.

Even the most conservative commentators (Smith 1982) recognize that science fiction is a literature of ideas, with a serious philosophical content and a distinct tendency to moralize. The dividing line between conservative and other critics, however, concerns the relation between the fantastic, the magical, and the strict genre of science fiction. Thus, Nicholas Smith argues that "absurdist, existentialist literature, the type in which human beings are inexplicably transformed into cockroaches, does not qualify as science fiction" (Smith 1982, 9). I beg to differ with his reductive approach. Smith recalls the traditional standards of judgment Todorov discusses, namely that even fantastic literature must not seriously threaten the morphological normality and the moral normativity of the humanistic worldview. Metamorphoses are fine, as long as they are kept clean and in control, that is, as long as they are anthropocentric and moralizing. All the rest does not deserve serious consideration. I will, instead, defend the idea that science fiction displaces our worldview away from the human epicenter and that it manages to establish a continuum with the animal, mineral, vegetable, extraterrestrial, and technological worlds. Science fiction points to a posthumanist, biocentered egalitarianism.

As Laurie Anderson wittily comments, science fiction's anti-anthropocentrism allows it to dispense rapidly with the question of "human nature" and its psychological repertoire, so as to move toward the exploration of other possible worlds. The emotions commonly associated with the human condition are not eliminated, as much as decentralized and diffused throughout the text. Science fiction provides the means to mirror and even magnify the cultural crises of our time.

What distinguishes contemporary science fiction from nineteenth-century science fiction is that, rather than offering utopian scenarios, it reflects our sense of estrangement regarding the rapidity of current change. Science fiction, in other words, defamiliarizes the present, not dreams of possible futures. It both reflects and provokes unease. Science fiction, therefore, becomes a vehicle for reflecting upon our limitations regarding cultural, ideological, and technical closures. By provoking such reflection, science fiction (especially texts Ursula Le Guin, Joanna Russ, Marge Piercy, and Samuel Delany produce) becomes self-referential in that the genre reflects upon its limits and circumstances. Science fiction mirrors the fundamental sense of disbelief of an entire culture toward itself—"How can this be? Is it real?"—and thus it echoes perfectly the doubts of well-meaning progressive people confronted with large-scale social transformations. Hence, science fiction paradoxically reintroduces a utopian element into the mode of autoreferentiality.

Like Deleuze, I think that neither in science fiction nor in any other text is there a master plot to be unveiled or revealed by the simultaneous deployment of world history and individual psychic processes. There are, instead, only debris and sets of hazard meetings and ad hoc intersections of events (Deleuze calls these intersections points of crossings) rather than Freud's libidinal redestination or Marx's teleological process. Therefore, however close to Deleuze in terminology, Jameson's project (1982) is conceptually and affectively different from the nomadology. Jameson applies a modernist philosophy of time to the analysis of the socioeconomic cultural conditions of late postmodernity. He adopts the lexicon of poststructuralism, not its syntax, which thrives on fragments and discontinuities without falling into the indulgence of self-pity, the hysteria of panic, or the dubious luxury of anxiety and melancholia. Poststructuralism is a pragmatic philosophy that rejects the ghosts of metaphysical interiority, the "hauntology" of missing presence. It specifically rejects the tyranny of a signifier that forever refers to something else, which is never "there" and never "that" anyway. What you see is what you get. What you see—as Walter Benjamin said ever so lucidly before the Nazis pushed him to commit suicide —is but the debris heap often called progress.

Feminist Science Fiction

As adventure-minded and action-oriented tales of exploration, war, conquest, and destruction, science fiction coincides with relatively traditional gender narratives; it is quite a male-dominated adventure story. As Sarah Lefanu states, however, science fiction as an experimental genre came of age during the 1960s to challenge the stock conventions of both realistic and fantastic literature. Eminently political, in both a dystopian and a utopian sense, it destabilizes authority in all its forms, and as such, it exercises a fatal attraction for feminist writers bent upon challenging the masculine bias of literature and society. The number of female science fiction writers has consequently grown rapidly (Lefanu 1988).[3]

Science fiction writers locate their historical roots in the nineteenth-century Gothic tradition, which is one of the few genres of the period that allows women to play active roles as travelers, murderers, thieves, and adventurers. That most Gothic heroines are eminently wicked certainly attests to their intelligence and wit. One of the direct links between the Gothic and science fiction is the idea of travel through space and time; outer-space travel is conducive to fantasies of escape into alternative systems. Gender relations, sexuality, child bearing, and alternative ecological and technological systems are currently all part of the postnuclear trip. Science and technology, therefore, remain the most direct reference point. Even at its most dystopic, as in Margaret Atwood's *The Handmaid's Tale* (1985), feminist science fiction is essentially technophilic. It distances itself from the feminist tradition of opposition to biotechnology, best exemplified by Gena Corea's notion of "the mother machine" (also known as "the reproductive brothel"; 1985), where women are totally subordinated in relation to mechanical procreation.

Shulamith Firestone's *The Dialectic of Sex* influenced both the theoretical and political practice of the second feminist wave and the fiction of Suzy McKee Charnas, Joanna Russ, Marge Piercy, and Sally Miller Gearhart. Firestone represents the "technophilic" trend in feminism, which assumed a minority position until the late 1980s when more "cyber-minded" feminists emerged. Cybernetic feminism relies on the use of technologies in every aspect of social interaction (including reproduction) in order to relieve women from drudgery, the oppressive patriarchal family, and masculine violence. Technology exists within Firestone's Marxist utopia to remove humanity from its enslavement to an obsolete natural order. The reproductive utopia of technobabies is part of this aim, and it is related to collectivist politics, social utopianism, and 1970s radical feminism.

Another important insight Lefanu brings to this discussion is that of a structural analogy between woman as the second sex—what Luce Irigaray (1993) calls the "Other of the Same"—and the alien or monstrous Other. Her analogy is assimilated within the general category "difference," understood as a term of pejoration. Lefanu extends this insight to describe a deep empathy between women and aliens that, within science fiction, favors exchanges and mutual influences. As a matter of fact, in science fiction written by women, women love aliens and feel connected to them by a deep bond of recognition.

The striking feature of feminist science fiction, then, is less the affirmation of the "feminine" (in an essentialist and moralist manner) than the questioning and the deconstruction of the gender dichotomy itself. Feminist science fiction erodes the cultural foundations of notions such as "woman" and "man." Marleen S. Barr, in her work on feminist literary postmodernism and in dialogue with Robert Scholes (1975), coins the expression "feminist fabulation" to describe science fiction, utopian fantasy, and the mainstream fiction of Virginia Woolf, Gertrude Stein, Djuna Barnes, and Doris Lessing, which share in restructuring patriarchal narratives, values, and myths (Barr 1992). According to Barr, these texts contribute to the postmodern undoing of master narratives and challenge literary hierarchies.

Science fiction is about sexual metamorphoses and mutations. In the manner of Woolf's Orlando, Angela Carter's New Eve changes from man to woman. Joanna Russ's "female man" opens new possibilities when she navigates between sexual polarities. Ursula Le Guin's protagonists determine their sexual characteristics depending on with whom they happen to fall in love. Most of these mutations function as methods to explore sexuality and desire in situations of extreme duress—for example, just before or after the collapse of civilization and the end of recorded time.

A great deal of these physical and morphological mutations are expressed in the language of monstrosity, abjection, and horror; in fact, science fiction shamelessly ransacks and recycles the whole Gothic repertoire. What horror fiction fundamentally concerns is the lifting of categorical boundaries between humans and their Others: racialized or ethnic Others, animals, insects, and inorganic and technological Others. The main function of horror fiction, consequently, is to blur fundamental distinctions and to introduce a sense of panic and chaos. The monstrous body fulfills the magical or symptomatic function as an indicator of the register of difference. Hence, the monster can never avoid a blind date with women. In the postnuclear cybernetic era, moreover, the encounter between the maternal body and the technological apparatus is so intense that it calls for new frames of analysis. Contemporary "monstrous Others" blur the dividing line between the organic and the inorganic, thus also rendering superfluous the political divide between technophobia and technophilia. The issue becomes how to redefine the techno–body in such a way as to preserve a sense of singularity, without falling into nostalgic reappraisal of an essential self. The boundaries–of–identity issue raises its monstrous head. Are

Corea's nightmare world of "gender–cide" (1985) and Atwood's dystopia of the technobrothel (1985) possible future scenarios pertinent to the year 3000?

In summary: within the contemporary imaginary, the monstrous refers to the play of representation and discourses that surround the bodies of late postmodernity. The monstrous expresses a deep anxiety about the bodily roots of subjectivity that foreground the material/maternal feminine as the site of monstrosity. I tend to view this cultural penchant as a counterpart and counterpoint to the emphasis hegemonic postindustrial culture places upon the construction of clean, healthy, fit, white, decent, law-abiding, heterosexual, and forever young bodies. This emphasis, aimed at perfecting the bodily self and at correcting the corporeal self's traces of mortality, creates the need for plastic surgery, dieting, and the fitness craze. Other techniques for disciplining the body also simultaneously help the body to supersede its "natural" state. What we witness in popular culture is almost a Baktinian ritual of transgression. The fascination with the monstrous (or, the freaky body double) is directly proportional to the suppression of images of both ugliness and disease. It is as if what we chase out the front door (the spectacle of the poor, fat, homeless, homosexual, black, dying, aging, decaying, leaky body) actually creeps back in through the rear window. The monstrous marks the "return of the repressed" of technoculture, and as such, it is intrinsic to it. These monstrous representations not only express the negative or reactive anxieties of the majority. They also, often simultaneously, exemplify the emerging subjectivities of former minorities, thus tracing possible patterns of becoming.

Thus, while the monstrous feminist haunts the imagination of the creators of the antifeminist backlash, feminists who want to redefine difference positively undertake a less destructive reappraisal of the monstrous Other. Multiculturalism and the critique of Orientalism and racism also contribute to rethinking the cultural and scientific practices surrounding monstrous bodies. The need has emerged to create a new epistemology to deal with difference in nonpejorative terms. In this case, the freak/monstrous Other becomes emblematic of the vast political and theoretical efforts directed toward redirecting human subjectivity away from the persistently logocentric and racist thinking that characterized subjectivity in Western culture.

Confronted with such a discursive inflation of monstrous images, I reject the nostalgic position that tends to read them as signs of the cultural decadence of our times (also known as the decline of "master narratives" or the loss of the great canon of "high culture"). I am equally opposed to the paranoid and misogynist interpretations of the new monsters. The proliferation of a monstrous social imaginary calls, instead, for adequate forms of analysis. More particularly, this proliferation requires a form of philosophical teratology that Deleuze is in a unique position to provide. I argue that a culture (both mainstream and feminist) in which the imaginary is so monstrous and deviant, especially in its cybernetic variants, can profit greatly from Deleuze's philosophical nomadology. Deleuze's emphasis upon reconfiguring the positivism of difference, his philosophy of becoming and his emphasis upon thinking about changes and the speed of transformation, provides an illuminating way to approach the complexities of our age. There is a profound sense of relevance in both Deleuze's political and aesthetic sensibility; it is as if he is indeed attuned to the most problematic contemporary questions.

From a cultural perspective, Deleuze's intensive approach to contemporary creativity—be it conceptual, scientific, or artistic—casts a significant light upon some of the most unprecedented aspects of advanced postindustrial cultures. Among them I include the desegregation of humanistic subject positions and values, the ubiquitousness of drug practices and cultural artifacts derived from the drug culture, pervasive political violence, and the intermingling of the biological with the technological. These features, which are often referred to as the "posthuman" universe, can be understood more positively if they are approached from the perspective of Deleuze's philosophy of radical immanence. Deleuze enables multiple patterns of becoming to overthrow the humanistic parameters of representation; he avoids relativism by grounding his practice into a tight spatiotemporal framework.

Beyond Metaphors: Philosophical Teratology

I have argued that the reason the monstrous is a dominant part of the social imaginary is that it offers privileged mirror images. We identify with these images because of either fear or fascination. This identification may also explain the peculiarly reassuring function that the representation of freaky bodies fulfills in relation to the anxiety-ridden contemporary imagination. As Diana Arbus (1972) suggests, freaks have already been "through it" and have come out at the other end. If not quite survivors, freaks are at least resilient in regard to their capacity to metamorphose and thus survive and cope. Many present-day humans may instead harbor serious doubt about their capacity to cope, let alone survive. In the case of monsters, the accident or catastrophe, to paraphrase Brian Massumi (1992), has already ensued. These events can provide welcome relief from the generalized political economy of fear, precisely by incarnating fully its destructive potential; they can also exemplify the virtual catastrophe by embodying it. The effect is cathartic, erotic, and deeply emotional; with a sigh of relief would-be suburban monsters rush to embrace their potential Other self. Contemporary horror and science fiction literature and film portray an exacerbated version of anxiety in the form of "Otherness within": the monster dwells in your embodied self and it may burst out at any minute into unexpected and definitely unwanted mutations. The monster is inside you, ready to erupt. The monstrous growths spreading within one's organism, as Jacky Stacey (1997) reminds us, in the form of cancer or other postnuclear diseases, are variations on the "enemy within" theme.

The monsters are "metamorphic" creatures who fulfill a kaleidoscopic mirror function and make us aware of the mutation that we experience in these postnuclear/-industrial/-modern times. For example, Sontag (1976) argues that Arbus's photos of human oddities are troubling not so much because of their subject matter, but because of the strong sense of the photographer's own consciousness and involvement with them. The fact of Arbus's suicide adds a tone of tragic authenticity to her images, and it testifies to the metamorphic power of freaks—that is to say the extent to which freaks captivate Arbus and psychically ambush her. Arbus's representation of freaks embodies the paradox of the contemporary teratological imaginary: on the one hand, they familiarize us with the human oddities and thus lower our threshold to tolerate the horrible. On the other hand, they keep a cold and unsentimental distance from her representations, displaying them as utterly un–self-conscious and quite autonomous. In fact, Arbus's pictures of freaks utterly lack irony and the stiff respectability of Victorian portraits; they paradoxically ultimately reinforce our sense of alienation from them. Her pictures become neutrally self-referential and, hence, fail to convey any possible moral message.

The metamorphic power of monstrous Others illuminates the thresholds of "Otherness" and displaces their boundaries. As I argued earlier, this process mobilizes issues of embodiment, morphology, and sexuality—scrambles the code of phallogocentric, anthropocentric representation in which they are traditionally cast. For instance, Fiedler's analysis of the typology of contemporary monsters classifies them in terms of lack, excess, and displacement of organs. Noel Carroll (1990) also points to hybridity and categorical incompleteness as defining features of monsters. This means that monsters superimpose features from different species, alternately displaying effects of excess or staggering omissions. The detachability of bodily organs is crucial to this effect. Carroll analyzes it in terms of complete lack of shape—as in the gelatinous blob-like entities—which effaces all meaningful morphological reference points. This effacement also involves fusion and fission of body parts. Bodily juxtaposition of this sort blurs such distinctions as living/dead, male/female, human/animal, insect/machine, and inside/outside. Fission/fusion displaces the attributes of these categories over other entities, creating body doubles, alter egos, and other forms of displacement of familiar traits. A variation on this theme is the evocation of abject monstrosity by metonymy: vermin, skeletons, and decaying body parts that represent the monstrous entity without actually portraying the monstrous entity.

This representation facilitates creating an analogy with the feminine. As psychoanalytic feminist critics have successfully argued (Wright 1992), the feminine also bears a privileged relation to lack, excess, and displacement. By being posited as eccentric vis-à-vis the dominant mode, or as constantly off-center, the feminine marks the threshold between the human and its "outside." This outside acts as a multilayered framework that at once distinguishes the human form and connects it to the animal, vegetable, mineral, and also the divine. As a link between the sacred and the abject, the feminine is paradoxical in its monstrosity. In other words, the feminine functions via displacement, and its ubiquity as a social or philosophical "problem" is equal to the awe and horror it inspires. Metamorphic creatures are uncomfortable "body doubles" or simulacra who simultaneously attract and repel, comfort and unsettle; they are objects of adoration and aberration. As I mentioned earlier, in science fiction texts written by women, a deep complicity exists between the male Other and the Other of the entire human species.

Another historically continuous analogy between women and monstrous beings concerns the malignant powers of women's imagination. Ever since antiquity, the active and desiring woman's imaginative powers have been represented as potentially lethal—especially if the woman is pregnant. A great deal of critical commentary exists regarding the destructive powers of the pregnant woman's imagination.[4] Marie-Hélène Huet (1983) uses a psychoanalytic framework to interpret the fear of the maternal imagination as a variation of male castration anxiety. The pregnant woman literally has the capacity to undo the father's signature—to "un-create" life. Mary Ann Doane (1987) and Linda Williams (1989) find the same mechanism at work in classic Hollywood cinema where "when the woman looks" with desire, trouble is never too far away. These feminist critics argue that, within phallocentric culture, the desiring females' lethal gaze expresses a general fear and mistrust of female desire and subjectivity.

Psychoanalytic feminist theory also casts an interesting light upon this aspect of the monstrous imaginary. First, women who are caught in the phallogocentric gaze tend to have a negative self-image and to dread what they see when they look in the mirror. Virginia Woolf and Sylvia Plath, for example, saw monsters emerging from the depths of their inner mirrors. Women, who represent difference in their cultural productions in terms of aberration or monstrosity, often experience difference as negative. Gothic literature can be read as a female projection of an inner sense of inadequacy. According to this perspective, the monster primarily fulfills a specular function, thereby playing a major role in the definition of female self-identity. *Frankenstein*—the creative product of the daughter of a renowned feminist—is also the portrait of a deep lack of self-confidence and an even deeper sense of displacement. Not only does Mary Shelley side with the monstrous creature, accusing its creator of avoiding his responsibilities, but she also presents the creature as her abject body double; this presentation allows her to express self-loathing with staggering lucidity.

Gilbert and Gubar (1979) argue that within English literature women have often depicted themselves as vile and degraded. Thus, they read *Frankenstein* as Mary Shelley's anti-Prometheus response to Milton and also as a tale of self-hatred. The latter reading is especially true for creative women, the women whom Virginia Woolf urged to "kill the angel in the house" and confront their inner demons so as to stretch their resources to the limit. I read Frankenstein's monster as mirroring essentially the process of literary creation: he is isomorphic in relation to the structure of Shelley's book—which is also rather badly conceived and shapeless. The monster, then, confronts readers with the auto-referentiality that Jameson considers to be the key to science fiction's power to make us experience our limits. I find Shelley's text to be affected by deep malaise which, via many flashbacks and detours, forms an uneasy epistolary format. The effect upon readers is one of unrest and torment. Moreover, Shelley, on several occasions, deliberately compares the text to her protagonist's monstrous body. The text is analogous to a horrible, unfinished product that portrays writing as doomed to failure and basically unfulfilling. The monster is Shelley's "becoming-writer"—and he is a most imperfect writing machine. His difficulties with comprehension and communication reflect the circular logic of the writing process itself that mirrors the pursuit of its own clarity. Writing, a game of seduction and repetition, is eroticized analogously to the agony of longing; but it offers little relief and even fewer rewards. The constant confrontation that Shelley establishes between human heterosexuality and the sterile pleasures of the anthropomorphic monster stresses the point that writing does not pursue the sublime; writing, instead, courts disaster and crime.

Thus, Shelley primarily criticizes the hubris of the scientists who play God by creating artificial life. She insinuates that these scientists are crazy little men locked up in their dungeons and masturbatory chambers who fall prey to matrix envy while trying to turn shit into gold or petrified matter into new life; they swap anatomy to pursue a new destiny. The ontological jealousy of the fallen angels who work maniacally to capitalize on time and space to achieve self-reproduction also haunts the writer. And a comparable folly inhabits the creative spirits who endlessly spill their fluids upon white pages in an endless inescapable process of self-birth. The circularity of the writing process expresses a delirium of self-legitimization. All writing is simultaneously predatory, vampiristic, and self-serving—and no significant distance separates the creator's gloved hands from the hideous claws of the monster. Through *Frankenstein*, Shelley herself becomes such a writing device—a depersonalized entity, a "bachelor machine." Chris Baldick explains that Shelley's masterpiece achieves a double self-referentiality, "both in its composition and in its subsequent cultural status miming the central moments of its own story" (Baldick 1987, 30). The process of artistic creation, the status of motherhood, and the birth process —via a remarkable case of "bibliogenesis"—all mirror each other and constantly overlap. When the reader remembers that Shelley's mother, Mary Wollstonecraft, died as a result of giving birth to her, the text, body, and mother become one ungovernable heap of excessive meanings; these characteristics propel *Frankenstein* outward, into a mythic dimension.

This metamorphic dimension fulfills an important function. The monstrous as a borderline figure blurs boundaries between hierarchically established distinctions (between human/nonhuman, Western/non-Western, and so on) and also between horizontal or adjacent differences. In other words, as Jane Gallop explains (1989), the monstrous triggers the recognition of a sense of multiplicity contained within the same body. The monstrous is an entity whose multiple parts are neither totally merged nor totally separate from the human observer. Thus, by blurring the boundaries of differentiation, the monstrous signifies the difficulty of maintaining manageable margins of differentiation between boundaries separating self and other.

As Irigaray maintains, the problem with boundaries and differentiation lies at the core of the mother/daughter relationship. Any daughter—that is, any woman—has a self that is, rather than being completely individuated, constitutively connected to another woman—her mother. "Mother" is already quite tangled and complex; it is the site of a symbiotic mix-up, which—according to Lacan—requires the ordering power of the Law of the Father to restore boundaries. Barbara Johnson (1982) pursues this argument in "My Monster/My Self" (which, of course, alludes to Nancy Friday's popular *My Mother/My Self*). Is the mother or the self the monster? Or, does the monstrous lie in the undecidability of what ensues in-between? The inability to answer such questions involves the difficulty of negotiating stable and positive boundaries with one's mother. The monstrous feminine is precisely the signpost of this structural and highly significant problem.

What is important to note here is that during the 1980s feminist theory cele-brated both the ambiguities and the intensity of the mother/daughter bond in positive terms. ("Ecriture féminine" and Irigaray's paradigm of "the poli-tics of sexual difference" epitomize this trend.) By the late 1990s, however, the maternalist/feminine paradigm was well under attack, if not discarded. This shift from gynocentric psychoanalytic feminism toward a definitely negative attitude directed at the mother coincides, as often is the case regarding femi-nism, with a generation gap. Silvia Kolbowski notes (1995) that Melanie Klein's "bad" mother replaces the Lacanian-inspired "vanilla sex" representation of the M/other as object of desire. Accordingly, in feminist theories of difference, parodic politics replaces strategic essentialism and other forms of affirmative mimesis. Nixon reads the anti-Lacanian climate of the 1990s (best illustrated by the revival of interest in Melanie Klein's theory of the aggressive drives) "in part as a critique of psychoanalytic feminist work of the 70's and 80's, privileg-ing pleasure and desire over hatred and aggression" (Nixon 1995, 72). I would like to situate the new alliance currently being negotiated between feminists and Deleuze in this context of the historical decline of Lacan's theory of desire as lack and the revival of Klein's theory of drives. A colder and more aggres-sive political sensibility dominated the 1990s. However, I share neither in the rejection of the mother nor in the denigration of the material/maternal femi-nine that this rejection entails. This does not mean that I am thrown back into the murky depths of uterine essentialism. My rejection of a position allegedly beyond gender, or beyond sexual indifferentiation, is, instead, framed by philo-sophical nomadism. This means that I value processes of change and trans-formation as methods to actualize a virtual feminine in a network of intercon-nections with other forces, entities, and actors. Like Massumi, I do not regard Deleuze's ideas as an incentive to abandon politics but, rather, as a method to add complexity to politics by imbuing politics with movement, dynamism, and nomadism. This open-ended, multilayered virtual feminine matrix is neither flesh nor metal, neither destiny nor teleology; it is motion, in spatial as well as temporal terms.

Hal Foster argues that, during the late postmodernism of the 1990s, ad-vanced technological cultures moved beyond the notion of the death of the subject toward "traumatic realism" (Foster 1996, 131). There is a return of the "real" subject that opposes the excessive emphasis the 1980s placed upon tex-tual models of culture or conventional notions of realism. In reaction to the AIDS crisis and the general decline of the end-of-the-millennium welfare state, a growing disillusionment with the psychoanalytic celebrations of desire as ex-perimentation and mobility is also palpable. What is significant, argues Foster, is that this cultural dissatisfaction is expressed as a return to the shocked subjectivity of a traumatized subject. Given that, as Arbus notes, freaks are born with their traumas written all over them and that they embody the actualized catastrophe, they emerge as a revived cultural paradigm. Cindy Sherman's artistic trajectory is telling in this regard: from her early romances, to her history portraits, to her present-day abject disaster pictures, Sherman signals the shift from a fascination with signs and the effects of representation upon reality to the fear that a gaze disengaged from any symbolic system cannibalizes the whole body.

The horror genre (in Kristeva's sense of the blurring of boundaries) returns; this return involves a cultural fascination with the amorphous, the shapeless, and the obscene. It assumes the negative form of the cult of wounded, diseased, traumatized bodies. Foster describes these bodies as a contemporary type of advanced melancholia that expresses a real fatigue with the politics of difference and an equal fascination for indistinction and death. Aesthetically, the return of horror produces both the ecstatic fascination for a body that the technological gaze invades and the fear of this invasion that leads to real despair —and to a sense of loss.

I argue that technological culture expresses a colder and more depersonalized sensibility. The arena within which this discussion takes place is the social imaginary—a highly contested social space in which the technoteratological body double, supported and promoted by postindustrial societies, is pervasive. Whether we like it or not, we are made to desire the human/machine interface. I consequently argue that, given the importance of both the social imaginary and the role of technology in coding it, we need to develop adequate forms of representation and resistance. Conceptual creativity is called for; new figurations are needed to help us negotiate the maze of technoteratological culture.

What also emerges from a closer analysis of the cyberteratological imaginary of advanced cultures is the crucial and highly strategic role the maternal feminine plays within it. There is especially one aspect of the quasi-isomorphic relationship between the technological tool and the maternal body that I find quite significant. This relationship has less to do with the classic technophobic objection that the machines are "taking over" the womb (Corea 1985), than with a shift in the position of female reproductive powers. In a context of disruption of the time/space continuum of humanism and of generalized postnuclear anxiety, popular culture highlights the threat of the collapse of paternal authority under the impact of female power's excessive growth. This collapse positions the suburban nuclear family as the privileged stage of a horror show (Greenberg 1991). Such staging has been a part of popular culture ever since

The Exorcist appeared, and it was already explicit in Hitchcock's *Psycho* (as well as, of course, in Romero's *Night of the Living Dead* and *Alien*). Monstrous gestations are a means to upset the monotonous normativity of the suburban family.

How does this situation apply to women?

Women are not only reduced to maternal power; maternal power is also redirected toward technology-based and corporate-owned reproductive production systems. Corporations, in some respects, are the real moral monsters science fiction and cyberpunk films portray; corporations ruthlessly corrupt, corrode, exploit, and destroy. The global incubators are the cybernightmare *The Matrix* depicts—and this nightmare speaks for itself.

In other words, "Mother" has been assimilated within the technoindustrial system; reproduction—especially the replication of white, male babies—is a primary asset in the postcapitalist cash nexus. The maternal body in late postmodernity is, therefore, positioned at the heart of the political economy of fear. The mother's body simultaneously reproduces the possibility of the future and must be made to inscribe this future within the regime of high-tech commodification (that is, within today's market economy). Holding the maternal/material feminine in this double bind creates excessive turbulence. This situation causes empirical females, as Camilla Griggers (1997) points out, to suffer a high degree of discontent, pathology, and disease.

The immediate effect of this topos is to disengage the child, fetus, and embryo —and even the ova—from the woman's body. Much has been written about these "fetal attractions" (Franklin 1997; Petchesky 1987) as well as the fetus's presence as an independent item in popular imagery. These images are also, as *The Silent Scream* demonstrates, instrumental regarding the impact of anti-abortion campaigns involving intimidation and terrorism. Sofia Zoe (1984) attentively analyzes embryological images; she recommends that they be kept within the context of nuclear technology and the threat of extermination: "To the list of technologies we commonly think of as reproductive, like abortion, birth control and other more exotic techniques like gene-splicing and editing, cloning etc. we add artifacts like radioactive waste and toxic poisons which also directly intervene in life chemistry and embryology" (Zoe 1984, 48).

According to Zoe, the extraterrestrial embryological imagery that abounds in science fiction film expresses the intense uterus envy that is built into technological culture. In *2001: A Space Odyssey*, for instance, maternal imagery codes the spaceship's main computer. (I especially think of the umbilical cord that connects the astronaut to the ship.) Zoe defends the hypothesis that, via the male abdomen, a clear displacement from female uterus to paternal brain occurs. This displacement produces a contemporary version of the myth of Athena's birth: fully armed, emerging from the father's head, she bears on her breastplate the image of Medusa's forever-frozen horrific gaze. Zoe also notes the recurrence of the father/daughter dyad in science fiction: from Rotwang and Maria in *Metropolis,* to Dr. Morbius's girl Alta in *Forbidden Planet,* to Rachael in *Blade Runner* (who is the brainchild of a corporation). These films exemplify the penchant for imagining Athena-like figures of young warriors who serve the system upon whom the father/scientist/corporation projects the animated remains of what used to be the female mother/nature (which is by now cannibalized into the company-owned technomatrix). The brain/womb of the corporation produces the "star child" located in a crystalline Cartesian geometrical space: high-tech supermoms integrated in advanced computer circuits. There is no sticky or messy "wetware" here. Fortunately, the pure light of reason also reveals nightmares: slimy evil alien creatures that shiny warriors fight to the bitter end. (Ripley in *Alien* comes to mind.)

Confronted with such maternal corporate high-tech power—and such ominous examples of women's free will—men are represented as the heroic resistance fighters. In *Terminator,* the male prophet descends to Earth to pave the way for the Savior and to ensure that the elected female saves humanity by reproducing the future Messiah. An entrenched anxiety about reestablishing the paternal line of filiation translates into a new masculine determination to make women do the right thing. Spielberg and Lucas are the principal creators of this fundamentally conservative approach to the corporate-run vision of reproduction: they tuck the technological apparatus safely away within a maternal role. Fortunately, other directors do not follow Spielberg's and Lucas's examples. Cronenberg, for instance, highlights the vulnerability of the male body.

Conclusion

Contemporary social imaginary, in a twist that strikes me as rather misogynist, directly blames women for postmodernity's crisis of identity. In one of the double binds that occur so often in regard to representing those people marked as different, women are portrayed as unruly elements who should be controlled —represented as so many cyber-Amazons in need of governance. Women are also, however, depicted as already complicitous with and integrated within the industrial reproductive complex. "Mother the bitch" is also the "serial mom" who uses and abuses her power over life. Sofia Zoe succinctly describes this tendency: "Superman has incorporated and taken over female functions to become a high-tech super mom, who feeds and fertilizes us with junk food, spermatic images and silicon chips, and who tempts us with terminal apples" (Zoe 1984, 51).

Translated into the Deleuzian language of the "becoming-woman," the maternal/material feminine simultaneously appears as the despotic face of the majority and the pathetic face of minorities. Postindustrial culture fights the battle for its renewal upon the mother's increasingly contaminated body. To survive, advanced capitalism must incorporate the mother—effectively metabolize the mother's offspring. This incorporation is also known as the "feminization" of advanced cultures and what I call the "becoming-woman of men." (My term brings Joanna Russ's "female man" to mind.)

Tania Modleski (1991) discusses this tendency in contemporary postfeminist American culture as a whole. For instance, women are identified with the most popular (that is, lowbrow) cultural consumer goods (such as talk shows and soap operas). This identification leads to defining the "feminization of culture" as a synonym for lack of high culture. Men, however, continue to be represented as creative and autonomous spirits. In some ways, this cultural tendency reflects the nineteenth-century tradition of structural ambivalence toward women. Huyssen (1986) lucidly analyzes this tradition in that he understands it as a paradoxical masculine identification with women. Flaubert's "Madame Bovary, c'est moi" coincides with the effective exclusion of real women from literature. Such exclusion also takes the form, in Flaubert as well as in soap operas, of representing women as avid consumers of pulp. Women symbolize the vulgarity of mass culture; creative high culture and tradition remain the firmly entrenched prerogatives of men.

The *Alien* films therefore function as welcome feminist interventions. The series turns the "new female monsters" that late postindustrial technosocieties engineer into heroic subjects who are most likely to save humanity from techno-induced annihilation. The feminist becomes the last human. J. H. Kavanagh (1990) argues that *Alien* celebrates the rebirth of humanism appearing as progressive feminism. The struggle is internal to the feminine; it occurs between an archaic monstrous feminine the alien represents and the postfeminist emancipated woman Ripley/Sigourney Weaver represents. The alien is a *phallus dentatus* born from a man's stomach; it stands grotesquely erect most of the time and often uses its phallic tail to try to commit oral rape. Ripley emerges, in contrast, as the life-giving, postfeminist principle. She is warrior with a heart of gold who rescues pets and little girls—as well as life in the galaxy. She is the new humanist hero: woman as the savior of mankind.

It would be far too predictable an ending, however, if an intergalactic Joan of Arc bearing Sigourney Weaver's ghostly white face[5] represented everything feminism can accomplish for a species experiencing an advanced state of crisis. Saving humanity is not an unworthy cause; it is a role that women have historically often been called upon to play—especially during war, invasion, liberation struggles, or other forms of daily resistance. Women have, however, seldom drawn real social benefits from their episodes of heroism. When the third millennium dawns, women's participation in ensuring humanity's future will consequently need to be negotiated rather than taken for granted. As Barbara Krueger states: "We don't need another hero."

Moreover, in the context of the feminism of difference that I defend throughout this essay, it is a defeat merely to reverse the dialectics of the sexes to benefit women—that is to say, mostly white, highly educated women—and to leave power structures unchanged. It is more productive to allow tensions that are built into the millennial crisis of values to explode within feminism—and, hence, to reveal feminism's paradoxes. Because feminism is definitely not about a search for final authenticity (a quest for the golden fleece in the form of truth), I believe that at the start of the current new millennium (and at the inception of all new millennia to come), we need to acquire a flair for complicating the issues that will enable us to equal the complexities of our age. I would like feminists to avoid repetitions without difference as well as the blatant recomposition of genderized and racialized power differences. I would also like feminists to avoid the equally unsatisfactory assumption of a morally superior triumphant feminine defining the one-way road to the future.

There is no denying that, during late postmodernity, various brands of nihilism are circulating. A whole philosophical style based upon catastrophe is popular among several prophets of doom who contemplate the implosion of humanism with tragic joy.[6] Nothing could be further removed from the ethics of affirmation and the political sensibility of posthumanist subjects than the altered states proposed by those people whom I call "narco-philosophers"; these individuals celebrate the implosion of sense, meaning, and values. They produce histrionic renditions of the delirious megalomania against which Deleuze posits firmly and rigorously a sustainable definition of the self. It is clear to me that a culture in the grip of a technoteratological imaginary occurring during a time of intense social and historical change is a culture that badly needs *less* abstraction and hype. This suggested diminishment concerns the economy of the spectral—that is to say, the forever living dead the media's representation system perpetuates. Images live forever—especially during the age of digital manipulation; images circulate within a continuously present ghastly/ghostly economy of vampiric consumption. This postmodern Gothic element is consequently overwhelming within today's highly mediamatic societies. The iconic stars live on: Marilyn and Diana, who will always appear forever young and dead, return endlessly to our attention.

I believe that a concretely embodied and embedded reading of the subject as a material, vitalistic, and anti-essentialist (and sustainable) entity can function as a profoundly sane reminder of the positive virtualities that lie in store regarding the crisis and transformation we now experience. I refer to a question of style (in the sense of a political and aesthetic sensibility). To assuage end of millennium stagnation, it is crucial to nurture a culture of affirmation and joy. To cultivate the art of complexity—and the specific aesthetic and political sensibilities that sustain it—I plead for working with an idea of the subject as the site of composition for multiple becomings. It is against the contemporary forms of nihilism that a critical philosophy of immanence needs to disintoxicate us and to reset our agenda in the direction of affirmation and sustainable subjectivity. In this project, the presence of monsters can provide both solace and a model. I hope that monsters will accompany those who witness the next new millennium's inception.

NOTES

1. Teratoxicology (Glamister 1964) is the branch of molecular biology that involves biochemically-induced birth defects and mutations that have been monitored in the wake of the Manhattan Project. By extension, teratoxicology triggers in humans the desire to represent the unrepresentable (and to think the unthinkable), which results in an advanced state of machine envy and the desire to imitate the inorganic or nonhuman.
2. See also White (1995).
3. Lefanu argues that the number of women science fiction writers has increased dramatically. There were no female winners of the Hugo Award between 1953 (the year of the award's inception) and 1967. Between 1968 and 1984 there were eleven female Hugo Award winners.
4. For a more detailed explanation see Braidotti (1994; 1996).
5. Anneke Smelik comments on the analogy between Ripley and Joan of Arc, especially in *Alien III* (Smelik 1996).
6. See Kroker and Kroker (1987).

WORKS CITED

Arbus, Diane. 1972. *Diane Arbus*. New York: Millerton.

Atwood, Margaret. 1985. *The Handmaid's Tale*. Toronto: Seal.

Baldick, Chris. 1987. *In Frankenstein's Shadow: Myth, Monstrosity and Nineteenth Century Writing*. Oxford: Clarendon.

Barr, Marleen S. 1992. *Feminist Fabulation: Space/Postmodern Fiction*. Iowa City: University of Iowa Press.

Baudrillard, Jean. 1995. *The Gulf War Did Not Take Place*. Sydney: Power Publications.

Becker, Susanne. 1999. *Gothic Forms of Feminine Fiction*. Manchester: Manchester University Press.

Braidotti, Rosi. 1994. "Mothers, Monsters and Machines." In Braidotti, *Nomadic Subjects: Embodiment and Difference in Contemporary Feminist Theory*. New York: Columbia University Press.

———. 1996. "Signs of Wonder and Traces of Doubt." Pp. 135–52 in *Between Monsters, Goddesses and Cyborgs*, ed. Rosi Braidotti and Nina Lykke. London: Zed.

Carroll, Noel. 1990. *The Philosophy of Horror: Paradoxes of the Heart*. New York: Routledge.

Corea, Gena. 1985. "The Reproductive Brothel." Pp. 38–51 in *Man-made Women: How New Reproductive Technologies Affect Women*, ed Gena Corea et al. London: Hutchinson.

Deleuze, Giles, and Felix Guattari. 1980. *Mille Plateaux. Capitalism et Schizophrénie II* Paris: Minuit. Translated by Brian Massumi (1987) under the title *A Thousand Plateaus: Capitalism and Schizophrenia* (Minneapolis: University of Minnesota Press).

Doane, Mary Ann. 1987. *The Desire to Desire: The Women's Film of the 40's*. Bloomington: Indiana University Press.

Fiedler, Leslie. 1979. *Freaks: Myths and Images of the Secret Self*. New York: Simon and Schuster.

Foster, Hal. 1996. *The Return of the Real*. Cambridge, Mass.: MIT Press.

Franklin, S., C. Lury, and J. Stacey. 1991. *Off-centre: Feminism and Cultural Studies*. Ithaca, N.Y.: Cornell University Press.

Franklin, Sarah. 1997. *Embodied Progress: A Cultural Account of Assisted Conception*. London: Routledge.

Gallop, Jane. 1989. "The Monster in the Mirror: The Feminist Critic's Psychoanalysis." In *Feminism and Psychoanalysis*, ed. R. Feldstein and J. Roof. Ithaca, N.Y.: Cornell University Press.

Gilbert, Sandra, and Susan Gubar. 1979. *The Madwoman in the Attic*. New Haven: Yale University Press.

Glamister, T. W. 1964. "Fantasies, Facts, and Foetuses: The Interplay of Fancy and Reason in Teratology." *Medical History* 8:15–30.

Greenberg, Harvey R. 1991. "Reimagining the Gargoyle: Psychoanalytic Notes on *Alien*." Pp. 83–106 in *Close Encounters: Film, Feminisms and Science Fiction*, ed. Constance Penley, Elizabeth Lyon, Lynn Spigel, and Janet Bergstrom. Minneapolis: University of Minnesota Press.

Griggers, Camilla. 1997. *Becoming-woman*. Minneapolis: University of Minnesota Press.

Haraway, Donna. 1992. "The Promises of Monsters: A Regenerative Politics for Inappropriate/d Others." Pp. 295–337 in *Cultural Studies*, ed. L. Grossberg, C. Nelson, and A. Treichler. London: Routledge.

Huet, Marie-Hélène. 1983. "Living Images: Monstrosity and Representation." *Representations* 4:73–87.

Huyssen, Andrea. 1986. "The Vamp and the Machine: Fritz Lang's *Metropolis*." In Andrea Huyssen, *After the Great Divide: Modernism, Mass Culture and Postmodernism*. Bloomington: Indiana University Press.

Irigaray, Luce. 1993. *An Ethics of Sexual Difference*. Ithaca, N.Y.: Cornell University Press.

Jameson, Fredric. 1982. "Progress versus Utopia; or, Can We Imagine the Future?" *Science Fiction Studies* 9:47–158.

Johnson, Barbara. 1982. "My Monster/My Self." *Diacritics* 12, no. 2:2–10.

Kavanagh, J. H. 1990. "Feminism, Humanism and Science." Pp. 73–81 in *Alien Zone*, ed. Annette Kuhn. London: Verso.

Kolbowski, Silvia. 1995. "Introduction" and "A Conversation on Recent Feminist Art Practices." *October* 71:49–69.

Kroker, Arthur, and Marilouise Kroker. 1987. *Body Invaders: Panic Sex in America*. New York, St. Martin's.

Lefanu, Sarah. 1988. *In the Chinks of the World Machine: Feminism and Science Fiction*. London: Women's Press.

Massumi, Brian. 1992. *A User's Guide to Capitalism and Schizophrenia*. Boston: MIT Press.

Modleski, Tania. 1991. *Feminism without Women: Culture and Criticism in a "Postfeminist" Age*. New York: Routledge.

Nixon, Mignon. 1995. "Bad Enough Mother." *October* 72:71–92.

Penley, Constance, and Andrew Ross, eds. 1991. *Technoculture*. Minneapolis: University of Minnesota Press.

Petchesky, Rosalind P. 1987. "Fetal Images: The Power of Visual Culture in the Politics of Reproduction." Pp. 57–80 in *Reproductive Technologies*, ed. M. Stanworth. Cambridge: Polity.

Scholes, Robert. 1975. *Structural Fabulation: An Essay on Fiction of the Future*. London: University of Notre Dame Press.

Smelik, Anneke. 1996. "Middeleeuwse Maillots en de Passie van Ripley Verfilming van Jeanne d'Arc." *Jaarboek Vooe Vrouwengeschedenis* 16:133–41.

Smith, Nicholas, ed. 1982. *Philosophers Look at Science Fiction*. Chicago: Nelson-Hall.

Sontag, Susan. 1976. "The Imagination of Disaster." Pp. 116–31 in *Science Fiction: A Collection of Critical Essays*, ed. Mark Rose. Englewood Cliffs, N.J.: Prentice Hall.

Stacey, Jacky. 1997. *Teratologies: A Cultural Study of Cancer*. London: Routledge.

Vance, Carol. 1990. "The Pleasures of Looking: The Attorney General's Commission on Pornography versus Visual Images." Pp. 38–58 in *The Critical Image: Essays on Contemporary Photography,* ed. Carol Squiers. Seattle: Bay.

Warner, Marina. 1994. *Six Myths of Our Time: Little Angels, Little Monsters, Beautiful Beasts, and More.* New York: Vintage.

White, Eric. 1995. "Once They Were Men, Now They're Landcrabs: Monstrous Becomings in Evolutionist Cinema." Pp. 226–44 in *Posthuman Bodies,* ed. Judith Halberstam and Ira Livingston. Bloomington: Indiana University Press.

Williams, Linda. 1989. *Hard Core: Power, Pleasure, and the Frenzy of the Visible.* Berkeley: University of California Press.

Wright, Elizabeth. 1992. *Feminism and Psychoanalysis: A Critical Dictionary.* Cambridge: Blackwell.

Zoe, Sofia. 1984. "Exterminating Fetuses: Abortion, Disarmament, and the Sexo-Semiotics of Extraterrestrialism." *Diacritics* (Summer 1984): 47–59.

———. 1992. "Virtual Corporalities: A Feminist View" *Australian Feminist Studies* 15:11–24.

four

FUTURE CRITICAL

"You Must Have Seen a Lot of Changes"
Fiction beyond the Twenty-first Century

patrick parrinder

How much will human life change in the next few centuries and the next few millennia? Writers—deliberately or inadvertently—give very different answers to these questions. Here are two examples from 1950s "Golden Age" science fiction. First, the biographical entry on Isaac Asimov's Hari Seldon in the *Encyclopedia Galactica:*

> HARI SELDON— . . . born in the 11,988th year of the Galactic Era: died 12,069. The dates are more commonly given in terms of the current Foundational Era as −79 to the year 1 F.E. Born to middle-class parents on Helicon, Arcturus sector (where his father, in a legend of doubtful authenticity, was a tobacco grower in the hydroponics plants of the planet), he early showed amazing ability in mathematics. [. . .]
>   . . . Undoubtedly his greatest contributions were in the field of psycho-history. Seldon found the field little more than a set of vague axioms; he left it a profound statistical science. . . . (Asimov 1960, 7)

And then the words of Henry Kuttner's mysterious time-traveler from "[s]everal thousand years in the future. Your future"—

> Hard to know what to say in new time-world. You have no conception of our advanced culture, sorry. Hard to get down to same place with you. Civilization moved fast, fast, after your century. (Kuttner 1954, 138, 139)

Kuttner's future has moved very much faster than Asimov's. Not only do the denizens of the Foundational Era still smoke tobacco and use a printed encyclopedia, but they also share exactly the same conceptual basis (indicated by phrases such as "middle-class," "vague axioms," and "profound statistical science") as Asimov's readers circa 1950. Yet Asimov is ostensibly representing the far future (though the *Foundation* series could be set in a parallel world). Kuttner's future is vague, ambiguous, and probably hallucinatory. Complete lucidity is normally only a property of stories using a simple extension of our own present timescale and set in the near future—and not in all of those. For a clear sense of what Isaac Asimov, for example, may have anticipated or wanted for human life we need to turn from the *Foundation* series to his robot stories. These stories begin from the Three Laws as set out in the fifty-sixth edition of the *Handbook of Robotics* published in 2058 A.D. (Asimov 1968, 8).

Near, Far, and Intermediate Futures

Science fiction is stuffed with future dates, so much so that a chronology bringing together all the genre's futures would fill an enormous and rapidly expanding volume—more an encyclopedia, in fact, than a handbook. What literary purposes are served by these dates? They are not indispensable, since a substantial proportion of late-twentieth-century science fiction is set either in undated futures or in futures with parallel or alternative dating. Novels adhering to the single, unbroken arrow of time along which (for example) H. G. Wells sent his time machine to the year 802,701 may be said nowadays to have a slightly old-fashioned look. Yet writers who use future dates vary enormously in the nature and degree of their attachment to precise, pedantic chronologies. All that may be ventured at this stage is that attention to dates—even if they are as farfetched as 802,701—links the text in one way or another to conventions of historical and political realism. Outright "speculative fantasy" tends to employ undated and parallel-dated futures or multiple timelines. "Realistic Future-Scene Fiction" as advocated by Robert A. Heinlein (1969, 22) is a formalistic category obscuring the difference between what might be called the private and domestic fiction of the future, and fiction incorporating a public record of supposed historical and political events. In the latter case, dates are more or less essential, but they may be used for solemnly prophetic, playful, or openly satirical effect.

In fiction that evokes a conventionally linear, historical future, the distinction between "near" and "far" is almost unavoidable. Two articles by Brian Stableford in the *Encyclopedia of Science Fiction* set out this distinction very suggestively. The "Near Future" article begins as follows:

> Images of the near future in science fiction differ markedly from those of the far future in both content and attitude. The far future tends to be associated with notions of ultimate destiny, and is dominated by metaphors of senescence; its images display a world irrevocably transfigured. It is viewed from a detached viewpoint; the dominant mood is—paradoxically—one of

nostalgia, because the far future, like the dead past, can be entered only imaginatively, and has meaning only in terms of its emotional resonance. The near future, by contrast, is a world which is imminently real—one of which we can have no definite knowledge, which exists only imaginatively and hypothetically, but which is nevertheless a world in which (or something like it) we may one day have to live, and towards which our present plans and ambitions must be directed. (1995b, 856)

Under the rubric of "Far Future," Stableford excludes "images of the historical future which will grow out of human action in the present day" (1995a, 415). The far future instead is the "future of destiny," an eschatological body of fiction often featuring the end of the world. Such fiction has its imposing landmarks, above all in the works of Olaf Stapledon, but (as Stableford rather ominously observes) it has also been found unduly limiting: "The theme does not lend itself readily to conventional plot and character development" (1995a, 416).

In the present context, the most obvious feature of Stableford's definitions is that they produce an excluded middle. I want to suggest, therefore, that a date such as the year 3000 is neither "near" nor "far" but typifies what I will call the intermediate future. The next millennium is not exactly a world toward which our present plans and ambitions must be directed; but neither is it purely a matter of destiny that is beyond the end of foreseeable history. What opportunities are there for plot and character development in the intermediate future? Can we simply extend our present culture into the next millennium, or will all continuity of historical memory have been lost? To understand why intermediate-future fiction is such a puzzling and liminal category, we need to appreciate the part played, until very recently, by a particular construction of the near future in the fiction of the last two hundred years. That is, we need to confront the history of fiction about the twenty-first century.

A very brief selection of twenty-first-century dates drawn from British and American science fiction and utopian writing follows:

2000 Julian West wakes to discover Boston, Massachusetts, transformed into a socialist utopia. (Edward Bellamy, *Looking Backward,* 1888)

2003 Rebuilding of Thames bridges in fourteenth-century style as part of the greening of socialist London. (William Morris, *News from Nowhere,* 1890)

2008 Susan Calvin, Ph.D., joins U.S. Robots as a robopsychologist. (Isaac Asimov, *I, Robot,* 1950)

2025 Fifty years after their first arrival, satanic Overlords inaugurate Golden Age on Earth. (Arthur C. Clarke, *Childhood's End*, 1953; events postponed to c. 2055 in revised second edition, 1990)

2027 First official party of colonists from Earth lands on Mars. (Kim Stanley Robinson, *Red Mars*, 1992)

2030 American continent abandoned due to failure of energy supplies; U.S. government-in-exile set up in Berlin. (J. G. Ballard, *Hello America*, 1981)

2035 Soviet army of occupation puts down attempted nationalist rebellion in England. (Kingsley Amis, *Russian Hide-and-Seek*, 1980)

2040 End of technological era and breakdown of European civilization. (Sheila Sullivan, *Summer Rising*, 1975)

2050 Newspeak scheduled for final adoption in totalitarian state of Oceania. (George Orwell, *Nineteen Eighty-Four*, 1949)

2050 Planet Lithia, fifty light-years from Earth, exorcised by order of Pope Gregory VIII and destroyed by United Nations nuclear explosion. (James Blish, *A Case of Conscience*, 1958)

2059 Declaration of Mégève sets up World State and inaugurates new phase of human history. (H. G. Wells, *The Shape of Things to Come*, 1933)

2076 Lunar colony declares independence from Earth. (Robert A. Heinlein, *The Moon Is a Harsh Mistress*, 1966)

2100 Lionel Verney, sole survivor of the plague that has wiped out the human race, greets the "last year of the world" from the pinnacle of St Peter's, Rome. (Mary Shelley, *The Last Man*, 1826)

There is a certain sameness about these predictions, none of which (I would guess) will actually be fulfilled. More examples would mean more repetitions of the basic theme, which is that—ever since Mary Shelley and her contemporaries—the twenty-first century has been the apocalyptic century. Once the classic setting for the arrival of the socialist millennium, it later became the favored period for the development of space travel or, alternatively, for the collapse of modern technological society. The point can be still more forcefully made if we extend the twenty-first century a little at both ends, to make what historians would call a long twenty-first century. In Ernest Callenbach's *Ecotopia* (1975), for example, the Pacific northwestern states secede from the Union in 1980 and by 1999 have built a stable utopia. Margaret Atwood's *The Handmaid's Tale* (1985) portrays a slave society set in the United States in the 1990s. It would be tempting to end the long twenty-first century at 2137, the date at which we are shown the feminist utopia of Mattapoisett in Marge Piercy's *Woman on the Edge of Time* (1976), although Piercy's novel suggests more than one possible future timeline. At all events, apocalypse beyond the long twenty-first century—but still in intermediate historical time—is very much rarer. Nearly all fictional visions of the twenty-first century portray a world that, whatever the revolutions or catastrophes it has undergone, retains quite strong links to the writer's own world. Historical memories remain, as do material artifacts connecting the new society to the unparalleled industrial production of the nineteenth and twentieth centuries. Often there are characters who dabble in antiquarianism or nurse a "junk habit" that makes them hoard the detritus of the past. Ironically, now that the year 2000 has come and gone, this whole genre of the "apocalyptic twenty-first century" in fiction is likely to be left to the literary historians.

Historically speaking, then, the twenty-first century in fiction has been both Stableford's "near future" and a "future of destiny." Logically, the twenty-second century ought now to take on this role. Beyond it lies the intermediate future, which must now be said to start in 2300 or thereabouts. But much intermediate-future fiction could be said to belong to an extended near future, due to the recurring prediction that the dynamic turbulence of present-day industrial capitalism will soon give way to a long reaction in favor of social stability or actual stagnation.[1] In this view, the world in (say) 2200 may be very different from now, but not much will happen between 2200 and 3200 or even later. Not surprisingly, a pervasive influence in this fiction is the thousand-year Rule of the Saints foretold in the Christian Apocalypse and revived in Adolf Hitler's post-Christian Thousand-Year Reich.

To take a straightforward example, Katharine Burdekin's dystopia *Swastika Night* (1937) is set in the "year of the Lord Hitler 720" (Burdekin 1985, 11) —presumably 2653 A.D. But most writers of intermediate-future fiction, unlike Burdekin, foresee a long-lasting new epoch that has not actually begun at the time of writing. The new epoch appears to be static because it is beyond the historical process as we understand it. Earth is no longer divided into competing separate nations, empires no longer rise and fall, social mores and behavior remain stagnant, and technological progress has either fizzled out or been exported into space. Post-holocaust stories belong to this category: once present-day civilization has been devastated by a nuclear war or other catastrophe, the number of centuries that it takes for a new society to emerge from the Dark Age hardly matters. The old society (our society), where it is remembered at all, is now regarded as a form of antiquity. A few post-holocaust fictions take the form of future histories, but usually the movement that matters in these stories is spatial rather than temporal: from the spaceship to earth and back in

Octavia E. Butler's Xenogenesis trilogy (1987–1989), or from the evil city of men to an all-female society in many feminist novels. Characteristically, the spatial novel of the future is illustrated by a map of the new terrain rather than a timeline chart; see, for example, the maps at the beginning of Suzy McKee Charnas's *Walk to the End of the World* (1974) and *Motherlines* (1978), and of Sally Miller Gearhart's *The Wanderground* (1980).

In extreme cases, this vision of a becalmed intermediate future can become the basis of far-future fiction. Arthur C. Clarke's *The City and the Stars* (1956) opens with a breathtaking sweep of far-future time in which nothing whatever happens:

> Men had built cities before, but never a city such as this. Some had lasted for centuries, some for millennia, before Time had swept away even their names. Diaspar alone had challenged Eternity, defending itself and all it sheltered against the slow attrition of the ages, the ravages of decay, and the corruption of rust. . . . For [the people of Diaspar] had lived in the same city, had walked in the same miraculously unchanging streets, while more than a thousand million years had worn away. (Clarke 1957, 9–10)

While *The City and the Stars* speculates in billennia, Clarke's later work—thanks above all to the success of *2001: A Space Odyssey*—forces us to consider him, more than any other contemporary writer, as the chronologist of the next millennium. The *2001* series offers a sequence of graduated steps into the future, three out of four of which are conservatively located within the twenty-first century: *2001, 2010, 2061*. The conclusion of the sequence was originally planned as *20,001: The Final Odyssey* (Clarke 1984), but the work that eventually appeared was dated 3001 and, as I shall show, could have been set much earlier. This self-conscious chronological foreshortening is one of the features that makes Clarke's work particularly illuminating as an example of contemporary intermediate-future fiction.

Satire and Historical Memory

Writers of intermediate-future fiction from Louis-Sébastien Mercier's *L'An 2440* (*The Year 2440*, 1771) to Aldous Huxley's *Brave New World* (1932) have used forward projections of between five hundred and a thousand years to startle the reader with a jolt in perspective and sharp, satirical contrasts. A survey of the historical origins of this subgenre will serve to introduce more recent fiction in which familiarity, not strangeness, becomes the keynote of the projected future.

L'An 2440 is recognized as the first example of the fiction of uchronia—the utopian or anti-utopian society set in the future. The Paris of 2440 is an "ideal city in an ideal society" (Alkon 1987, 118) based on the governance of reason. Mercier's descriptions of the systems of rational administration and rational education may strike us today as extremely bland, but the tone of the book changes—although there is no evidence of satirical intent—in chapter 28, concerning the royal library, where we learn that utopian rationality leads inevitably to a massive burning of books. Much of the literature of the past has been sacrificed in the name of "truth, good sense, and good taste" (Mercier 1999, 165) —and, we might add, of public decency. Among the authors thrown on the bonfire are such proverbial libertines as Sappho, Aristophanes, Catullus, and Petronius. Others, like Horace and Ovid, have been extensively bowdlerized. The main task of utopian literary criticism is to reduce the number of books in the world and, especially, the ranks of (and the opportunity for) literary criticism. Thus the works of Corneille, Racine, and Molière have been preserved, but not the commentaries on these authors (Mercier 1999, 171). The sole remaining book of criticism, *Des réputations usurpées*, sets out the reasons why each book has been destroyed. Mercier thus uses the temporal distance between 1770 and 2440 to construct a society wholly detached from contemporary values and sentiment—a society determined to minimize, if not entirely to abolish, the contaminations of historical memory. History and the cultural past are, by and large, superfluous baggage in an age of perfect reason.

In anti-utopian fiction set in the intermediate future, historical memory has often been perverted and distorted beyond accurate recovery. Emile Souvestre's *Le monde tel qu'il sera* [*The World as It Will Be*] (1846) is one of the earliest dystopian novels (Alkon 1987, 194) and, perhaps, the first novel actually to portray the year 3000. Souvestre's novel (which had considerable success and was translated into several languages—though not English) transports a contemporary progressive thinker and his bride to the eve of the fourth millennium, of which they have high hopes. Since what they find is a capitalist nightmare in which humanity is enslaved to the machine and civilization is about to collapse, Maurice and Marthe undergo a bitterly disillusioning experience. Paul Alkon has claimed that the dating of both Mercier's and Souvestre's visions of the future is largely meaningless (Alkon 1987, 227), and certainly Souvestre's novel is full of satirical barbs aimed at the author's own contemporaries. The historical novelist whose books are written by machinery and the national library starved of funds and not open to the public doubtless had their equivalents in nineteenth-century France (Souvestre 1859, 207, 216). The thousand-year future is put to more sensible use when we come upon an academician lecturing on the results of his fifteen years' research into ancient French culture.

The nineteenth century was a "semi-barbarous epoch" in which the vaunted military glory of the French was no more than a joke, and their supposed emperor Napoleon an outright fraud (Souvestre 1859, 200–203). The academician also constructs a ludicrous picture of everyday life in this forgotten past, based on his reading of the melodramas of Alexandre Dumas and Eugène Sue. Anticipating numerous later novels, Souvestre implies in these passages that one of the main reasons for traveling to the intermediate future is to meet its historians and discover their inhabitants' total incomprehension of our own culture.

The antiquarianism of the future is the main target of Edgar Allan Poe's well-known satirical story "Mellonta Tauta" (1848), a twelve-page gossipy letter written on board the balloon *Skylark* on April 1, 2848. Poe's airheaded narrator reports extensively on the archaeological obsessions of her husband, Pundit, a student of ancient philosophy and of the nineteenth-century "Amriccans." Democracy has long given way to autocracy in the New World (just as it did in ancient Rome), and the island of Manhattan, destroyed by an earthquake in 2050, is now the site of an imperial pleasure palace. Just as the punctured balloon is on the point of falling into the ocean, Pundita tells of her husband's excitement over the discovery of a marble slab, engraved in memory of George Washington, by a team of workmen building a new fountain for the emperor—but her interpretation of the nineteenth-century inscription is pure learned gobbledygook. Unlike Souvestre's future savants, the intellectuals of Poe's 2848 are not even possessed of inadvertent insight into our contemporary world; they simply get it totally, utterly, and frivolously wrong. In "Mellonta Tauta," the future is, precisely, the epoch we would least wish to know about.

Early twentieth-century satirical dystopias set in the intermediate future tend to portray a totalitarian state that has all but obliterated the memory of the past. In Yevgeny Zamyatin's *We* (1921), for example, the only name surviving from the twentieth century is that of F. W. Taylor, the inventor of time-and-motion study and prophet of the conveyor belt. According to Zamyatin's narrator, D-503, the "greatest literary monument" preserved from the past is the book of railway timetables (Zamyatin 1972, 12). D-503 is a citizen of the One State, which has been in existence for a thousand years (Zamyatin 1972, 1). Before the foundation of the One State came the Great Two Hundred Years' War, a "war between the city and the village" (Zamyatin 1972, 21) that might be supposed to have begun with the outbreak of the Russian Revolution in 1917. Thus, though there are some small inconsistencies in Zamyatin's dating, the novel is apparently set in the thirty-second century.[2]

The One State was made possible by the invention of petroleum-based synthetic foods (Zamyatin 1972, 11) and inaugurated by the sealing off of the city from the surrounding countryside. Seven hundred years later, free love was instituted by means of a law giving every "number" the right to everyone else "as to a sexual commodity" (Zamyatin 1972, 21). Since these twin "peaks of human history" (Zamyatin 1972, 22), nothing has happened. Life before the One State is seen as the preserve of the semibarbarian "Ancients," whose sole apparent memorial is the Ancient House, a museum of unspecified date. The museum's caretaker, a typical Russian *babushka,* is the only character in this world who does not seem to be nubile and sexually active. "It seemed incredible that she would still be able to speak," comments D-503, implying that she must be as old as the Ancient House itself (Zamyatin 1972, 75). In the event, she says very little. The wisdom of grandparents, much treasured in some late-nineteenth-century futuristic utopias and again (as we shall see) in recent intermediate-future novels, is simply of no account here. *We* is comparable in this respect to Katherine Burdekin's *The End of This Day's Business* ([1935] 1989) and to Huxley's *Brave New World.*

The End of This Day's Business portrays the world in 6250 A.D., after four millennia of matriarchal rule that have succeeded the twentieth-century Fascist upheavals and the eventual victory of Communism. The survival of a 4,000-year-old political system reflects the stability of this "female world" which, we are told, is "safe, reasonable, uncruel, loveless, and dull" (Burdekin 1989, 105). (Male civilizations, by contrast, quickly degenerate without the stimulus of constant change.) Grania, Burdekin's exponent character, is convinced that stagnation has gone too far and that it is time to release men from their servile, submissive roles. Unlike most of her contemporaries, Grania is also fascinated by the new state's distant origins and undertakes a lengthy analysis of the twentieth-century political crisis. This evidently reflects Burdekin's most pressing concerns in writing the novel (and may also explain her failure to publish it). Nevertheless, the rebirth of historical curiosity in the figure of Grania significantly coincides with what may become a decisive challenge to four thousand years of matriarchal oppression.

Burdekin's novel was unpublished in her lifetime, and the fifty years of oblivion that it has suffered contrasts oddly with the fate of *Brave New World* —surely the most famous and widely read of all intermediate-future fictions. Huxley's setting is the year A.F. 632, with "Our Ford"—who chose to call himself "Our Freud" when he spoke on psychological matters (Huxley 1955, 41)—as the source of the system of dates. (In all probability 1900, the date of *The Interpretation of Dreams,* and 1903, when the Ford Motor Company was founded, have been elided in setting the chronological baseline for Huxley's World State.) In his 1946 foreword to the novel, Huxley suggested that *Brave*

New World might have been better conceived as a near-future vision of the twenty-first century:

> All things considered, it looks as though Utopia were far closer to us than anyone, only fifteen years ago, could have imagined. Then, I projected it six hundred years into the future. To-day it seems quite possible that the horror may be upon us within a single century. That is, if we refrain from blowing ourselves to smithereens in the interval. (Huxley 1955, 14)

This rather reckless comment seems designed to support Huxley's retrospective reading of *Brave New World* as the work of an "amused, Pyrrhonic aesthete" (Huxley 1955, 8)—that is, as an ironical fable in which, however real and frightening the social tendencies to be caricatured, the dating is completely arbitrary. It is true that Huxley's future world is no millennial state like Zamyatin's and Burdekin's, but its motto nevertheless is "Community, Identity, Stability," and it boasts of having achieved the "stablest equilibrium in history" (Huxley 1955, 178).

The power of the World State derives from its total control of a genetically engineered and educationally and culturally infantilized population. Old age has been abolished; the average life expectancy is less than in our own time. The "moribund sexagenarians" in the Park Lane Hospital for the Dying have slim and upright bodies and youthful and taut-skinned faces, giving them the "appearance of childish girls" (Huxley 1955, 159). Theirs is a life of "[y]outh almost unimpaired till sixty, and then, crack! the end" (Huxley 1955, 92). All this might be imagined in the twenty-first century, at a stretch, but the wiping of historical memory in *Brave New World* suggests a more remote future. Thanks to Henry Ford's "beautiful and inspired saying . . . History is bunk," the past has been abolished as if with an "invisible feather whisk" (Huxley 1955, 38), leaving behind only a few mythical names, such as Ford and Freud, Lenin and Marx. As in Mercier's utopia, there has evidently been a wholesale burning of books; but those in the most privileged ranks, such as the Resident World Controller Mustapha Mond, have access to forbidden books. The ordinary people are taught that historical facts are simply "unpleasant" (Huxley 1955, 30), and Mond himself fervently believes in the suppression of history.

The Caliban of this new world is John the Savage, bred on the reservation in New Mexico and set apart by his obsession with Shakespeare. A copy of the dramatist's complete works has been miraculously preserved on the reservation, while in the World State itself the Western literary tradition has been deliberately destroyed. That "curious old writer" and authoritarian socialist Bernard Shaw is "one of the very few whose works have been permitted to come down to us" (Huxley 1955, 31). Asked by the Savage why Shakespeare must be prohibited, Mustapha Mond replies that the principal reason is "[b]ecause it's old. . . . We haven't any use for old things here" (Huxley 1955, 172). The society that Mond controls is an infantile utopia that worships youth and beauty, fears and scorns age, and uses artificial stimulants to guarantee happiness. Its intermediate-future setting is justified by the near-oblivion to which it has consigned our own very different society. Yet—skipping fifty years of science fiction's history in which the dystopian model typified by Huxley was very widely imitated—continuity with the past and the veneration of old age are strong features of the intermediate-future fiction of the late twentieth century.

The Slowing Down of Time

In Kim Stanley Robinson's *Icehenge* (1984), a young man meets an older man at dawn on New Year's Day 2590, and the following casual conversation takes place:

"You must have seen a lot of changes."

"Oh yeah. Not as many, though, these last couple of centuries. It appears to me things don't change as fast as they used to. Not as fast as in the twentieth, twenty-first, twenty-second, you know. Inertia, I guess."

"Slower turnover in the population, you mean." (Robinson 1997, 184)

The veteran, a retired ship worker, is 515 years old. One of the reasons for the stagnation he detects is a totalitarian political system, but the dialogue illustrates how developments in gerontological science and the slowing-down of human aging can be used to make the future seem more familiar. Given a normal human life span of several hundred years, future-history novels spanning the next millennium can be written with a much smaller cast of characters than would otherwise be necessary. "Golden Age" pulp science fiction, in which most novels were fix-ups or collations of short-story sequences, often had a highly episodic narrative with frequent changes of scene and protagonist. Part one of Arthur C. Clarke's *Childhood's End,* for example, centers around the negotiations between UN Secretary-General Stormgren and the master of the hidden Overlords, Karellen; part two, set fifty years later, begins with the Overlords' long-delayed appearance before the people of Earth, an event that Stormgren would dearly like to have seen. But he was fifty when the Overlords first arrived, and Clarke is not willing to have him live to a hundred. Later in his career, Clarke would most likely have prolonged Stormgren's life rather than introduced new characters.

Much contemporary science fiction is either set in the near future, or in fantastic parallel worlds, or in a future without dates. Robinson and Clarke, however, stand out as authors who employ precise future dating while relying on characters whose presence, by one means or another, spans much of the next millennium. Judged by the succession of generations, Huxley's 2532 is very much more distant than Robinson's 2590.

In *Icehenge*, Hjalmar Nederland is involved as a child in the revolt of 2248, which destroys the city of New Houston on Mars. Three hundred years later he returns as leader of an archaeological expedition to New Houston. He finds the diary of Emma Weil, a participant in the 2248 revolt who subsequently disappeared, and he suspects that she may still be alive. Weil is subsequently tracked down, or so we are invited to believe, by Nederland's great-grandson Edmond Doya in 2610. Doya persuades the woman he thinks is Weil to finance an expedition to Pluto, in which Nederland, still the dean of interplanetary archaeology, refuses to take part. In the rivalry between Nederland and Doya, Robinson replaces the usual Oedipal conflict with one between a great-grandfather and great-grandson who are, nevertheless, each other's contemporaries.

Icehenge uses a highly self-conscious series of narrative enigmas and discontinuities to obtain the kind of episodic and disruptive effect that could have been obtained, in earlier future-history novels, by a simple succession of generations.[3] The central question in *Icehenge* is whether the mysterious megalith found on Pluto is a genuine monument from the twenty-third century or a twenty-sixth-century construct designed to hoax the archaeologists; either way, it is clearly a human artifact. *Icehenge* is to some extent a spoof on Arthur C. Clarke's fiction, although the novels it most resembles, *2061* and *3001*, were actually written later. The Monoliths of Clarke's *2001* series are, as is well known, alien artifacts left behind in the solar system by the altruistic "Lords of the Galaxy" (Clarke 1997b, 3). It is to the later novels in the series, and especially *3001*, that I shall now turn.

2010: Odyssey Two (1982) ends with an epilogue dated 20,001, in which the Monolith left on Europa (one of the moons of Jupiter) has prompted the emergence of intelligent life there. From the Europans' somewhat myopic observations it seems that human space travel and space colonization is still flourishing (Clarke 1993, 293). But, as previously mentioned, Clarke decided not to pursue the far-future scenario set out in this epilogue. Instead, *2061: Odyssey Three* (1988) ends on Earth in 3001, long before the emergence of Europan civilization. The world of Clarke's next millennium is, at first sight, eerily familiar. The UN headquarters in New York may have been coated in a preservative layer of diamond, but "[a]nyone who had attended early meetings of the General Assembly could never have guessed that more than a thousand years had passed" (Clarke 1997a, 299). This sentence deftly adopts a transmillennial perspective, being focalized through the figure of a UN veteran who is also a time-traveler. In *3001: The Final Odyssey* (1997), Clarke sustains virtually a whole novel set in the next millennium through a similar time-traveling perspective. Moreover, not only Clarke's protagonist but also his imagined world as a whole look remarkably familiar to twentieth- or twenty-first-century eyes.

The opening sentence of chapter 1 of *3001* — "Captain Dimitri Chandler [M2973.04.21/93.106//Mars//SpaceAcad3005] — or 'Dim' to his very best friends — was understandably annoyed" (Clarke 1997b, 7) — typifies the studious banality of Clarke's future setting. For all the clutter of letters and figures after his name, Captain Chandler still holds an archaic naval rank, he is known by a typical twentieth-century diminutive, and his annoyance is as readily understandable to the present-day reader as it may have been to his own contemporaries. Sitting in his "space-tug" beyond the orbit of Neptune, Chandler has the photograph of a famous steamship from the history of twentieth-century Antarctic exploration in his cabin. "And what would those Antarctic explorers of a thousand years ago have made of the view from *his* bridge?" he asks (the word "bridge" is itself a giveaway), and he has no difficulty answering his own question (Clarke 1997b, 9). The bearded, swaggering Captain Dim strikes Clarke's protagonist as an "anachronism" (Clarke 1997b, 100), but this is somewhat misleading in a novel of the next millennium where "anachronism" is pretty much the norm.

3001 consists of a prologue, epilogue, and forty short chapters, in all but six of which the focal character is Frank Poole, a character miraculously brought back to life after vanishing in space during the original mission to Jupiter in *2001: A Space Odyssey*. Rescued by Chandler's ship from the cryonic state in which he has been drifting in deep space, Poole wakes up in a hospital some two thousand kilometers above the Earth, on one of the lower floors of the 36,000-kilometer-high space elevator that allows for easy communication between Earth and its colonies in the solar system. But this is only a very moderately disorienting experience, since after his thousand-year sleep the nurses (female) still wear the "immemorial uniform of their profession" and the doctor (male) exhibits the "confident bedside manner . . . of all doctors, in all places and all ages" (Clarke 1997b, 13, 16). Once revived by the medical team, Poole feels, awestruck, that "[t]here was so much he would have to learn in this new world" (Clarke 1997b, 19); but Clarke makes it easy both for him and for the reader. Poole is equipped with an electronic braincap, and Clarke's narrative doggedly insists on the familiarity — not the strangeness — of 3001. Not only is the fourth millennium brought to us through the perceptions of one of our contemporaries, but detail after detail suggests that the new world has been designed to make Frank Poole feel comfortable there.

In 3001 there are still old *Star Trek* movies, television sets (admittedly, these are regarded as rather antique), plastic smart cards, and Swiss army knives. The braincap is "wired" (!) to a "piece of equipment that could easily have been mistaken for a twentieth-century laptop computer" (Clarke 1997b, 40). Thirty-first-century computer diskettes, although the "end-product of more than a thousand years of electro-optical technology," are the same size as present-day diskettes but twice the thickness (Clarke 1997b, 44–45). Later Poole is issued with a personal organizer "not much larger than the hand-held personal assistants of his own age" (Clarke 1997b, 100). This is scarcely a gee-whiz world. A television documentary explains why 3001 is not nearly as shocking to a visitor from 2001 as our contemporary world would be to the people of 1001. People in 2001 "would have *expected* satellite cities, and colonies on the Moon and planets. They might even have been disappointed, because we are not yet immortal, and have sent probes only to the nearest stars" (Clarke 1997b, 35). (The first millennium did not produce science fiction writers; the second one did.) But this hardly explains why the everyday world of Clarke's 3001 is so totally lacking in innovation, adaptation, and enterprise. The fact that so many electronic gadgets look exactly the same as ours suggests that the profession of industrial design has been on vacation throughout the intervening millennium. Moreover, the mental climate of the population has not perceptibly altered, and where technological changes have been made they seem to have no discernible impact.

In a half-hearted gesture of technological innovation, Clarke tells us that there is a new standard computer keyboard: "that QWERTYUIOP nonsense" was discarded eight hundred years ago (Clarke 1997b, 110). This is hard to believe, since when one of the characters tries out her "new Thoughtwriter" she types out a hoary old sentence that has no meaning except in the context of QWERTY keyboard training: "now is the time for all good men to come to the aid of the party" (Clarke 1997b, 112). All future fiction makes some use of "familiarity tropes" to help readers identify with a new world, but in *3001* the familiarity trope is completely out of control. Moreover, the ultimate challenge facing humanity at the start of the fourth millennium is still that of solving the mystery of the Monoliths discovered by their ancestors a thousand years earlier. And to solve it — so far as humans can solve the enigma at all — the people of 3001 turn back to two members of the original *Discovery* mission revived from the dead, Frank Poole and Dave Bowman.

In a conversation with the director of astronautics at the Smithsonian — an institution which, predictably enough, "still exists, after all these centuries" (Clarke 1997b, 47)—Frank Poole learns that his new colleagues are still obsessed by the three twenty-first-century space odysseys. The only major discovery since then was the excavation of a Monolith at the famous prehistoric site of Olduvai Gorge in 2513. ("And it was hard to believe that, by this year 2513, there was anything left in Olduvai undug by enthusiastic anthropologists," Clarke's narrator feebly remarks [Clarke 1997b, 56]. He can say that again.) The result is that Poole, regarded by the rest of the crew "rather like a holy relic" (Clarke 1997b, 108), is sent on another mission to Europa, the Jovian moon on which a Monolith has been placed and where contact was made with Dave Bowman nine years after his disappearance in 2001. At the climax of *3001*, Poole and Bowman, or "Halman" as he is now called (his identity having fused with that of the famous computer), make contact again—an encounter for which the world has been kept waiting one thousand years. There is, of course, a reason for this: the Monoliths' "controller, or immediate superior" is 450 light-years away (Clarke 1997b, 215), so that it must take nine hundred years to get a message there and back. Clarke's portentous moralizing at the end of the story cannot disguise the thinness of his underlying pretext for setting the final odyssey in 3001 rather than several hundred years earlier:

> Poole had often cursed Einstein in the past; now he blessed him. Even the powers behind the Monoliths, it now appeared certain, could not spread their influence faster than the speed of light. So the human race should have almost a millennium to prepare for the next encounter—if there was to be one. Perhaps by that time, it would be better prepared. (Clarke 1997b, 246)

Clarke, as we have seen earlier, is well aware of science fictional expectations that by the fourth millennium humanity will have discovered immortality and sent probes throughout the galaxy. His message is more sober. Faced with the millennium festivities in a thousand years' time, he reports that "everyone had become heartily sick of all the events planned to celebrate the end of the 2000s. There had been a general sigh of relief when 1 January 3001 had passed uneventfully, and the human race could resume its normal activities" (Clarke 1997b, 9–10).[4] The problem, not peculiar to Clarke, is one of a general loss of confidence in the fiction of the intermediate future. If, rationally (and barring a once-for-all change in civilized life sometime in the next century), we can only predict that what to us appear the "normal activities" of the human race will still be going on a thousand years from now, then what is the point in setting fiction in such far-fetched—yet, it seems, banal and uneventful—times?

There is, then, a hint of artificial longevity, not to say cryonic rigor mortis, about the contemporary future-scene realism of writers such as Robinson and Clarke, impressive though many of their achievements are. Within the limitations of the Einsteinian universe as spelled out by Clarke, the now traditional Space Age preoccupations with exploring the galaxy and searching for extra-terrestrial intelligence seem to have reached an impasse. Some other basis for intermediate-future fiction is needed. The antecedents of this subgenre, going back to the eighteenth century, show that—though writers' conceptions of the next thousand years and more have always remained within fairly strict limits —these limits have changed quite substantially as science fiction has evolved. What intermediate-future fiction perhaps now needs is a return to Earth, since paradoxically the future-realistic novel set in outer space has come to seem so mundane. To explore human relationships in the genetically and cybernetically engineered contexts now foreseeable beyond the twenty-second century might lead once again to a kind of fiction in which the following dialogue would not be out of place:

"You must have seen a lot of changes."

"Hard to know what to say in new time-world. Civilization moved fast, fast, after your century."

NOTES

Quotations from the novels by Mercier and Souvestre are in my own translation.

1. Hugo Gernsback's *Ralph 124C 41+: A Romance of the Year 2660* (1911–1912) is a curious example. Serialized in the magazine *Modern Electrics* and meant to forecast the rapid advance of technology, it actually portrays a snail's pace future in which flying is not expected to become commonplace until the late twenty-first century and the photoelectric cell will not be invented until 2469. In the New York of 2660, an inscription commemorates the death of the last cab horse to ply its trade in the city streets; the date given is June 19, 2096.

2. D-503 describes his totalitarian ancestors as living "some nine hundred years ago" (Zamyatin 1972, 10) and speaks of F. W. Taylor as "that prophet who was able to see ten centuries ahead" (Zamyatin 1972, 33). To make sense of the latter reference, we should have to date the start of the Two Hundred Years' War back to the beginnings of the Industrial Revolution. But, whether F. W. Taylor saw ten or twelve centuries ahead, Mark R. Hillegas's description of the setting of *We* as a "Wellsian superstate of the twenty-sixth century" (1967, 99) is certainly unacceptable.

3. In the more conventional epic framework of his later *Mars* trilogy (1992–1996), however, Robinson uses the longevity of the early Martian colonists to hold his story to-

gether; the trilogy differs from *Icehenge* in being a hugely detailed near-future history ending in the year 2212.

4. The author of *2001* obstinately continues to date the new millennium from the year one, not the year zero. In other respects, these words published in 1997 are a very good prediction of the year 2000.

WORKS CITED

Alkon, Paul K. 1987. *Origins of Futuristic Fiction*. Athens: University of Georgia Press.

Asimov, Isaac. [1951] 1960. *Foundation*. London: Panther.

———. [1950] 1968. *I, Robot*. London: Panther.

Burdekin, Katharine. [1937] 1985. *Swastika Night*. Old Westbury, N.Y.: Feminist Press.

———. [1935] 1989. *The End of This Day's Business*. New York: Feminist Press.

Butler, Octavia, E. 1987. *Dawn: Xenogenesis*. New York: Warner.

———. 1988. *Adulthood Rites: Xenogenesis*. New York: Warner.

———. 1989. *Imago: Xenogenesis*. New York: Warner.

Charnas, Suzy McKee. 1974. *Walk to the End of the World*. New York: Ballantine.

———. 1978. *Motherlines*. New York: Berkley.

Clarke, Arthur C. 1953. *Childhood's End*. New York: Ballantine.

———. [1956] 1957. *The City and the Stars*. London: Corgi.

———. 1984. "Arthur Clarke Schedule." Typescript dated 3 August (private copy).

———. 1990. *Childhood's End*. 2d ed. London: Pan.

———. [1982] 1993. *2010: Odyssey Two*. London: HarperCollins.

———. [1988] 1997a. *2061: Odyssey Three*. London: HarperCollins.

———. 1997b. *3001: The Final Odyssey*. London: HarperCollins.

———. [1968] 1998. *2001: A Space Odyssey*. London: Orbit.

Gearhart, Sally. 1980. *The Wanderground: Stories of the Hill Women*. Watertown, Mass.: Persephone.

Heinlein, Robert A. 1969. "Science Fiction: Its Nature, Faults and Virtues." Pp. 14–18 in Basil Davenport et al., *The Science Fiction Novel: Imagination and Social Criticism*. 3d ed. Chicago: Advent.

Hillegas, Mark R. 1967. *The Future as Nightmare: H. G. Wells and the Anti-Utopians*. New York: Oxford University Press.

Huxley, Aldous. [1932] 1955. *Brave New World: A Novel*. Harmondsworth, U.K.: Penguin.

Kuttner, Henry. 1954. "Shock." Pp. 138–57 in Kuttner, *Ahead of Time: Ten Stories*. London: Weidenfeld.

Mercier, Louis-Sébastien. [1771] 1999. *L'An 2440: Rêve s'il en fut jamais*, ed. Christophe Cave and Christine Marcandier-Colard. Paris: La Découverte.

Piercy, Marge. 1976. *Woman on the Edge of Time*. New York: Knopf.

Poe, Edgar Allan. [1848] 1977. "Mellonta Tauta." Pp. 212–25 in *The Road to Science Fiction: From Gilgamesh to Wells*, ed. James Gunn. New York: New American Library.

Robinson, Kim Stanley. 1992a. *Red Mars*. London: HarperCollins.

———. 1992b. *Green Mars*. London: HarperCollins.

———. 1996. *Blue Mars*. London: HarperCollins.

———. [1984] 1997. *Icehenge*. London: HarperCollins.

Souvestre, Emile. [1846] 1859. *Le Monde tel qu'il sera*. In *Oeuvres complètes*, vol. 37. Paris: Lèvy.

S[tableford], B[rian]. 1995a. "Far Future." Pp. 415–16 in *The Encyclopedia of Science Fiction*, ed. John Clute and Peter Nicholls. New York: St. Martin's.

———. 1995b. "Near Future." Pp. 856–58 in *The Encyclopedia of Science Fiction*, ed. John Clute and Peter Nicholls. New York: St. Martin's.

Zamyatin, Yevgeny. [1921] 1972. *We*, trans. Mirra Ginsburg. New York: Bantam.

What Was Science Fiction?

eric s. rabkin

Science Fiction: Literal Narrative and the Adolescence of Humanity.
Lagrange Historical Collaborative. Oxford, Europe: Oxford U D. 2999.
SciFiUniverse: How We Became Human. La Familia Crick. Heinlein,
Mars: University of Mars D. 2999.

As all but the most nostalgically filtered know all too well by now, Earth tradi-
tionalists currently count themselves as fast approaching the fourth millennium. (We know, we know: if they are so nuclear traditional, you'd think that
they would take New Millennium's Eve to coincide with New Year's Eve EY3000
and not EY2999, but you don't have to be naked to know that disseminators always exploit every compulsion they can ferret and after all these centuries of
rationalism there still remains something atavistically compelling about numbers ending with zeros.) So scholars, making much of nothing, have been min-
ing our Solar Culture to discover millennial moments of the past. Hence the
dissemination of a spate of virtexes on Earth-limited topics including religious
millennialism, racism, and now that ancient pleasure known as science fiction.
Both the Lagrange Historical Collaborative, a group led by Billy-Bob Bacon
on Lagrange 3, and La Familia Crick, a clone clan nexused right here through
Heinlein, Mars, acknowledge, of course, that science fiction criticism is a dry
realm usually interesting almost exclusively to specialized scholars; however,
at this supposedly millennial moment, they collaborate mightily—although nuclear differently—to create fascinating justifications for requesting our time with
their ostensibly common topic.

Science Fiction is, we must admit, a bold experiment. Its defaults are set—
unalterably!—to mimic a twodee, which is a type of dissemination that hasn't
been widely popular since the twenty-second century. For those who have never
experienced a twodee, we should explain that it is not only planar in display, as
its name implies, but also limited just to text, graphics, movies, and sound.
There are no holos, no smells, no tactos, and certainly no direct stims or inter-

acts. Of course, there is hyperlinking within a twodee, just as within an ordinary virtex, but while virtual experiences respond to eye movements and brain waves, twodees respond only to touch and voice. When you experience *Science Fiction*, it doesn't matter where you look or what you think: retinal tracking is off and brain wave amplification falls on deaf sensors. Perversely perhaps, such formal restriction can be exciting. Just as haikolos limit themselves to seventeen interacts in hyperlinked groups of five, seven, and five, and thereby enforce an aesthetic compression that can be quite powerful, so the twodee becomes more than a mere hobbled virtex; it becomes an artifact the experience of which pulls us into the vanished world of science fiction itself, at least according to the LHC, which identifies the realm of science fiction exclusively with literal text.

To honor the LHC, and to give our expers, too, a sense of both the LHC's approach and subject, we have set much of this review's defaults to literal text, that is, we represent with nothing but letter symbols and those letter symbols may merely be read. Go ahead: think for the definition of a word. Nothing happens! Amazing, isn't it? And in that world, says LHC, science fiction flourished.

Of course, sometimes this trick is too precious. When you want to know what a "steam engine" felt like, it seems silly to have to touch the words and then be rewarded with only a chugging movie that goes on and on, always ignoring the exper's wishes. True, the point is made that before we and our artifacts were all bound in the biosm, machines once functioned independently of humans, but frustrating an exper is not the same as making the experience of frustration aesthetically rewarding. At least, not again and again.

Still, *Science Fiction*, a dissemination rife with nuggets and extended analyses, provides truly fascinating crap. For example, few people today know that the very word "crap" took on its modern meaning through science fiction. Apparently the original term "krappe" (c. EY1400) was a Dutch (Earth) word for the husks of grains, the unwanted outer covering of the edible seeds of a family of preindustrial food plants. By extension of this sense of worthlessness, "crap" came to mean excrement. According to the LHC, science fiction was a realm of literal text produced by people called writers. That is, their works, like much of this review, were made of letter symbols only, as opposed to multimedia texts or interactive texts and certainly far from virtexts, meaning virtual texts, which, since they lacked tactos and interacts, among other functionalities, should not be confused with our virtexes. In the mid-twentieth century, Theodore Sturgeon, a science fiction writer, apparently in defense of science fiction against elite critics, is reputed to have said, with a long internal pause, "95 percent of science fiction is crap . . . but then, 95 percent of everything is crap." This became known as "Sturgeon's Law." In the late twentieth and early twenty-first centuries, when science fiction, then known as SF, became not only accepted but thoroughly admired, people would say of it, "this is excellent crap," until finally "excellent" was assimilated into the core concept of "crap." Thus, "this SF is crap" and finally "my life is crap" took on the happy, approbative sense they enjoy today.

The underlying historical argument of *Science Fiction* depends on four propositions. The first is that SF should be properly viewed as a subset of literal text. In standard histories of SF from the later twentieth and early twenty-first centuries, it was common to claim that the first true and extended work of SF was Mary Shelley's novel *Frankenstein* (EY1818), source of the word and myth we still apply to ill-planned individual projects. According to the LHC, the last work of SF was the Venus Settlement House's *Cooking with Genes* (VY0235 [EY2251]), a tongue-in-cheek travelogue-cum-cookbook that satirically discusses ways to mutate Venusian resources into gourmet human food. Indeed, the works have much in common. *Frankenstein* ends with an ugly, huge, quasi-human creature carrying its creator's corpse across the frozen Earth Arctic, having promised to build a funeral pyre on which to consume the dead man's body. *Cooking with Genes* ends with an ugly, huge, quasi-Venusian creature carrying its human creator's flesh, this time as "stew," to a freezer vault, having promised to shape him into edible ice sculpture. Both the building of the pyre and the shaping of the sculpture are acts of religious significance, and each expresses, in its own cultural context, contrition and loss. Of course, the true history of human colonization of Venus contained no incidents so artful or kind; hence the satire. But more importantly, the real Venusian colonization and the imaginative gengineering were sufficiently close in content—although not in style—that it was all but impossible—and certainly trivial—to argue that *Cooking with Genes* was SF in particular rather than simply satire from the world of mainstream literal text. And this leads us to the second proposition.

According to *Science Fiction*, SF was a historically bound art form that arose from the literary mainstream and ultimately subsided into that mainstream, framed, at least emblematically, by literal texts disseminated between EY1818 and EY2251. While during this period there were elements that the public associated with SF ("ray guns and rocket ships/mutants and biochips," to quote the vestigial lyrics of a nursery rhyme dating from the late twenty-second century), those elements progressively populated the nonfictional world until the role of SF writers fell to others with less fictional intent: analysts, proponents, and planners. When Shelley wrote, toward the beginning of the so-called First Industrial Revolution, the consequences of that revolution were by no means clear, but they certainly included much that provoked anxiety. Imagine what it must have been like to live in a world so primitive in its communication infrastructure and so limited in its abilities to replicate experience that a single person might make a discovery and hoard it, misuse it (whether intentionally or not), and even lose it to the detriment of the species. No wonder people were frightened. And they addressed those fears in literal texts that were known collectively as SF.

The third proposition of *Science Fiction* is that literal text was uniquely appropriate for expressing the concerns of this historically bound art form since literal text symbolized in many ways the isolation of the individual. Before the popularization of moveable type by Gutenberg (c. EY1440), literal text was not a part of the lives of average individuals except insofar as it served as a record of laws or contracts that could be consulted by power elites; literal text was a technology devoted almost exclusively to control. From Gutenberg until the diffusion of the so-called Internet (c. EY2000), while literal text pervaded the lives of average individuals, it was not producible by average individuals. It remained a technology of control, of course, but much of that control depended upon diverting the masses with verbal art, novels for example, the products of writers. Still, while the number of readers became vast and the availability of literal texts became common, writers were few and publishers (disseminators of literal text) much, much fewer. Thus most people found their range of intellectual freedom still constrained by elites, but now most people were painfully —and restively—aware of this control. It was in this period, particularly after the Gutenberg Revolution took hold (c. EY1700), that SF arose. The LHC sees this in satires from the mid-seventeenth century on, such as those by Cyrano de Bergerac (EY1655) and Jonathan Swift (EY1726). By the time Shelley wrote, technological anxiety was itself a cultural element worthy of separate focus.

Also, the LHC reminds us, literal text was designed to be consumed in isolation. One did not link with a literal text as one does with a virtex. The only minds one sensed during reading were the reader's own and traces of the writer's. Here was a medium in which questions, cries, kudos, and complaints went unheard. Literal text not only expected individual isolation but also encouraged it. To consume the literal text of SF, then, was to replicate in one's own life the situations SF explored.

Of course, communication media have developed enormously since the twenty-first and even since the twenty-third century. By the mid-twenty-first century, as is well known, virtexes began to include the resident AIs we have all come to know, artificial intelligences that react to our thoughts and feelings about what we experience. Even in the late twentieth century, so-called computer games, the vast majority of which adopted the subject matter and motifs of SF, involved networked humans, so that experiencing these hypernarratives was no longer a necessarily isolated experience.

The fourth proposition of *Science Fiction* pursues this development. According to the LHC, the infancy of humanity was the period from speciation (c. –EY100,000) until the development of agriculture (c. –EY12,000). Agriculture brought humanity into its childhood, during which it developed cities and nations and rudimentary tools. When the tools became sufficiently powerful, the Industrial Revolution began, the period the LHC calls "the adolescence of humanity." The LHC points out that in the infancy of an individual human (before the coming of brain wave amplification, of course), the individual is largely isolated, interacting only with those people within eyeshot and earshot. Later, in childhood, one learns that one is part of one or many groups: a family, a clan, a nation, a culture, a lingua, a discipline. But in adolescence, one returns toward isolation, each adolescent seeking desperately for personal, individual answers to that age-old question, "What will I be when I grow up?" There are so many possible answers—or at least there were after the advent of the Industrial Revolution—and so little obvious constraint. How can the individual become again a fit part of some group? Adolescents look to each other, to their elders, to their imaginations. They invent; they tinker; they risk. But unlike isolated and experimenting infants, adolescents are powerful. From Gutenberg to the Internet, humanity was adolescent, a congeries of individuals, each seeking to define the future, each alone, each with power but no firm sense of how best to use that power.

By the twenty-third century, of course, with the ubiquity of the biosm, adolescent isolation became a matter of choice or historical curiosity. Now we all can share or not with others at any time, tap into the experiences of other intelligences both natural and artificial, into the ideas of others, into the skills of others. To experience a popular virtex is to dip into human society at large. If anxiety arises, the means for allaying it can be found easily. When humanity learned to augment its minds and allow ourselves voluntary interconnectivity, we reached species adulthood, life in the biosm. And thus the need for SF ended, and SF with it. To experience this at all, of course, today requires some trick, such as the dissemination of a twodee.

SciFiUniverse offers a completely different approach. Not only is this work a standard virtex, but it also defines SF much, much more broadly than literal text. According to La Familia Crick, "science fiction" was a Gestalt that snapped into focus in April EY1926 and, once focused, became visible back to the Ancient Greeks. This story is still, in its beginnings, one of literal text, but it is a nuclear different story.

A man named Hugo Gernsback, in an effort to propel himself into the economic elite, began publishing a monthly (that is, luna-monthly) compendium of literal text called *Amazing Stories*. In its first dissemination, he asserted that the content of *Amazing Stories* would be "scientifiction," that is, fiction motivated by and concerned with the impact of science on the human world. Although Gernsback's term did not enjoy success, it quickly transformed and spread as "science fiction." In that very first issue, Gernsback reprinted some earlier stories that his readers immediately recognized as appropriate in kind. SF was born and with it its own history.

La Familia Crick adopts the view that SF is not so much a genre of literal text as it is an intellectual movement, akin, say, to "Romanticism" or "Modernism" or "Atavism." They metaphorize it as a river that they see gathering tributaries and becoming the main source of movement and sustenance for humanity in the twentieth century. Fairy tale is one tributary, going back to preliterate humanity, a psychological tributary that focuses on the possible transfer of power from one generation to another, from the authorized individual to the un- or not-yet-authorized individual. Two great twentieth-century movies make this clear. In the more obvious case, *Star Wars* (EY1977) tells of a rural lad, with the blessings of a princess, acquiring the battle skills of his father and thus saving an empire. In the less obvious case, *2001: A Space Odyssey* (EY1968), the main human character bids a long-distance farewell to his mother, passes through a simulation of a past moment of elegance reminiscent of an ancient castle, and emerges as a "space child," an enormous fetus floating above Earth with all the future yet to decide.

Utopianism is another tributary, a social science tributary LFC claims, going back at least to Plato's *Republic* (c. −EY380). Here again the question is power: what shall be the relationship of the individual to the group? Beginning with the Gutenberg moment, La Familia Crick invokes the same facts as the Lagrange Historical Collaborative, but LFC puts these facts into a larger context. They see SF as a branch of the fantastic, that branch that artistically justifies its world against a backdrop of science. According to that understanding, literal text SF is SF, of course, but there is also SF in all other media, from the Druidic architecture of Earth's first Stonehenge to "the music of the spheres," a mystic concept idealized by ancient philosophers and influencing sonic composers from circa EY1650 on. By the late twentieth century, the dominant medium of SF became movies (both recorded from life and created by drawing or machine generation). There was enormous hybridization between producers and consumers of SF literal text, SF movies, SF music, SF industrial design, and so on. But, again, according to LFC, with the advent of the Internet, new human connectivity made a crucial change. To the LHC, this change obviated SF; we no longer needed fictions to handle our fears when we had come to embrace the sources of our fears. To LFC, this change absorbed SF. New human connectivity was the fulfillment of yearnings explored by SF from the inception of the species; it was "how we became human." If SF was the dominant intellectual movement of the twentieth century, LFC claims, a movement of concern for the relations between and among people in a world of constant material change, that movement won: it established itself as a permanent part of all Solar Culture just as the significance of the individual had earlier established itself as a permanent part of all Western (Earth) Culture, and it did so by integrating material culture into the infosphere of every human.

Both *Science Fiction* and *SciFiUniverse* see the beginning of the end of traditional SF at about EY2000. Thus the end—whether seen as subsidence or as apotheosis—is a millennial moment: enter the Internet and everything begins to be transformed. They agree that works of specialized SF have not been created for centuries. But which of these scholarly explorations of ancient SF, one might ask, is better today, which more worth one's time?

We must admit, the thesis of *SciFiUniverse* seems to us by far the more compelling. Once one comes to understand ancient SF, especially in its multimediated diversity, one recognizes it in every aspect of Solar Culture. We are living what our ancestors only imagined. They wrote stories; we create plans. SF has triumphed and is now everywhere, incarnate in the human biosm. But perhaps, some would argue, like mitochondria in human cells, SF is so much a part of us that it is no longer reasonable to speak of it as anything other than us. There are no mitochondria in the wild and there is no SF anymore.

Well, then, what about the experience of the two works? Which is more worth one's time? Again, we begin by nodding toward *SciFiUniverse*. What fun it is to watch 1,000-year-old movies in a spellbound virtual theater, to play primitive computer games with a network of "nerds," to use virtual "Captain Video decoder rings" to pass messages among friends, and to walk the lanes of the first "World's Fair" (EY1851). The point of *SciFiUniverse* is that we have achieved full humanity only through the realization of the visions of SF. *SciFiUniverse* lets us visit those visions, but we go there as ourselves. *Science Fiction*, on the other hand, by imposing on us the crippling constraints of the twodee, provokes an anxiety humanity has not felt for centuries, the same anxiety that spawned SF. If one wants to play at SF, yes, even to enjoy it, experience the virtex; but to feel what humanity felt for hundreds of years, to live the anxieties imposed by staring into the face of implacable and pervasive human-made uncertainty, for that there is only one choice. You must read *Science Fiction*.

Eric XIX Rabkin
U-M (University of Mars [Heinlein]) &
U-M (University of Michigan [Ann Arbor])

Science in the Third Millennium

kim stanley robinson

Science in the Third Millennium, by J. S. Khaldun
Scientific Careers 2001–3000, by AI 80004 "Ferdnand"

The twelve preceding volumes of Professor Khaldun's study articulate his belief that science has been the driving force in human history for the last fifty millennia at least, an idea sometimes criticized as containing too broad a definition of science to be useful. His latest book, however, brings him into an era in which the idea can be tested for its explanatory power.

It's also a period that illustrates Khaldun's contention that science was always a politics by other means, a utopian and unself-aware revolution attempting to shift power from residual aristocracies to the general populace. What early scientists took to be neutral and necessary aspects of the scientific method, such as reproducibility, falsifiability, Occam's razor, peer review, and so on (cf. Khaldun, 580–935), were actually political institutions all along, attempting to regulate human action with the ultimate goal of alleviating suffering. The invention of science as a method for understanding nature obscured for centuries the realization that it was also the optimum mode of social regulation. Only the population overshoot crisis brought scientists to an awareness of this.

The overshoot, as Khaldun reminds us, was a dangerous time. Humanity found itself in a race to invent a sustainable way of life before its reproductive success and primitive technology severely damaged the carrying capacity of the planet. Global warming and an anthropogenic major extinction event did occur, but it could have been worse: a full six billion of our ancestors existed simultaneously at the tip of an unsustainable technological prosthesis, and the social system facing this situation was the late feudal phase known as capitalism. Many technical advances of the era therefore did nothing to mitigate the ongoing ecological disaster or, worse, added to it; even the great leaps in the biological sciences, reinforcing health and initiating the ongoing assault on senescence, only exacerbated matters, as humanity entered the age of longevity still enmeshed in a dysfunctional social system.

In describing this crux Khaldun rehearses again his theory of history, in which social systems consist of clashes between residual and emergent elements: feudalism he reads as a clash of traditional command economies with emergent capitalism, capitalism a clash of feudalism with early permaculture, and our late permaculture a clash between residual capitalism and some poorly modeled emergent harmony that for biological reasons may be approachable only asymptotically. In the overshoot Khaldun sees this struggle expressed as a conflict between science, representing the emergent permaculture, and capitalism, representing residual elements of feudalism. Capitalism attempted to maintain a hierarchy in which science would serve as pet monkey, cranking out new commodities and increasing life spans; science resisted this impulse not only because of the practical danger of the overshoot to the progeny of scientists but also because science itself would be threatened if the residual elements succeeded. Thus scientists of the era, despite the lack of a paradigm describing them as historical actors, set to work transforming capitalism into a system of practices they recognized as more rational, universal, lawful, and pragmatic — that is to say, more scientific. The resulting ecological reorganization of the economy and increasing advisory power of science in the political realm initiated the institutional mutation toward the system identified retroactively as permaculture, which now seems to us so natural. Adequate food, water, shelter, clothing, health care, and education for all; increased longevity; the stabilization of Earth's ecologies; the inhabitation of the solar system: these and other major achievements of the millennium all followed from science's successful transformation of the social system of that time.

Whether macrohistories like Khaldun's can still convince is doubtful. His "metameme narrative" of residual and emergent smacks of Hegelian teleology, in which progress happens no matter what people choose to do. A useful corrective to this kind of metaphysics is the recent "hyperannalist" work of the computer archeologist AI 80004. Excavations in the enormous mass of data remaining from the overshoot period enabled 80004 to list all scientists working at that time; their careers are summarized, then analyzed in a series of tables and graphs charting their profits and investments, their political actions, their child-rearing, the ecological utility of the scientific content of their careers, and so on (cf. 7378–9417). Close perusal of these tables will indeed reveal which scientists contributed to the survival of the overshoot and invention of permaculture and which did not; but one sees in the tables no teleology, no residual or emergent elements, no grand battle of metamemes—only small individual actions, spread across the whole range of possibility. Khaldun might claim that these actions "summed over history" reveal the beliefs that motivated scientists, and thus the powerful existence of the metamemes. But this would be a subject for yet another volume, called perhaps "History Judges You."

Black to the Future

walter mosley

I've been reading fantasy and science fiction since I was a child. From "Winnie-the-Pooh" to *Tom Swift and His Jetmarine;* from Marvel Comics to Ray Bradbury to Gabriel García Márquez. Any book that offers an alternative account for the way things are catches my attention — at least for a few chapters. This is because I believe that the world in which we live is so much larger, has so many more possibilities than our simple sciences describe.

Anything conceivable I believe is possible: from the creation of life itself (those strings of molecules that twisted and turned until they were self-determinate) to freedom. The ability to formulate ideas into words, humanity's greatest creation, opens the door for all that comes after. Science fiction and its relatives (fantasy, horror, speculative fiction, and so on) have been a main artery for recasting our imagination. There are few concepts or inventions of the twentieth century — from submarine to Newspeak — that were not first fictional flights of fancy. We make up, then make real. The genre speaks most clearly to those who are dissatisfied with the way things are: adolescents, postadolescents, escapists, dreamers, and those who have been made to feel powerless. And this may explain the appeal that science fiction holds for a great many African Americans. Black people have been cut off from their African ancestry by the scythe of slavery and from an American heritage by being excluded from history. For us, science fiction offers an alternative where that which deviates from the norm is the norm.

Science fiction allows history to be rewritten or ignored. Science fiction promises a future full of possibility, alternative lives, and even revenge. A black child picks up a copy of *Spider-Man* and imagines himself swinging into a world beyond the limitations imposed by Harlem or Congress. In the series of "Amber" novels, Roger Zelazny offers us the key to an endless multitude of new dimensions. Through science fiction you can have a black president, a black world, or simply a say in the way things are. This power to imagine is the first step in changing the world. It is a step taken every day by young, and not so young, black readers who crave a vision that will shout down the realism that imprisons us behind a wall of alienating culture.

In science fiction we have a literary genre made to rail against the status quo. All we need now are the black science fiction writers to realize these ends.

But where are they?

There are only a handful of mainstream black science fiction writers working today. Octavia E. Butler, winner of a coveted MacArthur "genius" grant, and Samuel Delany, a monumental voice in the field since the 1960s, are two major figures. Steven Barnes and Tananarive Due are starting to make their marks. There are also flashes of the genre in such respected writers as Toni Morrison and Derrick Bell. But after these notables the silence washes in pretty quickly.

One reason for this absence is that black writers have only recently entered the popular genres in force. Our writers have historically been regarded as footnotes best suited to address the nature of our own chains. So if black writers wanted to branch out past the realism of racism and race they were curtailed by their own desire to document the crimes of America. A further deterrent was the white literary establishment's desire for blacks to write about being black in a white world, a limitation imposed upon a limitation.

Other factors that I believe have limited black participation in science fiction are the uses of play in our American paradise. Through make-believe a child can imagine anything. Being big like his father. Flying to the moon on an eagle's back. Children use the images that they see and the ones that they are shown. Imagine whiteness. White presidents, white soldiers, the whitest white teeth on a blond, blue-eyed model. Media images of policemen, artists, and scientists before the mid-1960s were almost all white. Now imagine blackness. There you will find powerlessness, ignorance, servitude, children who have forgotten how to play. Or you will simply not find anything at all—absence. These are the images that have made war on the imagination of black America.

Only within the last thirty years have positive images of blackness begun appearing in even the slightest way in the media, in history books, and in America's sense of the globe. And with just this small acknowledgment there has been an outpouring of dreams. Black writers, actors, scientists, lawyers, and even an angel or two have appeared in our media. Lovers and cowboys, detectives and kings have come out of the fertile imagination of black America.

The last hurdle is science fiction. The power of science fiction is that it can tear down the walls and windows, the artifice and laws by changing the logic, empowering the disenfranchised, or simply by asking, What if? This bold logic is not easy to attain. The destroyer-creator must first be able to imagine a world beyond his mental prison. The hardest thing to do is to break the chains of reality and go beyond into a world of your own creation.

So where are the black science fiction writers? Everywhere I go I meet young black poets and novelists who are working on science fiction manuscripts. Within the next five years I predict there will be an explosion of science fiction from the black community. When I tell black audiences that I've written a novel in this genre they applaud. And following that explosion will be the beginning of a new world of autonomy created out of the desire to scrap five hundred years of intellectual imperialism. This literary movement itself would make a good story. The tale could unfold in a world in which power is based upon uses of the imagination, where the strongest voices rise to control the destiny of the nation and the world. Maybe, in this make-believe world, a group is being held back by limits placed on its ability to imagine; its dreams have been infiltrated by the dominant group, making even the idea of dissent impossible. The metaphor of this speculative and revolutionary tale could be language as power—the hero, a disembodied choir that disrupts the status quo. "Jazz in the Machine" could be the title. Black letters on a white page would suffice for the jacket design.

Marleen S. Barr is a visiting scholar at Columbia University. Her most recent book is *Genre Fission: A New Discourse Practice for Cultural Studies.*

Rosi Braidotti is professor of women's studies in the arts at the University of Utrecht. Her most recent book is *Metamorphoses: Towards a Materialist Theory of Becoming.*

Harlan Ellison's most recent book is *The Essential Ellison: A 50-Year Retrospective.*

James Gunn is professor emeritus of English at the University of Kansas. His most recent book is *Human Voices: Science Fiction Stories.*

Walter Mosley's most recent book is *Bad Boy Brawly Brown.*

Patrick Parrinder is professor of English at the University of Reading. His most recent book is *Learning from Other Worlds: Estrangement, Cognition, and the Politics of Science Fiction and Utopia.*

Marge Piercy's most recent book is *Sleeping with Cats: A Memoir.*

Neil Postman is professor of culture and communications at New York University. His most recent book is *Building a Bridge to the 18th Century: How the Past Can Improve Our Future.*

Eric S. Rabkin is professor of English at the University of Michigan. His most recent book is *Fantastic Worlds: Myths, Tales and Stories.*

Kim Stanley Robinson's most recent book is *The Years of Rice and Salt.*

Pamela Sargent's most recent book is *The Mountain Cage and Other Stories.*

Darko Suvin is professor emeritus of English at McGill University. His most recent book is *Lessons of Japan: Assayings of Some Intercultural Stances.*

George Zebrowski's most recent book is *Swift Thoughts.*

Library of Congress Cataloging-in-Publication Data

Envisioning the future : science fiction and the next millennium /
edited by Marleen S. Barr.

p. cm.

Includes bibliographical references.

ISBN 0-8195-6651-9 (cloth : alk. paper) —

ISBN 0-8195-6652-7 (pbk. : alk. paper)

1. Science fiction, American—History and criticism.

2. Science fiction, American. 3. Prophecies in literature.

4. Future in literature. I. Barr, Marleen S.

PS374.S35E58 2003

813'.0876209—dc21   2003052547